Praise for the work of E. J. Noyes

Alone

E. J. Noyes is easily one of the most gifted writers pulling us into whatever world she creates making us live and feel every emotion with her characters. Definitely, loudly, vehemently recommended.

-Reviewer@Large, *NetGalley*

Alone is an absolutely stunning book. This book is not a 5-star, it is well above that. You don't see books like this one very often. Truly a treasure and one that will stay with you long after the final page.

-Tiff's Reviews, *goodreads*

For being one of my most anticipated books to read in 2019, this one sure had a lot of expectations to live up to! I can say with full authority that it met or exceeded every single hope that I had. Noyes has done it again, cementing her place as a "must-read" author. *Alone* lived up to all the hype, and is easily one of the best books of 2019!

-Bethany K., *NetGalley*

There are only a handful of authors that I will drop everything to read as soon as a new book comes out, and Noyes is at the top of that list. It seems no matter what Noyes writes she doesn't disappoint. I will eagerly be waiting for whatever she writes next.

-Lex Kent's Reviews, *goodreads*

There are only a few books out there so compelling they seem to take control of you and force you to read them as quickly as possible. You can't put them down. You just want the world to go away and leave you alone until you can finish this story. *Alone* by E. J. Noyes is that book for me. This novel is absolutely wonderful.

-Betty H., *NetGalley*

Not only is this easily one of the best books of 2019, but it has worked its way onto my personal all-time top 10 list. There is not one formulaic thing going on, and it's "unputdownable."

-Karen C., *NetGalley*

I cannot give this anything more than five stars, but damn I wish I could. I would give it 15.

-Carolyn M., *NetGalley*

Ask, Tell

This is a book with everything I love about top quality lesbian fiction: a fantastic romance between two wonderful women I can relate to, a location that really made me think again about something I thought I knew well, and brilliant pacing and scene-setting. I cannot recommend this novel highly enough.

-Rainbow Book Reviews

Noyes totally blew my mind from the first sentence. I went in timidly, and I came away awaiting her next release with bated breath. I really love how Noyes is able to get below the surface of the DADT legislation. She really captures the longing, the heartbreak, and especially the isolation that LGBTQ soldiers had to endure because the alternative was being deemed unfit to serve by their own government. I applaud Noyes for getting to the heart of the matter and giving a very important representation of what living and serving under this legislation truly meant for LGBTQ men and women of service.

-The Lesbian Review

E. J. Noyes was able to deliver on so many levels… This book is going to take you on a roller-coaster ride of ups and downs that you won't expect but it's so unbelievably worth it.

-Les Rêveur Reviews

Noyes clearly undertook a mammoth amount of research. I was totally engrossed. I'm not usually a reader of romance novels, but this one gripped me. The personal growth of the main character, the rich development of her fabulous best friend, Mitch, and the well-handled tension between Sabine and her love interest were all fantastic. This one definitely deserves five stars.

-ceLEStial books Reviews

Turbulence

Wow… and when I say 'wow' I mean… WOW. After the author's debut novel *Ask, Tell* got to my list of best books of 2017, I was wondering if that was just a fluke. Fortunately for us lesfic readers, now it's confirmed: E. J. Noyes CAN write. Not only that, she can write different genres… Written in first person from Isabelle's point of view, the reader gets into her headspace with all her insecurities, struggles, and character traits. Alongside Isabelle, we discover Audrey's personality, her life story and, most importantly, her feelings. Throughout the book, Ms. Noyes pushes us down a roller coaster of emotions as we accompany Isabelle in her journey of self-discovery. In the process, we laugh, suffer, and enjoy the ride.

-Gaby, *goodreads*

This was hot, steamy, even a little emotional…and I loved every second of it. This book is in first person. I know some don't care for that, but it works for this book, really. Always being in Isabella's head, not knowing for sure what Audrey was thinking, gave me almost a little suspense. I just love the way Noyes writes. I know I am fan-girling out a bit here, but her books make me happy. All other romance fans, I easily recommend this. I just hope I don't have to wait too long for another Noyes book.

-Lex Kent, *goodreads*

The entire story just flowed from the first page! F. J. Noyes did a superb job of bringing out Isabelle's and Audrey's personalities, faults, erratic emotions, and the burning passion they shared. The chemistry between both women was so palpable! I felt as though the writer drizzled every word she wrote with love, combustible desire, and intense longing.

-*The Lesbian Review*

Gold

This is Noyes' third book, and her writing just keeps getting better and better with each release. She gives us such amazing characters that are easy for anyone to relate to. And she makes them so endearing that you can't help but want them to overcome the past and move forward toward their happily ever after.

-*The Lesbian Review*

This book is exactly the way I wish romance authors would get back to writing romance. This is what I want to read. If you are a Noyes fan, get this book. If you are a romance fan, get this book. I didn't even talk about the skiing… if you are a skiing fan, get this book.

-Lex Kent, *goodreads*

If the Shoe Fits

When we pick up an E. J. Noyes book we expect intensity, characters with issues (circumstantial and/or internal), and a romance that builds believably. Considering this is Ask, Tell #3 we expected all of the above layered with epic seriousness. We were pleasantly surprised and totally floored by the humor in addition to what was already expected!

Reaping the Benefits

About the Author

E. J. Noyes lives in Australia with her wife, a needy cat, aloof chickens and too many horses. When not indulging in her love of reading and writing, E. J. argues with her hair and pretends to be good at things.

Reaping the Benefits

E. J. Noyes

BELLA
BOOKS
2020

Bella Books, Inc.
P.O. Box 10543
Tallahassee, FL 32302

Printed in the United States of America on acid-free paper.

First Bella Books Edition 2020

Editor: Cath Walker
Cover Designer: Kayla Mancuso

ISBN: 978-1-64247-139-7

Acknowledgments

Writing this book was an adventure, and by adventure I mean sometimes fabulous, sometimes death-defying, sometimes asking myself why the *bleep* I embarked upon the journey. First up, I should probably say thank you to everyone who follows me on social media for putting up with me being so annoyingly cryptic complaining about writing this book in third person for the last however many months.

My gratitude to Wee Linter for somehow managing to give me both an ass kicking and a pep talk all in one, and who managed to change my mindset with one simple sentence. Pal, you rock.

American Kate – thanks much for your never-ending and unwavering support, your beta eyes and otter gifs. I still can't believe you won the bet.

Jae – thank you for your support while I was flailing, for pointing out exactly what I knew was wrong but couldn't unravel, and for being so gosh darn polite about it.

Thanks to Claire, who was not only a fabulous cheerleader, pom-poms and all, but who was so excited to read this that I got excited too.

Christina, having your quiet optimism and willing ski-chat around is such a wonderful safe space for me, and I'm eternally grateful.

Bella Crew – all your hard work makes it work. Four-ish years ago I thought I'd be lucky if you wanted one, and here we are at seven and still counting. Go, team!

Cath, without you I'd have nothing but a pile of (too many) words. I'm so glad you know what you're doing, and understand that I really don't…

Pheebs, thanks for the title. Such wit! I adore you five thousand, and can't think of anyone I'd rather spend eternity with. Actually, I probably could. But, but, um, I doubt they'd be as amazing as you. Phew, nice save, E. J.

CHAPTER ONE

Only an idiot would try to have one hundred and twenty-three afterlife packages checked, approved, encrypted and uploaded by the end of the day. Clearly, Morgan Ashworth thought, I'm an idiot. An idiot who should know better by now. Stuffing potato chips into her mouth in a desperate attempt to quiet her grumbling stomach, Morgan pulled a black tablet from the bottom drawer of her desk.

She swiped across the Theda logo—a tasteful, stylized T that Cici La Morte regularly grumbled about. Apparently the logo looked far too much like the "stupid scythe" of Death folklore. It did look exactly like that, which Morgan had known when she'd designed it over a hundred years prior. Despite the fact she was actually Death, Cici *hated* her Grim-Reaper image, and the logo was one of the few things Morgan could use to tease her boss.

Slowly scrolling down a list of names, Morgan upended the bag until the remaining chips cascaded into her mouth. She was contemplating opening a second when her phone rang. Cursing the name on the display, she frantically chewed and swallowed, then answered with a faux-cheerful, "Olivier. To what do I owe this pleasure?" As if Olivier doing something wrong or complaining—either of which, or both, would be the only reason for his call—could count as *pleasure*.

The man who responded did so in a baritone accented with a mongrel mix of pretty much every European language imaginable. "Morgan, this damned program of yours keeps telling me there's an input error for one of my contracts and will not allow me to submit it to you."

"Well then, there's an input error and you can't submit it to me until you've fixed it. Simple." Contemplation turned to conviction, and she grabbed another bag of chips from the snack stash in her middle desk drawer.

Morgan could visualize him puffing himself up as he rebutted with an indignant, "I don't see how. The package was administered exactly the same way I've been doing it for the past one hundred and sixteen years."

"Did you run a verification protocol?"

The long, silent pause told her he hadn't.

Morgan imagined banging her head on her desk would produce less of a headache than the one this conversation was giving her. "Olivier, the afterlife package protocol is very simple. Visit the recipient, explain your purpose, give them the package to complete. Run the verification protocol before you leave to ensure nothing has been missed and then consolidate the data ready to forward to me. The same way you've been doing it for, what is it that you just said? One hundred and sixteen years?" Another few chips were sacrificed to try and appease her annoyance.

His refusal to answer told her he'd tried to shortcut the process yet again. His deflection using a pointless question confirmed it. "What *are* you eating?"

"Potato chips."

Olivier sniffed. "You Americans are so uncouth." Disdain dripped from every word.

"Yes, I have heard you say that before. And technically I'm a Briton, as I know you know." It's not like the British accent wasn't obvious. The way she formed words had remained with her despite centuries of inhabiting countless bodies, each one with a different voice.

Another deflection, this one weaker. "Every time I telephone you, you're eating."

She usually was eating something, so he wasn't far off the mark. "That's because unlike you, I'm required to realm-hop more than a few times a year, and as you know it expends a great deal of energy. In fact, more days than not I have to make multiple trips to Aether."

Morgan crunched another few chips extra loudly. "Because I need to give La Morte updates on her Minions, their completion percentages, their successes and of course, their *failures*."

He spluttered and mumbled a few random syllables before he eventually managed to articulate weakly, "Well...some of us travel around multiple countries many times a day."

Morgan hmmed. "Yes, I'm aware of how much every one of La Morte's Minions travel, and you clock up no more interstitial transit than anyone else." She paused, waiting for him to rebut, and when he didn't she told him something he already knew. "The verification protocol won't work because too much time has passed between implementing the person's afterlife package and when you're trying to verify it. Go back, *apologize* to them for the inconvenience and have them open their package file as if they wish to make a change. You should then be able to complete the verification protocol and send the package to me as normal."

"Okay. Yes. I will do that," he said stiffly.

"Good, thank you. And, Olivier, this is the fifth time you've had an issue this quarter. I haven't spoken to Cici about it yet because it's been nebulous, but if another mistake like this happens again, I will tell her and I will recommend disciplinary action."

Olivier sounded like he was being strangled with one of his Italian silk ties. "Yes, okay. Goodbye then."

Her reply was given in the polite *you're an idiot* tone she'd perfected over the centuries. "Excellent, thank you. Goodbye, Olivier." Morgan was certain she heard him say *Bitch* in Czech under his breath as the call cut off. Chuckling to herself, she murmured, "That's Boss Bitch to you."

She'd finished her second bag of chips and uploaded two afterlife packages—one hundred and twenty-one to go—when a data packet pinged through from the Oceanic region. Morgan's sigh sounded more like a goat being strangled. Make that...three hundred and sixty-four afterlife packages to check, approve, encrypt and upload.

"Damn you, Bethany...effing...Harris." Ugh. All month, Morgan had watched the Minion responsible for the Oceanic region climb higher and higher in her turn-in percentages, and in the process inch her way closer and closer to the Minion of the Year Award.

The nerve of Harris! She'd only been doing the job for thirty-six years. She was a newbie, a greenhorn, a pup, a...a...cheater, obviously. Somehow, she'd managed to tweak her completion rates to show the highest of any Minion, when she only had a total population of forty-two-point-three million people under her care. Morgan scribbled a note on her blotter. *Audit Harris's figures?*

If high blood pressure was an issue, Morgan would have exploded by now. Not only was she responsible for overseeing all Cici's Minions, ensuring the validity and integrity of every completed afterlife package worldwide and running the facility that housed the data, but for the past ten months she'd been traveling almost daily to multiple locations within North, South and Central America to issue said afterlife packages. All because the Minion previously in charge of The Americas had declared out of the blue that he was done, burnt out, over it—for real this time—and had asked to be relieved of duties indefinitely.

And according to Cici, explained through pouting lips and accompanied by fluttering eyelashes, Morgan was the *obvious* choice to cover the region until a replacement could be allocated, because she was the only person Cici fully trusted. And nobody, mortal or immortal, in all the realms could resist Cici La Morte when she turned on that charm. Oh, Morgan had tried. But her weak protests had been smothered by Cici's trademark flattery, charm and an appeal to her ego. Sneaky.

Morgan crumpled the second empty chip bag into the waste basket. "Oh it's nothing, Morgana!" she said, adopting a high-pitched voice. "Not even a billion people total. I neeeeed you, my darling. Besides, you're more than capable of balancing The Americas *and* your regular duties. You could do it in your sleep. It doesn't matter if you get a few hundred thousand contracts behind, the next Minion can easily dedicate a year to catching up—isn't that why *you* insisted we have such a large buffer between contract administration and death? Think of the end of year award. Kiss kiss, bye now, love you." Okay, so maybe Cici hadn't sounded *quite* like that, but close enough. "Not even a billion people," Morgan grumbled. Bethany Harris probably didn't even know what a billion was.

Morgan knew the moment she reached for her teacup that the tea was stone cold. Perfect. One couldn't function without hot tea. She carried her tablet to the corner of her office that housed a neat alcove with a small bench and sink, kettle, her favorite bone-china cups and teapot along with her precious stash of Assam tea she collected from the London Tea Exchange every time she made a trip home.

Home. Morgan frowned. Could you call a place home if you hadn't lived there in over three hundred years and if home was the specific place you'd made with the only woman you'd ever truly loved?

She'd lived in San Francisco for centuries and it still didn't feel like *home*. Perhaps home was merely an abstract concept. "Perhaps," she mumbled. "You should stop having existential thoughts when you should be concentrating so you can get back to work." She filled the electric kettle, scooped a careful measure of tea into the teapot, and while water boiled, read through an afterlife package on her tablet.

By the time the kettle had clicked off, Morgan had uploaded one more data packet. Wonderful. At the rate she was going, she might have them all done by close of business. Close of business the day after the day after tomorrow that is. She poured water into her teapot with the same loving care as always, collected a fresh cup and saucer and set everything on her desk. The tea needed to steep, which she knew from experience was just enough time to grab something more filling than chips.

The staff kitchen down the hall was empty save for Jorge, one of Theda's tech staff, who sat slumped at a modern IKEA-esque table, nursing a steaming cup of coffee. The newborn baby at home probably explained why he looked like he needed a solid thirty-hour block of sleep. As she approached, he straightened, offering a smiling yet exhausted, "Ms. Ashworth."

"Good morning," she said warmly, bee-lining for the cookie jar. "Is everything okay? Where's the rest of the team?" Morgan fished out a handful of choc-chip cookies and dropped them on a plate. She studied the pile, then added a few more.

"Out for an early lunch. Except for Jane." His thick, dark eyebrows furrowed. "We've been having trouble with server bank three. It's nowhere close to an emergency, but it's still running a few degrees hotter than we're comfortable with. She's down there now, rummaging around and muttering to herself." His face relaxed into a knowing smile. "We thought it best to give her some space, so…early break."

"Ah. Of course. Very good idea." Jane Smith, Morgan's Head of Data Integrity, was a tyrant when it came to *her* servers and *her* data. She was also an incredible team leader, well liked and respected by the other staff who also knew exactly when to leave her to work her magic. As did Morgan. "Well, good luck. Perhaps you should take her some chocolate or something as an offering?"

"I might try that if she bites my head off again for not handing her the flashlight fast enough," he deadpanned.

"It's more serious than I thought, better make it chocolate and a coffee then…" Morgan popped a cookie into her mouth, and smiling around the mouthful, made her exit. But not before she'd nabbed one of the two dozen cupcakes an employee had brought in and left for everyone to share. Morgan had already eaten three.

She'd approved and archived another seventeen afterlife packages and almost finished her tea when movement outside the glass that made up two of the four walls of Morgan's office drew her attention away from her screen. The glass was both blessing and curse. Cici had insisted upon it, stating emphatically that a boss being visually available was a steady comforting presence for employees. Given the number of Minions Cici had had over the centuries, Morgan supposed she knew what she was talking about. But seeing her reflection when she looked up sent a slow roll of unease through her and she avoided the glass as much as she could.

Jane walked past with her head down, focused intensely on her tablet, mumbling to herself. Tucked tightly under her arms were assorted cables, hard drives and a motherboard in a plastic sleeve. Jane paused to tap frantically on the tablet screen, and from within the confines of her office Morgan watched a cable work its way loose from under Jane's right elbow. It slid free inch by inch, despite Jane's contortions to keep it in place, and after a few seconds the cable dropped to the ground like a snake falling from a tree. Jane looked to the ceiling, shook her head and bent down to collect the offending piece of hardware.

Of course, the movement had her bending over with her ass directly in Morgan's line of sight. Oh boy. That was, ahem. She'd once overheard a new employee—who she'd let go for the unnecessary and judgmental comment—describe her as *Plain Jane*. Clearly they'd never paid attention, because Jane Smith was anything but *plain*.

If you paid attention, which Morgan had to admit she often did, then you would notice Jane's brown eyes were kind and shone when she spoke of things she was passionate about, like her love of wrangling data and servers, her family and some pop culture Morgan didn't understand.

You'd notice the way her glossy hair curled around behind her ears, and the shine of red through it. You'd notice the genuine warmth in her smile and the way it made her eyes and nose crinkle. You'd notice Jane came across as confident and concise while directing her team but she could turn instantly into a quiet, watchful and attentive listener.

And you'd notice—

Jane straightened and with comical slowness turned around until she was staring directly into Morgan's office. Morgan, who if she'd been paying attention instead of ogling an employee's ass, would have realized Jane had caught her boss in the act of checking her out.

Morgan's gaze snapped back down to her desk. Yes, very busy and important in my office doing ordinary everyday data storage things that a human would do. Not checking out your very nice, ahhhh… that's so inappropriate…ass. She made some gestures with her pen and tapped her tablet, hoping it looked like working, and at the edge of her vision Jane made a hasty retreat.

When she was sure Jane had gone, Morgan looked up again, letting out a long breath. She was getting sloppy, being caught out like that. Not that she made a habit of checking Jane out but, well…actually, what constituted a habit? At least once per day wasn't a habit, was it? And it wasn't like she was objectifying her, but more that Jane had some *thing* that always drew Morgan's attention and not just visually.

She reminded Morgan of Hannah in some ways—smart, tenacious, tender, attractive, quietly witty. Oh no, stop that line of thought right there. Morgan gave herself a metaphorical head shake. Less fantasizing about the employees, and more focusing on approvals and archiving so you can get to Aether and back again before tomorrow's sunrise.

An alert on her tablet signified a fresh afterlife package to be actioned in The Americas. Joy, another thing to do. Raising her teacup to her mouth, Morgan swiped to check the identity and location of the person she'd have to see to administer the package. Maybe the person wouldn't mind if she turned up at one a.m. the second Tuesday four months from now which was probably the only time she had free in her schedule. Morgan read the name and birthdate, stared at the accompanying identification picture and almost choked on her mouthful of tea.

Well, this might be awkward.

CHAPTER TWO

The best part about the open floorplan was that Jane had an unobstructed view right into Ms. Ashworth's office, and she took advantage of the sightline at every opportunity. The second-best part was that the location of Jane's cubicle meant she could see people approaching, giving her plenty of time to pretend she wasn't ogling while working. Movement in her periphery alerted her to a visitor and Jane ducked before Leah's stack-of-paper swat found its mark. Squirming, she held both hands up to ward off another attempt. "Hey! What's that about?"

"Stop it." Leah held the papers to her chest, her face a mix of exasperation and pity. Mostly pity.

Jane kept her hands up until she was confident that Leah wasn't about to launch another sneaky attack. "Stop what?"

"You're daydreaming about her right now. I can always tell. You get that look."

"I don't have a *look*," Jane mumbled. "I'm just thinking. About work stuff." She glanced at her boss's glass walls, then just as quickly forced her gaze back to her desk when she realized what she'd done. Thinking about work stuff was right, except it wasn't her job she was thinking about. It was Morgan Ashworth, at her desk, teacup in one hand and the other absently tugging her left earlobe.

"Uh, yeah, you do have a look. It's a little dreamy, a little horny and a little sad." Leah leaned down to speak quietly near Jane's ear. "But mostly, it's pathetic. Woman up and ask her out, or move on. My strong vote is for move on. She's your boss, actually more than that, she owns a very successful data storage company and is smoking hot. She could screw anyone she wanted. And she probably does. Ten bucks says she has some hot, rich model boyfriend or girlfriend waiting for her at home." Leah straightened and glanced into Ms. Ashworth's office. "Actually, make that twenty bucks. She has fresh flowers delivered every day."

Jane's tone was drier than dust. "Thanks for the ego boost." And the depressing mental image of Morgan Ashworth and her wealthy, model-perfect partner. She made a mental note, yet again, to actually use her gym membership and try to eat more salads. Maybe win the lottery? Jane cheered up marginally when she pointed out, "As for the daily flowers, they're also in the break room and bathrooms, so I think it's that she just likes flowers." And not that aforementioned hot, rich, did I mention hot, partner sent them to Ms. Ashworth every day like some Hallmark declaration of love to tide her over before she went home for hot rich sex every evening.

"Maybe." Leah raised a placating hand. "But I'm just being a realist and a friend. I really think you need to get over this. You should get *out* and meet women, be a human instead of a robot communing with computers all day."

Jane snorted out a laugh. "Right. I barely have time for the necessary things in my life at the moment without adding trying to get to know a woman to the mix. Did you know, every date I've been on in the past three years, the moment I mention Mom I can literally see their eyes glaze over, like it's all they can do to not run screaming then and there. Actually, you know what? One did run. Not screaming, but she ran."

"Newsflash. People are selfish dicks."

"Yeah, they are," Jane agreed, trying not to sound as down as she felt about the idea. "It's not like I'm asking them to marry me plus my mom as a package deal. I just want someone to spend time with, doing normal things and to help with my, um, urges."

"What about a hookup? Trawl dating sites or go to a bar and find someone to help you blunt the edges of those…urges." Leah bounced her eyebrows.

Jane laughed again, but it was one of disbelief instead of humor. "Oh sure, I can already see how that's going to go. Thanks for the orgasm, now I have to rush off so I can go home and get my mother into bed."

"Do it during the day then," Leah shot back. "You have an hour for lunch, plenty of time to satisfy any urge you might have. Trust me." Grinning, she nudged Jane's shoulder with her hip. "Are we still on for drinks after work?"

"Sure, why not. I could use some more emotional evisceration." Jane tried for a self-deprecating smile but had the feeling the expression looked more like she was constipated.

"It's for your own good. Every time I see you staring at our boss instead of actively trying to find yourself a girlfriend, a little piece of my soul breaks off and floats away. I'll come by once I'm done with payroll and drag your ass away from that tablet."

"My ass in front of this tablet is the thing that keeps all the servers running. No servers running means no Theda which means no cushy job for you."

"Yeah yeah, hero of the day. Your medal is in the mail." Leah's head pat was a perfect mix of grateful and condescending. "I'll see you later. Try not to wear your eyeballs out thinking about work." She air-quoted the last three words. "You'll need them tonight to check out hotties at the bar."

Jane offered a mock salute as Leah backed away and then turned to walk down the hall. In the fracas of trying to avoid Leah's paper swatting, her Wonder Woman figurine had been knocked out of line. Jane turned the figure so she stood at an angle to Batwoman. Tipping Wonder Woman forward, Jane whispered, "Kate Kane, your strength is only outmatched by your beauty."

Jane dropped her voice a register, adding some gruffness. "Diana of Themyscira, indulge me with some grappling. Of the Sapphic variety." She scoffed and moved both figurines so they were facing forward again. "Nice come-on lines, Jane. No wonder you're single."

When she looked up to make sure nobody had overheard her roleplay, she noticed the seat behind her boss's desk was empty. Ms. Ashworth had probably ducked out of the office for her usual lunch break, where she obviously didn't get lunch because she always came back and ate two grilled cheese sandwiches—one of her favorite snacks judging by how many of them she ate. That, and the ever-present teapot on her desk seemed to comprise her diet. She must have a killer personal trainer to keep a body that…well, utterly incredible.

Jane had to stop herself banging her head against her desk. Leah was right. She was pathetic. She snatched up her tablet to check the temperature in the server room and then moved on to monitoring data transfer rates. Exactly what was needed—something requiring concentration to take her mind off her hot boss. Scratch that. Very hot boss.

Her very hot boss appeared by her side so suddenly that Jane barely suppressed her squeak of surprise and only *just* managed not to gawp. Morgan Ashworth was attractive in a way that was almost unreal. And unfair. Blessed with a bone structure you'd sacrifice a kidney for. Full, sensuous mouth. And those eyes. The brightest blue like a clear summer sky. Her boss was immaculately attired in one of her suits—a skirt today which showed off killer legs—with flawless makeup, and blond hair down and curling around her shoulders.

She was the kind of woman that made Jane feel simultaneously aware of her neglected libido and self-conscious about her own appearance. Despite the fact her beauty was cool and glacial, Ms. Ashworth was never anything but warm and friendly, kind and professional. It was more that she felt unattainable, set slightly apart from everyone else. Set slightly apart from her, as in so far out of Jane's league she was practically on another dimension.

Ms. Ashworth placed her left hand flat on the desk, inches from Jane's. Jane glanced down at their almost-touching hands, her attention drawn to the ring her boss always wore on her pinky. It looked like cheap costume jewelry made from dull gold, if it was even genuine. A chipped, unevenly cut milky blue stone was set in the claw on the weirdly shaped band, and made no sense on the finger of a woman who clearly didn't lack money.

"Jane, can you come and see me before you leave this afternoon?"

As usual, when she heard that voice, Jane had to suppress a small shudder of pleasure. Her boss was undeniably British, the accent carried by a voice that was warm and low, calm and soothing. She swallowed the nervous lump that had taken up residence in her throat. Jane congratulated herself when her response was both steady, and somewhat articulate. "Yes, sure, of course." Articulate *and* repetitive. Well done.

"Wonderful." Ms. Ashworth paused, her brows creasing in the middle. "I heard there've been some issues with server bank three today. Have you managed to wrangle it into submission?"

"Hmm? Oh! Uh, not yet, no. The temperature is steady, but still higher than I want. The server room temperature is spot-on, so it's definitely a hardware issue. If it doesn't behave soon then we may need to take it offline to get a closer look."

"Whatever you think is best." She smiled warmly. "I'll see you later this afternoon." Then she was gone in a swirl of expensive-smelling perfume, leaving Jane feeling like an idiot teen with a crush.

Groaning, she dropped her forehead onto her desk. Wonder Woman toppled over, landing against her right ear. Perfect.

Everyone but she and Ms. Ashworth had left for the day—Leah to lip-pursed disapproval at the news Jane was staying back, and would meet her at the bar later—when Jane logged off her computer and tablet, and set the latter on to charge in the small fireproof room where all portable company devices lived overnight.

Jane knocked on her boss's open door, startling Ms. Ashworth who was eating a huge cookie, the last bite of which she hastily stuffed into her mouth before brushing crumbs off her desk into the waste can. "Jane, come in and take a seat." Smiling, she straightened the purple silk scarf knotted like a floppy bowtie around her neck.

Scarf days were Jane's second favorite day. Her favorite day was when Ms. Ashworth wore one of her three-piece suits complete with tie and pocket square, somehow managing to look dapper and feminine all at once. Dapper, feminine and so sexy it almost stole Jane's breath.

Ms. Ashworth drew in a long audible breath, looking strangely discomforted. "I need to discuss something important with you, and uh, I'm afraid I've been put in a somewhat unusual and unexpected position. Frankly, it's thrown me for a bit of a loop."

"Are you firing me?" It came out both incredulous and terrified, and very loud. Jane fought to dial herself down a notch. "Because I've only been late a handful of times, and it's because of my mom and I've always worked through my lunch hours to make up for it."

Ms. Ashworth's eyebrows shot up, and her hands shot out as if trying to stop Jane's rambling speech in its tracks. "Oh, goodness no! Nothing like that. I apologize for startling you." She collected a black tablet from the edge of her desk and came around to sit next to Jane who tried very hard not to notice the way her boss's skirt slid up to expose an expanse of smooth, toned thigh. "I thought you knew that I'm incredibly happy with your work. You're an asset to the company and I greatly value your assistance." She smiled, her eyes creasing at the edges which made her seem even younger than what Jane guessed to be not-even-thirty. Leaning in, Ms. Ashworth confessed, "Between you and me, you're indispensable to Theda."

The panic eased to mild concern. "Oh...well thank you. I really enjoy working here." And staring at you in your office while indulging in fantasies, she finished off in her head.

Ms. Ashworth sighed, seeming almost reluctant to continue. "Jane, there's no point in dancing around the subject, and I regret having to do this here in a work environment, but for the sake of efficiency, I'm left with no alternative."

For a brief, hopeful moment, Jane thought her boss might be about to follow up with an *I'm attracted to you* speech, but instead Ms. Ashworth passed her the tablet which displayed an open document. "It's time for you to fill in your afterlife questionnaire package."

Jane's face felt like it had melted downward. "I'm sorry. What?"

"Your afterlife package. Surely you know what that is?" It came out with not a small amount of incredulity.

Of course Jane knew what it was. Everyone in secondary school learned about Death's Minions and their afterlife packages. And if kids didn't attend school, a representative made a home visit with a handy information packet to help the parent or guardian explain that afterlife packages ensured Death placed you in an appropriate afterlife realm.

"Yes, no, I mean, I know about it, but why are *you* giving it to me?"

Ms. Ashworth held out her hand. "Morgan Ashworth, Head of Transition Operations for Death." With the hand still outstretched, she waggled her fingers.

Jane took the offered hand, simultaneously aware of how warm and smooth her boss's skin was, and that she was holding Morgan Ashworth's hand. What she'd just been told registered in some deep part of her brain, but she couldn't quite make the pieces fit into a logical picture. She released the hand, spluttering, "Wait, you're... you're, one of them?" Her voice squeaked embarrassingly. "You're a Death's Minion?"

Ms. Ashworth straightened. Her expression was haughty, as if she couldn't believe Jane was asking such a thing. "Yes. But I'm more than *just one* of them. I'm in charge of all of them." She ran both hands down her stomach, smoothing her blouse. "Both a liaison and a supervisor would be the best way to define my role."

"But...you're...you," Jane said, well aware of how idiotic it sounded. She paused, frowned and sifted through a dozen thoughts, before eventually asking, "How can you be one of them?"

"Yes, I'm me. And as to how I can be one of Death's Minions, that's easy. I simply am. What were you expecting?" She flashed a teasing smile, her voice dropping to sepulchral tones. "A demonic being? Horns and capes and fire and swirly brimstone gas?"

Jane's cheeks heated. "No, I mean, I don't know. I'd never really thought about it. But, I didn't, I mean…" She puffed out a breath. "Ms. Ashworth, if you'll excuse me and the fact my brain seems to have fallen out of my ears, but it's not every day you're handed your afterlife package and are also told your boss is one of Death's Minions. I mean, obviously I know they, um, you exist, but not…right in front of me." Oh God, she'd had a crush on one of Death's Minions for the past eight years. Jane swallowed hard.

The teasing smile softened. "That's true. I'm sorry to spring it on you this way, but as I said, I felt it best for expediency sake."

"Expediency?"

"Yes. These packages are somewhat time-sensitive."

Time-sensitive. Jane's heart double timed and her throat felt as though someone had grabbed her and begun to squeeze. The words rasped out. "Am I about to die?"

Ms. Ashworth reached over to give her hand an encouraging pat. "No, you're not about to die."

"Then why now?"

"Because I'm very busy, Jane, and I have quotas to keep up."

Quotas. Of dead people. What a morbid concept. "What if I just don't fill it in and sign it? I mean, I still die, right?"

"Yes, of course you'll die. But you will remain stuck in what people call Limbo." She air-quoted that last word. "And will become what is commonly referred to as a ghost." Ms. Ashworth's eyebrows drew together. "Most importantly, you'll affect my completion averages in a negative way. And I *really* can't afford to let that happen. I've won the Minion of the Year award every year since its implementation one hundred and eighty-three years ago and I'll be damned if I let Bethany Harris take it from me this year."

She'd won what award when and who was doing what now? Jane fumbled for an answer and managed a weak, "Oh. Um, congratulations?"

"Thank you." She brushed lint from her shoulder. "I know it may seem silly to you, Jane, but I deserve this award. Not only do I work harder than all the Minions combined, it was I who brought this whole process into the modern era. No more messing around with triplicate copies of paper or physically delivering the packages to every afterlife sector upon a person's death. Now it is all tablets and servers and automation, and my mistress can find what she needs in the fraction of a second."

Realization dawned in a wave of excitement and panic. "This… isn't a data storage facility for hire is it?"

Ms. Ashworth smiled indulgently. "No. You are head of data integrity for the facility that stores all the world's death contracts for past, present and future."

"Shit," Jane breathed. Then came a louder, panicked, "Shit! I need to get another backup routine in place, snapshots every half hour instead of every hour. We need more physical storage capabilities. I want to set up another fire-and-quake-proof server housing and physical backup room. We need more system redundancies in case of primary data restoration failures, housed in multiple locations even."

Her boss's eyebrows were slightly raised, the edges of her mouth lifted as she listened to Jane's runaway thoughts. "We've been doing okay with what we have already, and it's survived a few natural disasters. And besides, you have no idea what it was like when rooms full of paper contracts went up in flames. Compared to three hundred years ago, we have an abundance of data security."

"Yes but that was *then*, and now I know what's *on* the servers. I just…" She made a helpless gesture. "I would like it to be better, safer."

Ms. Ashworth rested the tablet on her thighs. "Well then, whatever you think we need, at whatever cost."

"It could get expensive." Her brain had already tallied past six figures.

A dismissive wave. "That doesn't matter. Theda houses an essential, irreplaceable service for the world's population, and I have unlimited resources for whatever I need. Send me your ideas and a meeting request to get the process rolling."

"Unlimited? Like…that's not an exaggeration?"

"No. Literally unlimited funds, manpower, work and storage space." She leveled a gaze at Jane. "There is no way we could do what's required of us if we were constrained by something like *finances*."

"I see," Jane said. Death apparently had perks.

Smiling, Ms. Ashworth turned the tablet around, holding it up like a magician who'd just performed a trick and was waiting for applause. "So, here it is. Are you ready to begin?"

Jane stared at the screen which displayed a basic form with details already filled in—her name, birth date, social security and other important personal details. It looked exactly like the sample they'd been shown as adolescents, which confirmed this whole thing wasn't just some practical joke. "I…no, I'm not."

Ms. Ashworth turned her head, leaning in as if she were hard of hearing. "Pardon me?"

"I said, no I'm not ready to begin. I can't just make a snap decision about where I'm going to be when I'm dead. I need to take some time to think about this and look over my options."

Her boss clearly tried to suppress a sigh and failed. "How much time exactly?"

"I don't know. A few days? A week maybe?" Jane straightened, squaring her shoulders. "With respect, you've just dumped something rather big on me. I don't think it's unreasonable for me to request some time to think about it."

The barely concealed exasperation broke free in a slightly terse, "Fine, okay. But people don't tend to *take time* with this, Jane. You are the first person in a very long time who has ever asked for an extension, might I add without even listening to an explanation or seeing the documentation. I have an excellent spiel, very informative, one I've delivered literally millions of times."

"I'm sure you do, Ms. Ashworth. And I'd love to hear it, but perhaps when I'm not trying to process the whole other issue of… who you are in the scheme of things."

Ms. Ashworth massaged the bridge of her nose. "Fine. But I must impose a deadline. Let's say one week from today. I need this done. Otherwise…" She trailed off, letting what remained unspoken linger between them.

Ghosts.

Jane did not want to be anything resembling a ghost. Trying to ignore her churning stomach, she nodded in confirmation. "One week."

"Wonderful." Smiling, Ms. Ashworth tapped the screen and moved to the printer in the corner of her office which had begun spitting out a multi-page document, leaving Jane to sit dumbly and stare at her hands.

The more Jane tried to process what had just transpired, the more confused she became. So she focused instead on the sounds behind her. Her boss—wait, no Death's Head Minion…Minion… was she even human?—humming cheerfully as she flicked through and straightened papers, a stapler crunching, then the slow rhythm of heels on the wooden floor.

Ms. Ashworth handed her a sealed envelope. "Here's a copy of the questionnaire for you to peruse."

Jane held the envelope to her chest. "Thank you. I'll check it out ASAP." She knew she was blushing and felt heat creeping up her neck. "Um, is that all you needed to see me about?"

"Yes, that was all." Ms. Ashworth smoothed her skirt down as she slipped around the desk to her high-backed leather chair. "Before you go, can you please check everything's clear for upload on banks two and six? I'm going to have some large packets of data going through tonight. And let me know what you're going to do with bank three so I can plan accordingly. Oh, and don't forget to send me a meeting request to discuss strengthening the data security and hardware and whatever else you feel necessary."

Jane's blink of disbelief felt like it was done at half speed. Surreal didn't even begin to cover it, as if this was nothing out of the ordinary for Ms. Ashworth, when Jane felt like her life had just been turned on its ass. "Sure...I'll get right on all of that."

Ms. Ashworth flashed her a winning smile that would have ordinarily turned Jane weak-kneed if she hadn't already felt so wobbly. "Marvelous, thanks so much." When Jane made no move to leave, she added, "That's all for now."

"Okay...thanks." Jane forced a smile, then rushed from the office feeling like a complete fool. Well. That had been as far from an *I'm attracted to you* speech as you could get. What an idiot she was.

CHAPTER THREE

Morgan was on to the last bite of her second grilled-cheese sandwich when a tentative knock sounded on her open door. Exactly half-past twelve—Jane, and right on time for the meeting she'd requested earlier that morning. Jane closed the door behind her as if she thought it might break and sat down as Morgan flipped to a new notebook page. She wrote the heading UPGRADES then glanced up expectantly. "I'm all ears." And eyes. The small freckle above the left side of Jane's upper lip drew her attention like a beacon. Morgan licked her lips, forced her gaze up and away from Jane's mouth. "What changes would you like to implement?"

Soft brown eyes widened. "Oh, I'll have hardware recommendations and cost estimates to you by tomorrow. This is, I, um wanted to talk to you about that…other thing we discussed yesterday." Jane's voice lowered to a near-whisper. "My afterlife package."

Well that was more like it. Morgan straightened, before leaning forward eagerly. "You're ready to fill it in?"

There was the briefest pause before Jane said, "Actually no, I'm not. I haven't even looked at it yet," she added in a mumble.

An eyeroll would come in handy right about now. Morgan resisted but couldn't prevent her question coming out a little clipped. "And why is that?" She liked Jane a great deal—okay, more than liked—but thinking someone was cute and had a great personality didn't mean you couldn't be frustrated at their inability to deal with something that was a normal part of life. Particularly when Jane's inability to deal with the inevitable affected Morgan.

Jane fiddled with the tablet on her lap, turning it around and around as she spoke. "Well, I've been thinking about this whole, um, death agreement thing. Pretty much all night, actually." She finally stopped fidgeting, squared her shoulders and seemed to be screwing up her courage to say, "I need some information about all of this, about you. And also, I want you to help me."

Morgan arched an eyebrow. "Help you with what exactly?" She dropped her pen, pushed the now pointless notepad aside and rested clasped hands on top of her blotter.

Jane paused, and on an exhalation spilled, "My bucket list."

Morgan swallowed her dismay. A bucket list? Really? She wiped her expression and voice to neutrality. "Pardon?"

"My bucket list. You know, things I want to do before I—" She air-quoted. "Kick the bucket."

"No, I know what a bucket list is. But why do I have to help you with the items on it?"

"Because I was lying in bed last night, unable to sleep because of this whole afterlife thing, and all I could think about were all the things I want to do with my life but haven't been able to because of…reasons. Considering you're the one responsible for shoving my mortality in my face, I don't think it's unreasonable for you to help me. Plus, you don't want to miss out on your Employee of the Year award, right? It's simple really. I want your help, you need me to complete this afterlife package. Fair trade." The explanation came out quickly and without pause, as if Jane had drafted it out, reworked it and then practiced saying it for hours.

Morgan leaned back in her leather executive chair, adopting her best in-charge expression, though all she wanted to do was smile, thinking of Jane working up the nerve to challenge her. Jane had found a weakness and expertly exploited it. Who would have thought? It was rather well done, and under other circumstances Morgan would have told her how impressed she was. Instead, what she said was, "I don't think that's a fair trade at all." Bethany Harris's smug face flashed behind her eyes and she clamped her lips closed on saying no way, no how. "What it is, is bribery," Morgan said flatly.

"I prefer a mutually beneficial arrangement. You have the means to help me do all the things I want to do before I die, which I unfortunately now know could be...I don't know, next week? And I can get you one step closer to your little award. It's a logical trade."

"It's not a *little award*, and it's the principle of it more than anything," Morgan ground out. She worked harder than any of Cici's Minions. Didn't she deserve a pat on the back in the form of a tacky trophy and a party in her honor? "And your death is not imminent. The minimum timeframe we allow between package administration and actual death is six months. But in ninety-nine percent of cases, the gap between the two events is years, decades even."

"So I'll be dead in a few years then?" Jane's voice squeaked up. "Possibly even six months?"

"Jane..." She lowered her voice to soothing. "What makes you think you'd be the one percent? Trust me, it's best not to think of these things."

Jane exhaled a long breath. "Okay, fine. But you know what would help me not think of these things?"

"Let me guess," Morgan drawled. "Completing your bucket list?"

"Partly, yes." Jane's voice lowered to soft persuasion. "Ms. Ashworth, we both want something. You have the resources to help me get what I want and in return, I have something you need. Simple."

Well, who knew? Not only did soft, kind, quiet Jane Smith have a steel backbone, but she knew how to bargain. Sighing, Morgan shook her head. "I can't believe you have a bucket list."

"Ms. Ashworth—"

Morgan held up a hand. "You can call me Morgan. If you're going to try to extort me, we should at least be on first name basis," she said drolly, relieved when she saw Jane had taken the joke.

"Okay, Morgan." Smiling, Jane glanced down at her lap. "So, we have an agreement?"

Morgan frowned. "I don't think so, no." She tried to make the refusal sound as gentle as she could. "I'm sure your bucket list is a more than worthy cause and it's not that I don't want to help. I do but, Jane, it's simply too much. All that for one contract? It's not a fair trade and there's no way I could convince my boss to approve expenditure of that magnitude outside of the scope of my duties. I'm happy to answer any questions, but aside from that I can't help you. I apologize."

"Oh. Okay then. I mean, I suppose you're right but I just thought..." Jane looked like she'd been shot down asking someone for a date. "I thought you really needed me to complete it for your award."

"I do, but I just can't justify this to my boss. I am really sorry."

"Sure thing. I get it." Jane grabbed her things and rocketed up from the chair. Her cheeks were red, either with embarrassment or anger, Morgan couldn't tell, and her smile was tight. "Sorry to bring it up. It was rude of me to assume."

"Jane—"

"It's fine. I'm sorry to chat and run but I, I…really need to check on bank three."

She was out the door before Morgan could say anything more.

* * *

Morgan rather enjoyed the slightly inebriated feeling of cross-realm travel, which was fortunate given she went to Aether at least once a day. Cici La Morte avoided visiting the earth realm as much as possible. Her many excuses included too busy, always waylaid by sights and sounds and chatting to people and somehow—oopsies—always came back with a plaything, or two. Valid enough reasons, but Morgan suspected it was more that Cici just couldn't be bothered and enjoyed regally sitting in state and having people coming to her.

The thing Morgan didn't enjoy about the journey to Aether was the intense, system-shocking cold. Though only lasting a few seconds, it always felt like she'd been dunked in an arctic pond. The shimmering down her back dissipated as she appeared in the heated lobby of Cici's mansion.

The concierge, a sharply pressed young man in his mid-twenties, jumped up from behind his desk to escort her but Morgan was already striding across the marble floor toward the east wing. "Is she in her study?" she asked, glancing back over her shoulder.

"Yes, Ms. Ashworth." He smiled knowingly as he added, "And she's just been served a light meal."

"Thank you, Jonathon." Briskly rubbing her arms, she made her way down the long, carpeted hallway toward her boss's private wing—a place no other Minion was permitted. The interior of the mansion was decorated in true original Victorian style, and Morgan always felt like she'd stepped back in time. Given most of the furniture was centuries old, the feeling wasn't surprising.

Reclining on her antique chaise longue, Cici La Morte was, as usual, impeccably presented. In this human form, which she'd once told Morgan she'd kept for millennia, she was blessed with a face to make an artist weep—cheekbones that could cut glass, full sensual mouth, delicate nose and chin, dark arched eyebrows and piercing green eyes that changed color from a deep emerald to a pale peridot depending on her mood. Her hair, a brunette that reminded Morgan of the color of bear's fur (though of course she could never utter the comparison aloud) framed Cici's face and curled loosely around her shoulders.

Cici wore a dark gray sleeveless Haute Couture dress, and her feet were encased in a surprisingly tame pair of two-inch heels. The woman really did have a body and face to die for, Morgan mused to herself, smiling inwardly as always at her joke. She could say such things with certainty, given she'd spent three-quarters of a century enjoying that body, and Cici hers.

Despite La Morte's languid appearance, Morgan knew her boss was mentally sorting through at least four dozen cases for immediate transfer approval to their afterlife, and would continue to do so without breaking stride while sipping wine and holding a conversation. *Nobody* could multitask like Cici La Morte.

"Good evening." Morgan placed a hand on Cici's shoulder, bending down to kiss her cheek. She was one of the few who were allowed to touch La Morte. Not for sinister reasons, but simply because her boss was selective with whom she allowed close.

After lifting her face to accept the kiss, La Morte flashed her a warm smile. "Evening," she said, her voice its usual low, almost lazy tone that was brushed with an accent Morgan could never place. The best she'd ever come up with was *sounds kind of Scandinavianish*, when in actuality it was probably an accent mash-up of many languages that no longer existed. Cici's eyebrow slowly rose as she studied Morgan. "What has you turned inside out?"

"I had to contract an employee of mine. First time since I took over from Marcus and it's not going as planned."

Cici grimaced. "Oh. How very awkward."

"You're telling me. So of course, now she knows what I am." Morgan poured herself half a glass of red from the crystal carafe on the side table, paused, reconsidered and filled it to the brim. Calories, right?

"Well our existence isn't a secret, Morgana." Slender fingers tipped with ruby nails played over a fruit platter before selecting a ripe apricot. She paused. "So, who is it?"

It took a moment for Morgan to catch up. "My Head of Data Integrity."

"Ahhh, Jane Smith." The corners of Cici's mouth edged down into the faintest frown—her thinking face. "It's not such a bad end date for her."

"Bad enough," Morgan countered immediately.

Cici leveled a look at her, the frown exchanged for a smile. "Is she alarmed?"

"No. Surprised but accepting would be the best description." Morgan sipped. Crossing the realm into Cici's domain was worth the effort for her substantial wine collection, and the snacks always on hand. She palmed a handful of nuts into her mouth, hoping it'd quiet her growling stomach, and dropped into the chair opposite Cici's chaise.

"Surprised is natural. What is the issue then?" Unlike Morgan's uncouth display, Cici bit delicately into her apricot. She could afford to be delicate. She hadn't just expended a massive amount of corporeal energy crossing realms. Not that Cici ever seemed to be bothered by interstitial travel. Everything was easy when you were Death.

"The issue is she won't sign because being handed her afterlife package has made her aware of her mortality, and she wants me to help her with her bucket list. *And* Bethany Harris is already creeping ahead of my numbers so I can't afford to have any unsigned contracts go through this quarter."

"Always so obsessed with winning. It's unhealthy, darling." Cici sniffed. "And as for bucket lists? What a ridiculous concept. Anyone would think the afterlife is terrible instead of a place with no stress, no worries and no obligations." A dismissive wave. "If Jane Smith wishes to spend her afterlife in a tedious nowhere realm with a bunch of misfits, stuck in the interspace, then let her."

Morgan bit back her annoyance. Not at Jane's lack of cooperation, but at Cici for suggesting that Jane should live out her life after death in such an unpleasant way. Morgan frowned, suddenly aware of the implications. If she didn't agree to Jane's proposition then Jane wouldn't complete the package and she'd end up stuck in Limbo. If she helped her, not only would she have to justify everything to Cici and The Accountant but it set a dangerous precedent. "Jane doesn't deserve that," she eventually murmured.

Perception flashed across Cici's face then just as quickly disappeared. "So, you've made a bargain then? You're going to help her with her list of pointless activities and get your tally mark?"

"Well, actually no. I said it wasn't worth it, not a fair trade. I mean, as much as it kills me to let a contract slide, one person isn't going to tip me over the line." She raised her chin, squared her shoulders and tried to look confident instead of concerned.

Cici's smile held a touch of slyness. "Haven't you heard the saying every vote counts? I think you should agree to the trade. Especially if this person whose welfare you seem to care about is at stake. Unless you think she's bluffing."

Morgan had no idea if Jane was bluffing or not, but the steel she'd glimpsed in Jane told her she might hold out, simply from pure stubbornness. She sighed. "Helping her is likely to cost a fortune. Those lists are always extravagant."

La Morte shrugged. "And why is that an issue, Morgana? If you need to hear the words—you have my permission to do and spend what you wish, not that you ever require my permission for that. If you *really* need this contract and helping your employee is the only way you'll get it, then go ahead."

Morgan hmmphed, gnawing around a pear as if it were a corn cob.

"Would you like me to get you something more substantial to eat?"

Morgan wiped juice from her lips, exhaling a grateful sigh. "Yes please, or I'll probably fade out midway between realms and you'll have to rescue me." Though infrequent, sometimes she simply ran out of energy after weeks of constant corporeal travel and got stuck in the disgusting gooey-feeling material that made up the space between realms. Most unpleasant. Given she'd been burning the candle at both ends all week, a fade-out was looking more likely with every day unless she did something to forestall it.

Years ago, they'd employed various scientists and discovered that a trip to and from Aether burned around two-thousand calories, and each jump from place to place around the world burned around five hundred. Corporeal fatigue was no joke, and Morgan had learned early on that the best way to combat it was to eat. A lot. Constantly.

"What would you like? Or need I even ask?"

"Grilled cheese would be fabulous. Maybe two? And a strawberry milkshake with extra ice cream please and thank you."

Smiling, Cici picked up the telephone. She swapped the wineglass for her tablet, swiped and peered expectantly at Morgan. "What else do you have for me?"

Morgan rattled off facts for five minutes. "Everyone is steady, their packages coming in on schedule except for Olivier who had another verification issue this week. I told him there would be disciplinary action if it happens again." She paused so Cici could make a note.

"Projections show a point-zero-eight increase in the Pacific for next month."

Cici input something into the device. "Europe has had an influx of births that require offsetting, so I believe this will balance nicely."

Morgan nodded her agreement as Jonathon arrived with two perfectly browned grilled sandwiches, the cheese oozing from the edges of four even triangles—just how Morgan liked—and a huge strawberry milkshake. Bliss. There were benefits to her position, even if it was only something as simple as the best food ever created across all realms. She slurped a long mouthful of shake and had barely swallowed a bite of sandwich before mumbling, "I can't believe you're letting her get away with this."

"Are we back on Bethany Harris, my dear? You really need to move on. And I don't let anyone do anything. It's hardly my fault if she's becoming more efficient than you." There was a teasing sparkle in Cici's eyes.

Morgan raised two fingers to her boss as she chased down the sandwich portion with a mouthful of milkshake. "It's unfair, and you know it. Her region doesn't even compare for population size with The Americas. And even if it did, and even if we exclude my temporary gig running The Americas, I'm still working harder than anyone else. It's like giving her a ten-lap head start in an eleven-lap race."

"There is nothing wrong with a little healthy competition, darling."

"Are you *trying* to work me to death? Is that it? I work my ass off for you and I bloody well need a carrot here and there."

"Very funny." Cici crossed one long, shapely leg over the other. "You get many carrots, Morgana. I can't believe you think some tacky trophy is worth raising your blood pressure."

"My blood pressure is fine. And it's not the actual trophy, Cici. It's what it represents."

"What it represents is some stupid arbitrary reward designed to keep the masses happy and working productively." She raised an eyebrow. "Don't tell me you subscribe to the notion? I should never have let you compete with them but you gave me that look and I was helpless to say no to you."

Morgan grunted, gobbling another grilled-cheese triangle.

La Morte's voice softened. "Did it ever occur to you that I might be trying to do the opposite of what you think I am?"

Morgan swallowed, stared. "What do you mean?"

"My darling, you have been by my side longer than any of *Mes Minions*. Maybe I'm worried about you. Maybe I think you need a break before you burn out."

"I'm not going to burn out and I don't need a break."

"I think you do. You shoulder more than anyone, and you always have. I *need* you. And I'm going to need you for the rest of time because frankly you're one of the few people I trust. What's wrong with taking a little time here and there to relax, recharge your batteries?"

"Oh, my. Is that what I think it is? An admission of caring?" Morgan feigned shock, a hand over her heart. "Goodness, Cici, it's only taken you how many centuries?"

La Morte's wave was dismissive. "Oh, as if you didn't know," she said, smiling like a cat who'd stolen cream.

Morgan grinned. "Of course I know. But it's still nice to hear the words."

"Then I shall attempt to say them more than once every several hundred years." Her voice lowered to sincerity. "You really are my favorite person."

"I'd appreciate it. And thank you, you're my favorite person too. Now, I really need to get back to work." Morgan kissed her chastely on the mouth. "I'll see you tomorrow."

"I can't wait. And do think about what I said. All work and no play makes Morgana a dull, dull Minion," was the laughing echo surrounding her as Morgan dissolved through space, back to her apartment.

CHAPTER FOUR

In the two days since she'd learned Morgan's real identity, Jane had been trying, and failing, to pin down exactly how she felt about the bombshell revelation. And she had been trying to forget about what a huge fool she'd made of herself trying to bargain with one of Death's Minions. Eventually she'd decided she was surprised and very interested, and if she was honest, she also felt a little duped. And felt ridiculous for feeling that way. Morgan Ashworth didn't owe her anything, didn't owe anyone honesty about who she really was. She was still her—a hardworking, kind, compassionate and caring woman. All the other stuff didn't matter.

Morgan had lowered her office blinds to half-mast which everyone knew meant *I'm busy but if you really need me I'm available.* Jane debated if it was worth bothering her boss. Her boss, no. Death's Head Minion, yes. Since Morgan's refusing her proposal, Jane had been fighting an unsettling trepidation. She still wanted answers, and her curiosity was greater than her concern. Jane wound her way through the staff cubicles to Morgan's office.

"Yes?" came the call from behind the almost-closed door.

Jane opened it a little more and stuck her head through. "Do you have some time for me, Ms.—Morgan?"

Morgan had turned her chair around, a genuine smile already in place. Smiling was good, smiling hopefully meant she didn't think Jane was a complete idiot. "Of course, come in. Take a seat." Morgan turned back to her desk to continue writing, murmuring an apology and promise that she was almost done.

Despite the fact they were a technology-based company, Jane had noticed almost from her first day that Morgan still handwrote a lot and then transcribed into one of her many tablets. Jane watched her finish up her list and the moment Morgan had penned her last word, she looked up. A half smile raised the edges of her mouth as she focused on Jane who'd been watching her intently. "What is it?"

"Nothing, just…I um, I've always thought you had really nice writing." She paused, debated, then elaborated, "Elegant and well, you know, like it should be used as the benchmark of handwriting."

Smiling fully now, Morgan set down her pen. "Ah, yes. Well I did learn to write back in the days of Ye Olde English," she deadpanned. Morgan ran her hand over a forearm then began to roll up the sleeves on her crisply starched white shirt. The shirt with the pearl buttons. The shirt that clung to her torso in ways that made Jane squirm. Did Morgan not realize how *hot* she looked with her sleeves rolled up to expose those tanned forearms? Did she sit at her desk all day squeezing a strength ball to get forearms like those? She was already sex on legs, and rolled sleeves just made her look smoldering. Casual yet elegant. Gurgle.

Jane knew she was blushing, something that had been happening far more frequently in the last few days, and managed a very articulate, "Wait, Ye Olde? How old are you exactly?" She knew the Minions didn't age the same way as humans did, but what Morgan was alluding to was more than *a few extra years*.

"Don't you know it's rude to ask a lady that?" Morgan teased, but answered without further hesitation. "I was born in Britain in 1325. My given name is actually Morgana but it was dated and out of place in modern America so I dropped the *a* in the early eighteen hundreds and now I am simply Morgan."

Jane did some math, did the math again, and then again to be sure. "Wait, hold on a moment. So you're…almost seven hundred years old."

"Yes. Six hundred and ninety-five to be exact. I'm actually the oldest of Cici's Minions by quite a few centuries. This job has a rather high burnout rate. And as for my Ye Olde English, I actually never went to school. When I was a child, schooling was only for those who could afford it, which my family certainly could not. And certainly not for girls. Cici taught me to read and write properly instead of just deciphering basic market words which was the limit of my knowledge to that point. First English, then Latin and Greek, and then…well, you get the idea. She helped with my arithmetic and mathematics and even supplied a tutor for me, a man who traveled with us for many years until I was confident with languages and numbers."

Languages. Plural. "How many languages do you speak exactly?"

"Fluently? Not including English, forty-three, including three different sign languages. And another eighteen spoken languages passably."

"Shit. Um, that's a lot. How old were you when you met Cici?"

While Jane had been talking, Morgan had been rummaging in her desk drawer. She pulled out a roll of Oreos, fingers pausing at the seam as if she'd only just remembered she had company. "Sorry, do you mind?"

Jane shook her head to indicate she didn't care if Morgan ate, and then again when Morgan offered her the package. Morgan quickly popped a cookie into her mouth. "I was nineteen. She came to my village for business and I thought her the most glamorous thing I'd ever seen. I'd always been attracted to women and had had a few *very* secret dalliances, but she was beyond beautiful. She asked for help with directions, then asked me to join her for a meal. She told me why she was there and I still don't know why, but I wasn't bothered by her revelation. Maybe that's why she asked me to join her. I accepted almost immediately because I couldn't see a life for myself there beyond a village girl eventually married to a village man." Morgan grinned. "And because she's incredibly charming, persuasive and attractive."

Jane tried to turn the notion over, to imagine leaving everything behind to run off with a woman who was practically a stranger. "Did you ever tell your family that you'd, um, changed into what you are now?"

"No," Morgan said softly. "The Plague of 1349 wiped out my home village. My whole family died before I could tell them of my new life. That's why Cici was there, preparing for the first wave." She cleared her throat. "I traveled back to see them sporadically, gave them money, but…I grew busy. I should have made more time."

Jane's throat tightened around the words as she uttered a quiet, "I'm sorry."

"Thank you." Morgan waved, not exactly dismissively but in a way that made Jane feel as though the events had lost some of their sting. Another cookie was inhaled. "What else do you wish to know?"

Jane ran down her mental list. "Do you have social security? A birth certificate that says 1325 would be a bit conspicuous."

Morgan's burst of laughter was loud and rich. "It would be indeed. We have a worldwide agreement with governments. Think of my job like a sort of diplomatic post. We perform an essential function, no different to trash collection or snowplowing the streets. It allows us to get the things we need to function in society."

"Like…endless wealth. How do you get all your money? I mean, this isn't a publicly traded company with shareholders or anything."

"Worldwide governments, a tithe type system. Our expenses are tabulated and then proportioned out based on population percentages, in addition to a set fee for our services. There's also some deft market investments going on in the background that I'm not entirely sure of as it's not my area of expertise." She ate another cookie.

"How many Minions are there exactly?"

"There used to be over one hundred thousand of us to cope with the growing population. In addition to the original tiresome administration work, we had to personally escort everyone to their final place and physically hand over paperwork. Now that we've advanced into the technological age, there are thirteen Minions plus myself, each of us handling a region. Or in my case, handling those who handle. I anticipate, with the way the world is going, after a catastrophic climate event culls the population, the number of Cici's employees will dwindle yet again." Morgan must have caught Jane's expression. "Don't worry, it's quite a few centuries away yet."

Something had been niggling, and it finally twigged. "Why are you called *Minions*? You don't seem unimportant at all, and definitely not like servants."

Morgan smiled indulgently. "No, we are not. We enjoy a measure of autonomy and self-reliance and we certainly don't wait on Cici hand and foot. It was a small dig at Cici, made well before I was born. Hades mocked her for having *Minions* following her around and it stuck."

"What about all those who were Minions but now…aren't? What happened to them?"

"Cici rewards her staff generously and the offer of continued *immortality* remains as a reward for their service." Her voice dropped, grew thoughtful. "But most choose to return to a normal, human lifespan."

"But why?" Jane spluttered. "If you had a life that was never ending, then why would anyone give that up?"

"Jane," Morgan said gently, almost tenderly. "This job is tremendously hard, and as I said, the burnout rate is exceptionally high. You watch everyone you care about die, while you're left to mourn them for an eternity. Few people are able to deal with that kind of emotion for decades upon decades." The expression of softness faded to one of distress before Morgan seemed to gain control again, and Jane wondered if she'd imagined the transition.

The slight tremor in Morgan's lips and the tautness of the skin around her eyes told Jane it had been real. *Left to mourn them for an eternity.* Who did Morgan mourn? She thought about asking, and just as quickly discarded the idea. Way too intrusive.

Morgan popped the last Oreo into her mouth and sighed wistfully as she crumpled the empty package into her waste basket. "Those darn things are never big enough."

* * *

Jane found her mom in the den, playing a game on her tablet, and she tilted her head up as Jane bent to kiss her forehead. "Your hair looks fabulous. Where'd you go for lunch?"

"Veronica and I went to Menlo."

Veronica, her mother's main daytime caretaker, was more like a friend than a paid assistant. "You're a spoiled woman, Pamela Smith." Jane pulled her hair from its ponytail and wrapped the band around her wrist as she walked into the kitchen. "Unlike you, I didn't have a fancy lunch and I'm absolutely starving."

Her mom maneuvered her motorized chair to follow Jane into the kitchen. "What's up, Janie?"

"Just a weird few days at work, that's all." She ran both hands through her hair, dragged it back and then released it again. "I had my afterlife contract questionnaire thing this week."

Her mom didn't even bat an eyelid. "Oh, those things. I'd completely forgotten about that."

"So you've done yours?"

"Oh yes. Years ago when we were still living in Michigan. You were just a baby, so it would've been late in 1988. It was given to me by a gentleman who was a dead ringer for Elvis, and I was trying to do this thing and you were fussing and crying. He was very nice about it all, even held you for me while I filled in the paperwork, and you know, you settled right away."

"Ah. Well, here's something interesting for you. It turns out Ms. Ashworth is not only one of Death's Minions who are responsible for such things, but she's in charge of all of them." Jane made a sweeping gesture. "Death's right-hand woman. And the company I work for isn't a data storage facility. Well it is, but not really. It's actually housing the data of millions and millions of those afterlife package things." She frowned, suddenly realizing she may have said too much. Morgan hadn't seemed alarmed by Jane knowing these matters, but Jane knowing and Jane blurting were perhaps two different things. "Um, maybe don't mention that to anyone? I'm not sure how secret it all is."

"I see. That's fascinating. And why would I tell anyone?" She reversed back a few feet. "Veronica left a plate for you in the fridge."

"Mom! I just told you I've been given my after-death questionnaire, and that my boss is in fact one of those basically immortal Minion things, and you're talking to me about dinner? Aren't you at all shocked? Surprised?"

"Janie, very little shocks or surprises me these days. I mean, have you looked at the news lately? Now, eat." Her expression made it clear that any and all discussions were on hold until Jane had dinner.

She spotted a cling-film wrapped plate of gnocchi smothered with white sauce. "Is this the white wine, cream and garlic sauce?" At her mother's nod, Jane breathed, "Veronica is a fucking goddess."

"Language, Jane!"

She offered an automatic, "Sorry."

"I'm doubtful of the sincerity of your apology. I can only conclude your potty mouth comes from the man who contributed half of your genetic material, since it definitely isn't from me."

Jane's father was rarely mentioned, and it was usually an offhanded comment. Her mom had once said why bother wasting breath talking about the man who had gotten her pregnant the night she lost her virginity at age eighteen and one quarter—oops, sorry, old condom—and then hightailed it out of town and never looked back. She'd raised Jane while finishing college, and once she'd graduated they'd moved interstate for jobs until her mom found her niche in Portland. She'd taught history and women's studies right up until her accident.

After plonking the plate in the microwave, Jane observed, "I don't think swearing is a genetically inherited trait. I heard you say *fuck* once when I was eleven and that woman cut you off and stole your parking spot. So I actually think it was you, that one time, who gave me my potty mouth."

The lines around her mother's mouth deepened. "You're lucky I'm in this chair, or I'd spank your butt. Don't think you're too old for some discipline."

Jane grinned. "Oh I know I'm not. I still remember you chasing me last month because I said…an expletive."

"Mmm. And don't think I won't do it again." Her mom made a limp-wristed gesture. "So did you do it?"

"Do what?"

The words came out on an exasperated sigh. "Your afterlife package thing."

"Oh. No. I haven't even looked at it." The microwave dinging gave her a few seconds of stalling time. Jane stirred her dinner, recovered it and sent it around for another minute.

"Why not?"

"Because I'm not ready to think about it, and also because I was too freaked out by Ms. Ashworth being Head Minion Honcho."

"Why would you be freaked out? Has anything else changed? Did she suddenly turn to an otherworldly being or undergo a complete personality change?"

Jane laughed dryly. "Oh no, she's as gorgeous and personable as ever." Her mother was well aware of Jane's attraction to her boss, and thankfully only teased her about it every other week.

"Well that's good. So what's the issue?"

"I don't know. Just…unexpected I guess. I've spent years thinking one thing and it wasn't true." She poured a glass of white wine, then collected her dinner. "Do you need anything?" she asked, waiting until her mom had indicated *no* before settling at the table.

Her mother moved to her usual spot at the head of the table, expertly guiding the chair right up to the edge. "She hasn't lied about it, it's simply something that's never needed to be revealed until now. She's been very good to you, Janie. Especially after my accident."

"I know." Morgan had been more than just good. Jane had never given her boss the specifics, just that her mom had been in an accident and that Jane needed some time off. And every time she was late because of an appointment, or the few times her mom had pneumonia or some other illness, Morgan had accommodated.

"She's a lovely person. So helpful and generous." Her mom was practically gushing, and over a woman she'd never actually met.

"Mhmm," Jane agreed around a mouthful. Morgan was helpful and generous, but she clearly had limits. Time to turn the conversation around before she inadvertently disclosed the bucket list fiasco. While

Jane ate dinner they talked about her mother's day out, then settled in for some shared television time. By nine p.m., her mom's voice had grown drowsy. Jane turned off the TV. "Come on, bedtime, young lady."

The fact her mother didn't argue told Jane that her day had taxed her more than she'd let on. After the accident, Jane had the study on the ground floor converted into a bedroom for her mom, and now they had their routines down to a fine art. Leah could go on as much as she wanted about Jane "needing" a girlfriend, but Jane already knew that women generally weren't excited about a woman who came with a quadriplegic mom. A mom who required assistance with bedtime every night. Sure, she didn't need assistance from Jane specifically, but a 24/7 caretaker was not only expensive and unnecessary, but unfair to her mother.

Jane unhooked the CPAP/BiPAP machine from its stand by the bed, and waggled the headpiece. "Ready for your octopus?"

The machine really did look like an octopus suctioned to her face, with a full headpiece, nose mask, and assorted hoses snaking everywhere. But it helped with breathing difficulties overnight so as far as Jane was concerned, the machine could look like whatever it wanted.

"Yeah. Love you," her mom mumbled.

"Love you too." Jane brushed hair from her forehead, then helped fit the headpiece and position the mask snugly on her mom's nose. She put the tablet and other assorted electronics on to charge, plugged in her chair and then with another *love you* and final check that everything was in order, turned out the light and pulled the door closed.

Time to take care of the thing she'd been avoiding for days. The afterlife package. While she'd been watching television, she'd been thinking about her mom's afterlife questionnaire and what she could put for hers, wondering if she could make her answers so they'd be in the same place. She would forget ever mentioning the bucket list and just complete the package. Fuck—uh…sorry, Mom—*screw* ending up in some creepy ghost afterlife. She collected the papers from her leather satchel, poured herself the remaining wine and settled on the couch.

At the top of the first page was the heading *Religious Affiliation* with more options than Jane had ever thought possible, three rows filling the entire page. She flipped the page and skimmed down. The questionnaire read like one of those annoying personality quizzes that asked the same question five times but in slightly varied ways.

Jane read the first question, murmuring, "On a scale of one to ten, ten being strongly agree and one being strongly disagree, do you…" She ran her index finger down the list.

Enjoy being alone.
Dislike change.
Think groups of people are enjoyable.
Consider yourself introverted.
Fear the unknown.
Enjoy being busy.
Think racism is acceptable.
Consider yourself extroverted.
Love sports.
Don't care if others aren't as well off as you.
Consider your political views aligned with the "left wing".
Enjoy the arts.
Define yourself as an animal lover.
Believe family is important.
Think culling "undesirable portions" of the human population is a good thing.
Find yourself easily bored.
Describe yourself as "liberal" politically.

Jane sighed, gulped some wine and picked up her pencil to draft out her answers.

CHAPTER FIVE

The previous evening, La Morte had queried how proceedings were going with Jane and the bucket list. And when Morgan pointed out there were no proceedings, Cici had been very insistent Morgan accept Jane's proposal. Strangely insistent actually, even going so far as to reiterate that she was not only fine with it but thought one of the hardest working staff at Theda deserved help of this kind. She'd smiled benevolently, and shooed Morgan off with the command that she was to get things for Jane's bucket list underway as soon as possible.

Overruled by the boss. Brilliant.

The moment she'd arrived home from Aether, Morgan had sent Jane three meeting request options and almost immediately received confirmation for the meeting slot before work.

Jane arrived with her usual punctuality an hour before the rest of the staff came in, her door knock tentative. "You wanted to see me? I have those costings for upgrades ready if you'd like to see them."

"Wonderful. You can send them through and I'll peruse the estimates today." Jane hadn't moved from the doorway, and Morgan gestured she should come in.

"Okay. I'll do that." Jane quickly sat opposite, tablet resting on her lap. She didn't look wary so much as forcibly neutral, and the thought that Morgan had somehow upset Jane was discomforting.

Despite declining to help with the bucket list, she *thought* they had been interacting as normal. Heck, she'd even answered some of Jane's questions. Now the tension radiating from Jane sent reciprocal disquiet through Morgan. Time to turn it about. Hopefully. "About your other proposal." At Jane's dazed confusion, Morgan clarified, "Me helping you with your bucket list in exchange for you signing my contract. I've spoken to my boss and she has no issues with it. If you still wish to make an agreement then it's fine."

The change in Jane was immediate, as if Morgan had just given her a gift, and her reply was hasty. "I do. Wish to make an agreement that is, if you're really sure."

"I'm sure. You can reap the benefits of my position, and in return I get your completed afterlife package. Then, in return again, you will be able to rest comfortably knowing your afterlife needs will be well taken care of. Really, you're in a double-win situation." She stretched a hand across her desk and Jane took it. Morgan held on for a few seconds, aware for the first time of how delicate and fragile Jane's hands were, before reluctantly letting go. "So we have a deal then."

"Yes. Great. That's really great. Thank you. I appreciate it." Jane nodded slowly, as if talking herself through something. "If I'm going to be doing these bucket list things, then I'm going to have to give my mom some sort of explanation. Any suggestions?" She cleared her throat. "I'm sorry, it may have slipped out who and what you are. She's pretty perceptive and I was feeling out of sorts and forgot to put brain before mouth."

"It's fine, really. I mean I'd prefer the whole world didn't know exactly who I am, simply because I enjoy my privacy, but a few people here and there knowing isn't an issue."

"Okay, good. I mean, she's not the gossiping type, so she's not going to put up a billboard on Market Street saying 'Morgan Ashworth is a Bigwig Death's Minion'."

Morgan almost choked on her laughter. "A bigwig. That's hilarious. I must tell my boss." Cici would die laughing. Delicately, Morgan wiped the edges of her eyes. "As for what to tell your mother, I believe the truth is always best. That said, I would prefer what we're doing to be kept as quiet as possible, simply because I don't want every human trying to bargain with me."

"Got it," Jane said instantly.

Morgan pointed at the tablet on Jane's lap. "Now, do you have that bucket list on there for me?"

"Um, sure, let me just bring it up." Jane frantically swiped and tapped, moved something on the screen and after almost thirty seconds, passed the tablet over.

Morgan started skimming down the list which contained about fifteen items. So this was what Jane thought most important to do before she died. An interesting insight into Jane's life, about which she was mostly private.

1. Visit Hobbiton in New Zealand.
2. Go to Everest Base Camp.
3. SCUBA dive on the Great Barrier Reef.
4. Fall in love.
5. Share a bottle of 1959 Dom Pérignon Rosé with Mom.
6. Climb the Eiffel Tower (sunset).
7. Take Mom back to Connecticut for her 50th birthday.
8. Ride *Valravn, Kingda Ka, The Smiler, Gravity Max, Takabisha*.

Morgan glanced up. "What's number eight? The ride those names?"

"Roller coasters," Jane said immediately. "The first two are in Ohio and New Jersey, the rest are overseas. The UK, Taiwan and Japan."

"Okay then." Morgan kept skimming. Do this, see that, meet some presumably famous person. One thing stood out in glaring detail—there was no number twelve on the list. "Is twelve your unlucky number?"

A pink flush appeared at the base of Jane's neck. "Pardon?"

Morgan turned the tablet around, pointing. "Ten, eleven, thirteen. You're missing number twelve."

"Am I?" she squeaked. "I hadn't, I mean. Oh, I…um, that one wasn't a…it was, I just…" The pinkness on her neck rapidly spread upward to her cheeks.

Interesting. Jane's spluttering nervousness had caught Morgan's attention immediately, and on a hunch, she hit the *undo* command. Words appeared on the screen between 11. and 13. As she read them, Morgan's world seemed to stutter, then grind to a halt. A low thrill of excitement turned her stomach over. Number twelve was *not* what she'd expected at all. But it was something very interesting.

12. Sleep with my boss.

Sleep with my boss. *She* was Jane's boss. Unless this was an old list that Jane hadn't kept updated and that's why she'd deleted it so Morgan didn't think it was her. Or maybe it had nothing to do with her and was just a sexual fantasy, person non-specific as long as they were in a position of work-related power.

Morgan cleared her throat, debating if she should say anything or just move past it as if she hadn't seen it. She wanted to mention it, wanted to point out that she would be *more* than amenable to helping with that item, but Jane's pink flush was now more like fully red embarrassment. She'd clearly realized that her attempt to scrub number twelve from the list hadn't been as successful as she'd thought.

Right, time to move briskly past it as if it were nothing out of the ordinary. Morgan passed the tablet back. "I see nothing here that would be a problem. I assume you have a valid passport?"

The response was barely audible as Jane held the device to her chest. "Yes, I do." If it were possible, her voice got even softer. "I've never used it though. It was just…in case I could. One day."

Morgan's heart almost melted at the thought of Jane making preparations to do all these things she'd dreamed of, yet never quite getting there. She cleared her throat. "Wonderful. Can you SCUBA dive, or will you need to learn?"

"No, I know how," Jane said, still in that small voice.

"Great. Now there's just one small snag. I need to have this done by the end of May. Otherwise it'll be too late."

"Too late? End of May? But that's only six weeks away?"

"Yes it is. That's when our reporting period ends and it's my last chance to get in as many afterlife packages as I can. Otherwise this whole thing is pointless."

"Oh. I uh, maybe I should just pick half of the things?" Jane stared at the list, eyes wide with panic. "I…shit, I think I just realized what a huge long list of expensive stuff that is. It's just stupid things, I mean—"

"If that's what you want to do," Morgan interjected calmly before Jane could run away with her thoughts. "Whatever you need to do to satisfy your requirements for you to complete the afterlife package for me." She pulled a fresh notebook from a drawer. The sooner she made plans, the sooner this would be done and she could move on with getting ahead for next year's award. "When is your mother's birthday? Does that item fit within my timeframe?"

"Next month, so that's fine. But there're issues."

Morgan arched an eyebrow. "There is no such thing as an *issue* for me, Jane. Simply something that requires more planning and effort in order to make it happen." She gestured at the tablet which Jane still held against her chest. "Most of those items seem to be nothing more than booking travel and accommodation."

Jane reached across the desk and softly touched Morgan's hand, the movement so unexpectedly intimate that Morgan's pen stilled. "Morgan. My mother's a C-eight quadriplegic. Getting her to Connecticut may not be practical."

Morgan had the sudden sensation she was being held underwater, flailing desperately to surface so she could take a breath. "Jane, I'm so sorry."

"It's okay, really. She was hit by a drunk driver while cycling home from work almost seven years ago now. They said she wouldn't make it two years but she keeps on giving the doctors double middle fingers."

That certainly explained all the personal and vacation time Jane had taken not long after she'd started working at Theda. Morgan came around to Jane's side and leaned against her desk. Reaching down, she took one of Jane's hands. "Will it put your mum's health at risk to take a flight?"

"I, well I don't know for sure." She frowned. "She has her motorized chair, some hand function and weak sensation, made better by nerve transplants. Her breathing is generally okay, but she uses oxygen sometimes. She has a lot of sensation issues, pain and that sort of thing." Jane's eyebrows knitted together. "Buuut, she *was* transported from Portland to San Fran to live with me after the accident, and she's improved and stabilized out of sight since then, so now that I think about it, it'll probably be okay?"

Morgan's heart clenched and she had to consciously make herself take a deep, slow breath. "Okay well first things first. Let's get medical clearance and we'll go from there." She stretched over and scribbled *Medical flight company* on her notepad. "Is this why you've never tried to do anything on this list before? Even the easier, not cost-prohibitive things?"

"Mhmm, partly. I don't want to leave her for weeks at a time while I'm traipsing around the world. And even if I *could* afford such a vacation, I can't afford to pay an overnight nurse. I'm not wealthy like you are."

"I have no personal wealth either, Jane," Morgan corrected quietly. "Simply resources at my disposal. It's nothing more than a benefit of my position."

"A huge benefit," Jane said under her breath.

"Well yes," she agreed. Morgan tapped the edge of the tablet Jane held. "Obviously some things on this list are beyond my control. Number four for example. Fall in love? Sorry but I can't interfere in things like that. I'm not Cupid."

Jane's head snapped up. "Cupid's real?" she squeaked out.

"Of course not. Love is emotional, biological and nobody or nothing can interfere with that. It was a joke." Smiling, Morgan extracted the tablet from Jane's grip so she could skim the list again. Immediately, she caught sight of the item that made her stomach do an excited roll when she thought about it. "As for number twelve…"

Jane's face went blank. "Uh."

"Of course, I'm making a leap in assuming that I'm the boss being referred to?"

Jane bit her lower lip, and after a long pause, nodded. "I, well it was just a…never mind. Damn. Just ignore it."

Morgan went utterly still. "What if I don't want to ignore it?" she asked, surprised by the low intimacy of the question.

"Um, I…but…"

Jane seemed as if she were about to pass out, or hyperventilate, so Morgan charged forward in a slightly less *take me to bed* tone. "I enjoy sex and I find you attractive. So why not?"

"You do?" Jane's voice squeaked up an octave on the second word. The squeaking was incredibly cute.

"Which one? Enjoy sex or find you attractive?"

"The second one. Both."

"Yes I do. To both," Morgan said honestly. "I had no idea you were even…you know."

Jane's eyebrows shot up. "A lesbian? Really? Did my canonically queer comic book figurines not give me away?"

"Well, no. But I'm not up on the latest movies or television or comics so it was never going to twig for me based on that alone."

"Ah, well, yes I am. Very much a lesbian."

"All right then, excellent. We're on. I look forward to it." Despite the conviction in her words, she felt an odd emotion nestled alongside the excitement of possibility. Uncertainty. Despite her centuries, Morgan had had exactly twelve lovers—one of whom was Death, one of whom was her soulmate and the rest were mostly forgettable months'-long flings. Not exactly a female Casanova. What if Jane was expecting some otherworldly experience and Morgan couldn't deliver?

Jane's expression grew disbelieving. "But why? I mean, I'm just… average, ordinary."

"Jane," Morgan said, her voice oddly breathy, almost wondrous. "You're *anything* but average or ordinary." An unexpected and unwanted image flashed through her mind and she had to force Hannah away, force herself to tease and be light. "And besides, it's just sex. Scratching a mutual itch. It's not like we're proposing marriage."

"No, you're right."

Her ready agreement should have made Morgan feel relieved. But Jane's apparent dismissal of sleeping together as nothing of deep consequence, just a physical thing and nothing more, was upsetting. Morgan moved back around to sit behind her desk. A small barrier between them might help her regain some control over her feelings. "Now, what more do you wish to know about me and the process?"

Jane went still, almost unnaturally so, and when she raised her face to meet Morgan's gaze, she looked like a small child. "Um, when will it happen? Me dying."

"I don't know. Only Death knows the exact date." A small lie. Every afterlife package contained a code that only Death's Minions could see—a year of death, and that was as much as Morgan knew. But telling Jane that she knew what year she was going to die was pointless and cruel.

Jane reached up to tuck a wayward strand of her long bob back behind an ear. The color of her hair reminded Morgan of the rich red-brown of conkers. Beautiful. "Right." Jane took a moment, seeming to digest this information before launching into her next question. "How exactly did you get this job?"

"I honestly don't know why Death chose me. Perhaps she realized my aptitude for organization, paperwork and empathy. Maybe she just wanted a new plaything to amuse herself." Morgan smiled to herself. "We were both very amused, for a time at least, but that relationship ended many centuries ago."

Jane didn't bother disguising her incredulity. "Your ex is Death. And Death is a woman?"

"Yes and yes. There is *no* way a man could multitask well enough to do everything that's required of Death. And technically she's a few exes ago." She lowered her voice to add, "Cici's not very good with monogamy."

"Death's name is really *Cici*?" The disbelief was evident both in Jane's tone and her comically confused expression.

Morgan nodded. "Cici La Morte. Actually, her full name is currently Cecilia Helena Immortata La Morte."

"Wait. Wait." Jane frowned, mouth working silently. "Her name is like…the immortal death?"

"It is. I mean, she's been around since the beginning of humans, no exaggeration, so I think she's been called many things over the millennia. Her name evolves as she sees fit, but it is always some form of the word *death*." She leaned forward. "I can summon her here now and you can ask her yourself. And even better, she can tell you her original name which I find utterly impossible to pronounce because it's in a tongue that predates any known spoken language."

Jane stiffened. "Ohhh, nonono, that's fine, no need to do that. I'm good, thanks."

Morgan grinned. "What? Afraid to meet Death herself? She's actually very nice. Charming, personable, witty and very easy to talk to. Just don't ask about the black robes and scythe and swirly clouds and Grim Reaper title. She *hates* that. She is basically the exact opposite of the Grim Reaper."

"Right. Okay. I'll just take your word for it." Jane moved forward to the front edge of the chair. "Um, do you actually do it? Kill us?"

"No. And neither does she. It's a myth, that Death herself comes to you at the very end to take your soul or whatever you want to believe. Like Death touches you and poof you're dead. Her role, and by extension her Minions' role, is administrative. Making sure everything's recorded and filed. The I's are dotted and the T's crossed. She has to approve the death before it can actually happen but she's not there at the actual moment, because that would simply be too complex and frankly, impossible."

"Then why exactly do we need a contract and the questionnaire package?"

"To facilitate a smooth and successful transfer from this realm to whichever plane you'll be spending your afterlife on," she said matter-of-factly. "Jane, you have no idea how much paperwork one person moving from life to death generates. When the time comes, the administrative team will take the package I designed, and everything will be smooth and easy for the journey to your afterlife realm."

"Sounds like you've got it all figured out." Jane cleared her throat. "So you're really almost seven hundred years old?"

"Yes, I am."

"I really can't wrap my head around that. I mean you just don't *seem* that old. Even if I ignore the obvious fact that you look barely thirty, you don't act like a—" She paused, eyebrows dipping before she continued, "Sept…centurion. Sept-centenaryian? Do the Minions age at some super *super* slow rate?"

"Thank you." Morgan inclined her head graciously. Her current form was one of her favorites—a twenty-eight-year-old Swiss adventurer who'd suffered cerebral edema while attempting to summit Everest. She was going to miss this body when she had to give it up. "It's partially because my language and speech patterns have evolved over time, which I suppose is good, because it'd be fairly noticeable if I still spoke the way I did in my youth. But I seem barely thirty because this body was twenty-eight when it died and I took it over."

Jane blanched. "I'm sorry, what? Took it...over?"

"Yes." Sensing this might be a tricky thing for Jane to take in, Morgan made sure to enunciate. "This isn't my original body, not the body I was born into. Minions can inhabit any human's body, if they're already dead."

"Oh. Okay." Though pale, Jane didn't look like she was about to run screaming. A good sign? She blinked a few times. "You'll need to explain this to me. Slowly. You can really look like anyone you want?"

"Anyone who's died. And not look, *become*, as in their body is now mine until I decide to change it. Just like slipping into a new casing. Do you recall all that fuss about Elvis being alive? Actually almost any *famous* person who is always spotted skulking around in the shadows once they've died?"

Jane nodded. Blinked. Gulped.

"Well technically he was. Just not in the traditional sense of the word. So now, we try not to take famous people. But sometimes it's just too tempting. I tried Marilyn Monroe for a few days. It was interesting." Interesting was an understatement. Mostly because having never seen one of her movies, she couldn't quite understand the fuss. Until she inhabited that body. Then she understood very well.

Jane's question was tentative, as if she was afraid to hear the answer. "Are you human?"

Morgan smiled indulgently. "Yes. Flesh and blood." She was about to leave it at that, but Jane seemed so overwhelmed that she felt a sudden urge to soothe her. "Here." She stretched over and took Jane's unresisting hand. Morgan placed it on her wrist, curling Jane's fingers around the pulse point. "Feel that?"

Jane nodded slowly, cheeks pinking, and her reply was barely above a whisper. "I feel it. You're warm."

Morgan felt it too, but it was more than just a simple touch. The gentle grip, the warmth of Jane's hand around her wrist was immediately soothing, and she had to force herself to think of what she was trying to say instead of the softness of Jane's skin and the immediate sense of rightness that accompanied their physical connection. "Yes I am. All that heartbeat and blood flow and internal organs working as intended. You know, a very alive and human thing to do."

Jane smiled, then seemed to register that her hand still lingered on Morgan's wrist. She withdrew it slowly, then rubbed her fingertips over her palm. Without looking at Morgan, she asked, "Can you take a man's body?"

Morgan absently turned the ring on her left pinky in an attempt to distract herself from the unusual sensation of goosebumps gliding up her arm. "I could. But why would I want to? I've been stuck in one as a last-minute emergency, against my will, but other than that I can't think of a good reason to be in a man's body." She clamped her molars together, trying to ignore the unease of recalling each of those nights, centuries ago, where Cici would arrive, without fail, to *save her*.

Jane looked poised to ask her to clarify, but thankfully Morgan's expression seemed to divert her. "What if you pick a body with say cancer or an incurable disease or something?"

"If it's not too advanced, it goes away when I inhabit the body. The moment I'm in there, the aging process, and the progression of any disease halts." Morgan held up a hand. "Don't ask me how. I don't know the exact reason or science behind it. I imagine it ties in to whatever Cici does that gives us the ability to move between realms and through time and space. I've always thought a little of what makes her *her* is passed to us."

"Why do you even change? I mean if what we were told in high school is correct, Minions don't die. So why is there any reason?"

Morgan hesitated for a few moments. "We change because it can cause issues if you stay in the same place, looking exactly the same for too long. But the main reason is that sometimes bodies break and can no longer do this job for which we need to be physically capable. I'm immortal in the vague sense of the word, but I am not indestructible."

"How does that work? You don't seem like you're made of stone or whatever."

Morgan rolled her eyes. "I swear fiction is the most annoying, unrealistic pain in my butt. We just confirmed that I'm a human with a heartbeat and blood and organs working like everyone else, did we not?"

Jane nodded.

"Do you remember how I said Death must approve all deaths as they happen? She just doesn't allow ours. I can get hurt like a regular person and I have before, trust me, but things that would ordinarily kill me just…don't. I'm stuck as I am, injured, until I can either move myself into a new body, or Cici does it for me."

Jane's eyebrows knitted adorably together. "Right, okay. So you just pick someone who's newly dead and away you go?"

Such a wonderfully simple way of putting it. "Pretty much. Certain types of deaths are preferable, things where organs are intact otherwise it takes me too long to heal them. I can't overcome massive organ failure, the overwhelming amount of cell damage caused by aggressive or end-stage cancer, decapitation, spinal injuries or dismemberment or anything like that. Drownings or smoke inhalation are the best— anything that causes brain death but where organs are functional, because my Animus reanimates the brain."

"Animus." Jane drew the word out over a few seconds. "And it reanimates dead bodies. So…you're like a zombie?"

It'd come out so hopeful, as if Jane really believed in such things, that Morgan laughed. "I suppose you're right."

"So what is Animus exactly?"

How to explain Animus to someone like Jane who dealt in data and absolutes? "It's, well…I suppose the easiest explanation is it's our life force. A soul maybe? I really don't know exactly what it is but it's the thing that keeps living things living, and somehow allows me to move myself into a dead bag of tissue and make it live again."

Thankfully Jane seemed to accept Morgan's clumsy answer, or at least she pretended to. More likely was that Jane was storing this information to research later. "Where is it exactly? Is it cells, or part of your blood or an extra organ you have?"

"Nobody knows where Animus lives." Morgan twisted her hands together, surprised by her unusual nervousness. "It's not in your brain, I know that much."

"How do you know that?"

"I just…do." Morgan felt an unexpected shudder run down her spine, and had to consciously force it, and unwanted memories, away. She cleared her throat. "What else do you want to know?"

"Ummm." Jane tapped her fingertips on the arm of her chair. "How do you get all these afterlife packages done in time when there's billions of people in the world?"

"Billions, yes but if you exclude the under-fifteens which is roughly one-quarter of the world's population, and consider that administering and uploading packages is a constantly rolling process, it's not hard to imagine. A package I check and upload today may have been administered last year for a person who won't die for another five or ten. We're very efficient and we can travel anywhere in the world or across realms in seconds. The easiest way to describe it would be teleportation."

Jane gaped for a few seconds before asking in a voice that held more than a little disbelief, "You can teleport?"

"Yes."

Jane squeaked out yet another, "How?"

"I suppose pinching the fabric of time and space would be as accurate as I could get. I really don't understand the nitty gritty of it." Morgan laughed. "Theoretical physics isn't as *theoretical* as most people think."

Jane was silent for almost a minute. "What does teleporting feel like?"

Not the question she was expecting. "Around earth it's warm, kind of humid and gooey feeling. Traveling to Aether, the plane where Cici lives, is absolutely freezing."

"Can you take people with you?"

"No, but I can take small things if I'm carrying them or have a bag. Only Cici can move people around earth or across realms."

They sat quietly for a while, Morgan watching Jane who seemed to be working through everything she'd just heard. After a few minutes Jane exhaled a long breath. "Okay, so if you want to go somewhere, you just blink yourself there and if you need a new human body, you just put yourself into one. Sure, okay, makes…sense?"

"I understand this must be a lot to take in." Morgan offered a patient smile. She clasped Jane's hand, squeezing reassuringly. "Jane, you're going to have to trust me when I tell you that some things just *are* and are unexplainable to someone who hasn't experienced life the way I have. The life I live is somewhat transcendent. Not exactly supernatural, but close."

"Okay, I get it." She nodded a few more times as if collecting her thoughts, then drew in a breath. "Is there anything you can't do?"

"Time travel. Nobody can do that. I always burn every cake I cook. I'm terrible at poker," Morgan deadpanned.

A smile flickered across Jane's lips. "That's actually not a lot in the scheme of things. What did you look like before all of this? When you weren't a Minion?"

"Similar to the way I do now, though nowhere near as attractive." There was no point avoiding the truth that she was considered good-looking. "The older I get, the more I find myself afflicted with vanity, but I've always chosen bodies that are blond-haired and blue-eyed. It feels better to me, makes me feel more like myself." Morgan frowned, trying to recall her first body. "I was far shorter, maybe around five feet two? My hair was more straw-colored and now that I think about it, I think my eyes were a lighter blue."

Jane's voice lowered to an almost intimate softness. "Does it bother you at all? Like…not really being you, physically?"

"The first hundred years or so, yes it did. Now I've grown accustomed to it. It's a necessity." The last word came out more harshly than she'd intended, but Jane either didn't catch the tone or chose yet again to move past it.

Jane ventured another tentative question. "And does everything like, work the way a human body does?"

"Yes. I *do* have ridiculously high energy requirements though, call it a fast metabolism or whatever, because I cross-realm travel frequently, and have been traveling daily around The Americas for the past ten months or so too. But biologically, I'm human. A robust human. I'm a little stronger and faster, slightly better sight and all that. But not much. Like if the average woman scores a ten, for those things I'd be a twelve. Just a little better but not like a superhero."

"More than a twelve," Jane said under her breath, probably thinking Morgan couldn't hear her.

But Morgan did. "Thank you."

The pinkness of Jane's cheeks turned to a cute redness. "So you like, uh, use the bathroom and menstruate and things like that?"

People were fascinated by the minutest details, things that were irrelevant in the scheme of things. "Yes, I do all the human stuff, because I'm human, remember?"

"You could have kids?"

She stiffened. "I suppose I could, but I've never considered it."

Jane fidgeted. "Would they be human or Minion?"

"They would be very human and another mortal for me to leave behind when they reached the end of their life. That is why I will not do it. I left someone behind once, and once was enough." The pain had arrived as expected, and Morgan couldn't help the terseness of her explanation.

Jane was either incredibly perceptive, or not at all attuned to others' emotional states, because she moved past Morgan's reaction as if it were non-existent. "What happens when people start noticing you never look any older? Fifty years is still a very long time to look the same."

"I tell them I have a fantastic surgeon and assortment of effective skincare products, along with an excellent diet and exercise regime." Morgan raised a shoulder. "When I have to change bodies, I tell my employees that unfortunately the company is moving in a new direction and they are all given generous redundancies. Then I swap my form for a new one, sometimes change my middle initial, and hire new people. I've only had to do it twice in this modern era, but the process has worked well so far."

Jane fidgeted nervously. "Um, when are you due to get a new body?"

"Fifteen years or so."

Jane nodded slowly as if she were working through some complex math. "Okay. That's okay." The inward focus turned outward, and she studied Morgan as though she held the key to an unanswerable question. "What's it like? Getting a new body I mean."

"It takes a few weeks or a month to get comfortable, depending on the physical differences of height and mass. The voice is always different which is interesting—I can't change physical attributes like vocal cord length and pitch but I always retain my accent. A few times I've had to swap for a new body within a few days because I couldn't stand the way I sounded. But what's really strange is occupying slightly different dimensions in space. It totally messes with my proprioception and takes me some time to adjust. Until I do, I'm constantly tripping, or misjudging distance. I spend a lot of time in a gymnasium until I feel like myself again."

"That sounds really annoying."

Morgan shrugged. "It's part of the job."

Jane gestured vaguely. "I'm still having a hard time wrapping my head around the whole body swap and superhuman healing. So what happens if you like...I don't know, are in a serious car accident and your insides are outside?"

"Unpleasant but not unfixable. I don't know what it is but something allows me to heal faster than normal people." She held up both hands in a placating gesture. "Sorry, again I really don't know how. But if it's something that's going to affect our ability to perform our jobs then it *has* to be a new body."

"Like what?"

"I broke my back in 1858 in a riding accident. My horse spooked at a bear and ran me into a tree. Paralyzed me." Morgan drew her fingers between her breasts. "About here. Cici carried me to a new host and that was that." Morgan decided there was no point in elaborating on the other times when she was unable to move herself to a new host and needed Cici's help. She already felt vaguely sick after alluding to it earlier.

Jane's reply was surprisingly acerbic. "Everything comes so easily to you, doesn't it? Broken body, just get a new one. You've never had a hardship in your life, have you?"

Though she understood Jane's anger, given her mother's circumstance, and was annoyed with herself for being so careless in mentioning it, Morgan couldn't help bristling. She tried to keep the bite from her reply, and failed. "Yes I have. Quite a bit actually." She stood with an abruptness that surprised her. "I think that's enough for one day. Everyone will be here soon. I have work to do."

CHAPTER SIX

A takeout delivery driver arrived at the office ten minutes after the last person—save for Jane and Morgan—had left the Theda office for the evening. After the abrupt and awkward end to their meeting yesterday morning, Jane had been dreading this planning session but since then Morgan had acted like their exchange about paralysis had never happened and had been as friendly and easygoing as ever.

Smiling widely, Morgan held up two huge brown paper bags. "I ordered Japanese. I hope you like it? Sorry I should have asked but you were down in the server room and I was starving. Am starving."

"I do like Japanese, very much." Jane stared at the bags. "Is someone else joining us?"

Morgan's eyebrows crinkled. "No? It's just us." She started hauling out containers of heavenly smelling food, setting them on the table in the staff room. "I wasn't sure what you liked so I just got a whole bunch of things. And I'll eat everything you don't."

Jane stared at her boss's slender, borderline too-thin frame, trying to imagine her consuming all that food. Before she could police herself, she blurted, "Are you secretly three starving kids dressed up inside an adult costume?"

Morgan nearly choked on a gyoza. Coughing and laughing at the same time, she covered her mouth until she regained control again. "I am not. My life is basically nonstop eating so I have enough energy to get to my next destination." Her smile was self-deprecating, almost exasperated. "And no, it's not as fun as it sounds, *having* to eat all the time."

Jane had been about to joke about it, but that smile which hadn't touched Morgan's eyes stopped her. "I've never really thought about it, but I could see it getting kind of tedious."

"It does. Once, I was so desperate for energy, I ate butter. Just butter on its own, spooning it into my mouth like it was ice cream or something."

Finding Morgan's wide-eyed embarrassment adorable, Jane prolonged it by asking, "What was it like?"

Morgan dipped another gyoza into sauce. "Actually not bad. Slippery." She winked and ate the gyoza in one surprisingly delicate mouthful. "Come on, let's eat before all of this gets cold."

They sampled each other's dishes, which wasn't as weird as Jane would have thought. And they talked. Or rather, Jane asked and Morgan answered without hesitation.

Jane deftly chopsticked udon noodles into her mouth, barely containing her groan of pleasure. So good. "I've always wondered about *Theda* because it's such an odd name for a data storage company. It's an acronym right? The...data?"

"No, it's not an acronym." Grinning, Morgan reached for her notebook with the Theda logo and company name across the top. She turned it sideways so Jane could see, and on the first line she wrote D, and crossed out the D in Theda. Morgan did the same for the E and the A...

It was then Jane saw it—it was an anagram. She laughed, took the pen from Morgan and finished the word. DEATH.

Morgan golf clapped. "That's it. Cici hates it almost as much as she hates the, and I quote, *stupid Death scythe logo* I designed." Morgan tapped the top of the page.

Jane laughed. Now that the origin of both logo and company name had been pointed out to her it seemed embarrassingly obvious, especially for someone so detail-oriented. "It really was under my nose all this time."

"Yours and everyone else's." Morgan's voice softened. "People tend to see what they wish to, what fits into their narrative. For instance, you stopping to consider other possibilities, like the fact I could be attracted to you?" Her smile managed to be both flirtatious and sad. "It doesn't fit because you already have an image of who I am in your mind. Everyone does. The body I inhabit, the clothes I wear, the car I drive. But none of that is *me*." By the time she was done explaining, she seemed almost distressed.

Jane felt overcome with a sense of social inadequacy. Time for comforting fallbacks—change the subject, or move right along as if nothing is awkward or weird. "Why do you have a car if you can teleport anywhere you want to?" Morgan drove a flashy, near-new black BMW convertible beside which Jane parked her Mazda some mornings.

"Because suddenly arriving and disappearing every day would be a little odd, don't you think? I mean our existence isn't a secret but at the same time we don't go around advertising ourselves. And I quite enjoy driving. Or speeding, rather."

"What about *hell* for bad people? Is that actually a thing?"

"Hell is a very broad term, and not an entirely accurate one. There are many realms, all with varying functions. As I said, our role is simply to facilitate the smooth passage from one realm—this life, into the other realm—the afterlife. We don't actually get to say who goes where." Morgan frowned. "Actually, that's not entirely true. Through history there *have* been a few dozen or so people that the Afterlife Committee, which is all the leaders of every afterlife realm and headed up by Death, have unanimously decided should be...flung out into space for lack of a better phrase." She lowered her voice. "I'm sure you can imagine who those people are."

Still chewing, Jane nodded.

"As for everyday pieces of shit, they're afforded the same rights as everyone else." Morgan cleared her throat. "Of course, sometimes there are administrative errors, or the connection glitches while transferring the data, and people don't *quite* end up where they thought they would. Unavoidable really when you're dealing with roughly one hundred and fifty thousand people dying worldwide on a daily basis." Her smile was a touch sly. "I'm only human after all."

Jane picked up on what she hadn't said right away. "So you just decide out of rapists and murderers and whatever who should be sent to the bad place and who shouldn't?"

"Cici has the final say, and sometimes we disagree. It's not black and white, and I do the best I can with the knowledge I have. There is an appeal process which again, goes through the Afterlife Committee, but in all the centuries I've been doing this I've only had four people transferred from a…" She air-quoted. "Bad realm they shouldn't have been in. *Four*, in how many billions?" Morgan's tone turned almost defiant, combative. "I know people. I'm *very* good at what I do."

"I'm sorry, I didn't mean to sound like I don't think you do the right thing or you're making mistakes. It's just, how do you decide? Like a guy who beats his wife but, I don't know, donates to charity and rescues stray animals as well or something?"

Morgan shrugged. "What can I say, Jane? Sometimes people who do bad things in their life don't get what the people they wronged think they deserve. We do the best we can, and like I said, it's a committee process. The criteria have been in place for an extraordinarily long time and have worked very well so far."

Jane maneuvered more noodles into her mouth in an attempt to buy herself some time to ponder. But all she could think about was the drunk guy who'd paralyzed her mom. The guy who'd changed both of their lives forever. He'd been drinking on the first anniversary of his wife's death, decided to drive home after his day at the bar and had received a prison term for what he'd done.

By all accounts he was a decent guy who'd made a mistake, so did he deserve to live his afterlife in some horrible place because of this one thing that had changed lives? Before, she would've said unequivocally yes. But now…now she wasn't sure. The mouthful she'd swallowed felt stuck in her throat and she had to force it down. "What about kids? I mean if they can't do their contracts and stuff then where do they go?"

"Under the age of fifteen they all go to the same, wonderful place. Personally escorted by Maria, our head of child care. Between fifteen and eighteen they are generally segregated from adults. That's the simple version of course." She pushed her empty container to the side and nabbed another of sesame chicken, tilting it toward Jane. "Would you like this?"

Jane shook her head. With a contented smile, Morgan began scooping up food. They finished eating in silence, and though Morgan had eaten three times as much as Jane, she'd managed to do it delicately. Or so Jane had seen the few times she'd snuck a look at her. There was something oddly sexy about watching Morgan Ashworth eating.

Morgan scraped her chopsticks around the inside of the takeout container, stared longingly at it then set it aside. She wiped her mouth with a paper napkin. "Now, Jane." Her voice lowered to a soft purr.

"Have you decided on your absolute must-dos for your bucket list? I'd like you to get this underway as soon as possible."

Mercifully, Jane managed to ignore the tone to focus on the actual question. As it was, all she managed was, "Yes, I have."

"And?"

She'd spent hours thinking about what she most wanted to do, about what were the most unattainable without Morgan's financial assistance, and had managed to narrow the list to six. Six choices which meant leaving the one she thought she wanted the most off the list.

Number. Twelve.

Jane tried not to think about it, failed to not think about it, *really* thought about it and finally engaged a non-lusty part of her brain to splutter out her answer to Morgan's question. "I'd like to do Hobbiton, SCUBA diving on the Great Barrier Reef, the champagne with my Mom, the roller coasters, taking Mom back to Connecticut, and the Eiffel Tower. I really want to do Everest Base Camp but if we have a time limit then I don't have enough time to train and acclimate." Jane looked up, feeling suddenly nervous, as if she'd made the wrong choices on a multiple-choice quiz. "Are those okay?"

Morgan's expression softened the moment they made eye contact. "Of course they are. I told you, any you want." Morgan paused. "But, what about number twelve?"

Yes, what about it? Oh nothing much except the fact *number twelve* was basically at the top of her want to do list and had been on her mind almost every day since she'd first laid eyes on Morgan. "Uh, I um…just didn't think it was a good idea."

"Why not? My ego could get rather bruised here, Jane," Morgan said, but she was smiling. Actually, not smiling so much as smirking, her expression slightly predatory.

"Because. The others seemed more, well…" She knew her face was bright red and the knowledge only made her blush further. "Attainable."

"Attainable." The word sounded like silk. "And you think what exactly? That I'm unattainable?"

"Yes," she admitted. "It was just a silly thing, something I knew would never actually happen, and the things for my mom seemed more important."

"So you would put another person's wants above your own?" Despite the slightly formal wording of Morgan's question, it was asked so tenderly that Jane couldn't think of how to respond. Morgan leaned forward. "The things for your mother are more important than what exactly?"

"They're more important than me, um, enjoying myself."

"Ah, I see. But what if *I* want you to enjoy yourself? What if I want to enjoy myself?" Her lips quirked, and before Jane could fumble out an answer, Morgan murmured, "Tell you what. I'll throw number twelve in as a freebie. Think of it as an incentive to get this finished as quickly as possible."

Jane had no idea why, but she found herself saying, "You don't have to. I mean we made an agreement and this is stepping outside the predetermined rules." Oh, shut *up*. She was being handed sex with Morgan Ashworth on a platter and she was basically saying oh yes please but also no thank you. Jane wanted to slap her inner voice for being so dumb.

That right eyebrow came up. So sexy. "You don't want it?"

Jane swallowed and answered in a voice hoarse with anticipation, "No. I do, but…"

"But what?"

"But nothing, I suppose." Except the whole job thing and how the hell was she supposed to work near Morgan Ashworth after they'd slept together. Jane made a mental note to bring up HR documentation to avoid a sexual harassment suit. Later. When Morgan wasn't looking at her like she was her last meal.

"Good. So do I. Want it, that is. Very much." Despite the fact they were alone, Morgan leaned close to murmur in Jane's ear, "I thought I already made that clear."

Jane suppressed a shudder. She had no idea how Morgan managed to go from a calm and controlled CEO to a smoldering, sensuous seductress in a matter of seconds. "You did," she said hoarsely.

"Wonderful. Then it's agreed." Morgan moved back and offered her hand to seal the deal.

Jane took it, noticing immediately that instead of shaking her hand, Morgan simply held it, her thumb softly stroking the back of her hand. Jane went still, aware of the movement and able to do little more than just hold on. Swallowing hard, she nodded. "Sounds good," she managed to get out.

"I concur." With a final squeeze, Morgan released her and leaned back in her chair.

Jane pushed her own chair back a few inches, desperate for some distance before she embarrassed herself even more. "Are you always this forward?"

Morgan seemed taken aback. "Well, yes. I have no need to skirt around details, and I've learned over my many years that honesty is generally the best course of action. Unless it's hurtful." Her expression transformed to one of concern. "Are you hurt by my admission?"

Jane couldn't help laughing. "Hurt? Oh not at all. I'm flattered, very confused, a little nervous, but definitely not hurt." She was a lot more besides all of that, but the admission of just what she was feeling wasn't appropriate for now.

Morgan exhaled. "Good. Then let's get started on planning." She rummaged in the paper bags, turned them upside down and sighing, asked, "Do you mind if I have some dessert delivered?"

CHAPTER SEVEN

The moment she'd kissed Cici hello, Morgan blurted, "I've now seen The List. Jane's bucket list," she clarified at Cici's momentarily blank expression.

"I see. And why do I need to know?"

Morgan plonked into a chair and reached for a pre-cut wedge of brie. "It's going to be expensive. I'm simply keeping you in the loop so you're prepared for The Accountant." The cheese was so good, she took two more and ate them in one mouthful.

"I appreciate that, and I already knew it would be a reasonable sum. No matter." Cici waved her wineglass in an expressive arc. "So, some international travel is on the cards for you then?"

Morgan frowned. "Well yes, but that's not unusual though."

La Morte laughed, the sound a rich melody that echoed and filled the room. "No, darling. I mean you'll be accompanying Ms. Smith during her travels."

Morgan almost choked on her response. And a fourth wedge of cheese. "What? No! Why would I do that?"

"Because how else are you going to finance this?"

"I'll give her a card loaded with funds, or transfer funds into an account for her to use," she said slowly, as if it were obvious. Which it was.

"Oh no no. No," Cici said flatly, both hands up, palms out as if to stop Morgan in her tracks. "Morgana, it is one thing to provide the means for Ms. Smith to enjoy her bucket list, which as I said I am more than happy to sign off on, but I am *not* wasting half of my day on the phone to The Accountant because this human can't properly account for her expenditure. Not to mention, if you're not accompanying her, then how can we technically expense it? I will not defraud the tax-paying humans of the world." She kept both hands up as if to forestall Morgan's rebuttal. "Yes, I know. And I know you know. And we both know what The Accountant is like, regardless of the fact nobody else in the universe cares. If she's unsatisfied with an audit I'll never hear the end of it, and you know finances bore me to death. So, you will go wherever Ms. Smith goes. Spend whatever you wish, of course, but bring back receipts."

Morgan managed a spluttered, "Really?"

"Yes, really."

"Ugh, I'm not a babysitter, Cici."

"No, of course you're not a babysitter." She raised a finger, her smile slow, almost coy. "Because Ms. Smith is not a baby, she's an adult woman. And what exactly is on this bucket list? Surely it won't take long to complete."

"The usual. Visit some overseas places, drink fancy champagne, do some things that would ordinarily be difficult because she doesn't have the funds, etcetera." The four words of number twelve were seared behind her eyes and she fought down a surge of anticipation. Morgan cleared her throat, hoping she didn't look as flushed as she felt. "This is a phenomenal waste of my time. And my talents."

"I disagree. It will be a walk in the park for you, and your many talents which you *will* utilize to escort Ms. Smith around the world as she merrily checks things off this list."

The battle had been lost before she'd even had a chance to put up a fight. Morgan ground her teeth. "Fine."

"Wonderful! I'm so glad you've agreed." Smiling, Cici raised the wineglass to her lips.

Agreed was a loose interpretation of what she'd done, but Morgan simply nodded, well aware that there was no point in arguing.

Cici eyed her, the smile turning mischievous. "You know, that was far easier than I expected. I do believe you're pleased by the prospect of joining Ms. Smith on her adventures. Excited even."

"Pardon me?"

But Cici simply mimed locking her smiling lips shut and throwing away the key.

"Sometimes you're insufferable." Morgan sighed, mind turning over details. "I'll make sure The Accountant knows what's happening so you don't have to waste any of your precious time speaking with her."

Cici cooed, "Thank you." She reached up and softly patted Morgan's cheek. "Always looking out for my happiness."

"Yes, of course," Morgan drawled.

La Morte leaned back, crossing her legs. "I really don't know why you're so opposed to escorting Ms. Smith. It's perfect. You'll be out and about among the people. *People*, Morgana. You are one of the few I know who like people, genuinely like them, and who is revitalized by being among them as if your engine is fueled by empathetic connections. It's adorable watching you interact with people, and it also means you're excellent at your job which you know makes me very happy."

Cici was right. Highly empathetic, Morgan was sensitive to others to the point where pleasure, happiness, enjoyment and the like of other people was almost like an energy recharge. And conversely, people with bad vibes tended to drag her down. She frowned, mind tracking back to what Cici had just said. "Adorable? Really? Like, a puppy?"

"Well that's not exactly what I meant, but now that you've mentioned it, puppy is rather appropriate. Cuteness aside, you're loyal, protective, sweet and friendly." She tapped her chin. "Hmm, yes." Cici straightened, now all business. "Now, tell me everything I need to know. And in…" A quick glance at the wall clock. "Ten minutes. I have someone to meet."

More like someone or someones with whom to sleep. Morgan acceded, set aside her frustration at her boss's deft underhanded maneuvering in making her an accomplice to Jane's bucket list, and quickly gave Cici the rundown of pertinent information.

Once she'd nodded her satisfaction at Morgan's report, Cici gathered her papers and tablet then rose from the chaise longue. She strode off in the direction of her quarters, leaving Morgan rushing after her, talking as she walked. "Now, if you're using conventional transportation methods then you're going to need a passport. Traveling on your diplomatic ID will cause more annoyance than help if you have to pass through security checkpoints."

Morgan had obviously never needed a passport before, because she'd never traveled internationally via conventional methods. She, like all Minions, had diplomatic immunity, with an identification card to negotiate her through any security issue. She threw both hands up.

"Fine. Whatever. I hope you're seeing now just what a huge pain in the ass making me go along with this is."

If she didn't know better, Morgan would have sworn that time slowed. Cici glanced at her. "Oh no. Not a pain at all, Morgana. In fact, I'd say it's serendipitous. Was I not just lamenting a few days ago that you're starting to look worn down and needed a break? And here it is, dropped in your lap." They'd reached the door of La Morte's bedroom, and her boss turned to face her. "Rather timely, I'd say."

"Timely? You told me you wanted me to work less, not more and you're sending me away from my work. I'm going to have to work twice as hard to keep up, and then catch up!"

"Oh please. Eighty percent of your work is mobile and as for the other twenty percent, I'm certain you're so on top of it that a few days is not going to cause any issues. You need a break, Morgana, and this is the perfect opportunity."

"You know what would give me a break? You finding someone to head up The Americas so I can focus on my *actual* job." Aware of her insolence, Morgan left her complaint at that.

La Morte waved dismissively. "I'm working on it. You know I can't just conjure a replacement from thin air. Do you recall the last time I appointed someone in a rush?" She arched an eyebrow. "We ended up with the disaster that was Frederick and the Finland Incident." Cici cupped Morgan's face in both hands and pulled her close to kiss her forehead. "I have utmost faith in you managing The Americas for me until I find someone to relieve you, *and* of your ability to make the most of Ms. Smith's travel situation. Now, if you'll excuse me, I have important business to attend to." With a wink, she slipped into the room and closed the door with a quiet *snick*.

Morgan resisted the urge to raise double middle fingers at the closed door, then spun on her Louboutin heels and stalked away. Her annoyance echoed down the hall as sharp clacks. She muttered under her breath, unable to stop the mocking singsong from creeping in, "Oh *you* can babysit Jane. It'll be so fun and exciting for you. You need to have a break, Morga*n*a, because dare I say it you're starting to look your age." She blew a raspberry.

As Morgan approached the concierge desk, Jonathon straightened even further, if that were possible. "Jonathon, I need you to tell The Accountant there's going to be a substantial increase in my expenditure for the next few months." She knew she didn't have to explain why—Morgan's budget was unlimited and her bank cards were never declined. "I want her to be aware there may be potential strange charges on my accounts so she won't bother Cici with questions, and also so she doesn't cross earth side to see me." She raised an eyebrow. "Having her charging into my office like last time doesn't look good in front of my employees."

"Yes, Ms. Ashworth. Of course. I'll take care of that for you," he said in his usual calm tone. He had his finger on the pulse of everything, intuiting what people needed without ever being unctuous or obsequious.

"Also, I need you to arrange a passport for me, please."

"Certainly. It should only take a few days." He penned something in his diary before looking up, eyebrows raised expectantly. "What nationality would you prefer?"

"British would probably be most prudent. And please make me seem youthful when you're putting in my birth year. About twenty-six or seven would be perfect." She eyed him before asking dryly, "I can get away with it, can't I?"

A smile broke free before he managed to arrange his features back into his usual professional face. "Of course. And yes, Ms. Ashworth, you most certainly can." Another note joined the first one. "When you have your travel arrangements finalized, please copy me in on your plans so that I can ensure there are no security issues with your check-ins. So many trips in succession may raise red flags with border agents, customs and the like. Especially internationally when Ms. Smith has never traveled abroad."

Morgan didn't even bother to ask how he knew Jane had never used her passport. He probably knew Jane's birthday, favorite drink and shoe size. "Thank you. Call me if you require any details, otherwise I'll see you tomorrow." Morgan smiled her thanks, said goodbye then summoned her energy and left Aether.

Decades ago, she'd learned that if she stood next to her refrigerator before leaving to visit Cici, she could cut down on the precious few seconds that would be used to move from her relocation position to the kitchen. The refrigerator door was in easy reach as was the tray half-full of leftover shepherd's pie that she'd left a spoon in ready for just this situation. It took no time to finish, and still chewing a mouthful of mashed potato topping, Morgan made her way toward her bathroom.

She turned on the bath tap, tossed her jacket in the direction of the dry-cleaning pile and as she passed the mirror, reflexively glanced at herself. A mistake. Morgan froze, staring at her reflection, tracing the shapes of eyes and nose, lips and chin, cheekbones and ears. The more she stared, the greater the whirl of anxiety. She stared some more, waiting, hoping for the emotion to pass.

It'd been this way since she'd made her first body change. A few times a year she would have this feeling, which she'd managed to categorize as disquiet. A strange sensation of not knowing who she really was anymore. Of not knowing the face she wore, the body she inhabited. It was ridiculous because of course she *knew*. But some deep primitive part of her was triggered to remind her that she didn't inhabit the body into which she was born. Occasionally she'd have an unwanted flash of some physical part of her original self—the birthmark she'd had on her left hip, the unevenness of her bottom teeth, the crooked angle of her right pinky from where she'd broken it in the mill—and the discomfort would well up again.

The strength of the feeling had eased over the centuries, and she'd learned to bring herself under control faster with every passing year. But she had never managed to rid herself of the sensation entirely. Looking at the reflected image of perfection staring back at her now only intensified the feeling.

Who are you, Morgan Rochefort Ashworth? Would Hannah ever recognize you? Definitely not physically. Perhaps not even emotionally. Morgan smoothed her palms over her breasts and down her stomach. Pressing her hands against her diaphragm, she made herself breathe slowly and deeply until the upset eased enough for her to think clearly again.

She glanced over her shoulder, checking the water level of the freestanding claw bathtub in the middle of the bathroom. Morgan stripped off the rest of her clothing, tossed those too onto the dry-cleaning pile. Her bath oil—a vanilla and coconut-scented mixture that one of Cici's handmaidens prepared weekly for her—was within easy reach. The heat in the bathroom already had her sweating and she began to slather the oil over her skin, massaging it into every centimeter of herself, even the skin between her toes.

A generous helping of bath salts dissolved into the hot water before she stepped in, sliding down into the long, deep tub until she was fully submerged with her eyes closed. Morgan let out her breath through her nose, a few slow bubbles at a time until her lungs had emptied and were burning in protest. She kept herself underwater until she physically couldn't bear it any longer and propelled herself upward, sucking in a deep gasping breath as she broke the surface.

Water dripped into her eyes and Morgan shoved her hair back, wringing it out before sliding back down until just her shoulders and arms were above the water. She let her hands float on the surface, waggling her fingers in the scented water. She traced the faint scars on her hands, the one on the outside of her right thigh, the one on her left knee. When she'd first slipped into this body, her fingertips had been rough and calloused. Given the manner in which she'd died, Morgan had to conclude that the woman had been a fan of all things outdoors and rock climbing in particular.

As she always did when changing bodies, she'd carefully examined her new self, mapped out every freckle and tattoo and scar. Then she'd concocted reasons for each one, something to make her feel more grounded and connected to this new shell. The scar on her knuckle was from a fist fight with the school bully, the one on her thigh from when she fell off her bicycle at age eight and was dragged ten feet down the road, the one on her knee was from roller skating on the path around her childhood park. Just normal things that would occur during a regular human lifespan.

Unexpectedly now, she found herself wondering about Jane. Her scars and birthmarks. How she might have acquired them. How she felt about them. Jane *had* lived a regular human life and the inevitability of it leaving marks was oddly fascinating. That thought turned easily to carefully undressing Jane, and Morgan's discovery of each of these marks.

Oh no, this was not the time to think of that.

Of course, she couldn't tell Cici that the main reason for her reluctance to join Jane was that the thought of spending so much time with a woman she was attracted to—especially with the inevitability of number twelve looming over them—was torturous. Sighing, Morgan stretched for the strigil on the shelf that straddled the end of her bath. Over the decades she'd had to have metalworkers craft new ones for her as the old ones wore down and rusted. She would present detailed plans for the size and exact arc of the curved blade and the angle of the handle. *Is it a fancy shoehorn?* was the most frequent question. And because "new" metals like stainless steel simply didn't work, she had to repeatedly insist upon bronze or iron which added another layer of confusion.

Morgan began to scrape the blade over her skin, starting with her shoulders and working down her arms. When they were lovers, Cici would sit behind her in the bath, scraping oil and sweat and dirt from her skin. *Bathing methods is one of the many things the ancient Greeks and Romans got right*, she'd say, smoothing Morgan's hair from her shoulders and sliding the instrument firmly over Morgan's body.

The sensation of someone else scraping her skin always made her shudder, and inevitably their bathing session would turn into hours of lovemaking.

One evening Hannah had watched Morgan bathing, then wordlessly shed her clothing and slipped into the bath to take over the task. Her voice was low, soft as she'd asked Morgan how exactly she should wield the instrument, how much pressure she should use, which direction to scrape. Her touch had been decisive yet soft and tender. Despite Hannah's caresses, their shared desire, they hadn't made love. Rather, Morgan, exhausted from a week of near constant inter-realm travel had leaned back against Hannah and fallen asleep. She'd been woken hours later by the cooling water, still in the same position, after Hannah had instructed their servants to stop bringing fresh warm cisterns of water so Morgan could sleep in their bed.

Morgan swallowed, the curved instrument pausing on her thigh as her thoughts took a confusing turn from memory into fantasy. Jane kneeling between her legs as she scraped and smoothed the instrument over Morgan's skin. Jane behind her, pulling Morgan back into the vee of her legs as her hands slid down over Morgan's oil-slick torso and then under the water. She could easily imagine it, the pleasure Jane's hands and mouth would bring. But also the safety, the comfort and trust afterward of being able to relax and let herself sleep in another's arms again.

Morgan shuddered. The strigil slid into the bathwater.

CHAPTER EIGHT

"I'm just finishing up here, take a seat," Morgan invited Jane without looking up. Jane sat as usual on the opposite side of the desk as Morgan signed her name—a round and smoothly formed *Morgan R. Ashworth* that Jane loved—before dropping the document into a tray.

"What does the R in your signature stand for?" Jane asked.

"Rochefort. It's actually my given surname." Morgan turned the fountain pen over and over in her fingers. "Ashworth was the surname of my…life partner. I took it after she died."

What could she say to that heartbreaking revelation except, "I'm so sorry."

Morgan glanced up, eyebrows already shooting toward her hairline. "You shouldn't be. It wasn't your doing." She paused, expression softening. "But thank you."

"I've often thought about changing my name," Jane blurted in an attempt to shift the mood. Morgan didn't seem upset so much as contemplative and withdrawn.

"Why not do it?" She capped the pen and set it down beside the blotter.

"Because I can't quite imagine myself as anything else." Jane laughed at the absurdity of her statement and added, "Can't imagine myself as anything but one of the most common name combinations. I might as well change my surname to *Doe*."

Morgan's smile formed like a flower opening to the sun—slow but resulting in brilliance. "I've always thought Jane Smith suited you."

Jane wanted nothing more than to lean forward, prop her elbows on Morgan's desk and ask her to elaborate on the *always thought*. Always thought as in she'd actually allocated some brain power to something as mundane as Jane's name? "Mom wanted to name me Gabrielle but after my dad left when she got pregnant, she said she didn't want him coming to claim me. So she hid me in this boring, common name. But she gave me Gabrielle for my middle name."

Morgan's expression softened. "Names are important, such an innate part of us, of how we define ourselves. I think I feel that even more so since I began changing my exterior."

Jane caught the underlying wistfulness but had no idea what to say, or how to provide some comfort. "If the Minions are changing bodies, and get different voices and all that then how do you recognize one another before saying your name or some…secret password or something?"

Morgan laughed. "Cici always knows immediately who we are, and I can usually tell fairly soon after seeing them again. A person may change their appearance but it doesn't change who they are. Mannerisms, speech patterns, habits, they all remain." Morgan tugged her left earlobe. "Like this. Almost seven centuries, and I can't seem to stop doing it."

Jane smiled. She'd often seen Morgan with an elbow up on her desk, head resting on her hand while she played with her left ear. "What if the person whose body you take was left-handed or vice versa?"

"It doesn't matter. All my memories and skills and ideals and everything that I am are there the moment I change. I suppose my Animus retains all those important details." She shrugged, reaching for the teacup by her right hand. After sipping, Morgan frowned. "Cold," she murmured, sliding her chair back and gathering the teapot, cup and saucer. As she walked to the small kitchen alcove in the corner of her office, she asked over her shoulder, "Did you want tea?"

"No thank you. I've never really developed a taste for it."

Morgan paused as she was emptying a small basket of tea leaves, her eyes widening comically. "Jane. On behalf of every tea-loving person everywhere, I'm offended." She grinned, tapping the upended metal basket against the edge of the trash can. "I'd wager it's because you've never had *real* tea."

"Probably. I mean all I've had is weak, milky sweet tea made from teabags. Mostly in the ICU waiting room. Made by my relatives," she said by way of explanation.

Morgan's expression softened into understanding. "Well then, it's no wonder." She began what looked like a practiced ritual of tea-making. "I now consider it my duty to convert you. You'll never go back to teabags ever again. In fact, you won't even be able to pass them in the supermarket without recoiling in horror."

"I look forward to that."

Smiling, Morgan turned back to her task. "I've spoken to Cici about financing your bucket list and I've run into a small...well, it isn't a snag but an unexpected twist. I have to come with you, because I have to pay and obtain receipts for The Accountant."

Jane's mind blanked except for one thought. Traveling with Morgan Ashworth. Shit. Exhilaration and Panic both held up fists, ready to do battle for which would win. Exhilaration threw a combination punch and knocked Panic out of the ring. Jane struggled for composure and was proud of herself for not sounding like a complete idiot when she said, "Why is that? Don't you have an infinite amount of money?"

"Yes, technically. But The Accountant is *stringent*, to put it mildly. Having our expenditure laid out concisely helps with budgeting and reporting to various government agencies so we can adjust their contribution each decade." Morgan laughed. "This little adventure is going to throw my entertainment expenses through the roof. The Accountant is going to have a stroke. Not literally," she added hastily.

"Damn, I'm really sorry about that."

Morgan waved dismissively. "No harm. But that's why I can't just transfer you a hundred thousand or so and send you merrily on your way."

Jane gaped, spluttered. "A hundred thousand dollars? Morgan, it's not going to cost that much, is it?"

"Why not?" Morgan smiled sweetly. "If you're going to do these things you've deemed so important that they must be done before you die, then why not do them in style? Even if I wasn't coming with you, I would have insisted upon it. And now that I'm joining you, it's a given."

"Why?"

"Because, can you imagine the watercooler gossip around the Minion offices if I didn't?" She mock-gasped, placing a hand on her breast as she adopted a high-pitched, American-accented voice. "Did you hear how much of a cheapskate Morgan was with that bucket list fiasco? Ohmygoodness she is *such* a hardass. If that were me, *I'd* have sent that poor human off in a private jet with all the caviar and Dom Pérignon she could handle, and nothing but five-star hotels and limousines all the way." Morgan was grinning as if she'd just given an Oscar-worthy performance.

Unable to suppress her laughter, Jane asked, "Really?"

Morgan dropped her hand, her voice resuming its usual knee-weakening accent. "Who knows, but I would not put it past them. Horrendous gossips, the lot of them."

"Okay, sure, I mean if you're going to insist then I'm not stupid enough to say no to traveling in style." She paused before asking a tentative, "Does it bother you that you have to come with me?"

Morgan's answer was a little too fast but sounded completely genuine. "No, it doesn't. I can work during flights and travel back and forth as needed to ensure everything continues to run smoothly."

Jane exhaled some of her trepidation. "Good, okay then, so we're settled."

"Yes, we are." Morgan poured just-boiled water into her teapot. "I was thinking too, perhaps you should look into some sort of travel insurance."

The implication of Morgan's suggestion hit her like a gut punch. "Why? Is something going to happen? Oh, God. What if by doing something on my bucket list, something that's dangerous, I end up dying?"

"Well, my thought was more along the lines of replacing potentially lost luggage and things like that." Morgan's smile was patient. "Jane, you can't die until at least six months after you're first presented with your afterlife documents, remember? Those are the rules." She carried the teapot and a fresh teacup and saucer to her desk.

Jane had the sudden urge to squirm, stand up, pace, do something to ease the tight anxious feeling that was making her feel vaguely sick. "I do, but now it feels like a paradox. Like, I didn't have the means to do these things before, and now I do. What if...I'm diving on the Great Barrier Reef and I get the bends and die a horrible painful death, or get munched by a shark, or get bitten by some venomous Australian thing?"

"The odds of that are tiny. Big sharks like that don't tend to come into the shallow reef and I think the whole *everything in Australia wants to kill you* is an exaggeration."

"Okay, but what if the plane crashes on our way overseas?" She lost the battle with her nervousness and hopped up from the chair, taking a few steps away from the desk.

"Jane, it's not going to—"

Jane spun around, startling at Morgan's sudden closeness. "How can you be sure? I'm screwing around with the order of things, aren't I? By moving all this stuff forward, or by doing things I might not have done before, I could be hastening my death."

Morgan grasped her shoulders, but for all the firmness of the grip, her fingers massaged with surprising gentleness. "For crying out loud. Am I speaking a foreign language all of a sudden? You. Aren't. Going. To. Die." Every word was punctuated by a soft shake. "Well, not within the next six months. After that…" Morgan shrugged. "You know the deal. Everyone dies. But I made you a promise, and Death's employees are nothing if not honorable. You and me? We are bucket listing together."

The grip, the smooth motion of Morgan's fingers and the proximity of the other woman broke some of Jane's panic. "Why are you even helping me when you originally said no? Why do you care when or if I die?"

"I'm helping you because I said I would." Morgan stepped even closer, her thigh brushing the edge of Jane's hip. She leaned down, her lips just whispering along the edge of Jane's ear, and murmured, "And I'm not going to let you die until I've had a chance to fulfill number twelve on your list." The lightest breath washed over Jane's neck. "Because I've been thinking about having you naked from pretty much the first day I met you, when you charged into my office telling me my hardware was outdated and my protocols were weak. You were so confident yet tentative all at once and I had a very inappropriate thought, wondering if you displayed the same confidence and tentativeness in bed. Is that a good enough reason for you?"

"Oh." Jane swallowed. "All right then."

Morgan straightened, and aside from the slight smirk it was as if she'd never said what she'd just said. "Good. Now I need you to give me an itinerary so that we may get this bucket list thing started as soon as possible." She sipped her tea and made a sound of almost sinful pleasure.

The quivering in Jane's stomach made it difficult to answer, and her words came out embarrassingly breathy. "Okay, but I'll need to talk to HR about my vacation time, and make sure I can get a caretaker to stay with my mom if I'm going to be away."

Morgan waved dismissively. "Don't worry about HR and your vacation time. I'll approve whatever you need to get these things done. And I can cover the extra care for your mum, simply let me know and I'll arrange it."

Even though Jane had pushed Morgan into the whole bucket list thing, it seemed that Morgan's willingness to accommodate went beyond simply wanting Jane to fill in her afterlife package. She'd always sensed Morgan had an innate desire to help, to be kind and accommodating, which was part of what had started her lusty crush. Lusting after kindness. How sexy. "Speaking of HR. What about the whole sex thing?"

Morgan's face blanked. "What about it?"

"Shouldn't we have some sort of documentation for, uh, legal purposes?" She felt ridiculous for bringing it up, and the timidity of her question made her cheeks flame. Though she wasn't typically aggressive or confrontational, she'd never considered herself a weakling or pushover either. Yet there she was, practically stammering out a question that she'd known from the moment Morgan said number twelve was happening, she'd have to ask.

"Oh. That." Morgan shrugged. "It's not an issue for me but we can if you like." She leaned in, smiling conspiratorially. "Jane, you've probably realized by now, given our conversations on this topic to date, that this is not a regular business and *regular* rules don't really apply here. But if it makes you feel better, I'll have the lawyers draft a document protecting you and your position in the company that not a single lawyer across any realm would be able to find fault with."

"Thank you," Jane breathed. "I'm sorry, I sound so stupid but... my mom...I really need this job, Morgan."

Morgan grasped her forearm, squeezed gently and reassuringly. "I understand and it's absolutely fine. And I would never want you to feel uncomfortable. I need you." She cleared her throat and hastily amended, "I mean, Theda needs you."

CHAPTER NINE

Morgan had always considered herself an excellent planner and administrator, but she was quickly learning that Jane Smith had exceptional skills of her own. The woman ran a tight ship, and their itinerary had been laid out to the minute with maps and directions and booking numbers aligned with every outing. Though Morgan supposed that if you had to fly and drive everywhere, you'd be used to keeping track of such things.

At Morgan's insistence, they'd stretched a few things out over two days to avoid rushing from activity to airport. If she had to accompany Jane around the world using human transport, the last thing she wanted was to be pushed around trying to make connections. What was an extra few hours here or an overnight there in the scheme of things? Plus, later when they went overseas it meant Jane would get to see more of the world, even if only a glimpse.

The thought suffused Morgan with satisfaction. Jane would likely not get the chance to travel like this for some time, so why not tack on a few freebies? Of course, the thought of those freebies made Morgan think of the other *freebie* she had offered and she had to forcibly set the thought aside lest she spend the day embarrassing herself by acting like a hormonal teenager.

Because of its proximity, their first bucket-list item was the *Valravn* roller coaster at Cedar Point Amusement Park in Ohio. Once Jane had her fill, they would catch a flight the following morning to ride the *Kingda Ka* in New Jersey, and jet back to San Fran late in the afternoon. Two amusement parks in two days. Morgan clamped down on a sigh at the thought of all the work she could be doing during that time.

But Jane's childlike enthusiasm for simple things like flying first class balanced her mild annoyance. She would never admit it aloud, but she felt a buzz of excitement about flying too. She'd only ever flown a few times before, with her last month-long girlfriend who wasn't aware that Morgan was capable of getting from point A to B by faster means.

As they drove the hour to the park, Jane chattered about the venue's other roller coasters and rides, and filled her in on their main reason for being there. She said the name *Valravn*—a two minute and twenty-three second, two hundred and twenty-three-feet tall, dual ninety-degree dive-drop, with multiple loops including one two-seventy degree roll ride of awesomeness—as though it were sacred to her. The whole thing was a foreign language to Morgan.

Before they could genuflect to the roller coaster god, Morgan needed to quiet the grumble in her stomach. Jane appointed herself as table-finder while Morgan collected her second breakfast. She barely hesitated before picking up her burger. "You're not eating?"

"Not before a ride, no. And definitely not…that." Jane eyed her, then stared dubiously at the tray which held fries, onion rings and a Caesar salad along with a huge vanilla milkshake. "Are you sure you want to eat all that before getting on a roller coaster? You might get motion sick, and it won't be pleasant for anyone."

Morgan hastily swallowed her huge mouthful of burger. "Yes, I'm very sure I want to eat all of this. I cross realms and travel thousands of miles daily. I've been to every post-life place you can possibly think of, more times than you can imagine, and let me tell you—some of those journeys are *rough*. I am not afflicted by motion sickness."

"Lucky."

Morgan grabbed a handful of fries, smiling angelically. "Indeed it is." She pointed to the track of the *Valravn* roller coaster looming in front of them. "Interesting that you've chosen this one. I'm sure you know that Valravns are part of Danish folklore—Ravens of the Dead who eat those slain on battlefields."

"I did know that." Jane paused. "Are they real?"

"They are," Morgan confirmed. "Real and one of the creepiest things I have ever seen. But they also do regular raven things like play in the snow and lull you into thinking they're cute." She slurped her milkshake. "And then they eat a corpse and stare at you like they'd go after you too, dead or alive and it's back to being creepy." Morgan pushed the fries toward Jane. "Not even one?"

Rolling her eyes, Jane took a few fries, and popped them into her mouth. "Happy?"

"Now I am. You need to keep your strength up," Morgan teased.

Jane shook her head, though she was smiling. "Good, now hurry up and finish that so we can ride."

It only took her a few minutes to inhale the contents of the tray, and when it was empty she stared ruefully. Damn. Another basket of fries would go down a treat. Morgan shook her milkshake cup again, confirming with dismay that it was indeed finished as well. "Okay, I'm done. Shall we embark upon the coaster adventure before you spontaneously combust from anticipation?"

Jane jumped up so quickly she was almost airborne. She grabbed Morgan's hand and dragged her in front of the track to a photo station that looked like a cross between a mock-up throne and fake battlements. Jane charmed a passerby to take a photo as they posed under the gold crown-wearing raven that spread its wings over the backdrop—how bizarre—and as the stranger fiddled with Jane's phone, Jane slung an arm around Morgan's shoulders. "Big smile!"

Jane's enthusiasm was so infectious that Morgan didn't even have to pretend. She instinctively wrapped her arm around Jane's waist, gratified when Jane relaxed into her, and was left feeling suddenly cool when Jane stepped away to take back her phone. Jane checked the photos, thanked the stranger repeatedly and then herded Morgan toward the stairs up to the boarding platform.

Morgan tuned out the excited nervous chatter around her and quietly confessed to Jane, "So, in the interest of full disclosure, I've never actually been on a roller coaster."

Jane spluttered for a few seconds before managing, "But you've lived for almost seven hundred years, Morgan. How can you have never ridden a roller coaster?"

"Just never felt the urge. When you can teleport around the universe, amusement rides don't hold much appeal."

Jane grinned as the roller coaster car came gliding to a stop in front of them. "Well, it's time to lose your coaster virginity."

The *Valravn* vehicle was one cart of three rows with eight people in each that sat across the track instead of along it. They were allocated the end seats in the front row and Jane's excitement was palpable as she settled on the very end. Morgan wondered how much effort it was taking her to remain still.

Jane practically squealed, "Best seats we could've gotten! This is awesome." Once the harnesses had lowered and locked into place, Jane leaned close, her voice teasing. "You wanna hold my hand?"

Morgan scoffed. "Please. I once told Lucifer he was being an asshole. I'm not afraid of this little rolling gravity machine."

"Alllll right then, if you say so. It's just you look...never mind. Wait, what did you say?" Jane's about-face was almost comical. "Lucifer is real?"

"He certainly is, and is a good guy for the most part, but he's absolutely *obsessed* with football...soccer, to the point of being a bit of an asshole about it. Hence why I told him he was an asshole. Top tip, if you should ever meet him, never mention the English Premier League, and if the subject somehow gets onto it, find a way to get off it as fast as you can."

"Noted. Not that I'll even meet Lucifer."

"Likely not, but forewarned is forearmed. And Jane? From now on, why don't you assume every place and every person and every event that I mention is real. I don't lie because I have no need for untruths." She smiled. "But thank you for the offer of a comforting hand."

Jane shrugged, but it seemed more forced than nonchalant, and Morgan could see the pulse beating hard in Jane's neck. Jane smiled broadly. "Means I can have both hands in the air. Always makes the ride feel so much better."

"I'll take your word for it."

They left the gate, rounding a curve before a *clunk-clunk-clunk* sounded as they rose up the incline. It reminded Morgan of a drawbridge being raised and lowered, and a sudden rush of memory hit her so strongly she felt as though she'd been slapped in the face. It was the sound of the bridge that guarded the village of Coleraine in Northern Ireland where she'd briefly lived with Hannah in a tiny house with a lumpy bed and a surly cat.

Her heart beat furiously and she had the irrational feeling that she wanted off this ride. But she couldn't go anywhere. She was stuck, in America, in the twenty-first century and with Jane not Hannah. Jane.

Sweet, kind, funny, beautiful, clever Jane. Morgan squirmed against the harness.

Jane leaned over as far as she could. "You okay? It's supposed to be tight."

Morgan nodded and despite the fact she'd declined a hand hold, as they reached the top of the incline, Jane reached over and grabbed hers. Jane's hand was warm and dry, and without a tremor of fear as it gripped Morgan's, and the anxiety eased immediately. She was here, with Jane.

Morgan turned to glance at her and was rewarded with a maniacal grin as ever…so…slowly they crested and then rolled along the flat around another corner. The coaster stopped. Paused. Rolled forward with more clanks and clunks until finally they tilted over the edge, staring straight down a vertical drop. Oh, well that's rather fun. The end seats they occupied seemed to dangle in space, with no track beneath them, and Morgan immediately twigged as to why Jane was so excited for her seat.

Time held still. Morgan was hyperaware of everything. Jane's hand in hers, and her excited breathing. The mechanical noises. The wind ruffling her hair. The sensation of being pushed forward into her harness, and then…what would happen if it failed. Nothing to her except pain and perhaps a new body, but Jane…

Morgan swallowed. Jane was very mortal.

Filled with sudden extreme panic, irrational for someone who knew when Jane would die—which was *unquestionably* not this day— Morgan gripped her hand tighter and stretched a leg over to hook her foot around Jane's ankle, readying herself to hold on should anything go wrong. Just because Jane wasn't going to die today didn't mean she couldn't be badly injured. Morgan could always rip the harness free and grab Jane, twisting her body so Jane would land on top of her and have her fall broken. She already knew that worked.

As if sensing what she was thinking, Jane raised her voice above the wind. "These things are super safe. Don't worry. Plus, remember what you said about the paradox?"

Morgan didn't get a chance to answer because they were suddenly plummeting straight down the track. Her stomach on the other hand, felt as if it'd been left at the top of the drop. Jane's joyous screaming beside her almost took her attention away from the intense, sudden nausea.

Almost.

After the first loop, immediately following the drop, Morgan regretted the burger.

After the second drop-loop combination, Morgan regretted the fries.

After the spinny-tilty-loop-flip thing, well…Morgan regretted everything.

She scrunched her eyes closed to concentrate on slow, deep breaths and not losing the contents of her stomach. It only took another ten seconds or so until the ride had completed its circuit of turns and lifts and twirls, and the car began to slow down a gentle incline. Morgan opened her eyes, blinking hard to try and chase away the nauseated vertigo.

Jane's yell carried over the other riders' excitement and the grind and hiss of the mechanics as they chugged into the loading bay. "Oh-my-god-that-was-so-incredible!"

All Morgan could do was nod weakly and gurgle something she hoped Jane would take as agreement. Even Jane's adrenaline and excitement couldn't override her overwhelming nausea. A few more deep breaths helped settle her enough to stand and exit the loading bay. Moving was not a good idea. Actually, it was a horrible idea. She paused for a few seconds, hoping to quell her queasiness. Oh no, being still was also not a good idea. Nothing was a good idea. Panic and nausea rising, Morgan rushed away from the ride and down the stairs until Jane finally caught up, grabbing Morgan's arm to slow her. "You okay? You look kind of…"

Morgan wrenched her arm free and raced to a semi-secluded spot where she bent over the garden, and promptly vomited up everything she'd consumed earlier. Charming.

"Shit." Quick footsteps to Morgan's side, then a hand strafed up and down her back. Jane carefully pulled Morgan's hair back, murmuring soothing words that she couldn't quite make out.

Once she'd stopped retching, Morgan straightened, swiping the back of her hand over her mouth. "Are you kidding me?" she exclaimed hoarsely. "I've been back and forth to Valhalla more times than I can count, millions of trips. Beautiful place, horrendous journey. Same for Annwn, Niflhel, Tartarus, Mag Mell and *thousands* of other afterlife realms. And this pissant roller coaster made me vomit? There is something seriously topsy-turvy with the world."

Jane's concern transformed to mild confusion and then amusement. "Will you be okay here for a minute?"

"Mhmm." Morgan leaned against the fence, praying she was done embarrassing herself.

Jane jogged off and returned a few minutes later, by which time Morgan had moved away from the remnants of her embarrassment to stand near the front of the *Valravn* gift store. Jane fished a water bottle from her retrieved backpack.

"Thanks." Morgan rinsed her mouth, spat as discreetly as she could into a trash can then drank a few mouthfuls of lukewarm water.

Jane offered her some gum and ran her hand down Morgan's forearm ending in a light hand squeeze. "How're you feeling?"

"Fine, thank you," she said quickly. After a beat, Morgan added, "But utterly mortified."

"Don't be. It's not the first time it's happened to someone on a roller coaster and it certainly won't be the last. People puke on and after coasters allll the time."

But Morgan wasn't an ordinary person, and to do something as uncouth as vomit in public was offensive to her dignity. She fought to regain composure. "Well. I suppose I'll chalk it up to physics and biology being at odds?"

"Mmm." Jane moved some strands of hair that had stuck to Morgan's damp forehead and tucked them behind her ear. "Are you ready to buy some useless crap to commemorate the ride?"

"I love useless crap," Morgan deadpanned, holding open the door to the gift store.

As Jane backed through the displays of *Valravn* goodies, her face lit with an excited grin. "Why don't you go grab our photograph? I'll check out the overpriced junk."

Morgan saluted and left Jane to her consumerism. Their ride photo was already up and Morgan's eyes were immediately drawn to the two of them among the group of riders. Jane's smile was huge, as though all of her joy and excitement had been poured into this single expression. Morgan on the other hand, looked exactly like she'd felt at that moment. Nauseated.

Laughing quietly, Morgan purchased two copies of the photo, cropped to exclude most of the other riders, as well as special ride-themed frames to put them in. By the time the photos were framed, Jane had finished shopping and was waiting by the shelves of mugs for her. Morgan handed her one of the frames. "Here you go. What did you get?"

"Thanks." Jane put the photo in her bag and fished out a few things. "Just a shirt and a travel coffee mug. And this raven toy for Mom."

"Oh that's so cute."

"And for you…" Jane rummaged some more, then with a flourish presented Morgan with ball cap in two-tone dark and light blue that had **VALRAVN** emblazoned on the front. "Sorry, I tried to find something that said 'I rode *Valravn* and puked in the garden afterward' but it seems they don't sell anything like that." There was the cutest teasing sparkle in her eyes.

"Isn't that a pity," Morgan said dryly. "Wait here a moment." She strode over to the cashier and deployed her best smile as she asked to borrow a marker. The teen behind the counter fumbled before handing one over, which she accepted with another smile that made him blush furiously.

Jane's slightly raised eyebrows rose higher as Morgan thrust the marker at her. "What's this for?"

"If they didn't have the thing you wanted to buy, then you can make one for me." She shook the marker until Jane took it from her.

"You want me to write on your cap?"

"Yes I do."

"You might regret it."

The answer came out before she could stop it. "I don't think I'll regret anything with you, Jane."

Jane's expression changed from surprise to pleasure. "Okay then." With tongue peeking out of smiling lips Jane carefully wrote on the ball cap. When she passed it back, it read:

I Rode
VALRAVN
(And Puked In The Garden After)

Morgan burst into laughter, barely able to speak around her mirth. "Absolutely perfect." Morgan set the cap on her head, gave the employee back his marker, then grabbed Jane's hand. "Let's go. I need something to eat."

"But it's time to ride the *Raptor*!" Jane protested, though she let herself be pulled through the store, outside and in the direction of a food stand.

Morgan's stomach felt not unlike it had on that first *Valravn* drop. "Really? Oh, uh, you know what? I might stay on firm ground for the other ones. You need on the ground photographic evidence and a, uh…cheerleader." Oh that sounded *so* unconvincing.

Jane snorted out a laugh. "I can't believe it. Morgana Ashworth, big bad boss of all of Death's Minions, teller-offer of Lucifer and who knows who else, conqueror of afterlife realms is scared of a widdle woller coaster?"

"Not scared," Morgan shot back petulantly. "I just don't like decorating the gardens, that's all. And someone needs to hold our purchases."

"I know. The lockers are that someone."

Morgan lowered her voice, ashamed to let passersby hear her admission. "Jane, I'm not sure I like roller coasters. I felt so bilious the last time."

"That probably had something to do with eating enough food for two pregnant women before you rode the coaster." She nudged Morgan gently in the ribs. "Come on. Your stomach is empty now. You'll be fine."

Morgan groaned. The problem was she had to accompany Jane so she could be there in case of emergencies. But the memory of *Valravn* sent a surge of nausea through her. A hand pressed softly against her lower back, fingers gently kneading either side of her spine as Jane stood on tiptoes to murmur in her ear, "If you *really* don't want to ride, that's fine. But if you do, trust me. I've got you."

CHAPTER TEN

Their hotel sported an indoor pool, a fabulous restaurant and bar, and an internal door connecting their suites that immediately conjured up images of sneaking into Morgan's room in the middle of the night. Or vice versa. Jane took a blissfully hot shower, during which she could hear—and tried to ignore the mental image of—Morgan showering on the other side of the wall. She had just finished dressing when a soft knock sounded on the connecting door. Jane checked she hadn't done something like put a shirt on inside out then called, "Come in."

Morgan had changed into a long-sleeved baby-blue tee, which along with the jeans and Vans sneakers she'd worn all day made her look like a college freshman. Her hair, hastily dried and pulled back into a messy bun completed the picture of youthfulness. She smiled apologetically. "I have to go see my boss."

Jane's disappointment rose unexpectedly and she chastised herself for her foolishness. What had she actually expected? That after spending all day with Jane, before she'd spend all of tomorrow with her, that Morgan would want to hang out at night? She adopted nonchalance. Or tried to. "Oh, sure. I was just thinking of getting some dinner. This is a stupid question I know, but are you hungry?"

Morgan's expression grew rueful. "Always. I just emptied the snack bar in my room. But I'll only be gone for an hour or so if you can wait? Or I'll just get something to eat while I'm gone if you're hungry now." She shrugged into a leather jacket.

"I can wait," Jane said, realizing immediately and embarrassingly that it'd come out rushed and super-enthusiastic. Time to dial it down. But how could she when Morgan plus leather jacket equaled bone-melting hotness. She forced herself to look relaxed, like the thought of sharing yet another meal with Morgan was tedious instead enjoyable. "I'm not *that* hungry yet."

"Then I look forward to eating dinner with you when I return."

"You know, I realized that I haven't asked where your boss actually lives, like where it is."

"Aether? It's just…around. You know." Morgan swirled a finger through the air. "Hard to explain. Why don't you check out the room service menu and decide what you want so we can order as soon as I get back. I'll be desperate for food." She laughed and added, "As you may have noticed, that's kind of my default state."

"Will do." Jane leaned forward, unable to contain her interest. "Can I watch?"

Morgan frowned, clearly puzzled. "Watch me eat?"

Jane laughed at the misassumption, though watching Morgan eat was fast becoming one of her most enjoyable things. She'd never paid much attention to anyone that way before, but Morgan was *beyond* sexy while chowing down. Sexy anytime, really. "No. Watch you leave."

Morgan's short laugh conveyed her embarrassment. "Oh! Of course, if you want. Um, but just a heads up—stay away from this area where I am now, and don't be naked or doing anything compromising while I'm gone."

"Why?"

Morgan's smile was slow and sensuous and her answer a low, husky tone that promised delicious things. "Because I don't want you to have all the fun without me." She backed up a few steps until she was almost against the wall and with a wink said, "Don't blink."

And then—

Jane *knew* she hadn't blinked but Morgan was just…gone. She rushed to the last spot she'd seen her, foolishly thinking maybe she'd just become invisible or some other Minion power she hadn't been told about. But Morgan wasn't invisible. She simply wasn't there. There was a warmth in the air where she'd been, and Jane stood there until the warmth faded to leave her feeling cold and disturbingly empty.

She ambled around the room for five minutes, checking out the amenities then slid the curtains back to watch planes landing and taking off at the nearby airport. After fifteen aimless minutes, Jane flopped onto the bed. Bad idea. She'd known the moment she stopped and allowed herself to think that her thoughts would inevitably stray to Morgan.

Morgan.

Outside their work environment, she was so different to what Jane had expected. It wasn't that she was an entirely new person but more that she dropped a barrier, became even more who Jane had always glimpsed behind the professional façade. Her humor and compassion along with her unexpected sense of fun and ridiculousness had drawn Jane in ever closer as the day progressed.

Morgan had worn the amended *Valravn* ball cap all day and offered huge smiles to everyone who reacted to the public declaration that she'd been sick after the coaster. She'd been in a teasing, cheerful mood all afternoon and the more time Jane spent with her as Normal Person Morgan instead of My Hot Boss Morgan the more she enjoyed it. The more she wanted…more.

Jane reached behind herself to grab a pillow and pressed it against her face to muffle her, "Argh!"

She had it so bad. All day, the admiration and lust she'd been comfortably carrying around for the last however many years, had turned softer, more connected. Oh sure, the lust was still there and as intense as ever, but now it was complemented by *liking* Morgan as well. She pulled the pillow away from her face and leaned over for the remote. Right, no more pathetic pining after her boss. Time for… no, no, maybe, no, hmm…a documentary about Australian wildlife? Might as well get a head start ready for their trip Down Under.

Morgan returned after an hour and twelve minutes—not that Jane had been watching the clock—and her appearance was as sudden as her disappearance. One moment nothing, then the next she stood in the same spot as when she'd left. Jane couldn't help her shriek. She sucked in a startled breath and pushed it out with a choked, "Ohmygod."

"Only me," Morgan said quietly. She shook her head, expelling a self-deprecating snort. "Obviously it's only me. Sorry, I wish I could give you some warning or something that I'm about to suddenly be there."

Jane dropped her hand from where she'd done a very clichéd alarmed-person T-Shirt clutch. "It's fine, just didn't expect it, that's all. Does it always happen like that, in the same spot?" Now that her heart had dropped by a hundred beats a minute, she was glad she'd heeded Morgan's advice and hadn't climbed naked into bed or indulged in some personal time. Though the thought of personal time being interrupted by Morgan...was a thought for another time.

"Yes, that's why I told you to stay away from that place. If I'm traveling around earth side I can hop from place to place as I please without issue, as though I have some kind of supernatural GPS. We get part of Cici and her talents or whatever you want to call it, and she has the *ultimate* cosmic navigation system." She unzipped her jacket. "But when I travel to Aether or beyond, I always return to the exact place I departed from. I think it's some sort of beacon, like my body marks its place in space and time when crossing realms so it knows that's a safe place to come back to."

"What if someone is in the spot you left from? Are they—" Jane fumbled for the word, "Displaced?"

"I always make sure I'm inside and somewhere I know so I don't just land in the middle of the street, like *Hi here I am out of nowhere sorry to frighten everyone.* When I come back it causes a kind of, uh, shockwave I guess you could call it that pushes anyone in that spot away." She smiled. "It happened a few times when Hannah forgot where I'd left from and I came back just as she walked on that spot. It was pretty funny." Despite her assertion of amusement, Morgan's smile faded like the setting sun.

"If you're moving around Earth do you ever land in a tree, or against a wall or anything like that?"

"No. There's a certain amount of intuitiveness to the..." She frowned. "...mechanism that allows us to transport."

"Was it the same amount of time for you? About an hour and a quarter?"

"Yes. Time passes the same everywhere." Morgan opened the door connecting their rooms, toed off her sneakers and kicked them into her room. "Have you had a good night?" She slipped out of her jacket and flung it through the door as well, leaving just the body-hugging long-sleeved tee covering her lean frame. She reminded Jane of a cheetah, lithe and sleek. What would that body look like *without* clothes? Oh help.

She cleared her throat. "I found the remote and got sucked into a documentary about platypuses. Platypi?"

"Both are technically correct," Morgan mused, a slow grin quirking her lips. As if sensing Jane was about to question her, she asserted, "Trust me. I have witnessed *a lot* of language evolution."

"Platypi it is." Jane heard the slight hopeful lift in her tone as she asked, "Do you still want to have dinner together or have you already eaten over in the other realm?"

Morgan was already reaching for the phone. "Yes I did eat, but unsurprisingly I'm still hungry. So if you're hungry, care to join me?"

Jane was aware of the warm spread of pleasure through her body the moment Morgan asked, and didn't even think before answering, "Love to."

The room service guy raised a surprised eyebrow as he delivered the cart with enough food for five people into a room obviously containing only two. Morgan thanked him profusely, handed him a large tip and rushed their dinner into the room. As well as the garden salad and pasta marinara Jane had ordered for herself, Morgan had chosen a spread of fried snacks, steamed vegetables, Polish meatballs and a ribeye steak that was so bloody it looked like it might get up and walk away. Morgan used a spoon to fish out the ice from her water, grumbling that she'd specifically asked for *no* ice in one of the waters.

"I'll take it," Jane offered.

Morgan gifted the ice into Jane's glass. "Thanks. I've never been able to get used to it. The modern age has many wonderful inventions but putting freezing chunks of water in your beverages is not one of them. How is one expected to drink around all those floating obstacles?"

They settled on Jane's king-sized bed with trays on their laps, and Jane was instantly aware that despite the abundance of space, they'd both shuffled to sit in the middle of the bed, almost touching. Trying not to dwell on the fact, she drizzled blue-cheese dressing over her salad. Morgan offered her basket of fries, and after Jane's head shake of *no thanks*, she shifted to reach into a jeans pocket and produced a handful of small packets which she tore open and shook over the fries.

An acidic tang hit Jane's nostrils. "Is that…vinegar?"

"Indeed it is," she confirmed, eyebrows furrowed as she squeezed out the last of the condiment.

Jane sniffed and coughed, trying to chase away the smell. "Sorry but that's disgusting."

Morgan smiled at Jane's eyebrow-raised expression, picked up a vinegar-drenched fry and popped it in her mouth. After swallowing she said, "I *am* British, Jane."

"Well yes, I know that. Fries are a pretty recent culinary invention, aren't they?"

"Mmm, but vinegar has been around for a very long time, well before I was born. People used to use it as a disinfectant, antiseptic and the like. Stings horrendously in open wounds." She grinned. "But yes, putting it on *chips* is a fairly modern notion. I still spend a fair bit of time in the United Kingdom." Morgan dragged a few fries through the puddle at the bottom of the basket. "I've also discovered that if you can train yourself to enjoy the taste of something like vinegar, it makes it easier when you *have* to eat something unpleasant." Still smiling, she ate a few more fries then turned her attention to the steak.

Jane tried not to watch. And failed.

Despite the fact Morgan practically inhaled her steak, she somehow managed to make it look dainty. It'd been the same way when Jane had watched her eat four full meals plus snacks during the day. Morgan had looked like she was in the middle of an etiquette class while chowing down on a burger she could barely get her mouth around.

Jane swallowed a mouthful of pasta. "Do you ever feel full? Like disgustingly full after eating all that?" Almost immediately she added, "Sorry, that sounded judgmental. It's just I think I'd hurl if I even attempted half of it."

"Not really no. I'm always burning energy, more than a regular person just existing, and I'm always running at a deficit. Kind of like filling your car with fuel while there's a hole in the tank and it's pouring out as fast as you put it in."

"Actually, that analogy makes perfect sense." Jane sifted her fork through her dinner. "What's your favorite food?"

Morgan hastily swallowed and wiped her mouth with the cloth napkin. "For taste or calorific utility?"

"Both."

"Grilled cheese," she answered immediately. "And the milkshake may well have been one of humanity's greatest inventions."

"Ah, yes I noticed the fact you had a milkshake with every meal today except this one."

Morgan grinned. "I plan to order one for second dessert later. Milkshakes are no good if they get warm."

"Second dessert?" Jane stretched, placing her hands over her belly and eyeing the two thick slabs of chocolate cake on the room service cart. "I'm going to need at least an hour before I can even think about *first* dessert."

With a knowing smile, Morgan offered her Polish meatballs to Jane, and when Jane declined with an *are you kidding me* look, she cheerfully started in. Before she'd begun each dish, she'd first paused to offer it to Jane, despite the fact Jane knew she had to be hungry and probably desperate to eat the meal herself.

Jane leaned over to set her empty dishes on the cart before settling back against the pillows. "I want to know more about your teleporting thing. Do you disintegrate into bits like—" Jane snapped her fingers a few times as she searched for the image. "That, um, uh, Mike TeeVee from the *Willy Wonka* movie."

"I'm sorry, pardon?"

"You know, where he breaks into teensy pieces and then forms into a person again after being shot across the room as microscopic television bits."

Morgan covered her mouth as she laughed. "No, I don't know that, and no I don't break into teensy pieces and get shot across realms and then resolidify on the other side. I've actually become stuck between realms before and had to summon Cici to help me. Just totally ran out of steam." She speared a meatball. "Hence, why I always try to make sure I have enough juice to get me wherever I need to go." The meatballs were chased down with what Jane knew from the menu was a really expensive red wine.

"Do you get drunk?" she blurted.

"I do. Technically human, remember? And I get hungover too, which is why I think you need to help me with this bottle." Morgan held it up, eyebrows raised in a silent question.

"Oh, sure, thanks. I just wasn't sure." The admission felt stupid, given how Morgan had offered her everything she'd ordered before she'd eaten a bite herself.

"There are two glasses, Jane. And it's not so I can have one in each hand," Morgan teased as she filled the second glass. As she passed it to Jane, she deliberately stroked the back of Jane's hand with her forefinger.

Jane had to suppress the small shudder at the sensation of Morgan's fingers softly gliding over her skin. "Thanks," she managed to get out before raising the wineglass to her nose. Oh boy, this was going to be good. She'd had good wines, but this was next level. She held the wine in her mouth, savoring the hints of cherry and spice, all too aware that it would likely be quite some time before she had another red this rich and full.

Morgan touched her arm and as if she knew exactly what Jane was experiencing, murmured, "It's good, isn't it? One benefit of living so long is you gain intimate knowledge of which vineyards produce the best wines." Smiling lazily, Morgan upended her wineglass toward her mouth. "Have you really never been in love?"

Jane's own wineglass froze in midair. "Excuse me?"

"Number four on your list." Morgan gestured vaguely. "Fall in love."

Jane's eyes widened. She took a few moments to collect her thoughts, though she knew she really didn't have to think about Morgan's question. "No, I've never been in love. Like, yes. Lust, sure. But never love."

"Lust…" Morgan raised an eyebrow as she added another half inch of wine to her glass. "Do tell."

"Mhmm," she managed to squeak out. Then the wine spoke for her, goddammit. "After you, since basically the moment we met, as I told you. Why do you think number twelve exists?"

Morgan inclined her head graciously. "I'm flattered. But I believe it's just this body, Jane. It's pleasing to look at. I had no part in making it this way, I simply utilized something available to me."

"Morgan, no. It's not just…" She felt like clapping her hand over her mouth to stop the words spilling out.

Morgan held a hand up as if to save Jane from herself. "It's okay, honestly. I know how you, I mean how *people* see me."

Jane wanted to clutch Morgan's shoulders, to shake her until she understood that she had it so wrong—the thing she felt for Morgan went *so* far beyond just physical attraction. But how could she explain that without making herself seem like a ridiculous lovestruck fool? She couldn't, so Jane chose the coward's response and deftly sidestepped. "Does it bother you when people make assumptions based on your looks?"

Morgan's eyebrows drew together, and the perturbed expression would've been comical if it weren't for the seriousness of their conversation. It took almost a minute before she admitted, "A little bit, yes. I know it's silly, and also somewhat arrogant and ungrateful of me given this attractive parcel I live inside. But it's just that, Jane. A parcel. Nothing more than nice wrapping paper. And even though I choose this and I enjoy having people admire the way I look and how that translates to something that's emotionally recharging for me, sometimes I want to remind them that bodies are nothing more than containers to hold all the wonderful stuff that makes up humans."

Jane reached over to clasp the hand closest to her, entwining their fingers, gratified when Morgan not only accepted the hold, but curled her fingers around Jane's. "You're absolutely right. And it's not just your outside for me, though the outside is very pleasing." She laughed, shaking her head as she clarified, "Okay, at first it was just the outside but then I realized it's also *you*. You're just…well you're pretty great, and I know this sounds clichéd but you're wonderful on the inside as well as the outside."

Though Jane knew it was impossible, she would have sworn something almost electrical crackled between their joined hands.

Morgan's grip tightened. "Jane…" That one word came out hoarsely, a plea and a demand all in one. Morgan turned toward her, the thumb of her free hand sliding softly over Jane's lower lip as she leaned closer. The thumb brushed over Jane's top lip and then the skin above. "This beauty spot," Morgan whispered. "Every time I look at you, I want to kiss it." She paused for the briefest moment, searching Jane's face as though asking for consent.

Jane didn't think, could barely breathe as she simply nodded yes. Yes, kiss me, please. Morgan was so close, Jane felt her breath caressing her lips. She ran her fingertips along Jane's jaw and up until they were woven in the hair behind her ears.

"You are so—" The sound of Morgan's phone made them both jump and unfortunately, cut off whatever Morgan had been about to say. And do.

Morgan pulled back. "Goddammit," she griped. "I'm so sorry but I have to answer." She rolled off the bed, tugging the phone from her back pocket as she strode toward her room. "Bethany, a pleasure as always. What can I do for you?" The door closed behind her with a quiet click.

Jane stared after her, heart thudding as the implication of what had almost happened hit her. Shit. Shit! She'd come *thisclose* to kissing Morgan Ashworth. This. Close. A millisecond and it would've happened. Jane pushed herself back, leaned against the stack of pillows and tried to calm her disappointment.

* * *

Morgan spent most of the early-evening flight back to California working on her tablet while Jane read the latest Jillian Keing thriller. Or tried to. She'd never noticed until this trip outside of work how magnetic Morgan was, how much people seemed to be drawn to her. Jane understood it, knowing how hard it was to keep her own gaze from constantly straying to Morgan.

Fellow passengers stared at Morgan, tried to catch her eye, and without fail she'd respond with a smile and a murmured word or two before moving on—a small acknowledgement that Jane knew would make them feel *seen*. It'd been the same in the airport, walking through the terminal and waiting in the lounge. She garnered attention, but Jane realized it wasn't always sexual attraction. Even kids seemed to gravitate to her and Jane had the sense that it was some innate, inexplicable human element that people were drawn to Morgan as a source of comfort. A pillar of strength and honesty even though they could never have understood the deeper reasons behind what they felt.

For a brief, panicked moment, Jane wondered if this was the only reason she'd always felt so drawn to her as well. Beyond her obvious attraction to her boss, lust or anything else, Morgan had always felt like a good place. Nice one, excellent description. *A good place.* Staring blankly at her page, Jane pondered the basis of her feeling, and eventually concluded that her connection to Morgan was deeper than anything that might be caused by her Minion-ness. It was real, and it felt incredible.

Jane glanced to her right, where in the first-class seat next to her, Morgan sat cross-legged and turned slightly toward her. Morgan's concentration on her tablet meant Jane could sneak as many peeks as she wanted. And Jane snuck plenty. They weren't touching, yet Morgan was close enough that she could feel the warmth of her body, and she longed to reach out and rest a hand on Morgan's jean-clad thigh.

She wouldn't have thought it possible, but Morgan Ashworth wearing faded jeans that accentuated the perfect swell of her ass—which Jane had congratulated herself on only looking at seven times while walking through the airport—coupled with well-worn black biker boots, a faded gray shirt with black block print proclaiming FEMINIST and that butter-soft leather jacket was even sexier than Morgan Ashworth in a corporate power suit.

Come to think of it, the jeans, polo shirt and sneakers combo she'd worn both days at the theme parks had been pretty hot too. So simple yet so damned sexy. Jane swallowed, recalling for the thousandth time, their almost kiss of the evening before. Of course, the mood had been broken and once Morgan had returned from her phone call she'd almost shyly said she had some things to take care of, set the cart and empty room service trays outside Jane's door and left her with the remainder of the wine. Which Jane had finished and which had unfortunately not dulled her as she'd hoped, but rather increased the hum of excitement their near-kiss had ignited.

The doting first-class flight attendant appeared at Jane's side. "Last call for food and beverages before we begin our approach. Can I bring you ladies anything?" Flying first class had been a two-for, ticking two things off the list at once, though number fourteen—Fly

First Class—hadn't actually made it to Jane's final six. But Morgan had done it anyway. Because as Jane was discovering, that was just the kind of person…Minion?…no, person, Morgan was.

Morgan's smile was charming, reassuring and grateful all at once as she answered, "Whisky, neat please. And another one of those sandwiches if there are any left?"

"Of course." He turned to Jane, his smile as genuine as it had been for Morgan. "And for you?"

"I'd love a Sprite. Thank you."

"Sprite," Morgan teased once the attendant had left. She twisted in the seat until her knee brushed Jane's thigh. "You could have almost anything to eat or drink, you know."

Jane pulled her tray down. "I know, but old habits I suppose."

Morgan's laugh was low and amused. She reached over to tuck Jane's hair behind her ear. "When you're with me, you're going to have to get used to new habits."

Once they'd collected Morgan's BMW from the valet, and Jane had queried why Morgan didn't just blink herself to the airport and back and Jane could've caught an Uber, Morgan had smiled patiently and said, "I can't carry all my bags. And the airport is busy and full of cameras so it's hard to be inconspicuous by just appearing and disappearing." She had answers for every question and the logic was obvious when she explained things in her calm, matter-of-fact way.

The conversation on the way to Jane's was easy, if not deep and meaningful—mostly work related and touching on a few aspects of their upcoming trip to Australia and New Zealand. Only five days and Jane would take her first overseas vacation. The fact that she was traveling with Morgan, something she'd discovered over these two days that she enjoyed immensely, was just the frosting on the cake.

Morgan slowly pulled into Jane's driveway, parked then rushed out and around to hold the passenger door open for her. While Jane fumbled with the backpack at her feet, Morgan collected Jane's bag from the trunk. Instead of handing it to her, Morgan set the bag on the driveway beside the rear tire. She seemed unusually lost for words, fidgeting with her keys and phone before shoving both into jeans pockets. "I'll see you at work in the morning."

Jane responded to the obvious statement with one of her own. "Of course. Thanks for this, it was everything I'd hoped for and then more." And almost even more again, if it weren't for the interruption of their kiss.

Morgan smiled faintly. "You're welcome. I had a really great few days, *Valravn* embarrassment and all."

"I'm glad to hear it. I'll convert you to coasters yet." Jane went to pick up her bag, but Morgan side-stepped to block her, and then blocked her again when Jane moved to the other side to get around the Morgan-obstacle.

Morgan took a step forward until they were almost toe-to-toe and Jane didn't have time to question what she was doing before Morgan spoke a single word. "Jane." Her name came out as if it were reverential. Morgan reached into the back pocket of her jeans and pulled out her phone, turning it to silent. "I don't want to be interrupted again. I'm going to kiss you." Morgan's voice was barely above a murmur when she added, "If that's okay." She stepped even closer and snaked an arm around Jane's waist, pulling her forward until their bodies touched.

Jane could only nod. If she spoke, she knew she'd say something stupid, like how good it felt to be snuggled against Morgan's body. How safe she felt. How much she'd been thinking about kissing her since almost the moment she'd first seen her, and how it was basically all she'd thought about since the almost-kiss the night before.

Morgan dipped her head, lingered teasingly close for a long moment before her lips brushed over the skin above Jane's upper lip. Jane didn't miss the quiet groan that escaped Morgan and then finally those soft, warm lips touched hers. Jane clutched the front of her leather jacket, keeping her close as Morgan's lips moved against hers with a sweetness Jane hadn't imagined possible.

Morgan tasted...fresh, like the cool, clear taste of rainwater. Her hands on Jane's face were warm and dry, cupping her cheeks as her lips and tongue gently explored Jane's mouth. Time stuttered to a halt. They could have stood there for hours, just kissing.

When they finally came up for air, Morgan swallowed hard. Her expression was part lust, part sheepishness. She shrugged, grinning shyly. "I just thought, if we're going to sleep together then we should at least get comfortable with kissing."

"Good plan. Clever." Tentatively she reached up to wrap her arms around Morgan's neck, fingers tangling in her hair. Morgan exhaled, as though releasing tension while Jane's fingers curled blond strands of hair around and around. Jane widened her eyes, feigning innocence. "You know, I think I'm still feeling a little weird about it. Can we try again?"

Their eyes met and held for a second before Jane kissed her, gratified when Morgan responded with enthusiasm. The way Morgan kissed her was like she felt they had all the time in the world. Soft lips, bold tongue. She pressed against Jane as though she wanted to merge their bodies into one, her hands roaming over Jane's back. She stroked, kneaded, tested, making small murmurs of appreciation as she explored.

When Jane melted against her, Morgan's strong arms wrapped around her back, holding her close. Holding her upright. Holding her together. Jane knew that when the time came, she was going to lose herself in this woman. And that she might never be found again.

CHAPTER ELEVEN

Their suite on Heron Island, a resort smack bang in the middle of Australia's Great Barrier Reef, was secluded among trees and overlooked the beach on the north side of the island. The moderately appointed lodging had one king bed, and a daybed in the living area which Morgan had quickly claimed. Given she hardly slept anyway, it wasn't fair to lay claim to the actual bed. Though when she saw how big it was, she was tempted to suggest they share it. Of course, sharing a bed with Jane would probably lead into number twelve, or get very close. Jane hadn't said anything more since their kiss goodbye the other evening. Nor had they kissed again since then. Five days, no kissing.

Despite Jane's silence on the matter, number twelve factored frequently in Morgan's thoughts. Every day she had some variation on the thought of *Sex with Jane*—passionate sex, giggling sex, rough sex, sweet sex, playful sex, and everything in between. And in every single fantasy, Jane's pleasure was Morgan's sole focus. Allowing herself to imagine Jane's hands and mouth on her was more than she could handle. It'd been so long since she'd done anything resembling number twelve that every time she thought about it, a small nugget of fear slid in beside the desire. And it was that fear that had kept her from making any further moves.

As soon as they'd unpacked, they booked Jane's SCUBA adventure for first thing the next morning, confirmed a pre-arranged dinner time and then settled on sunbeds by the pool overlooking the reef. They had three nights on the island, something to do with Jane being unable to fly within a time period after diving, an issue with nitrogen and pressure and altitude combining to make something bad happen. All Morgan had heard was Jane could get the bends, which would lead to her being very unwell, and she'd readily agreed. The moment she'd seen the views, she'd wished they were staying for three months instead of three nights.

Jane gestured to the vista of ocean. "I can't believe how incredible it is here. I mean I've seen pictures but this is just…" She lowered the level of her cider by half an inch. "Amazing."

"It is," Morgan agreed quietly. She dropped her sunglasses to take another look at the colors splayed out before them—an incredible mix of blues from the deepest sapphire to the brightest aqua. She sipped her dirty martini, a murmur of appreciation slipping past her lips.

"Are you sure you'll be all right while I'm diving tomorrow?"

"Perfectly all right," Morgan assured her. She held up a small square of paper with printed codes on it. "I've purchased wi-fi time for every day and the barman assures me it's semi-reliable twenty minutes out of every hour." She'd noted right away that signal on the island was basically non-existent, but oddly enough the thought didn't concern her. "Even if I can't push any data, I can still approve the packages I have downloaded and encrypt them ready to send through when we get back to civilization."

"You really don't know how to relax and take a vacation, do you?"

Morgan raised her martini. "Please. Look at me. I'm so relaxed I'm practically a liquid state. Like this excellent cocktail."

Jane let down her sunglasses half an inch and casually raked her eyes over Morgan's body. After her slow inspection, Jane pointed to the expanse of skin left bare between Morgan's bikini top and the wrap slung low around her hips. "That's a great tattoo, I've never seen it before."

Trying to ignore the heat on her skin left by Jane's gaze, Morgan arched an eyebrow above her oversized sunglasses. "Obviously, given I've never worn a bikini to the office." She glanced down at the tattoo inked above her right hip traveling toward her navel—a black heart rhythm line that became the jagged outline of a mountain before returning to the heart rhythm. After much staring back and forth between her belly and images of mountains on the Internet, Morgan had discovered it was the outline of Mount Everest. "This was already here when I took over. I've never actually *gotten* a tattoo, but I've had quite a few."

Jane drank another large mouthful of cider. "How many bodies have you inhabited?"

The question, while not intimate, had the potential to reveal far more about Morgan's past than she cared to at this moment. She affected a casual shrug. "Quite a few."

"Mmm, I'll bet." Jane stretched, slowly like a cat in a sun patch. "God this place is fabulous. I think I could stay here for weeks."

Morgan pushed her sunglasses farther up her nose. "Indeed." The moment she'd jumped from the seaplane into the shallow water and helped Jane down, Morgan had felt an immediate soothing calm.

"You're not really going to work the whole time we're here, are you?" Jane asked, concern coloring her query.

"No, of course not. But while you're diving and sleeping, I'll be able to tie up some loose ends and hopefully stop Bethany Harris from gaining anything more on me."

Jane frowned. "While I'm sleeping?"

"Yes. Perfect time to duck back to the office. They'll never even know I'm not staying in the same hemisphere. Plus I need to water my flowers," she added playfully.

Jane smiled in return, but it seemed forced. "That makes sense." She looked to the pool where a couple were canoodling in the water, then back to Morgan. "What do you want to do for the rest of the day?"

Morgan made a vague, lazy gesture. "Your list, Jane, therefore it's your call."

"I think…more of the same of what we're doing right now."

She raised her martini glass in toast. "Good choice." Fishing the olive from the glass, she used her lips to slowly pull it off the stick.

Jane stared. After a long pause, she cleared her throat. "I think I need another drink."

They spent the rest of the afternoon lounging around, testing the bartender's skills, exploring the small island, and talking to the rangers and staff about the reef's ecology before eating dinner. Jane had beaten Morgan at chess—played using two-feet-tall pieces on a huge board painted onto the concrete near the pool area—before they'd taken a walk on the moonlit beach to look for turtle hatchlings.

They'd seen nothing for two hours except other guests, clearly with the same mission, and around ten p.m. Jane had dejectedly suggested they call it a night because she needed to rest before her

SCUBA adventure the next morning. Once Jane had said her quiet goodnight, Morgan waited for thirty minutes before peeking through the door into the bedroom to check on her. Jane slept on her side, facing the door, the slow rise and fall of her ribcage a comforting rhythm.

Morgan wrote a quick note to remind her that she had gone but should be back before sunrise, and left it propped on the daybed. She allowed herself a few moments to listen to the water lapping at the beach and inhale the fresh ocean scent, and with a pang of reluctance, left for San Francisco.

Normally, Morgan loved being in the office. The quiet hum of the electronics hosting billions of important contracts and the chatter of her employees were soothing. But being at Theda away from Jane, she found herself struck with desperation to get back to the small quarters where Jane would be sleeping, a hemisphere away. She made a quick sweep of the server rooms, checked inputs and outputs and tidied up a few small housekeeping things before settling in her office with a pot of tea. Just like a regular day. Except it felt nothing like it.

Hours at work, more hours hopping around the USA, hours wishing she was with Jane. Finally, after visiting five people to complete packages, Morgan went home to her dark apartment, trying to ignore the low fog of exhaustion clouding her with a weak fuzziness. Quick hot shower, clean clothes and a huge bowl of sugary cereal. Not quite enough, but it'd have to do.

Sighing, she rinsed her bowl and spoon, wishing for what felt like the hundredth time that day that she was back in the small apartment suite on the Great Barrier Reef. Instead, she was about to travel to Aether. Just a few more things to take care of and she could go back to Jane. She closed her eyes and allowed herself a brief moment to blank her mind and think of nothing but *her*.

Morgan remembered the sparkle in Jane's eyes as they'd talked during their sunset beach walk and over dinner, the low intimacy in her voice as she'd leaned in to ask a question, her hand grasping Morgan's arm. And as they'd had drinks by the resort pool, her thinly disguised shape under the loose long-sleeved linen shirt Jane wore over her bikini.

Okay, that was enough. She shook herself like a dog shaking off water, as if she could shake off the lingering mental image. Linger was right. Jane was always somewhere in her thoughts. Morgan closed her eyes again, allowed herself one more thought of Jane, the heated gaze she'd given her that afternoon, and then left the earth realm.

As soon as she'd kissed Cici hello and flopped onto an adjacent couch, Morgan blurted, "Did you know female sea turtles will return to the same place where they themselves hatched to lay their eggs?"

"Yes, I did know that. Nature is incredible." Cici smiled fondly at her. "Are you thinking of becoming a marine biologist, Morgana?"

"No, though it's incredibly interesting. We spent some time in the information center on Heron Island this afternoon. You should see the reef, Cici, and this island is only a *tiny* part of it. Incredible. Jane's doing two dives tomorrow and then I think we'll snorkel the last day and hopefully see some turtle hatchlings at night."

"I see," Cici purred. "And how *is* Jane enjoying crossing items off her bucket list?"

"As you know, we've only ticked off a few things but she seems to be enjoying it a great deal. We'll have one night on the Australian mainland Friday before we fly to New Zealand Saturday morning and stay there for a few days so she can see that *Lord of the Rings* movie place, then we're done for a week or so I think."

"Hmm. Excellent." She raised her wine in salute. "Dare I say it, Morgana, you look almost…relaxed?"

Morgan laughed. "You try not relaxing when you're lying on a deck chair in the sun, staring out into the most amazingly blue ocean reef with cocktails being brought to you regularly." She drummed her fingers on the arm of the couch. "This whole thing has made me think that maybe I *do* need to take more vacations. I mean, not full vacations but get away more."

"Well I'm all for it. Relaxation looks good on you." After a reassuring hand squeeze, Cici's expression turned businesslike. "Now, tell me, what's going on in the world of those about to come under my care."

* * *

Morgan sensed Jane returning from her dives a few moments before she appeared in the open doorway of their suite. Jane had been asleep when she'd come back from Aether, and they'd barely seen each other that morning before Jane had rushed off for her SCUBA dives. And it was only now Jane had returned that Morgan realized that she'd felt the time apart as something physical, something missing.

"I'm not interrupting?" was Jane's quiet question.

Morgan set down her tablet, response dying in her throat. All she managed was a headshake and an indeterminate squeak. Smooth. Jane wore a towel wrapped around her hips which left the top half of her body, and the bright red bikini, free for her to see. Morgan only just choked back the unconscious low moan at the swell of Jane's breasts filling in the fabric of the bikini, and forcibly raised her eyes to Jane's face. Jane wore the indent of her dive mask around her eyes and nose, her hair was ragged, wet and salt-stiff and her expression was one of pure, unfettered joy.

That radiant expression not only shook Morgan out of her dumbfounded stupor, it told her everything she needed to know about how Jane's diving had gone. Desperate for a few moments to regain her equilibrium, she asked an obvious question. "How was it?"

"Absolutely incredible," she gushed. "I've never seen coral that bright, or so many fish and turtles and reef sharks. There was even a snowflake eel, and an octopus and a million other things. Morgan, it was…" Jane made a gesture like her head was exploding. "Just, wow."

"So you enjoyed it then," Morgan asked dryly.

Jane's laugh was loud and full of pleasure. "Just a little. And they were so helpful, sorted out all my gear, and when we came back to the dive shop between the dives there were snacks and drinks and candy waiting. I need to shower, and then I feel like I could eat half of the buffet."

Morgan tilted her head back to glance up at her. "Good. I'll eat the other half."

Jane grinned, pausing before she bent to bestow a light, far too brief kiss on Morgan's cheek. She dropped the towel and draped it over a chair then slipped into the bathroom. And Morgan most definitely did not stare after her. Much.

After their late lunch—where Jane fell far short on her promise of eating half of the buffet—and a stroll along the beach, Jane slipped out to read on the balcony and Morgan resigned herself to working inside at the coffee table. Funny how work, which was so much a part of her life and usually gave her no pause, suddenly made her feel so antsy. After twenty minutes inside, listening to the sounds of the beach and gentle breeze, Morgan grabbed her things and moved out onto the balcony beside Jane, overlooking the reef.

Perhaps not the best thing for productivity, but the idea was too tempting to resist. Especially when Jane glanced up from her novel and gave Morgan the most adorable smile of pleasure. Worth it. After an hour or so, Jane's quiet question broke Morgan from her intense concentration. "Did you want to take another walk before dinner?"

Morgan looked up, surprised that the sky had darkened to almost sunset. Jane's question required no thought, and she immediately stood and gathered her tablet and phone to lock them in the room safe. "Let's go."

They slipped barefoot onto the beach and made their way to the high-tide line as the sun dipped lower and lower until it had almost kissed the water, spreading a brilliant red-orange sky across the horizon. They'd walked for ten minutes into the darkening twilight when Morgan spotted tiny shapes about fifteen meters away, moving clumsily across the sand toward the water. She grabbed Jane's hand and pulled her to a stop. "Look. Hatchlings."

"Where?" The question was almost panicked, as if Jane thought she might miss them.

With her free hand, Morgan pointed up toward the dunes where more tiny dark shapes were moving toward the water. "There."

"Where?" Jane asked again, even more anxious now. "I can't see anything."

Morgan slipped behind her and wrapped both arms around Jane's waist. Jane's body went rigid for a few seconds before she relaxed and leaned back into her. "Here," Morgan murmured, pointing at the hatchlings. "Sight along my arm."

Jane leaned her cheek against Morgan's bicep and after a few moments whispered, "Oh! I see them." Jane's realization was a breathless, wondrous admission. "What did the staff say? Don't get in their way and stay still? Shit, what if they want to come over here and we're blocking their path?" She twisted around to look searchingly up at Morgan.

"They're at least fifteen meters in front of us, so I don't think they're likely to detour this way. I think they'll make their way straight down to the water to begin their life." She couldn't help herself, softly nuzzling the smooth skin behind Jane's ear.

Jane's inhalation was quick, her words husky and breathless. "I can't believe it! I didn't think we'd see them. Oh my God." She turned to face forward again and snuggled Morgan's arms around her waist.

"Me either. It's incredible." She softly kissed Jane's neck, letting her lips linger against warm skin.

Jane shivered and without thinking, Morgan pulled her even tighter against her front. "Cold?" Morgan murmured against Jane's ear.

Jane's response was a murmured and barely intelligible negative.

"Good." Morgan was dimly aware of a few other groups who'd stopped as well, but her focus honed in on Jane who still leaned against her, clutching the hands she had resting on Jane's stomach. The hands which roamed to lightly stroke Jane's belly.

Jane shuddered and made a small noise of either protest or acquiescence but regardless of the emotion, she didn't move. Morgan sighed against Jane's neck, the exhalation a contented realization of just how incredible it felt to have physical connection like this again. Without taking her eyes off the tiny moving shapes, Jane murmured, "What is it?"

For just the briefest moment, she considered not answering or answering with some brush off. But just as quickly came the awareness that she wanted to tell Jane, wanted to share another part of herself, as uncomfortable as it made her feel. Keeping her voice low, cheek against Jane's hair, Morgan confessed, "I haven't really had physical contact like this in a very long time. I don't have friends, and people who touch me usually only do so for a handshake. I mean, I touch Cici every day and even being near her makes me feel comforted and connected but..."

She nosed Jane's hair, inhaled the scent of her. "It's nothing like this simple human connection, Jane. I didn't even know that I'd been missing it until you, and it feels so utterly incredible that I'm afraid of losing it when this is all done."

And this was only the beginning—in the scheme of things, they'd barely even touched. What would it be like after number twelve?

Jane turned her head slightly so she could still watch the hatchlings, and not to raise her voice. The side of her face was shadowed by the rising moonlight. "It doesn't have to be the end. When we've finished my bucket list, I'll still be around. I'd still like to be your friend."

Friend. She turned the word over in her head, trying to decipher it. It felt wonderful and entirely unsatisfactory all at the same time. But admitting *that* sad lonely truth went beyond their arrangement and into territory Morgan didn't want to enter again. So she kept silent and together, they watched dozens and dozens of tiny turtles make their first journey to the ocean.

CHAPTER TWELVE

While Morgan was back in the States at the Theda office pretending everything was normal and she wasn't actually jaunting around the southern hemisphere, Jane was trying to summon the energy to sort through the videos and images from their trip. She was bone weary yet utterly elated after the Hobbiton tour, and desperately craving a beer. Morgan, bless her foresight, had insisted on a grocery stop after the tour.

The fridge in their apartment in Auckland's CBD was stocked with snacks, and what the grocery clerk had sworn was one of the best New Zealand beers—Mac's Sassy Red. One of New Zealand's best beers was apparently adult proof, and after fumbling with and swearing at the pull tab opening for a few minutes, Jane finally managed to open the bottle. Licking spilled beer from her hand, she nabbed her laptop and sank onto the couch with feet on the coffee table and amber ale in hand.

Slowly sipping the beer, which thankfully was worth the trouble it'd taken to open it, Jane waited for her photos to transfer. And waited. And waited. Okay, maybe she'd gone a little overboard. Morgan had been in good humor, feigning exasperation then holding out her hand for the camera to snap Jane posing by every building, sign, garden and pathway of Hobbiton.

She'd half-finished a second beer, which had been opened with marginally more aplomb than the first, when the images turned from hobbits to hawksbill turtles. They'd gone snorkeling on their last day on Heron Island, and Jane managed not to spend the whole time ogling Morgan who wore nothing but a dark green bikini.

She watched a bunch of short videos of parrotfish, rays, guitarfish, turtles and black-tipped reef sharks before starting up the last clip. The video followed a turtle then panned to Morgan who waved underwater, grinning around her snorkel. A loud burst of laughter echoed underwater and Morgan pointed off screen before the video swung to the turtle, who'd just crapped before swimming away. From the screen came the sound of Morgan's laughter as she surfaced. She'd been in hysterics when Jane had surfaced right beside her, barely able to talk around her mirth.

Jane scrubbed the video back to the start again, unsurprised by the sensation that began in her chest, then spread through her stomach. And lower. Jane paused the video before the marine animal crapping incident and covered her face with both hands. "Shit," she mumbled to herself. "Shit!"

This was more than just a physical thing, though the physical thing was still front and center, this was…shit, this was veering dangerously close to falling in love. She scoffed. Falling in love was a bit of a jump, especially after only a few trips with Morgan. But she was definitely falling in like, or somewhere between the two. Loke?

Since they'd embarked on Operation: Bucket List, it had become apparent just how much she hadn't known about Morgan Ashworth. And not just the Minion stuff, but who she was as a person. Every layer revealed, each discovery was like a tick in the "Pros" column of why she loved, errrr, *liked* Morgan. Oh come on, Jane. You literally just admitted that you thought you were falling in love.

Most surprising of all was that the thing that'd been at the forefront for so long, namely number twelve, had been pushed aside for the sheer pleasure of being around Morgan. Jane almost laughed at the thought. Not so much pushed aside as more fitting it in beside the enjoyment of Morgan's company. Number twelve was still *very* much on her mind, but *something* always seemed to get in the way. Mostly Morgan's work and the fact that no matter how hard Jane tried, and swore she'd be awake and dressed all sexily when Morgan returned from Minioning, she had fallen asleep every night they'd spent away together. Then woken in the morning cursing herself and trying to ignore the insistent reminder that she still hadn't crossed number twelve from the list.

The way they were going, between Morgan's workload and teleporting around the world and who-knows-where-else and Jane's screwed-up circadian rhythms, they were going to have to schedule number twelve six months in advance. And by then, maybe Jane would have wrangled her feelings so she didn't feel so pathetic for wanting someone who didn't even want her that way.

Morgan hadn't said it outright and she didn't need to, didn't need to say Jane had no chance beyond them scratching a mutual itch. Jane had seen it when Morgan mentioned Hannah. Had heard the pain in her voice, the intensity in her eyes when she spoke about her soulmate. Her seven-hundred-year-old boss was still in love with a dead woman. Jane couldn't compete with that. She didn't *want* to compete, because this wasn't a competition. But it would be nice to have made the team at all. She wasn't even on the bench.

Jane dropped her hands from her face and was treated to the wonderful image of Morgan's bikini-clad breasts not ten inches from her eyes. Granted, it was on a laptop and not in person but still, hello. Her fingers seemed to have a mind of their own as they gently traced the inner curve of Morgan's screen-breast. Mouth suddenly dry and other places decidedly not dry, she ran her fingers around the outside of the other breast. If she was quick there was plenty of time to...

She'd just put her hands on the waistband of her sweatpants when Morgan appeared in the kitchen of the open-plan apartment. Jane's thudding heart could have been the anticipation of what she was about to do, or the shock of Morgan's sudden reappearance. Hoping her cheeks didn't look as red as they felt, she rushed a, "Oh, hey." Did her voice sound as hoarse to Morgan as it did in her own ears? Oh God, it had to be *so* obvious that she'd been milliseconds away from masturbating to a picture of Morgan's boobs like some fourteen-year-old.

Morgan raised a hand in a feeble wave, mumbled hello, then turned to slump against the counter facing away from Jane, with shoulders hunched and head bowed. The arousal from seconds before was replaced by alarm as she rushed to Morgan's side. "Are you all right?"

Without lifting her head, Morgan nodded. "Yes, well no, but yes. I'm just a little bit tired. Lots of jumps from here to home and work and then around to administer some contracts then to Aether then back home again and then to here." The explanation came out flat and dull. "I almost ran out of juice on the way here from San Fran. Morrrrtifying," she slurred.

Jane failed to suppress her concern and her question came out rushed and high-pitched. "Have you eaten enough?"

"I had a quick snack before I left home for here and I've been munching all day, but…I suppose it was not enough. It's been quite a while since I hopped such distances without a break." Morgan raised her head and offered a smile that didn't reach her normally bright expressive eyes. Now they were dull, and she seemed pale and almost gaunt.

She grasped Morgan's arms and pulled her away from where she leaned against the counter. "Sit down and rest. Let me get you something to eat."

She'd meant for her to sit at the table, but Morgan slid to the floor like discarded clothing. Sighing she admitted, "I'm not hungry so much as utterly exhausted I think."

Jane rummaged in the fridge for one of the huge protein drinks Morgan had bought. "How many trips did you make exactly?"

"Here to home then office…" She closed her eyes and her fingers moved one by one to count. "Three trips in the USA for packages, then home then Aether then home again then here. I do not understand it. I shouldn't be out of shape for so much travel, but I have never been this wrecked before."

Jane lowered herself to sit beside Morgan, twisting the plastic cap open. "Drink this," she urged.

Morgan's fingers seemed to slide against the plastic bottle instead of gripping it and Jane's concern turned rapidly to panic. Morgan's eyebrows furrowed and she huffed out a sound of annoyance before she managed to get a hold on the drink. "Wow, now that is *really* embarrassing." She chugged the whole drink in a few long gulps then capped the now-empty bottle and set it on the floor beside her.

Jane thumbed the edge of Morgan's mouth where some chocolate protein drink lingered. "Better?"

"I will be in a minute." Despite her attempt at reassurance, she was still slumped on the floor and looking too unsteady to move. She turned a smile on Jane, one that reached her eyes this time. "Thank you."

Jane settled in a more comfortable position leaning back against the kitchen cabinet and slung an arm around Morgan's shoulders to pull her against herself. "Rest here for a while then I'll help you into bed."

"Bed," Morgan whispered, sliding her arm until it rested comfortably across Jane's waist. After a few moments she breathed,

"I've thought of little else than taking you to bed this whole trip, and now you're here and awake and you look so sexy in those sweatpants, and I'm just too damned tired."

Jane had to swallow before answering dumbly, "Oh? Really?" Well done, brain. Arousal is now back in the building.

"Yes, really." Morgan exhaled, drooping even more against her. The fingers of the hand resting on Jane's waist slid back and forth as if Morgan was testing how she felt. "Jane, I need to confess something. The thought of sleeping with you, having sex or making love or whatever we're going to do, is so overwhelming I've been, well not running away but staying away from you more than I normally would. Procrastinating, in Aether or home or whatever, even though I don't like being away from you." Morgan moved slightly so she could look up at her, her face a mask of earnestness as she quietly admitted, "I'm afraid."

Jane stroked her neck softly, lingering against warm smooth skin. "Why are you afraid?"

"It's just been a while I suppose. Don't know what to expect. Don't want to disappoint you." Morgan leaned back against Jane, fingers now resting against Jane's stomach. "This feels really nice," she said into Jane's shoulder, slumping even more into her.

"It does." Jane stroked her hair, twining strands around her fingers. "And don't worry about number twelve. We'll get there when we get there."

"I bet the destination is worth it." Morgan exhaled a sigh, then mumbled, "I'll get up in just a moment."

Then she fell asleep.

* * *

Still battling hellish jetlag—likely a consequence of only *just* getting over the jetlag from their flight to Australia before they'd left the southern hemisphere again—Jane sleepwalked through her morning server-maintenance tasks before turning her attention to the stack of messages and reports from her team. There was also a handful of messages, both handwritten and in the internal office private messaging system, from Morgan. The idea that Morgan had been in this office, and also with her on an island in the Great Barrier Reef and New Zealand within minutes of each other was still somewhat unbelievable.

Most of Morgan's messages were asking her to confirm data or core stats and asking questions about the new build they were planning, but there was one instant message that caught her eye.

The export rate on bank six seems to be a little slow – have asked Jorge to check on it but can you please follow up when you're back? You were talking in your sleep when I left and it was so cute and I can't stop thinking about it.

She read the message again, lingering on the intimacy of the last sentence. The way Morgan swung from professional to personal in the blink of an eye was incredible. But never when anyone at the Theda office would see—she was one hundred percent professional at work, not giving away anything by word or look or gesture that a week earlier they'd indulged in a kissing session that had left Jane feeling like Jell-O. Jane's eyes strayed unconsciously to Morgan's office.

Morgan wore her charcoal pinstripe skirt suit, a crisp white shirt and a sky-blue scarf knotted around her neck which Jane knew made her eyes seem intensely blue. She was on a phone call and paced slowly back and forth in front of her desk, gesturing with her free hand. The woman presented here was so completely opposite to the woman Jane had known less than twenty-four hours earlier. The woman in jeans and sneakers or biker boots and with whom she'd shared meals with and who'd fallen asleep against her.

Morgan had spent the entire flight from New Zealand to San Francisco making sporadic apologies for using Jane as a pillow until Jane had had to tell her it was fine, really. Then she'd done something stupid. She'd admitted that she'd liked it. Fortunately she had managed to hold her traitorous tongue before she said that sitting on the kitchen floor, holding Morgan while she slept had felt so natural, so *right*, that when Morgan stirred forty minutes after falling asleep, Jane had been overcome by a sharp pang of disappointment and something like loss.

Pathetic.

Leah arrived at just that moment to remind her, as she loved to do, of that exact fact. "Glad to be back so you can stare dreamily at Ms. Ashworth every day?" She fluttered her eyelashes. "How*ever* did you cope being away from her?"

"I coped just fine," Jane said automatically, turning her attention back to her laptop. Because she got to stare dreamily at Morgan every day. She felt the heat creeping up her neck and hoped Leah was more interested in teasing her than studying her.

"Mm, sure." Leah made an impatient sound. "Come on, how was trying not to get eaten by an Australian shark and geeking around Geek-town?"

"Very few divers get bitten by sharks, especially not while reef diving." Jane checked the screen one last time before looking up. "And it's called Hobbiton, thank you very much, and it was incredible. It's literally like being in the movies. So great."

"Riveting…" Leah mumbled. She hitched a hip onto Jane's desk. "Listen. Do you remember that new gym instructor I mentioned last month?"

Leah was many things, subtle was not one of them. "Vaguely," Jane hedged.

"Well, she made a pass at me yesterday and I mean, she's hot and all, but I had to tell her, well you know. Not into women like that." Leah nudged her, sing-songing, "But I may have mentioned my cute lesbian workmate friend."

The groan she'd been trying to suppress outmuscled her resolve. A set-up. Joy. "Really? Ugh, Leah, introductions like that are *so* awkward. And you know what else is awkward? When your straight friend gets hit on by more women than you do."

Said straight friend didn't bother to hide her smugness. "If you went out more, I'm sure that statistic would be reversed."

"I have been going out. I've just come back from an overseas vacation, remember?" Her traitorous eyes strayed again to the glass of Morgan's office.

Leah huffed out a disbelieving sigh. "Jane, seriously. May I present you with Exhibit A." Discreetly, Leah indicated Morgan who'd just paced back into view. "You can't even go half an hour without looking at her. This has gone on for long enough. You need to move on. And I have a woman with the most incredible, ripped six-pack lined up ready to meet my sweet, funny, nerdy friend."

"I don't really want a ripped six-pack." Just the quiet ripple of muscle she'd already been gifted, care of Morgan's bikini.

"Jane. Pardon my French, but are you fucking nuts?"

"No, I just…look, set-ups are so not me, and I'm not really looking to date right now. And can you honestly see me with a gym instructor? I don't even remember what the interior of my gym looks like."

"You're never looking to date," Leah countered flatly. "And it's because you're hung up on a woman who wouldn't give you the time of day outside of work."

It took every ounce of Jane's willpower to bite down on the words wanting to fly out. Morgan had done far more than give her the time of day outside of work. She offered a musing sound, hoping Leah would take it as Jane thinking rather than Jane agreeing with her.

"I mean I get it, even straight ol' me can tell she's hot. And she's kind and a really nice boss. Well, most of the time, but—"

Jane's head snapped up. "What do you mean most of the time? She's always a nice boss."

Leah raised both hands. "Whoa, calm down, staunch defender. Totally agree she is, normally, but she was really off this past week. Popping in and out of the office all day at weird times and grumpy like I've never seen her. It was like twelve months' worth of PMS all smooshed into one week."

"Really? She was fine when I—" Jane bit off the words *when I was with her* and made a hasty adjustment. "When I came in this morning."

Leah's shrug was the epitome of *whatever*. "I'm just worried about you, that's all. I don't want to see you wither and die under a pile of computer parts and confusing data crap."

What was she supposed to say? Oh, don't worry about me, Leah. I'm fine. Just pretty sure I'm in love with an immortal woman who is still hung up on a woman who died three hundred years ago. And by the way, I might be dead in six months, so I've got a bit on my plate at the moment and I don't really want to meet your gym instructor's six-pack. Have I mentioned I'm in love with my boss?

Jane made herself smile. "I appreciate the concern, really I do, but everything is A-Okay." She glanced at her watch. "Now, it's time for Elevenses."

"For what?"

Jane suppressed the urge to say it was not only one of a Hobbit's seven daily meals but also part of Morgan's twelve daily meals. "It's a geek thing. You wouldn't understand." She stood and pointed in the direction of the staff room. "Food time."

The toaster had been commandeered for bagels, which had popped and apparently been forgotten. Well, there went her dream of an English muffin. It was bad break-room etiquette to touch someone else's snack. Almost as bad as forgetting your snack and keeping the toaster out of commission. Time for microwave popcorn. As soon as Jane started the microwave, Leah pounced again. "Are you seriously not interested in the gym instructor?"

"No, I'm really not." Almost as an afterthought she added, "But I appreciate you looking out for my wellbeing and trying to set me up."

Someone cleared their throat and Jane and Leah both spun around at the sound. Well, there was another kind of English muffin. Morgan's expression was pleasant and welcoming...if you hadn't spent hours alone with her and perhaps pitifully learned the nuance of her expressions. The fine tension lines around her eyes, and the slight tightness at the corners of her smile told Jane she wasn't nearly as happy as she appeared, and the unexpectedness of the expression sent a small shudder of alarm through her.

But when Morgan spoke, her tone was as calm and friendly as ever. "Jane, Leah. How are you both?" She slipped around them and pulled the bagels from the toaster. "Sorry, I got caught up on the phone and forgot about these."

While Leah stared at Jane with an expression that bordered on alarm, Morgan used, what seemed to Jane, half a jar of peanut butter on her bagels. As she spread, she said conversationally, "Leah, I wanted to apologize for last week. I know I was short with you and I offer no excuses except personal issues. Actually, that's not even an excuse. Merely an explanation, and I'm sorry."

Leah choked out a, "No problem."

Morgan offered Jane the ghost of a wink, and immediately the tension in her stomach eased. Clearly, she'd overheard Leah. While Jane and Leah stared on, Morgan sliced a banana over the bagels then drizzled honey over that before smooshing the halves together to create two banana-PB-honey bagel sandwiches. After a quick, and slightly desperate bite, chew, swallow of one of her creations, Morgan asked, "And how was your overseas trip, Jane?"

"Really good," she managed to get out. Damn Morgan Ashworth's sexy eating.

"I'm glad to hear that. And you're off again next week for your cousin's wedding in the UK, right?"

"Mhmm, yep." She almost added a fake elaboration to make the lie about why she was going overseas again so quickly seem more believable, but had the feeling she'd probably fumble it.

Morgan's smile held a touch of mischief as she nodded her agreement. "There's few things more enjoyable than travel. Especially with a companion." She added a handful of cookies to her plate and with a "Have an enjoyable day, ladies!" left the break room eating one of her bagel-sandwiches.

The moment Morgan had turned the corner, Leah gestured after her, her mouth agape. "Seriously. How does she eat so much and look like *that*?"

Jane bit her lip on a smile, shrugged and said, "Must be supernatural."

"Mmm, has to be. Or she's out running marathons every lunch break." She nudged Jane in the ribs. "Also, may I draw your attention to her phrases *personal life* and *with a companion*? She's taken. So, hot gym instructor?"

Jane suppressed her sigh. "Still a no."

And also no, Morgan Ashworth is not taken. Unless you want to count by a woman who's been dead for three hundred years.

CHAPTER THIRTEEN

Morgan always enjoyed France—the culture, scenery, food and wine held a comforting familiarity. But being in Paris with Jane was something else entirely. Her enthusiasm and delight for seemingly ordinary things was infectious and for Morgan, gave Paris an entirely new layer, like someone had draped it in soft sensual pastels. What a ridiculous, sappy romantic thought. Yet ridiculous as it seemed, the thought refused to go away. But romance was not what they'd agreed upon for number twelve. Was it?

Shit. What if Jane's idea for number twelve was being wined and dined, swept off her feet with flowers and seduction? And all Morgan could really offer her was a one-sided empathetic bond, a whole lot of lust and desire and what would probably be a clumsy sexual encounter until she regained her bearings after decades of celibacy. She sighed inwardly. Perhaps it would be wise to discuss expectations with Jane before she made a fool of herself.

Ensconced at the table on the balcony of their Airbnb in Le Marais—an eclectic, queer-friendly district spreading across the 3rd and 4th Arrondissements—she sipped tea and watched Jane zinging around the apartment. The zinging had begun when Jane woke before dawn and two hours later, she showed no signs of chilling out. She'd bounced between rushing out onto the balcony that, if you were a contortionist, showed glimpses of the Seine and Notre Dame Cathedral, to the kitchen and then her room and back out again. When Morgan settled at the balcony table, Jane had joined her for about thirty seconds before jumping up again.

Jane leaned her head out of the open balcony doors for the fourteenth time. "Can we go out for breakfast? I'd love to find a tiny café somewhere and eat a French breakfast."

Morgan arched a brow. "Well you know I never turn down food but what exactly does a *French breakfast* entail?"

"I actually don't know," Jane admitted sheepishly. "But I'm imagining croissants and bread, pastries and fresh produce and deli foods and wonderful coffee and all that."

Sold. "Let me finish my tea, then I'm all yours. Shall we walk?"

Within twenty minutes they'd stepped out of the door and made their way to the bustling Rue de Bretagne to begin Mission: Find Jane a French Breakfast. Jane paused to peer in nearly every window at not-yet-open galleries and boutiques before smiling sheepishly at Morgan, apologizing and promising she was done…before stopping to look in the next window. And despite Morgan's protesting stomach, she didn't care about the delay.

They chose a corner café, and after Morgan's quiet plea, the server seated them at a free table by the front window so Jane could watch the bustling street. After a quick smile and a murmured *merci* to the waitress, she asked Jane, "What would you like to drink?"

"Just plain coffee please."

Once she'd ordered coffee for both of them and they were alone again, Morgan opened the laminated menu. "Do you need me to translate for you?"

Jane slid her chair closer until their knees were brushing. "Yes please. I have an app, but I think it'd just be quicker if you did it for me." She cleared her throat. "But say the items in French first."

"Why?"

Cheeks turned an adorable pink, Jane looked as if she were considering not answering before she shyly admitted, "Because listening to you speaking French is possibly one of the sexiest things I've ever heard."

Morgan leaned in, brushed a light kiss on each of those pink cheeks and murmured, "Then I shall be sure to do it as frequently as I can."

When Morgan's first espresso arrived, Jane's eyebrows shot up. "You drink coffee? I've only ever seen you with a death grip on a teacup."

"That's because American coffee is, well…it's not great." Morgan turned her cup around and around. "I tried bringing coffee beans back from overseas and making the coffee myself but it turns out I'm no barista. So I don't drink coffee unless I'm in a country where I know the coffee will be good." She grinned and with a wink said, "So basically everywhere except the USA."

It looked like Jane was mentally storing this fact away, and the thought that she cared so much about an innocuous thing almost made Morgan reach for her hand. Instead, she finished her espresso and asked, "Have you planned out the day?"

"To the minute. But I think I might be able to adjust some things so I can spend more time in this café with you…"

They lingered over their meal, or meals for Morgan, and multiple coffees until Jane declared it was time take a look around the city before their scheduled Eiffel Tower ticket time in the afternoon.

They meandered around Paris for hours, stopping at the Louvre, the Arc de Triomphe and what felt like a million other landmarks while Jane handed out Wikipedia facts. And she talked, questioned, marveled. The only time she pulled her hand from Morgan's was to take yet another photograph, or when they stopped for one of Morgan's many meal breaks. The sensation of wandering Paris hand in hand with Jane was achingly sweet and Morgan filed the feeling away, ready to drag out if ever she had a pang of melancholy.

Late in the afternoon, as they crossed the Pont de l'Alma over the Seine toward the tower, Jane asked, "What's your favorite century?"

"Hmm, that's a difficult one. I'm going to cheat and say the entirety of the Renaissance. It had already begun when I was born and it just kept growing and growing. Such a beautiful time to be alive, the openness of people to learn and teach and create, and unabashed delight in *knowing* was addictive." She grinned. "Though, I admit I do enjoy this modern era very much."

"Good answer. Now, least favorite?"

"You know, I don't think I have one. Things that would cause a person to loathe a particular time period, like disease or famine or poverty never touched me." She smiled self-deprecatingly. "I was not born with, but I was definitely *given* a silver spoon." With their joined hands, Morgan pointed to a spot just past the end of the bridge. "There's a great view here. Do you want me to take some photographs?"

Jane posed with the Eiffel Tower in the background, a smile splitting her face as she brushed back windblown hair. The deepening afternoon sun brought out the red in her hair and Morgan stared at the image on the screen, mesmerized before she remembered she was supposed to be photographing, not staring. Morgan offered Jane her phone back. Jane held it up questioningly. "Do you want some photos of yourself?"

"Oh, no I'm okay, thank you." She smiled. "I've been here many times before and I can always come again."

"Ah, of course." Jane's face fell for a moment before she seemed to catch it and exchange it for a smile.

It took Morgan a few moments to catch on, and she hastily added, "But we could have some photos together?"

Jane's response was casually nonchalant, but her face gave her pleasure away. "Sure. That'd be great."

They situated themselves in front of the tower, and Morgan used Jane's phone to take a few selfies. "Hold on one moment." She rushed up to a passing middle-aged man eating an apple and reading a book as he walked. Glancing at the cover, which was French, Morgan called, "*Pardonnez-moi, Monsieur!*"

He stopped, turned with exaggerated slowness, and sighed. His expression changed to one of forced patience, as if he knew what was coming and it happened regularly. But when Morgan drew closer, his expression changed. And as she apologized for disturbing his day then spoke with him in rapid French, he actually smiled and blushed as he agreed.

When he was done documenting the moment for them, Morgan thanked him profusely and wished him well, and Jane offered a shy and utterly adorable, "*Merci.*"

Morgan took Jane's hand and they walked toward the line waiting to scale the tower. Jane's smaller hand tucked into hers felt like a lifeline, an anchor and Morgan never wanted to let go of this tether to normality, the sensation she could only describe as *rightness*. They, like half the population it would seem, had the idea to climb the Eiffel Tower in time to witness the sun setting over Paris. She had no idea how Jonathon had managed to secure the tickets for this time at such short notice, and she made a mental note to thank him for this and everything else he'd done to help Jane fulfill her list.

Morgan's breathing barely changed by the time they made it to the second platform. Jane, on the other hand, was huffing and puffing. When Jane paused to catch her breath, she muttered, "You know, you really know how to make a gal feel inferior."

"It's unintentional, I assure you." Morgan laughed. "Always remember that I'm blessed with an unfair advantage—longer legs." She lowered her head to speak near Jane's ear. "Besides, I like listening to you out of breath and panting. It makes me think of how else I can make you gasp and pant…"

Jane's ears went red, her mouth opened and closed abruptly. She flashed Morgan a desperate look, then backed toward the elevator which would take them to the top viewing platform. Smiling at Jane's reaction, Morgan followed and squeezed into the elevator car. Jane had become stuck against Morgan, their bodies touching from torso to thigh. "Sorry," Jane murmured, shuffling to move away yet finding no free space.

"Don't be. I like it." *I like it*. What a wonderfully in-depth descriptor. Her arm stole tentatively around Jane's waist and she told herself it was just so she could help Jane balance during the long, unsteady elevator ascent. "Is this okay?"

Jane nodded, her eyes wide. Morgan pulled her closer, gratified when Jane practically melded her body against hers for the remainder of the journey. The mutual reluctance of having to break apart to exit onto the viewing platform felt almost like a cord between them, stretching but not breaking. Once they were free of the oppressive crush of other viewers, Morgan gave in and reached for Jane's hand, relief flooding through her as Jane threaded her fingers through Morgan's as she'd done for most of the day. She led them to a slightly less crowded area and positioned herself behind Jane to stop people pushing against her.

Staring out over the Parisian landscape Jane's *wow* was exultant. Morgan's tears threatened and she blinked hard a few times. The whole experience was beyond incredible, beyond anything she'd ever experienced. She could just make out the Notre Dame cathedral, a mere shell since fire had ripped through the structure the year before. The more she saw, the more she realized how much she'd not seen. How much she'd never paid attention to as she moved through her life. She'd forgotten to stop and smell the roses, when pausing to smell flowers had been the thing to bring her back to herself.

Jane's murmur was barely audible as she twisted around to look back at her. "It's beautiful."

Morgan glanced up, surprised to see her own emotion reflected on Jane's face, and she had to restrain herself from uttering *No, you are*. Jane's eyes were bright, her face alight with joy and wonder. Morgan wanted to pause time, take a photograph to capture it. She reached out, intending to cup Jane's cheek. But Jane turned her head and pressed the softest kiss into Morgan's palm.

Morgan let her hand fall. She cleared her throat. "I can't believe I've never done this. I mean, I've been to Paris countless times, I was even here when the tower was being built." She frowned at the unease trying to rise up again when she thought of everything she hadn't done. So much time and opportunity that she'd wasted.

"Well, you're here now," Jane said softly.

Morgan had to swallow the sudden rush of emotion before saying, "I'm here with you." She paused for the briefest moment before closing the space between them, but it was Jane who stretched up and pulled Morgan down until their mouths touched. The brush of Jane's lips sent the same thrill coursing through her body as it had when they'd kissed on Jane's driveway.

Though Morgan knew it impossible, she would have sworn that time slowed for them while everyone else rushed around. The background noise blurred to a hum as Jane's tongue caressed her lower lip, and when Morgan's lips parted, she gently stroked her tongue over Morgan's. She had no idea how a kiss could both scorch and soothe but when Jane made that low groaning sound, the sound of pleasure and borderline frustration, Morgan's knees turned to jelly. She clutched Jane's waist, pulled herself as close as she could to keep her balance. But the grasp which was meant only to keep herself upright soon turned into a want so deep Morgan felt dizzy.

With difficulty, she pulled away. Morgan studied Jane whose expression showed her want clearly. "What are you thinking?" Morgan murmured.

Jane's voice was little more than a husky whisper. "Number twelve…"

It was all she could to do to breathe and respond in her own, now-hoarse, voice, "Me too. Shall we go back to the apartment and cross that one off the list?" Morgan almost held her breath as she waited for Jane's response.

Jane's expression tightened and she stepped back from their embrace. "I, um…" She nervously licked her lips and in a low voice, elaborated, "I have my period, so probably not."

Morgan only just managed to hold on to her disappointment. "Oh. Damn. But I don't mind about that if you don't."

"Normally I wouldn't be concerned but this list is supposed to be all of my wonderful, fantastical things." Jane flashed her a rueful smile. "Period sex, while fun, doesn't really live up to the fantasy, and if I'm only going to get one chance then I want it to be as perfect as it can be."

"Ah. Well, it *is* your list. Your rules, your fantasy. I can wait if you can." They'd come so close, so many times but something had always stood in the way. Her fatigue, her work, Jane's biology. She felt like banging her head in disappointment against the steel of the tower. "And one chance? Thank you for putting pressure on me to perform, Jane." She had to tease to stop herself revealing her disappointment that she would only have one night, or day with Jane. What an awful notion.

"I don't want to wait, but also I do…" Jane bit her lower lip. "Typical, isn't it? My first time with a beautiful woman in one of the most romantic cities in the world, and I've been hamstrung by my own body."

Ah, a clue. "Romantic?" Morgan moved in, close enough to feel Jane's heat but far enough away that they weren't touching. She dipped her head, unable to resist the temptation of Jane's neck. She felt Jane shudder as she kissed it, before whispering, "Is that what you want when we sleep together? Romance? Slow and sweet and sensual?" Oh, now was such a bad time to think it, let alone verbalize it. Just the thought alone was turning her liquid with need, not an unexpected sensation yet somehow frightening all the same.

When was the last time I *really* wanted a woman, Morgan wondered. Wanted them in more than a casual way. Not since Hannah. She tensed, waited for the upset. But surprisingly, the expected twist of sadness never eventuated. Nor did that fear she'd been holding on to since the idea of sleeping with Jane had first arisen.

"I—" Jane shuddered, one hand gripping Morgan's waist and the other cupping the back of her neck to hold her in place. "I don't know. I just want."

Morgan shifted her attention to the other side of Jane's neck, lightly kissing the warm skin. Jane smelled incredible, like vanilla and citrus and Morgan breathed her in, felt the desire and comfort mix. She lowered her voice even more, keeping her words soft and quiet. "You *want*. It would help if I knew exactly what you want. Do you want to make love? Or do you want something more…primal? Hot and sweaty and rough? Fucking?"

"This is really unfair," Jane choked out, fingers tightening on Morgan's waist. "I want *all* of that."

A slow roll of relief flooded through her. "You know what they say about anticipation being half the pleasure." Morgan straightened, but didn't move away. She pulled Jane closer until their pelvises touched, her hand gliding down until it rested at the small of Jane's back. "And I don't know about you, but I've been anticipating this for quite some time." She bestowed a soft kiss on Jane's tempting lips then drew back. "But you're right, it's unfair. And not just to you."

Jane drew in a shaky inhalation. "Really?" Her disbelieving eyes grew wide, lips slightly parted as though they wanted to ask more.

"Yes, really. So why don't we do something wonderful to take our minds off the unfair. Climb back down this metal beast, find a fabulous restaurant where we can gorge ourselves on amazing French food and wine, and then we can take a walk around and see more of the city at night." And maybe then Morgan could forget about how much she wanted nothing more than to spend the rest of the night making sure Jane was thoroughly satisfied that the requirements for number twelve had been met. "What do you think?"

"I think that sounds incredible." Jane tucked her hand into Morgan's elbow, leaning close. "Lead the way."

Once they'd put feet back on solid ground again Morgan glanced up at the tower and the lights of the exclusive restaurant on the second platform. "Next time we come to Paris, we'll be sure to book well in advance so we can have dinner at Jules Verne."

Jane's voice was small. "Next time…*we* come to Paris?"

Morgan wanted to flee from the faux pas, brush it off as a slip of the tongue, a Freudian Slip, anything but what she knew was the truth. The thought of what she was about to admit was simultaneously thrilling and terrifying, and it took every bit of courage she possessed to nod and say, "Yes. Next time *we* come to Paris. You and me. Together. If you want."

"Yes. I want."

CHAPTER FOURTEEN

"Are you from around this area?" Jane asked when they were almost halfway through the fifty-mile drive from Manchester to the Alton Towers Theme Park. While Jane tried to ignore how weird it felt to be on the wrong side of the car and road, Morgan navigated the roads as if she drove them every day. Actually, Morgan just seemed comfortable all around. Jane had noticed that from the moment they'd arrived in the UK, Morgan's British accent intensified, as if being among *her* people brought it out more.

"No. I'm from Balsdean in the parish of Rottingdean. It's gone now, but it was a village about six miles east of Brighton, a seaside town that's right down the bottom of England. So...two hundred miles from here, give or take. Brighton is now known as the LGBTQ-plus capital of the UK." She turned to grin widely at Jane. "I like to think it was I who started the whole queer culture there."

Jane returned her exuberant expression. "You probably did." She twisted slightly on her seat. "Do you ever go back there?"

"Sometimes, but there's really nothing left from when I lived there. Just memories," she mused. "But I think all English countryside is beautiful and if you want to see some more, I can take a few quick detours?"

Jane's smile felt shy. "I would like that, very much."

Morgan's answering smile was luminous. "Excellent. Detours it is."

They passed through towns which dwindled to historical villages and the more they drove, the more Jane thought Morgan was right—the English countryside held quite possibly some of the prettiest landscapes she'd ever seen. The scenery was exactly as she'd imagined. She had no idea how anyone worked or did anything at all in this part of the world. If she lived here, she'd probably do nothing but walk around staring or spend her days lying down in the fields of thick grass.

Gradually the fields, hedgerows and narrow roads gave way to a highway again as they closed the distance to Alton Towers Theme Park, home of *The Smiler*. Morgan chattered the whole drive, pointing out various features with a fond enthusiasm she'd never shown anywhere before as she recounted facts and local anecdotes.

Lining up to enter the park, Morgan absently twirled her ponytail through the back of her doctored *Valravn* ball cap. She was dressed in what she called her Theme Park Uniform—jeans, a polo and sneakers. Jane was all for the uniform.

Morgan had declared she needed to watch the ride before committing to it, and they navigated through the park to the reason for their visit. She peered up at the coaster, watching two cars complete their circuit. "It looks like someone was drunk when they designed this thing." Her mouth was twisted, her expression part thoughtful, part horrified as she traced the riders' progress with her eyes. Leaning in, she mumbled, "This is the ride that had that bad accident a few years back, isn't it?"

"Yes."

"And you still want to ride it?"

"Yes, of course."

Morgan looked helplessly up at the track, then back to Jane. "Well, then I guess I do too," she said unenthusiastically.

"It's fine, really. I've ridden plenty of coasters by myself."

"Yes I know but that was then, before I…knew you better. I'm just worried, that's all. I can't protect you if I'm not with you."

Jane ran her hand up and down Morgan's bicep. "I thought we'd gone over the whole paradox thing. It'll be okay."

"I know, but you can still get *injured*, Jane." The statement was almost pained. "And yes, rationally I know it's unlikely but lov—" She stopped abruptly, paused then hastily blurted, "Sometimes worrying about something or someone isn't rational."

Jane nodded her agreement, her brain stuck on what Morgan had just said. Could Morgan have been about to say *love*? Jane dismissed the idea. There was *no* way Morgan could feel that for her, and she must've misheard. She forced herself to let go of Morgan's arm. "It's up to you."

Morgan took Jane's hand and placed it back on her bicep, patting it once as if telling it to stay put. She smiled tightly and her voice croaked when she said, "Let's go. And I'm not eating anything until afterward."

The Smiler was everything Jane had hoped for and more. Three thrilling minutes with a world record fourteen inversions, four-point-five Gs and a max speed of eighty-five kilometers, uh fifty-three miles an hour. Absolutely fabulous. She'd held on to Morgan's hand with one of hers, leaving the other to flail wildly and excitedly in the air, and with every passing second Morgan's grip had tightened uncomfortably.

Morgan didn't look green exactly, but her skin was definitely paler as she fumbled for something to hold, struggling to her feet. She drew in a few slow breaths, then offered Jane a shaky smile. "I'm not going to throw up," she said, though Jane wasn't sure if she was simply informing her of her plan, or talking herself out of it. Morgan's eyes widened. "I'm really not." Despite her assurances, she looked as if she might do just that.

Jane slipped her hand into Morgan's and pulled her away from the coaster. "Come on, let's walk. Just keep breathing and it'll pass."

Morgan let herself be led away, grumbling the whole time. "Jane, you probably don't believe me, but these gravity machines are literally the only time I've ever experienced motion sickness. In 1758, someone dared me to go out into the Bay of Biscay, one of the most dangerously rough and unpredictable parts of the ocean, during a storm in nothing more than a rickety sloop. I capsized. And I…" She made air quotes. "Died. And even *that* didn't make me sick. Even with the whole drowning thing, which was quite unpleasant but not sickening."

"Oh, really?"

Morgan gestured expansively at the coaster track then threw both hands in the air. "I simply don't understand why I can't get on one of these things without being nauseated. And I haven't even eaten anything in an hour and a half! I'm starving and it was all for nothing."

Jane's heart melted at her consternation. "Aww, but you tried. Come on, let's you something to eat."

Morgan's expression turned to helpless pleading. "But if I eat something, I can't ride any more coasters with you. I'll...get sick."

"It's okay, really it is. You don't need to ride with me. I promise it's fine. I promise *I'll* be fine," she reassured her for what felt like the tenth time that day. "The idea of being injured on a coaster has never occurred to me."

Morgan's face contorted and she blathered out a disjointed incoherent sentence. "But, I...this is not, my...Jane, I just..."

Watching her, listening to the rambling, Jane sensed that this was the first time in a very long time that Morgan Ashworth had encountered something she didn't find easy, or something she just plain couldn't do. "Trust me on this one?" Without giving her a chance to argue, Jane stood on tiptoes and left a lingering kiss on the corner of Morgan's mouth. "Now, snack time."

Morgan nodded, her features softening as if she had made her peace with whatever she needed to. She exhaled a relieved breath, then inhaled a few donuts as they strolled through the park to find her something more substantial. She bee-lined for a burger joint, fidgeted until her order was ready and then inhaled that meal too.

By three p.m. Jane had ridden every roller coaster at Alton Towers, some twice. Morgan had waited with her in line, all the way to the coaster boarding platforms. Then at each ride, she'd charmed the attendants into letting her stand with the other waiting passengers. Each time Jane rolled back to the platform post-ride, Morgan had been staring anxiously at the track as if reassuring herself that Jane had returned. Her agitation and concern were clear and Jane felt the tenuous thread that was keeping her from tumbling completely head over heels fraying with every passing second.

Even after detouring on the way home to a fast-food place and then a gas station for snacks, when they were just over half an hour from the hotel Morgan had pulled over again in front of a small café. She'd barely cut the engine before telling Jane she needed to come inside with her, where she ordered a pot of tea and scones with strawberry jam...jelly...and cream, and insisted Jane try at least one, mumbling something about how awful *bastardized American scones* were.

Morgan was correct, yet again. These "real" scones were unreal—flaky and light, moist on the inside while crunchy golden on the outside—and the fresh cream and fruit preserve turned a food Jane was usually ambivalent about to something she'd wanted to gobble down as fast as she could and stuff a few in her backpack for later.

On their way back to the car, Jane asked, "Why don't you pack snacks or a few sandwiches or something when you come out?"

Morgan seemed genuinely perplexed by the idea. "Because I can just go wherever I want whenever I want to get food? Honestly, I've never considered taking food with me anywhere."

When put like that, it made perfect sense. "Sure, okay. But if you're going to be driving places with me instead of teleporting, maybe it's a good idea to bring something with you in case we can't find food fast enough? I don't like the idea of you being hungry."

Morgan adopted her haughty expression, though it was made less effective by the pull of a smile at the edges of her mouth. "Are you saying you don't like it when I get, what's that phrase, hangry?"

Jane's backpedal was so quick she almost toppled. "No I'm not saying that at all! Just that I don't think it's good to be hungry, especially not you. What you need is a—" Mercifully, Jane managed to stop herself from saying *partner*, and mentally flailed for something more neutral, something that didn't scream *I want to be your girlfriend and I think I'm falling for you.* "You need a friend to look out for your dietary needs."

"Ah, are you offering to be that friend?" Her eyebrow flicked upward, for just a second, before settling. The way Morgan said it was as if she didn't like the way the word *friend* sounded coming from her mouth. She unlocked the car and opened the passenger door.

If Jane was honest, she didn't particularly like the way it sounded either, but friend was far better than nothing. She screwed up some courage and admitted, "Yes, I am."

Morgan's smile was unreadable as she gestured for Jane to get in the car.

By the time they'd driven back to Manchester and taken showers, it was almost seven in the evening. Jane was beyond hungry and exhausted, and judging by the expression on Morgan's face, their food stops on the way home weren't cutting it for her either in the stomach fulfillment department. Despite her exhaustion, Jane agreed they should go out for dinner instead of just ordering pizzas or something.

Morgan shrugged into her leather jacket. "I think we should go for something authentically British, other than scones, while you're here. Theme park food doesn't really give you a taste of the UK. Nor does McDonalds."

"What do you recommend?"

She smirked, then seemed to reconsider what she was going to say, though Jane had a fairly good idea of what *British* thing she was about to offer. Jane almost picked up the thread of innuendo and just as quickly decided it wasn't a good idea, not while she was still incapacitated by her uterus. She was all for anticipation, but there was only so much she could take.

Despite having apparently rethought her answer to something innocuous, Morgan's response was still full of laughter. "Dangerous question, Jane. You should know by now that there's very few things I won't consume."

"Then let's go find you something. Many somethings."

They exited the hotel and Jane glanced to her left and stepped off the sidewalk. A strong arm wrapped around her waist and she was practically lifted from the ground and pulled backward until her back was snug against Morgan's front. A car zipped in front of them from their right, and a low chuckle sounded against her ear. "Jane. Remember in some parts of the world, the cars come from the opposite direction."

Jane gripped Morgan's wrist. Her heart thudded, part adrenaline from the realization of what had almost happened, and part excitement at being held in Morgan's strong and comforting embrace. Her response came out breathy and weak. "Intellectually, I know that, really I do but it's just automatic."

"Mmm." Morgan briefly nuzzled Jane's neck before the arm around her waist relaxed. "Can I trust you not to do it again, or should I hold your hand?"

Jane twisted slightly to look back at her. "I'm feeling a bit forgetful," she said. "Might be best to keep hold of me."

"That's what I thought." Morgan twined her fingers through Jane's, her grip firm without being overbearing. "Let's go before you get into any more trouble." Under her breath she added, so quietly that Jane only just heard her, "Or before I do."

After strolling the streets for another ten minutes, peering into restaurants and glancing at menus posted outside, Morgan stopped in front of a small pub, the exterior dark wood inset with wide windows through which warm lighting shone out. "How about here? Authentic pub grub."

"Pub…grub?"

"Grub is food. Ergo, pub grub is food served in a pub." She placed her free hand on her chest, affecting a faux-appalled expression. "Jane, I am utterly shocked that you didn't research vernacular for this portion of our trip."

Our trip… Jane bit her lower lip on the smile and bumped Morgan with her shoulder. "Why would I when I have my own translator for anywhere and everywhere."

Morgan held open the door and ushered Jane inside the pub. "In that case, I should be charging you for my services."

"Oh, I intend to pay you. Very handsomely." She lowered her voice so the front of house woman wouldn't hear her say, "But I don't have any cash on me, so it'll have to be another means of payment. If you're agreeable."

"I think you'll find I'm agreeable in a great many ways."

The flush on her cheeks *had* to be noticeable, but thankfully the woman who showed them to their table in an intimate corner in the back said nothing. Morgan took barely any time perusing the menu before she picked a starter of scallops, chorizo and blood pudding, and after a quick menu skim, Jane ordered the same. Morgan seemed oddly delighted she was going to brave blood pudding and assured her she'd eat any part Jane didn't like. For main, Morgan chose fish pie, declaring she could never find anything that came close back in the States, while Jane decided on a rabbit dish. "I've never tried it before," she admitted, a little embarrassed. "It's not really something I've ever seen offered at home."

"Tastes like chicken," Morgan deadpanned. She held the wide-eyed innocent expression for a few seconds before bursting into laughter. "Really, it kind of does. Or pork, or lamb. Fine, okay, it just tastes like rabbit which is very good."

"Well, I suppose if I don't like it, I can always count on you to finish it for me."

Morgan's voice dropped a few decibels, grew intimate and seductive. "I'm always happy to eat anything you offer me, Jane." She wet her lower lip with her tongue, her eyes never leaving Jane's.

The comeback fell from her lips before she could second-guess it. "Then I'll be sure to offer something you'll enjoy."

Desire flared in Morgan's eyes, but the waiter arrived with drinks before she could respond. The air felt charged with electricity and it was all Jane could do not to reach under the table and run her hand up Morgan's inner thigh. She had to slide her chair a few inches to the side to stop herself from doing just that. And more.

While waiting, they chatted about their day and then their flight home early the next afternoon. The thought of yet again leaving this casual, fun, personal time behind while they returned to their regular life left Jane feeling disappointed. Their starters arrived, thankfully interrupting her despondency.

The food made Morgan's face light up as if she'd been presented with her first meal in a month, and Jane had to admit it wasn't as bad as she'd thought—as long as she didn't think about what blood pudding actually was. Still, she left most of that part to Morgan who happily reached over the table to fork it from Jane's plate, proclaiming with teasing glee, "Jane, come on. How can you not enjoy this delicious fatty protein?" When she was done, she leaned in, voice low and wistful as she confessed, "My mum's was better."

"I'll take your word for it." Jane set down her fork. "Do you miss your family?" As soon as she'd asked the question, she wanted to snatch it back again. "I'm so sorry, that was a dumb question and none of my business at all."

"It's not a dumb question. I do miss them but it's always felt like an abstract kind of loss and one that's unfortunately dimmed with time. Not like...Hannah." She cleared her throat and swallowed a large gulp of wine. "I hadn't even reached twenty when I left home, left my family and in the scheme of things, it's not that long to spend with people."

"Why did you leave? I mean I know Cici was irresistible and all, but leaving family like that is something I just can't imagine."

Morgan set her fork down on the plate then gathered Jane's and laid them next to each other before stacking their plates. She pushed them off to the side and drank a long, slow mouthful of wine. Jane knew stalling when she saw it, and she waited quietly until Morgan answered, "I was dissatisfied with my life, with what I knew to be my future, and was desperate to get away from that by any means possible." Morgan looked up, her expression so open and honest, she almost seemed naked. "Haven't you ever felt that way?"

After a few moments to ponder, Jane answered truthfully, "I'm not sure."

"No? Then why did you make this bucket list, Jane? Isn't it because there's things you've dreamed of doing? Because you wanted to get away from your life for a little while? Aren't there things you want for yourself that go beyond simple hopes or dreams?"

The notion of *leaving her life*, of running away from the things that weren't so pleasant—just as her father had done—had never occurred to Jane. Her answer was a little indignant. "But that's not why I made the list at all. I love my job. I love my mom even though taking care of her is tough sometimes. I'm not dissatisfied, not by a long shot. I mean, yeah sometimes I wish I had more time, more money to do some of the things I want to, like travel." She curled the cloth napkin into a cylinder. "And, yes I want things I don't have. I wish I had a partner to share my life and experience wonderful things with. But those things are all just…frosting on the cake when the cake tastes fine without it."

Morgan grinned, but her eyes were serious, watchful, as if she understood the deeper meaning behind what Jane was implying, though Jane wasn't sure even *she* understood it completely. "Mmm, food metaphors." The grin faded. "But don't you ever wish for something like a triple-layer, double frosted and extravagantly decorated cake?"

"Of course I do. But I haven't yet found someone to put frosting on my cake." Okay, now the food metaphors were just getting confusing.

The server appeared with their meals before Morgan could answer, and judging by her salacious expression, Jane wasn't sure she wanted to hear what euphemism she was going to spout about *frosting cakes*.

Morgan waited until Jane had taken the first bite of her dinner, a hopefully expectant expression lighting her face, as if she felt personally responsible for Jane's enjoyment, or not, of British cuisine. Jane's rabbit was indeed delicious, as was the fish pie Morgan insisted she try. "Why is this not a thing back home?"

Morgan shrugged. "Beats me. One of the many travesties I've encountered during my time away from my homeland." She offered another forkful to Jane, who only hesitated for a second before taking the second mouthful. "Tasty?" Morgan asked hoarsely.

"Delicious," Jane murmured.

Morgan opened her mouth as if to fire back something that probably wasn't safe for saying in public, but instead took another mouthful. The whole outing had turned into a great big flirting session, though thankfully they seemed to have reached a mutual, unspoken agreement that flirting any more over dinner probably wasn't going to help matters.

The conversation moved to more neutral topics, until Morgan glanced out the broad window into the evening light. Reluctance tinged her statement. "We should probably head back. Early start tomorrow."

Jane bit back her disappointment. She wanted nothing more than to stay in the cozy pub for hours and hours and talk and connect and just…be with Morgan, but she nodded and agreed that they should go back to their apartment. To the apartment and to sleep. Sigh.

Once Morgan had paid, she held Jane's long coat so she could slip into it, then held the door for her as well. Such a wonderful mix of feminine chivalry. Morgan paused outside the pub, staring at her reflection in the broad window. She took a small step as if to leave, then visibly shivered. Jane touched her back. "Are you okay?"

"Hmm? Oh, someone must have stepped on my grave." She turned away from the pub. "Let's go." They'd barely taken ten steps before the drizzle had Morgan reaching for her umbrella. Pressed together under the protective dome, Morgan slipped a hand around Jane's waist and pulled her even closer. Jane shuddered, and Morgan ran her hand up and down Jane's back. "You're cold? I thought you knew cold and or rainy are one of the UK's weather standards."

"I did," Jane choked out, unable to articulate that she wasn't so much cold as she was reacting to Morgan's closeness.

"Maybe I can help warm you up?" She kissed Jane's jaw, pressed more kisses on her neck. Morgan's hand roamed down, cupped an ass cheek and then moved back up as though she hadn't just had an ass grope in public.

The woman was simultaneously the sexiest and most frustrating thing Jane had experienced. With effort, she put a few inches between them. "Morgan. Still having woman issues here, and you're *really* not helping my self-control."

She blew out a long, loud breath. "I'm sorry. I seem to forget all of *my* self-control around you." Morgan's groan was strangled. "Let's call a truce. No more innuendo until it's time for innuendo." Her expression was almost pleading. "And it's almost time for innuendo, right?"

"Yes, it is almost time, but weren't you just saying the other day that anticipation is half the fun?" Jane said, surprising herself with the purr in her voice.

"Well yes, but not when it makes me feel like I'm about to combust."

"Combust, hey?" Jane slipped her hands under Morgan's coat and inside her shirt to stroke the skin of her back which was indeed warm, though not quite at combustible temperature. She tilted her head up for a kiss and was met halfway by soft lips. Morgan tasted as she had previously, only this time with a hint of spiciness under the cool cleanness of her.

Morgan pulled back but stayed close. She rested her forehead against Jane's, and when she spoke her voice was hoarse, almost choked. "Jane."

"Mmm?" A lock of Morgan's hair had fallen into her eyes and Jane carefully tucked it back.

"I, about what I said in Paris, I…um…"

The expression on her face made it easy to figure out Morgan was referring to the laughable idea that they would go back to Paris together some day. "It's okay, really. I understand. Heat of the moment type thing." Despite her words, the disappointment of not being wanted stung.

"No it's not that. I meant it. Really I did, but I'm just—" She raised both hands.

"Don't worry about it, we'll just cross that bridge if and when we get to it." Jane stretched up to kiss her again, and though it was quick and gentle, she felt the connection between them as if it were physical.

Heavy footsteps approached before an obnoxious wolf whistle cut through the night to ruin the moment and pull them apart. Morgan froze then straightened, turned around and positioned herself in front of Jane, who had to peer around her to see a stranger approaching. A slow roll of fear filled her belly, replacing the slow build of arousal she'd been enjoying moments earlier.

A heavyset man, perhaps in his mid-twenties, spat on the ground. "Fuckin' dykes. Fuck off, lesbos and take all ya lesbo friends wif you."

"So witty," Morgan drawled. She glanced over her shoulder at Jane, her sardonic smile making her seem almost menacing. "It seems our friend here wants to visit the island of Lesbos. I'd wager he's far more interested in *dykes* than he would like us to believe."

He took a step toward her, hands balling into loose fists, his expression one of clear confusion at Morgan's comeback. "What'dya say, cunt?" Jane couldn't quite make out his features—non-descript angry young guy with a coarse British accent was the best she could come up with. Wonderful, and so specific. British guy in Britain. Wasn't she so helpful in an emergency.

Morgan's voice was conversational. "I said—"

"Morgan!" Jane hissed, trying to pull her back and drag her away but Morgan had planted her feet and was as unmovable as stone. A quick, sharp fear filled Jane's belly.

Morgan gently nudged Jane back and slipped around to her other side, putting herself between Jane and the guy. "I *said* you seem quite knowledgeable about lesbians."

He squared up to Morgan, clearly having identified her as the target. "So yer a tough bitch, ey?"

"When I care to be." Morgan's voice turned icy. "Now be a good lad and do run along." As she stepped even closer to him, she made a shooing gesture with both hands. The man was only an inch taller than Morgan, but he was a good fifty pounds heavier. That fact didn't seem to register with Morgan who nudged him almost casually as if trying to brush him aside.

It all happened so quickly that Jane barely had time to register his elbow swinging around. Morgan faltered, her head snapping back as she tried to move out of the way of the elbow which clipped her on the jaw before she regained her balance. Then, with the strength of an NFL lineman, she grasped the front of his shirt, bent her body, and propelled him backward. He stumbled and grabbed at her, somehow managing to stay on his feet as Morgan drove him six feet away from Jane, who was rooted in place with no idea what she could or should do. Or if she *could* or *should* actually do anything at all that might help Morgan.

Indistinct grunts cut through the city sounds which had receded to white noise. The pair scuffled for a few seconds, and then Morgan was on the ground and the asshole, the fucking *bastard*, was kicking her. Kicking Morgan who did nothing except lie there, not even trying to protect herself or fight back. She just took the beating which made no sense because Jane knew she was more than capable of defending herself.

Actually, she was doing something. Something stupid and unexpected. She was taunting the guy, making fun of him, deriding his physical abilities, his masculinity and a whole bunch of other things that seemed to Jane to be nothing more than gasoline for a wildfire.

Jane didn't even have time to cry out for him to stop, or tell Morgan to stop being so stupid, or get between them or yell for someone to help or even *do* something—if she'd been able to figure out what to do—before more heavy footsteps and a deep-voiced yell of, "Oi! Oi! Sod off, you fuckin' lout!" interrupted the huge wind up of his next kick which was on track for Morgan's face. The guy beating the crap out of Morgan peered around nervously before aiming a foot into her ribs and sprinting off.

CHAPTER FIFTEEN

Well. That had escalated rather quickly. Morgan braced herself on the damp concrete and pushed up onto her hands and knees. The lance of pain through her ribs and the sharp ache of her face were familiar, almost comforting.

Jane knelt beside her, hands moving erratically over Morgan's back and shoulders as if she didn't know what to touch first. "Morgan?"

"Can I get a hand up please?" she asked roughly. Jane rocketed to her feet, a hand outstretched to help her stand. Upright once more, Morgan bent down to brush off her jeans, exhaling audibly as her torso contracted. Straightening, she flashed Jane a weak smile and a weaker, "Thanks."

A tall middle-aged gent wearing a newsboy cap skidded to a stop a few feet away, breathlessly blurting, "Sorry, saw what happened but couldn't get 'ere quick enough. You ladies okay?"

Morgan forced herself to smile brilliantly, like a game show host telling a contestant they'd just won a new car. "Yes, perfectly all right. Thank you." It even sounded steady and convincing, despite the fact she was holding her ribs as gingerly as if they were porcelain.

He peered around nervously. "Didja call the coppers?"

"Not yet, no. Too busy being assaulted and all that. But I will," she added quickly when his eyes widened and his lips parted. "Thank you very much for your concern, but I assure you we're fine."

He didn't seem convinced, but when Morgan offered him another smile, this one dialed up in intensity, he nodded and seemed to accept her explanation. "Well, aw'right then, love. If yer sure."

"I am," Morgan assured him. "And I appreciate your assistance. Thank you."

The man gave her a quick look-over, nodded and with a flick of fingers against the brim of his cap, strolled away. He glanced back at them once before crossing the street and then continued without looking back again. Jane glanced after him, the barely disguised anger on her face warring with obvious concern. "Who the hell just walks away and leaves a woman after she's been beaten up?"

Morgan laughed, then winced and pressed her palm to her stomach. A quick, forced smile formed automatically on her lips. "Jane, the number one rule of the British Empire is don't impose— politeness above all else. I guarantee that he's relieved right now."

"That's ridiculous." She cupped Morgan's face gently, taking her time to study her properly. "Where are you hurt?" Warm hands guided her head carefully from side to side, and Morgan noted with relief that it didn't hurt to move her neck.

"I'm not. Not seriously. My mouth stings a little and I think my ribs are going to be sore tomorrow but I'm fine."

Jane gawped before spluttering, "Fine? Are you kidding me? Morgan, he hit you in the face and was kicking you in the ribs. How can you be fine? I *know* you get hurt. Is this some ridiculous Minion stubbornness?"

"No, it's just…me." Her smile melted into a wince then a frown. Morgan dabbed at her lower lip, staring down at the blood on her fingertips. "Yes, my face and ribs hurt, but I guarantee I've had far *far* worse."

Apparently satisfied that Morgan was okay, Jane exchanged concern for outrage. "Why didn't you just walk away? He wasn't worth it. Why were you goading him like that? He could've had a gun!"

Morgan smiled again, trying to calm Jane. She licked the small cut on her lower lip which had begun a slow trickle. "A gun is unlikely here—more probable would be a blade. Even then, doubtful. He was just a moron who wanted to express his moronic opinion."

Her attempt to reassure Jane apparently did anything but. "Oh, wonderful! Then it's all fine. Get stabbed or beaten instead of shot. Antagonize away instead of just letting it go."

"But Jane, he was being an asshole."

"So? Let him be one."

Morgan sighed. "This really isn't a conversation to have in public. Let's get moving before I cause even more of a scene." She took a few steps, noted Jane hadn't moved, and turned around. "Are you coming?"

Jane hurried after her and they made their way back to the hotel with Morgan walking at three-quarter pace. After a minute, Jane's indignance rose up again. "You can't do that."

"Do...what?" She doubted Jane would accept her stalling tactic. She put her index finger to the cut on her lower lip and held it there.

"You know what. You just jumped in and put yourself in danger like that. It was stupid."

With an exasperated huff, Morgan pulled her finger from her lip. "Well it was better me than you. You can get hurt." Jane was so fragile, so...mortal. Her guilt finally eased, only to be replaced by a new emotion. Fear. *Not* the emotion she wanted.

"So can you," Jane pointed out.

"It's hardly the same thing," Morgan argued. "I'm fine." She took a slow wheezing breath. She turned to Jane, sheepishly caught in a lie.

Jane raised two helpless hands. "I didn't know how to help, how to protect you or do anything except just stand there like an utterly useless person. I even forgot the number for emergency services here."

"I would never want you to put yourself in a position where you might be hurt on my behalf, Jane."

"Well the feeling is mutual, you idiot." She stretched up to place a soft kiss on the ungrazed side of Morgan's jaw. "I just, like, what the hell were you thinking? Why did you do that?"

"Because he was rude to you. I couldn't stand it. And I was thinking about you, Jane," she murmured. "I'm always thinking about you." Morgan stiffened. She had definitely *not* meant to say that aloud.

"Me too," Jane whispered. She plastered herself to Morgan's side, wrapping an arm low around her torso and resting her head against Morgan's shoulder. "We need to find an emergency department."

"I'm not going to the hospital. There's no point," she hastened to add at Jane's renewed look of outrage. "It's only some scrapes and bruises, maybe a cracked rib if I'm unlucky. It'll be fine in a few days and I don't want the trouble of wasting time while they find their Minion Liaison on call and then trying to deal with paperwork." Nor did she want to discuss what had happened when Cici caught wind of it. She smoothed a hand over her ribs as though convincing herself of their integrity.

"Morgan…"

"Please, I just want to go back to our apartment and lie cuddled up in bed." After the briefest pause, she added a barely audible, "With you, until it's time to fly home tomorrow. Please. It's all right. I'm all right. I promise."

She couldn't offer any more, though Jane deserved answers. She deserved honesty, honesty Morgan couldn't give her because the truth of *why* was awful. She couldn't pretend she didn't know exactly why she'd behaved as she'd done, and Jane would never understand how she'd craved a physical hurt to try to stop the emotional hurt. How she sometimes craved pain, discomfort, *something* to remind her that she was forgetting about Hannah. The more time she spent with Jane, the harder it became to hold on to fading memories.

But how could she explain that to Jane? And how could she explain the surge of anger and intense protectiveness that had risen within her, sharp and dangerous and unexpected when that asshole had interrupted them? She'd had only one thought. Keep Jane safe—physically and emotionally. Everything else, reason and sensibility had been pushed away by that intense desire to keep Jane from harm. She should have just shielded Jane and guided her away from the guy. And once her Neanderthal brain had caught up, she'd realized that all she'd really done was put Jane in danger.

Morgan tried to reach the emotion from where she could sense it lingering just out of her grasp. It was something different, but as gut-wrenching as her guilt and shame. Something she never thought she'd have again, something she'd sworn she wouldn't.

Love.

Love was wonderful. So why did something as incredible as the prospect of loving Jane feel so bad? Rationally she knew there was nothing *wrong* with how she felt, but trying to override centuries of guilt and loss wasn't as easy as just telling herself it was okay to move on.

Jane's hand strafed down her back. "Morgan?"

She startled. "Mmm? Sorry? What was that?"

"I asked if you were okay. You look totally zoned out. Be honest with me, are you hurt?"

"No, I'm fine. I was just thinking." Her shoulders relaxed, the tension easing. "About you…"

* * *

Their first-class seats on the flight from London were actually a double suite that could be curtained off into two single cubicles for privacy. The curtain remained open in an unspoken agreement that neither of them wished to be cut off from the other. Morgan peered over at Jane, lying on her side with arms and legs sprawled everywhere like a possessed octopus. It was how she'd slept last night after she'd tentatively accepted Morgan's invitation to join her in her bed so they could do exactly what Morgan had said she'd wanted to—just cuddle up together.

For the second time while lying curled against Jane, Morgan had fallen asleep. Only this time, she hadn't startled awake after a short nap. She'd woken naturally as the sun rose to pour muted light through the curtains, and with Jane sprawled over her like she'd been doing calisthenics in her sleep and had eventually found Morgan a comforting mat to rest upon.

Morgan had lain quietly in the dawn light, enjoying the sensation of the gentle weight of Jane's limbs, her soft breath blowing warm against the exposed skin of her collarbone. Then Jane's alarm had blared obnoxiously and jerked her awake. She snatched her limbs from Morgan's body, rolled over and offered bleary-eyed blushing apologies for her intrusion into Morgan's sleeping space. She'd rushed into the bathroom before Morgan could assure her that it was fine, that she'd really...well, *loved it* seemed too strong a descriptor, but she'd definitely enjoyed it.

No. She really had loved it. Having Jane so close that way, sleeping together in an intimate, yet not sexual way, so trusting, had made Morgan feel more settled and comfortable than she'd felt in years. It eased some of the emotional discomfort of the events after the pub. Some of...

Now, Jane's face was soft with sleep again. The airline blanket had slipped from her shoulders to bunch around her waist, leaving her torso and shoulders uncovered. Morgan saved her monthly birth/death projections report, unbuckled and crossed the few steps to Jane's side. A passing flight attendant peered expectantly at her, and with a smile and headshake she assured him silently that they were fine.

Carefully, Morgan pulled the blanket up to cover Jane's shoulders. She had the inexplicable urge to touch her, to slide her fingers down Jane's cheek and feel the skin she knew would be warm and soft and smooth. Jane stirred and rolled over to face away from her, immediately dislodging Morgan's careful cover arrangement.

Morgan's second attempt to cover Jane produced the exact same result as her first attempt. Suppressing a laugh, Morgan gave up, allowing herself a quick final glimpse of Jane before she would return to her side of the suite. A *quick final glimpse* was a bad idea because watching Jane sleep segued quickly into thinking about sleeping beside Jane last night. Of course, that thought segued into *not* sleeping beside Jane, but instead indulging in long lovemaking, soft caresses, lazy kisses.

Kisses. Jane's kisses.

Such a bad idea, she really shouldn't be thinking about this. But despite what she'd just affirmed to herself, she closed her eyes and gave in to her weakness. She thought of Jane's expression when they'd stood atop the Eiffel Tower, the expectant hopeful look that'd flashed over her face moments before Morgan had given in and kissed her. Kissing Jane was like an out-of-body experience. Jane knew how to maintain the perfect balance of give and take, of lips and tongue and the occasional grazing of teeth. Morgan loved how Jane clung to her, the almost unconscious movement of fingertips negotiating their way over her body as they kissed.

And if Jane was that good at just *kissing*, what would she be like when the time came for number twelve? How would that mouth feel pressed to other parts of her skin? How would Morgan cope as Jane's tongue mapped her body to find every place that would make Morgan quiver? Places that nobody had touched in decades. Places she hadn't wanted anyone to touch. Until she'd met Jane...

The slow, warm roll of arousal wasn't entirely unexpected, but its intensity was. Morgan let the fantasy unravel a little further. She could almost taste Jane's skin, smell her scent and hear the sounds of pleasure she knew Jane would make when Morgan carried her to climax. Jane made the cutest sound when she kissed her—groan of frustration and helplessness all rolled up into the sexiest intonation Morgan had ever heard. What sound would she make when Morgan took her? And how in all the realms would Morgan control herself when they were naked?

She could almost feel it. Trusting. Begging. Needing. Giving.

Okay, that really was enough. Morgan forced her eyes open before she either slid into the small bed with Jane and nuzzled her awake to suggest they join the Mile High Club or closed the curtain around her own cubicle to indulge in something she hadn't done for...a depressingly long time. She swallowed hard, returned to her side of the suite, buckled herself back in and picked up her tablet. Work, yes. That was exactly what she needed.

Morgan sighed inwardly. This thing with Jane, this emotional bond was too intense, too sudden, too utterly and completely wonderful for Morgan to be rational. The smart thing would be to withdraw, maintain a professional distance. Of course, the smart thing was the thing she least wanted to do. But if they remained on this path… No, she couldn't think about that. That possibility was far too complex and frightening.

She allowed herself one last look at the woman beside her, then leaned over and pulled the curtain partway closed.

Despite the fact that Jane had slept on and off for most of the flight, once they'd landed back in San Francisco and been ushered swiftly through passport control, bag collection and customs—thank you, Minion diplomacy—and exited the airport she seemed to be flattened by jetlag, or coming down from trip excitement, or possibly a combination of both. Jane sagged against Morgan, who wrapped a tight arm around her waist to keep her upright while pushing the trolley with the other.

Jane mumbled something indistinct when Morgan guided her into the passenger seat of her car, then fumbled so much with the seatbelt that Morgan told her to stay still so she could belt her in. Jane giggled, almost drunkenly. "You touched my boob."

"It was an accident," Morgan said, adopting her best upper crust-tone before she clarified, "Unfortunately." She leaned close to Jane's ear to murmur, "Trust me, when I touch your boob for real, you'll know about it."

The motion of the car seemed to drag Jane out of her stupor and after fifteen minutes she straightened in the seat, ran her hands through her hair and retied her ponytail. From the corner of her eye, Morgan saw Jane scrub both hands over her face. She shook her head and mumbled into her hands, "I'm so sorry, I have no idea what that was about. I didn't feel like that when we came back from New Zealand and Australia."

"Different flights. The direction you fly can make a difference." She chanced a look at her. "Are you okay?"

"Yeah I think I am. Just felt like I'd been flattened by a bus. Adrenaline come down maybe." She turned slightly side-on in the seat. "Back-to-normality disappointment I suppose."

Morgan forced herself to smile, feeling something akin to what Jane had just described. "Sounds like it. So I don't need to carry you inside your house?" She slowed to stop at a traffic light and gave Jane her full attention.

"Mmm," Jane mused. "That would be so sexy. Maybe you should." Her expression transformed from devilish to thoughtful. "Except it might scare my mom if you burst through the door with me in your arms. She'll probably think I've passed out or been injured or something and you're heroically rescuing me."

They drove in contemplative silence, and once Morgan had pulled into Jane's driveway and taken her bags to the front door, she was overcome with sudden shy awkwardness. "Uh, I suppose I'll see you back at work on Monday then?"

"I'll be there with bells on." Jane smiled, paused a moment then with a hand on Morgan's shoulder she stretched up to place the softest, sweetest kiss on Morgan's lips. When Morgan opened her mouth in invitation, Jane chuckled and broke their contact. "No more, I don't think I could stand the teasing. See you Monday." She picked up her bags and then as if unable to help herself, pecked Morgan once more on the mouth and disappeared into her house.

Morgan slumped against the porch railing, not quite willing to let the connection go. As she heard the joyous reunion between mother and daughter, she felt the flood of love as strongly as if she were inside with them. The empathetic emotion emanating from the house helped push away the emptiness that had suffused her when Jane had gone inside.

Jane's teasing echoed through her head. ...*heroically rescuing me...* "Oh, Jane," Morgan murmured. "I think maybe it's you who's going to rescue me. If I can be brave enough to let you."

CHAPTER SIXTEEN

Jane wasn't entirely sure how it happened, but one moment they were packing up after a planning session for the Connecticut birthday trip and the next, Morgan had stood up and moved around her desk with her hand out. Her voice was low, and the tone both demand and desperate plea. "Jane. Come here." After a beat she added an almost shy, "Please. I don't know how much longer I can wait to touch you, to taste you. May I?"

Stunned, Jane could do nothing but move toward her. Morgan wrapped both arms around her waist and kissed her with such hunger that Jane felt turned inside out with desire. Morgan slid both hands down her back, cupped Jane's ass and lifted her up onto her desk. Jane groaned at the contact then groaned again as Morgan sucked gently on her lower lip before her tongue stroked briefly against hers.

Without breaking the kiss, she gently pushed Jane's knees apart, and then stepped forward into the vee of her parted legs. Jane tangled her hands in Morgan's loose hair, clutched her shoulders, her back, anything she could touch to try and anchor herself. When Morgan leaned into her as if to lay them both on her desk, Jane finally broke the kiss. She could barely breathe for wanting and if it wasn't for some small rational piece in her brain, she would have let herself be taken on her boss's desk. "Oh God, stop. Not here."

Morgan swallowed hard. Her usually calm blue eyes were stormy with want, her breathing ragged as she apologized, "Sorry. I'm so sorry. You just looked so...sexy and I...sorry."

Jane ran her hands up and down Morgan's back. "No, no, I want this but I want more, longer. I want you naked on top of me, me on top of you." She kissed the edge of Morgan's mouth, gave in and indulged in a slower longer kiss. "I don't just want a quick dry hump on your desk."

"Then let's go." Morgan's hunger was thinly disguised, and she looked as though her hold on her self-discipline was tenuous. She paused, inhaled slowly. "Unless you need to go home for your mum? We can...postpone this?" The breathiness of her words, and the fact her hands were still under Jane's shirt made it clear that postponing wasn't something Morgan wanted.

Even if the entire west coast was tumbled into the ocean by a magnitude ten earthquake Jane wasn't sure she could postpone either. "No," she said hastily. "It's fine, we're good for a few hours. She doesn't need twenty-four-hour supervision or anything like that. She has the fall sensors and her panic button if she needs anything. But we can't go back to my place." Jane's cheeks felt like they were on fire. "My...mom and stuff, and the caretaker will be there until six thirty."

Morgan wrapped both arms around Jane's waist and carefully lifted her down from the desk. She kissed her softly, sweetly, soothing Jane's anxiety. "My place then. It's closer anyway and I want you naked as soon as possible." Her eyes smoldered, her lust undisguised and so damned sexy. Morgan's voice lowered to a seductive purr. "And, Jane? I promise the only thing that's going to make me stop this time, is you telling me to."

Settled in Morgan's luxurious car, Jane texted her mom that she'd been roped into a last-minute social thing—not a total lie—and that she'd be home around ten or eleven to help her to bed. She'd received a message back to *Have fun and enjoy yourself like a normal person.* Gee thanks, Mom.

The whole drive, Morgan's hand ran up and down her thigh, fingers pausing to lightly knead high up on Jane's leg. Every time Morgan's fingers strayed tantalizingly close to where Jane most wanted them, Jane tensed, and Morgan chuckled or smirked then withdrew her hand to a more neutral location. But only for a few seconds before she did it again.

Oh, Jane was *definitely* going to enjoy herself.

She craned her neck to look at the apartment building, registering only a vague image of modern and expensive as Morgan steered into the underground garage. Morgan led Jane to the elevator, pressed the button for the top floor then took a half step to the side without retaking her hand. When Jane sidestepped closer, Morgan moved away again, turning so she faced Jane, a slightly sheepish smile curling the corners of her mouth.

Being so close yet not touching was torturous and Jane's imagination ran overtime, thinking of the time, soon, when she would be naked with Morgan, exploring every single inch of her. She let her eyes drift closed, the whirring hum of the elevator a perfect white noise to let her think. What would Morgan's skin feel like? Taste like? How would it feel to have Morgan's hands on her, inside her?

"Jane." The voice was rough, almost strained. "I can see you thinking…"

She opened her eyes and turned toward Morgan. Her response was barely above a whisper. "Can you blame me?"

"No." The ding of the elevator finally moved Morgan, who strode forward, grasping Jane's hand and pulling her down a wide, brightly lit hallway. She held her close to her side with an arm around her waist as she unlocked her front door, almost as if she was afraid Jane might run away. "Come on in," Morgan murmured.

The large open-plan apartment was clean and modern and immensely personal, but Jane immediately noticed one glaring detail missing among the usual furnishings you'd find in anyone's place. "You don't have a television?"

"No, I've never had one." Morgan grinned, then explained, "I like real people and their stories, and I really just don't have time for television."

"You mean…you've never watched any TV shows? What about movies?"

Morgan slipped out of her suit jacket and tossed it over the back of the couch. "I've watched portions of television shows on other people's sets, and yes I have seen a few movies."

"Like what?"

Morgan paused, eyebrows creasing together. "*Le voyage dans la lune—A Trip to the Moon* in 1902. Umm…*Cinderella* in 1914. *It Happened One Night* in 1934, then, uh…" Her eyebrows tried harder to meet in the middle of her forehead. "Actually, that's about it."

Jane couldn't help laughing. She hadn't expected Morgan to literally mean *a few* movies. Especially not such old ones. "Damn. You should really try it sometime. Movies have come a long way since the early nineteen hundreds, like being in color and having sound. Plus, there's something fabulous about snuggling up to binge a television show for hours at a time." Immediately, her cheeks heated. "I mean, I didn't mean to imply that you and me, or anything like that. Sorry."

Morgan's expression softened. "Snuggling on the couch sounds rather nice actually. I don't think I've ever done that." A decidedly naughty expression crossed her face. "I can think of another thing that involves *snuggling* together." She moved closer until Jane was pressed back against the wall. But Morgan still didn't touch her.

Jane's mind blanked and she flailed desperately for something to say. Despite having thought of this very moment almost constantly since it'd first been offered to her, she found herself fighting down butterflies. Actually, angry birds of prey would probably be a better description.

Morgan observed quietly, "You look nervous."

"I am." Quickly she clarified, "Only just a little."

"Is it me who's making you nervous?"

"Oh, God no! No, it's just, well, it's been a while since I went to bed with anyone. My last girlfriend and I didn't exactly part on good terms and I've been a little anxious about dating since." She pulled a self-deprecating face. "Plus with my mom, ladies aren't exactly lining up at my door."

"I find that hard to believe. If it makes you feel better, it's been a while for me too." Morgan smiled. "And I guarantee it's been longer for me than you."

"How long are you talking about here?"

"Let's just say you weren't born and leave it at that," Morgan said, then covered Jane's open mouth with hers, kissing her until Jane forgot her incredulity.

Every time Morgan said something like that so casually, as though not having sex for over thirty years when you looked the way Morgan Ashworth did was no big deal, it made Jane's brain stall. And as with the movie revelation, Jane was reminded again that Morgan was different. Nowhere near bad different. But different in a way that made her feel unattainable.

But she *wasn't* unattainable, Jane realized instantly. She was standing right there, her suit jacket off and her hands and mouth exploring Jane's body with casual confidence. She wanted to know why Morgan seemed to prefer being alone, why she didn't seek company or casual lovers but realized firstly that it wasn't her business, and secondly now was not the time.

Jane inhaled sharply as Morgan's hands slid under her extremely boring and not-sexy work polo top and lightly stroked her stomach. "Then I guess we can help each other remember what to do."

"Mmm, I imagine it will all come back to me once I touch you."

"Or when I touch you," Jane shot back.

Morgan let out a helpless moan and braced a hand on the wall beside Jane's shoulders, her lips departing to lightly kiss the edge of Jane's mouth, her chin, her neck. Morgan lingered to suck the skin at the base of Jane's neck, chuckling when she shuddered at the sensation. "Well in that case," Morgan murmured. "I'd be grateful if you could give me a quick refresher on what being touched feels like."

Jane angled her neck, offering herself. Morgan took the bait, and Jane inhaled sharply at the nip of teeth. "I might. If you ask me nicely."

Morgan's *please* was both desperate and forceful, sending goosebumps racing over Jane's skin. She ran her hands down Morgan's neck, over her shoulders, down her chest and carefully unbuttoned her blouse. Morgan's intake of breath was audible when Jane paused to cup firm breasts and thumb hard nipples through the plain black bra. "Like this?" she asked quietly.

This time, Morgan's *please* was choked.

Boldly, she reached down to unbutton and unzip Morgan's pants before slipping her hand beneath the waistband of her silk panties. Jane inhaled sharply, stunned by the warmth she found. "Oh fuck, you're so..."

"Wet?" Morgan breathed in her ear as her hips pressed forward into Jane's hand.

Jane nodded helplessly, catching her lower lip between her teeth. She couldn't help herself, sliding her fingers lower through wet folds to tease at Morgan's entrance before drawing her fingers back up over her clit. "I didn't think you'd be, I mean, I thought you weren't..."

"What?" Morgan's breathing caught, the rest of her words halting. "Do you think I don't really want this? That I'm only going through the motions to help you with your list so I can get the thing I need?"

Jane went very still, uttering a quiet, "Maybe."

"I'm not," Morgan insisted. "I want this. I want you. I thought I told you that I've wanted you from the moment you first spoke to me." Soft kisses made a path from her collarbone to her ear.

"You did say that." Yet despite the words, their current connection and everything Morgan had said and done in the past, Jane still couldn't quite believe it. Morgan wanting her felt almost dreamlike, but what she felt right now was most certainly not a dream.

Lips closed on her earlobe, tugged gently. "Jane. Didn't I say once before that I have no need to be untruthful? You need not ever question my veracity because I only say things I mean." A slow exhalation. "I'll admit that I'm afraid of the possibility but this, *us* right now, it feels… right." Morgan turned Jane's face to hers and kissed her.

They kissed, long and deep while Jane's fingers stroked through Morgan's heat. Every time she brushed her finger over Morgan's clit, the other woman jerked against her, and let out the sexiest, most toe-curling groan Jane had ever heard. She knew she was wet as well, could feel the deep pulse of arousal thrumming steadily between her legs. But it was more than just a biological response. She felt the tingle in her belly, the electrified sensation across her skin that she knew came with *connection*.

Morgan groaned, only this time it was frustrated. She broke their kiss, but her mouth remained a whisper away from Jane's. "I'm sorry, I'm being selfish. I told you I wanted you naked. And I do, I want it right now. I want you to come for me." Morgan disengaged from Jane's touch and in the sexiest move ever, lifted Jane exactly as she had to put her on her desk earlier. Only this time, she held on until Jane wrapped her legs around her waist. Nobody had ever picked her up like that, and the movement was…just, goddamn, that *little bit stronger than most women* was so incredibly hot.

Jane's arms went automatically around Morgan's shoulders, hands threading through thick golden hair as she bent her head to kiss her again. She could have a lifetime of kissing Morgan, and still feel unsatisfied. Without breaking their kiss, Morgan carried her effortlessly into her bedroom.

She sat on the bed, maneuvering Jane on top of her and pulling them both down to lie on top of the checkered gray and white bedspread. Jane didn't know who undressed who, but they were naked, entwined and twisting together in a slow, sensual dance. Jane took her time studying the lines and form of Morgan's body—her small firm breasts, the lean lithe shape of her. For the first time she felt no self-consciousness about her own nudity in front of a lover, possibly because Morgan's reflected gaze made her feel like an admired, worshipped work of art.

Hands roamed, tongues and teeth claimed, and with every touch Jane felt herself falling further and further and wondered how she was ever going to catch herself. Morgan's arms around her were possessive as they kissed, a deep and needy clash of lips and tongue. "Jane," she breathed. "I want you on top of me, underneath me, inside me." She swallowed, eyes glassy. "But this is your show. Your bucket list, your rules. Tell me what you want."

What she wanted was exactly what Morgan was giving her. She took her face in both hands. "Morgan?"

"Yes?"

"Make me come." Jane's heart double-timed at the thought. "And then it's my turn with you."

Morgan's uncertain smile turned slow and seductive. "Yes, boss." The hand on her belly slid downward with agonizing languor, until fingers found her wetness. Morgan's strokes were slow and soft, gentle thrusts along every sensitive spot, lingering for a moment before moving on. She held herself up on one arm, breasts brushing Jane's, her mouth gliding over Jane's as her hands explored and pleasured.

And with every touch, Jane unraveled further.

She'd expected something different, rougher or more vigorous maybe, instead of the sensuous web of pleasure Morgan was weaving for her. Such an incredible, intuitive and generous lover. Yet every time she touched her, Morgan pulled away, promising soon…soon, you first. Jane could hear the tightness in her voice, the desperation, the need. But she still kept herself away from Jane's desperate touch.

More pleasure, this time Morgan's mouth on her. Jane pushed up into the wet heat, chasing the orgasm lingering just out of reach but Morgan withdrew and raised her head to lock eyes with Jane, as one hand slid up Jane's stomach to gently cup a breast. "Is this what you want?" Her thumb stroked Jane's nipple, sending a curl of fresh arousal through her. "Is this how you imagined it for your…list?"

"Yes," Jane breathed. A million times yes, and so much more that she hadn't imagined.

Morgan's "Me too" was so quiet that Jane wasn't sure she'd heard her correctly. But she had no chance to ask before a hot tongue slid through her folds. Jane's response was an incoherent moan. Morgan licked and sucked, stroked and teased until Jane's entire body felt as though it was nothing more than desperate need, poised on the edge of exploding.

Jane reached down, hand fumbling for something to hold on to. Morgan's palm touched hers, her hand sliding upward until their fingers locked together. She tried to verbalize the sensations rippling through her body, tried to tell Morgan exactly how she felt, what she was doing to her, how much she loved it and never wanted it to end. But all she could do was whimper as the heat built into something uncontainable and she came, back arched and limbs moving helplessly as Morgan kept licking and sucking through Jane's climax.

She began to build again, a slow steady roll that she knew was leading directly to another orgasm. But instead of holding Morgan more firmly against her and allowing her to take her again and again, she began to squirm away, pushing Morgan's head from between her thighs. If she didn't move now she would have selfishly let herself be taken over and over again, when what she most desired was to feel Morgan's pleasure. "Wait, stop, mercy," she begged.

Morgan whimpered, indulging in one last light flick of her tongue against Jane's clit before she climbed up to lie beside Jane, propping herself on an elbow. Her lips curled into a devilish smile. "Why? You didn't enjoy it?" The sultry tone telegraphed her teasing, and that she knew *exactly* how much Jane had enjoyed it.

Jane's laugh felt unsteady. "I *enjoyed* it very much. More than I've ever enjoyed...anything like this." Jane stroked the quivering muscle of Morgan's belly, light and slow and inching ever downward until her hand rested just above what she most desired. "But now I want to feel your enjoyment." The question caught as she tried to ask it, then came out as a hoarse plea. "Can I?"

"God, yes. Please." Morgan offered herself, legs falling open as she begged Jane with her body. Her eyes were unfocused, breathing ragged and shallow under the hand that was clutching a breast.

Jane paused for a heartbeat before drawing her fingers through the slick heat, the copious wetness. She moaned at Morgan's arousal, the evidence that Morgan had enjoyed what they'd done just as much as Jane. "You kept pulling back," she whispered, aware of how self-conscious the statement made her feel.

The expression in Morgan's eyes was a mix of tenderness, incredulity and desire. Her hand tightened on Jane's hip. "Do you think what you're feeling now, what you felt inside my underwear before is just my body's automatic reaction? It isn't," Morgan insisted before Jane could answer. "I've been desperate for you to touch me but, embarrassingly I knew I wouldn't last if you did. I probably still won't. That's it, I promise."

"Really?"

"Yes, really." She kissed first her mouth, then each cheek before coming back to linger against Jane's lips. Morgan's tongue lightly stroked her lower lip. "I want you badly, almost *too* badly and that's all. What will it take for you to trust me when I say I want this, want you?"

"It's just—" Jane gestured between them with one hand, the other now lightly stroking up and down Morgan's ribs. "You're you and I'm just me. It feels kind of unnatural to me, that you and I are..." She flushed. "I mean I know you can make your own decisions, but it just feels so out there. I've imagined it so many times, so many ways and even now after the mind-blowingly good orgasm you just gifted to me, some part of my brain still thinks I'm dreaming."

"You're…just you? Jane." Morgan shook her head, disbelief evident in her expression. "You are sexy, smart, funny, kind and charming. Did I mention sexy? I nearly came along with you just before, just from listening to you, touching you. It's not a dream." Smiling, she gave Jane's thigh the lightest pinch. "Now please, I'm three seconds away from really begging here…"

"I think I'd like to hear you beg." In that instant, Jane wanted nothing more than to watch calm, controlled Morgan unravel. Scratch that, she wanted to be the one to make her unravel.

And she did. Inch by sensuous inch.

She delighted in the tight quiver of her muscle, the desperation in her cries, the utterly helpless look Morgan fixed on her as Jane kissed and licked and sucked her way over tight breasts and belly, pausing to lavish attention on a particularly enticing place before moving on.

Morgan's hand tangled in her hair, her vocalizations loud and completely unashamed and it was barely two minutes before she arched up against Jane's mouth, a hoarse cry escaping her as she climaxed. A rush of heat spilled down Jane's spine as she felt the evidence of Morgan's pleasure in her mouth and she didn't even try to suppress her own cry of pleasure.

Morgan's legs moved restlessly in the sheets, her hands fumbling for Jane until she finally managed to grasp her hand. Her breathing was short, raspy and Jane ran her fingertips lightly along Morgan's skin as if that might help her remember to take a deeper more fulfilling breath. She stayed on her stomach, face resting against Morgan's thigh for a few minutes until Morgan shifted and rolled over, pulling Jane up to lie beside her. She stroked along Jane's side, over her belly, her breasts, and after a soft and thorough exploration of everything she'd already claimed, she murmured, "Thank you."

Jane laughed quietly. "I feel like I should be thanking you. That was, well, I don't even think I have words for what that was."

Morgan's nose wrinkled, but she was smiling. "*That* was me finishing incredibly quickly. I'm so sorry but I couldn't help myself. You were so, so good."

Jane bent her head to kiss the inner curves of Morgan's breasts. "Don't be sorry, it was one of the sexiest things I've ever experienced. I feel like I should make a joke about that time you told me you were just a bit faster than regular humans."

Morgan tangled gentle hands in Jane's hair, pulling her close to kiss her again. It was a slow, thorough kiss—the urgency and hunger of before having eased for something soft and sensual. "You know, we could try again and see if I can bring myself back down to ordinary human speed."

"I'd like that very much." Jane thought her sneaky peek at her watch went unnoticed but Morgan gently grasped her wrist and twisted it toward herself to check the time too.

"But…" Morgan caressed the back of Jane's hand. "You need to go?"

"I should, yes. I really hate to screw and sprint, but Mom will want to go to bed in a few hours. And if we start again, then I'm never going to want to leave."

Morgan's smile seemed fixed. "Of course."

"Is it okay if I get a drink of water?"

"Absolutely. I just need the bathroom." Morgan rolled off the bed. "You remember where the kitchen is? Help yourself to anything." She leaned down to kiss her again, warm lips lingering, then sauntered to the master bathroom.

Jane quickly dressed. Conflicting emotions—the remnants of pleasure from such an incredible session of lovemaking sat alongside a pang of wistfulness that she'd never have it again. Morgan had more than held up her end of the bargain, a freebie bargain at that, and that was it. Done. Over. Orgasm delivered.

If nothing else, she reasoned with herself on her way to the kitchen, she'd now have some fabulous mental images to sustain her through self-help sessions. And then some. She wondered what exactly would have happened if she didn't have to leave and could take Morgan up on her offer of another round of lovemaking. On second thought, best not to think about that right now.

Jane already knew Morgan's dietary choices were basically anything she could get her hands on, but a study of the fridge and pantry told her that her boss really did eat like a college student. Actually, a college student probably ate better. Morgan's home diet seemed to consist of frozen pizzas and assorted pre-made meals, chilled protein drinks, a whole lot of cheese, potato chips, snack foods and candy. There were a few fruits and vegetables and large Tupperware containers of nuts, but they were far outweighed by junk. The whole bottom shelf of the fridge was nothing but tightly packed cans of Guinness beer—yuck. Clearly those immortal genes were good ones.

A warm body pressed to Jane's back, soft kisses were gifted to her neck, and almost as though Morgan knew what she was thinking, she explained, "Quick and easy calories okay? And this stuff tastes so good. Trust me. I've lived through times when beer was drunk for calories because it was so cheap and easy, and foods like offal and pease pottage was considered decadent. I mean, yes they're tasty but…" She laughed softly. "I cannot tell you the number of times I just couldn't move through realms because I didn't have the energy. Processed foods have literally saved my life."

"Hey, no judgment. Only jealousy."

"Mmm." Another neck kiss before Morgan turned her around and pressed her back against the counter. "I was thinking just now."

"What about?"

Morgan's answering grin was shy. "I'm worried that us having sex only once might not uh, satisfy your bucket list requirements. If you're amenable, I propose we try number twelve a few more times. Purely for thoroughness." Morgan's eyes grew wide, expression faux-serious. "I *really* want you to be satisfied that everything has been crossed off your list so I can get what I want. That's all. And…I'd also really like to show you that I'm not a short-fuse firecracker."

Jane offered a hoarse, "Sure. Sounds good. Whatever."

Morgan gave her a knowing look, then barreled on as if she hadn't just given Jane the ultimate gift. "Great. Give me a minute to grab my shoes and I'll take you home."

"Oh, no it's fine. I'll just order an Uber. I'm sure you've got Minion things to attend to, and you should sleep. If that frown line is any indication, you've had a long and stressful day."

Morgan pouted, making that exact frown line appear. "I do not have frown lines."

"You kind of do. And they're adorable."

"Mmph. Must have wrinkle lines because I'm *sooo* old." Morgan took Jane's face in both hands, thumbs caressing her cheekbones, and kissed her so tenderly Jane nearly melted. "I'm still driving you home. I really don't need to sleep much. A few hours every night is fine for me. Even less really. I only do it because it feels nice and I enjoy dreaming."

Jane raised both hands in surrender. "Fine then, superhuman."

Morgan flicked her fingers against her forehead in salute, then with a hand on Jane's back guided her to the doorway. On the wall beside the doorway hung a framed pencil sketch safely contained behind a sheet of glass that Jane hadn't noticed before. The drawing showed a young woman's face with vague, half-finished shapes surrounding her. The unsigned sketches were clear and bold on aged, yellowed paper.

"What's this?" Jane asked. "Or, who rather."

"Oh," Morgan said as she leaned down to pull on her shoes. Her voice held a hint of surprise, as though she'd forgotten the drawing. "That's me. Michelangelo drew that in 1502."

"Michelangelo," Jane said incredulously.

"Mhmm. Cici asked him to do a sculpture of me but he flat out refused. Brave of him to stand up to Death herself." She grinned. "He was working on *David* at the time, so I don't really blame him. I've never told Cici but I'm so relieved. Can you imagine? Forever immortalized as a nude sculpture in some public place? How embarrassing. I'd have to stay away from Europe for the rest of time."

"So this is you? The body you were born in?"

"Yes. Doesn't really tell you much but that's me. Morgan, version one."

Morgan *version one* had full lips shaped in the beginnings of a smirk, laughing eyes, an adorable upturned nose and wildly curly hair. Jane stared. "But this is almost two centuries past when Cici turned you, isn't it?"

"Yes."

Jane felt embarrassed as she asked, "Sorry but why are you still in your first body then? I thought you said you changed them every fifty years or so, or when you got hurt."

Morgan paused for the briefest moment, and if Jane hadn't become so attuned to her she wouldn't have even registered the pause. "Life expectancy was less, population density was far lower than now, and we also traveled quite a lot in those first three hundred years or so. Thus, I had no need to change my appearance. Nor had I..." She frowned as though weighing her next words. "Damaged myself enough to require a new host."

Jane studied her. There was something on Morgan's face, an expression of pain or regret that made Jane hastily change the subject. "Who's the most famous person you've ever met?"

The pained expression was exchanged for a patient smile. "Fame is so subjective, Jane. And notoriety doesn't necessarily equal fame."

"Okay then, who would you have loved to have met but never did?"

"Cleopatra," Morgan answered instantly. "Cici was very close with her and tells me the most incredible stories about that time. An astonishing woman, and so much power."

"When did Cici, um start? I mean when was she created?"

"She says she doesn't know, that she just came to awareness knowing her purpose. She didn't take an actual *human* form until hominids evolved millions of years ago." Morgan smiled. "There were no afterlife packages back then."

"Wow."

"Wow indeed. She's incredible. She's the world's smartest, most in-tune being. She's connected to every living person, and still has ties to those who've died. She's caring and compassionate, successful, purposeful." Morgan's smile was soft, almost sad. "She's my best friend. My only friend really."

The last statement tore at Jane. The bits and pieces Morgan had shared during their time together were sporadic morsels, but now it was painfully obvious to Jane just how alone Morgan really was. And she suddenly wanted nothing more than to be the one who would help her erase the loneliness.

CHAPTER SEVENTEEN

"Oh my, *finally*! You had sex," was the first thing Cici said the moment Morgan appeared in the doorway of La Morte's study.

"Perspicacious of you," Morgan commented dryly, hanging her coat on the free-standing coat rack just inside the door.

"Well yes, but mostly it's that you're incredibly easy to read." Cici sat up, swinging her feet to the floor. Her gaze never left Morgan's face. "You get this *look* for days afterward. Supreme joy because you've given someone pleasure, and enjoyed pleasure yourself, mixed with mortified guilt because it wasn't Hannah. Don't protest," Cici said as Morgan opened her mouth to do just that. Cici set aside her tablet and reached for her wine as though they were two pals about to have a chat. "It's been decades since I saw this expression on your face, Morgana. I *demand* details."

"Hello, Cici, nice to see you too. How's your day been? Mine's been busy but all in all, rather productive."

La Morte waved impatiently. "Yes, yes, lovely and wonderful being in each other's company and all that, haven't seen you for almost ten hours and it's been torturous every moment we've been apart. Now, details."

Morgan was all set to demur, until overwhelmed by a sudden urge to unpack what had transpired less than an hour before. "We had sex," she blurted. "Me and Jane. And agreed to have more." She sucked in a quick breath. "And it was utterly, mind-blowingly incredible." An entirely inadequate description.

"Good for you." Cici's raised glass was a salute. "It's about time." She poured another glass of red and passed it to Morgan. "Now, sit. Let's gossip."

Morgan settled beside Cici on the chaise longue. She drank the Cabernet slowly, taking the opportunity to enjoy the flavor and think. "About time? It's not like I've been celibate for the past three hundred years, Cici. It's just that nobody has ever come close to what Hannah and I had." Morgan stopped abruptly, her mood turning from dreaminess to devastation. "It does feel a little like betrayal, because… because I enjoyed it so much. Because I knew I would enjoy it, enjoy *her*, long before it happened."

"How does it feel like betrayal? Was it better?"

"Better? How do you compare the two things? Intimacy with a woman I've loved for centuries and intimacy with someone I could love. I really don't know, but I do know it's the best connection I've had with anyone since Hannah." She knew more than that, that it was the most…alive she'd felt in centuries. The most present, the most needed. And despite what Cici said about her expression—the intimacy had been noticeably free of the undercurrent of guilt she usually experienced during sex.

Cici pounced. "Someone you could love?"

Morgan hastily swallowed the wine she'd just sipped. "Pardon me?"

"You said, and I quote verbatim, intimacy with someone I could love."

She opened her mouth to protest indignantly that she most certainly had not said that, until she realized that yes, she had indeed said those very words. And it wasn't the first time she'd thought of the word love as it applied to Jane. It didn't feel wrong so much as confusing, because was she even capable of loving someone else? Was there room for both Hannah *and* Jane? She let out a soft huff and raised both hands helplessly, as if the gesture could encompass her confusion.

La Morte's hand came to her cheek. Her thumb touched Morgan's nose in a gesture that was both comforting and teasing. "Morgana, my darling. Are you going to wear your broken heart like a hair shirt for another three hundred years?"

"Maybe," she muttered petulantly. "Look, I know I'm being clichéd and pitiful. The poor broken woman who's hardened her heart against finding love because her first true love died. But you know what? I've been doing just fine with my clichéd pitifulness."

"You're not *doing just fine,* and yes, you are a cliché. So I'm going to give you another cliché. Do you honestly think Hannah would want this? Want you to be miserable and suffering because she's gone? You've grieved, some part of you will always grieve but you need to move on. I know that's what she told you to do, and I know you promised her that." It came out unusually rushed, as though Cici had been holding on to her thoughts for decades.

Morgan's jaw tightened, radiating pain through her skull. "That was a private moment. Why in all hell dimensions were you even there?"

La Morte looked horrified. "Of course I wasn't *there* there. Just... around and you know that I just know some things. And you seem to forget that I knew and was friendly with Hannah too and that maybe I might know her wishes. Things that even you don't know." Cici exhaled, setting down her wineglass. "Morgana, you hold on to her so tightly because nobody has ever given you a reason to loosen your grip."

"Don't you mean *let go?*"

La Morte's expression turned sadly understanding. "No, my love. You should know by now that you don't have to let go. You can hold on to many people, all at once or in different moments in time. But when you're clenching your fist so tightly, there's no room for you to grasp anything, or *anyone* else."

"She was the love of my life, Cici," Morgan said quietly. "A once-in-a-lifetime love."

"You've lived several *normal* lifetimes, and universe willing you'll live thousands more. Don't you think that the regular once in a lifetime isn't quite applicable here? You live more than one lifetime, surely you can have more than one love."

Cici dipped her head and when Morgan refused to make eye contact, she gently raised her chin with a forefinger. "I believe Ms. Smith is one such love. Every moment she is in your life, I see that tight hold loosening so that you can grasp her. I believe you need her, whether you can see that yet or not."

A muscle in Morgan's jaw jumped in annoyance, and she was all set to leap up and storm out. Until she remembered that she still had to make her evening report and that maybe, just maybe, Cici had a point. Even if Morgan set aside their intimacy, the things about Jane she loved—the overwhelming fact was that Jane's mere presence was a soothing comfort Morgan hadn't even realized she sought until Jane came near, and it was suddenly as though she'd been in darkness and now Jane was light. "Perhaps you're right," she finally mumbled.

Cici waved airily. "Of course I am." After a few moments she said, "I could take you to see Hannah if you wanted." Her tone was so quiet and gentle she sounded almost childlike.

Morgan froze. "I'm sorry, what?"

"You heard me. If seeing her, talking to her, will help you move on, then I'll do it. I'll call in favors and bear the aftermath of the complaints. For you, I would do it gladly."

None of Cici's Minions had ever been past the handover point of any afterlife realm, as it was strictly forbidden. Not only by her—the deceased were entitled to their eternal peace and to let Minions pass back and forth to see loved ones was cruel for all involved—but because the leaders of the afterlife realms disliked the intrusion. She would have to trade favors forever in order to mollify them. For Cici to offer such a thing, and without even being asked was monumental.

And Morgan couldn't accept.

"I…can't. I can't do that to myself or to her." Morgan gestured at herself. "I mean, look at me. She wouldn't even recognize this body." Despite rejecting the offer, her longing was so strong she almost doubled over.

"No, she wouldn't," Cici agreed softly. Despite the softness of her voice, her gaze was steady, penetrating. "You've changed, Morgana, whether you want to believe it or not, and not only physically. It's inevitable for those of us who live so long. All your core ideals and morals and whatnot are still in there, but other things have shifted. Expectations, memories, even your grief. It's like a glacier, tiny movement over a long period of time. So small you don't notice it until you pay attention. Then one day you look up and notice it's moved a hundred meters from where it was three hundred years ago."

A comfortable silence settled between them, the silence of longtime friends who don't need to talk in order to communicate. Morgan chewed over the conversation as Cici sipped her wine with slow pleasure.

Realization dawned like a sunrise, sudden and bright. "You're saying I've changed but haven't realized it because I've been holding on for so long. I'm holding on to my grief, to my loss because I think I *should* be, but what I'm holding on to is the idea of it, not the actual emotion?"

"Yes. And more to the point, I believe the real issue here is that you're bothered because you're not as bothered by it as you think you should be. Because you think you should feel worse about your imagined betrayal of Hannah. And I think if you stop to really think about it, you'll find you already know the reason why."

Morgan closed her eyes, knowing if she had to look at Cici's gentle and knowing expression she'd cry. "I'm already in love with Jane. I'm madly, deeply in love with her and this whole bucket list thing has solidified my feelings into something wonderful and utterly terrifying. When I'm away from her I feel like I can't see or breathe and the moment I'm near her again it's like she's filling my lungs and the sun has just come out after a year-long darkness."

When she opened her eyes again, Cici cupped her face in both hands, pulled Morgan closer and kissed her forehead. "Yes, I believe you are. Both in love, and you also simply love her. Morgana, you don't love the way other people do—you connect with someone and then..." Cici gestured as if vanishing something into thin air. "It's all over, you're head over heels and that is that. I've seen it only once before."

"And now?" she whispered.

"I think you know the answer. I think the thing that connects you to Jane Smith goes far beyond simple emotions like *lust* or *love*. And I believe you felt this way long before you took her to your bed."

The second admission came more easily. "I think I have." She made an expansive gesture. "So here I am in love with yet another fragile, dying human. I have quite the type, wouldn't you say?"

"Oh, darling. Yes you do." Cici smiled. "Smart, humorous, kind, sensual women who accept you in all your complex glory. Women who understand your intense empathy and love the kindness and humor and sensuality you return to them. Women who enjoy your generosity in a way that's not depleting but fulfilling. Jane Smith has *Made for Morgana Ashworth* written all over her. She is all of the above plus whip-smart, beautiful, quiet yet no pushover and most importantly— in need of someone to swoop in and help her. And even when you help her, you know she'll never let you own her. She'll own you and that's the way you like it."

Morgan couldn't disagree with anything La Morte had said. She ran her hands through her hair, gathered it back then let it fall about her shoulders again. "So what do I do with that knowledge? Loving Jane is going to kill me all over again."

"No, it isn't."

Morgan huffed. "Well no, not literally, but you know what I mean."

"I do, and as already expressed, I disagree. You've grown, changed and the way you love the two women is different. Jane Smith is a mirror to your emotion in a way Hannah wasn't."

"What do you mean?" Defensiveness bristled down her back. "Are you saying Hannah wasn't my soulmate after all?"

La Morte seemed almost offended by the accusation. "Not at all. Simply that Jane is not Hannah."

"Obviously."

"Don't be deliberately obtuse, Morgana. It's tiresome. And don't pout at me, you know I'm rendered helpless when you do that."

Morgan fixed her expression to something more neutral. "So you're saying because Jane is more...I don't know...in tune with me that she'll be able to what? Love me from the afterlife?" It seemed utterly absurd. And even if that were true, could she let go of her natural instinct and trust that somehow Jane's love would give her strength to continue after she was gone, when Hannah's had not?

"Basically, yes. That is the very abbreviated version." Cici let out an exaggerated sigh. "You should be leaping at this opportunity. You are quite the catch, Morgana Ashworth, and if I were a few millennia younger I might even make another play for you." Cici's wink managed to be both teasing and salacious. "But I think Jane Smith might challenge me to a duel at twenty paces."

Morgan scoffed. "Hardly. I don't think she's that invested."

"Oh yes she is. Do you really think that *you* of all people would feel so deeply if it were a one-sided affair?"

"You're right. I wouldn't." But her empathy could be mistaking Jane's lust for something more and magnifying her own feelings beyond the truth. Morgan chewed over it for a minute. No, what she felt was definitely real.

"Thank the universe you're so smart. As much as I love you, I'm afraid I don't have time to explain every nuance of your emotions to you right now. I have a meeting with the Committee and I need to prepare. You know how Hades gets when things don't run to schedule." She clapped gleefully. "Now that we've set you on the right track with your centuries of emotional baggage, why don't you give me your report so you may get back to your Jane and I can argue with people. We'll pick this up another time."

Her Jane. No, Jane wasn't hers. But maybe...maybe she could be? If Morgan could figure out what to do with the inevitable heartbreak.

It took twenty minutes to give her report, and the moment Morgan finished, Cici downed the last of her wine, leaned over and kissed Morgan's forehead. "I do not know how I would do this without you, Morgana. Now, I must get ready."

"Before I go, may I look in your alcohol cellar?"

Cici gaped, her hand coming to her breast as she feigned shock. "You don't trust my tastes anymore?"

"No, of course I do. But I need to find a rare bottle of Dom Pérignon and I thought I'd start with you."

"I see." Cici's eyebrow arched. "And if I have what you want, what makes you think I would give you this rare bottle out of the goodness of my heart?"

"Because you love me, and because this bottle is on Jane's bucket list. Most importantly, you are probably the most efficient route to this limited-edition, super-special, hardly-any-made, super-expensive vintage champagne."

Cici shrugged. "Fine. Do you need me to get it for you or can you find it yourself?" The fact she was already halfway to the door told Morgan that her offer was merely politeness.

"I've got it. But, thank you."

"You're welcome. Come to my quarters before you leave."

Cici's cellar contained thousands upon thousands of bottles of wine and champagne laid out by varietal, and then organized within each category by producer name and the vintage. Cici was aware of every bottle that nestled in the racks and Morgan cursed herself for not asking the specific locations of all her Dom Pérignon. Thankfully, due to Cici's slightly OCD organization, it only took Morgan ten minutes to find the bottle she wanted. There were two bottles actually, which didn't surprise Morgan. Her boss loved rare things, and she was a hoarder.

She transported to Cici's quarters, knocked and at the invitation opened the door to find Cici in front of her dressing mirror, arranging her hair. Morgan held up the bottle of Dom Pérignon. "Got it, thank you. And I even left you a spare."

Cici grinned at her in the mirror. "So thoughtful."

"Very. Even more thoughtful that you're not going to have The Accountant coming after you because I had to spend twenty-five thousand on one of these."

"Ah, yes. I retract my sarcasm. You are indeed thoughtful." Cici shuddered. "That woman is terrifying, and I say that as someone who's been to some pretty horrific places and seen the most horrendous creatures. You would think *unlimited resources* and full worldwide government cooperation would mean she could relax a little."

Morgan laughed. "Well rest assured my expenditure documentation, as always, passes the most stringent audit."

"I know, and that's part of why I adore you so much." Cici's brows drew together for a moment. "Oh, that's a shame," she murmured. "Such a marvelous actor." Then her face relaxed as if nothing had happened, and she resumed fixing her hair.

"Who?" Morgan prompted. She never asked when, because not only was it irrelevant, but Cici La Morte had no inclination to share the death dates of those under her purview.

"Marty Young. I suppose he won't be the next James Bond after all." Cici spun on her dressing stool and leveled a look at her. "Drugs are bad, Morgana."

The first sensation Morgan registered when she arrived back in her living room was the feel of cold glass in her hand, the trip from Aether having cooled the champagne to perfect drinking temperature. Morgan had planned to give the bottle to Jane the next day at work—carefully boxed of course so none of the other employees realized what it was—but now she had another idea.

It was still just before nine p.m. Jane would surely be awake and she could just give her the bottle to put in her refrigerator and leave. After a quick internal back and forth, Morgan closed her eyes and left her apartment for Jane's house.

She could hear the television and two women laughing and had to suppress the urge to stride up to the house and press her nose to the window to peek inside. Instead, Morgan jogged up the stairs, and feeling uncharacteristically awkward, rang the doorbell. It was a minute or so until she heard footsteps before the door was flung open.

There was no mistaking the surprise, and pleasure in Jane's simple greeting. "Morgan, hi."

There was also no mistaking how good Jane looked, having changed out of work clothes into faded jeans and a tee with three comic women on it. Morgan waved and immediately felt idiotic. She dropped her hand. "Hi," she said, feeling like a teenager about to ask a crush on a date. "Um, sorry to just arrive unannounced like this. Especially after, well…we, um…you know."

A flush of pink touched Jane's cheeks. "No problem at all." Jane closed the door behind her, stepping onto the porch, just out of the light above the door. She stretched up and kissed Morgan tentatively as if Morgan might move away. No chance of that.

"So, you like comics then?" Morgan pointed at Jane's chest, then realized exactly what she'd done and cringingly withdrew her hand. Wow. Less than three hours before, they'd been writhing naked in Morgan's bed crying out their mutual pleasure, and then agreeing to do it again. And now Morgan was acting like someone who'd never even touched a woman. Apparently admitting she could or did love Jane Smith had turned her into a fool.

Jane glanced down and laughed. "All the way."

"That makes sense, given your desk figurines." Then, aware of the added embarrassment of admitting that she watched Jane while at her desk, Morgan cleared her throat and held up the bottle. "I come bearing gifts."

Jane's eyes widened, her expression wavering between awe and disbelief. "Morgan, how did you get this so quickly? I thought it would have to be ordered from overseas or something."

"Had to sell my soul into a life of eternal servitude." Grinning, she added, "It's perfectly chilled from uh, moving between *there* and here so I thought I'd just drop it off now. I promise I didn't even shake it, so now would be the perfect time to enjoy it."

Jane laughed. "It's a Monday night."

"Champagne isn't dayist, Jane."

"I suppose that's true." Jane glanced behind her, then back to Morgan. "Mom's still awake too." Her expression was hopeful, with a strange and unexpected touch of apprehension. "Why don't you come inside and join us? It seems only right that you should share in the fruits of your labor. If you don't have plans, I mean I'm just assuming but—"

"I don't have plans." She lowered her voice. "All of my plans ended when you left my bed."

Jane bit her lower lip. "Mine too..."

"Mmm." She had to restrain herself from pushing Jane against the wall and initiating something unsuitable for such a location. Especially not when holding a rare and important vintage of champagne. She pushed those thoughts aside and smiled. "I would like to know what the fuss is about this bottle, and I would really love to meet your mum. So, I accept your invitation, thank you."

"Okay then. Great." Despite her invitation and apparent verbal enthusiasm, Jane's expression still bordered on panic. She swung the door open. "Come on in."

CHAPTER EIGHTEEN

Jane made quick introductions and ignored the sly smile her mom directed at her when she explained who Morgan was. Shit, maybe this wasn't such a good idea after all. Especially considering they were only a few hours past having sex for the first time, and there she was asking Morgan in to meet her mother like it was some sort of *now we're dating* scenario. One day, Jane mused to herself, she might stop acting so cringeworthy around Morgan. Probably not any day soon.

Morgan dipped her head and said cordially, "Hello, Pamela. It's a pleasure to finally meet you." She sounded like an overpolite child meeting a parent of a friend. The smile Morgan offered was worthy of a cartoon-ish sparkle animation and when she held out her hand, she placed it where Jane's mom would be able to easily grasp it.

Her mother shot Jane an accusatory glance. "You never told me she was British, Janie."

"I didn't?" Jane squeaked, trying to make a discreet *cut it out and stop being so embarrassing* gesture. "Must have slipped my mind the few times only that I've ever in all these years mentioned Ms. Ashworth to you."

Morgan, bless her, broke the awkwardness by raising the bottle of champagne, turning the label so Jane's mom could read it. "Yes, I am British. And in the tradition of my people who think it's criminally impolite to arrive empty-handed, I come bearing...well, nothing more than alcohol really."

Her mom studied the bottle, and when she spoke her voice was full of awe. "This is the 1959 limited-vintage Dom Pérignon Rosé my father used to talk about." She stared at Morgan. "Is it real?"

Morgan nodded, her expression shifting to earnestness the way it always did when Jane had asked if she was telling the truth. "Yes, of course it is." She passed the bottle to Jane.

Jane's mom gaped, her eyes moving between Jane and Morgan. "My father always said there were only three hundred bottles ever produced and they were never officially on the market." Her confusion turned to suspicion. "He also said it costs as much a car. Where did you get this?"

Jane glanced at Morgan before turning her attention back to her mom. "Morgan just happened to know a person who was willing to part with it."

"But why has she given it to you?"

Jane decided to go with the easy explanation. She lowered her voice, feeling so suddenly choked up she could barely answer. "Sharing this with you was on my list."

"Janie..." An unsteady hand swiped at her eyes. "This is incredible. Thank you. May I hold it?"

Jane offered her the bottle, resting it on the tray of her mom's chair for support and keeping her grip until she was certain her mom had a grasp on it. What a horrible thing if she dropped it now after the trouble it would have been for Morgan to obtain it. As if she knew what Jane was thinking, her mom peered up at Morgan. "This is a wonderful gesture, Ms. Ashworth."

"Morgan," she corrected. "And it really was no trouble. My boss is quite the collector of rare things, and she was more than willing to part with this for such a good cause."

Jane was surprised by the steady steel in her mom's gaze. "A good cause. Your generosity seems to go beyond a simple charitable donation. And you're responsible for my birthday trip to Connecticut, aren't you?"

"I'm assisting, but it's Jane's idea not mine," Morgan said carefully.

"Mmm, yes, but you're providing the means." Her gaze was shrewd. "Do you go to this much trouble for all the people you administer afterlife contracts to?"

Morgan softly touched Jane's back. "No. I certainly do not."

Mercifully, her mother remained silent, and Jane leapt in before she rethought the silence and made things seriously awkward instead of mildly awkward. "My grandpa was a history teacher," Jane explained. "He could probably tell you everyone who's ever touched this exact bottle."

Her mother laughed. "And he could also tell you every grape that went into it. Now, we should open this while it's still chilled." She flicked her fingers toward the kitchen. "Let's use the champagne bowls, not the flutes, Janie!"

"Fine, okay." Jane touched Morgan's forearm. "Will you be all right here for a moment? Do you need something to eat?"

Morgan's eyes flashed before she reined her expression to neutrality. "Yes, please," she murmured.

The implication in Morgan's tone sent a sliver of arousal snaking through Jane's body. "Behave."

A slow eyebrow arch told Jane that Morgan had no intention of doing any such thing. She raised her voice to normal speaking volume. "If you're offering a snack, then I'll happily accept." This smile was softer and more intimate than the dazzling one she'd offered to Jane's mother.

"Be right back. Can you open the bottle please?" After Morgan nodded her agreement, Jane leveled a pleading look at her mom. "And you, behave yourself please."

She heard quiet laughter and conversation, then a muted cork popping as she set about collecting and quickly cleaning three rarely used champagne glasses from the corner cupboard above the counter, before assembling a plate of cheese, crackers, salami and olives. Was that fancy enough for Morgan? Jane chuckled at her worry that it was fancy enough for Morgan, who had eaten what looked like weeks-old sandwiches, just waiting to bestow salmonella, from a gas station and had also admitted to eating butter.

Morgan nabbed the platter, breathing out a *thank you*, while Jane set the three glasses on the coffee table. "Mom, you're tired. Let me add a little thickener." Thickening powder added to liquid helped her mom with swallowing fluids. It only changed the texture, not the taste, and when they'd first begun using it they had played around, giggling as they added it to everything from chocolate milk to Bacardi and cola.

"You have got to be joking. Janie, I know how much this bottle costs and how rare it is. If you think I'm going to dilute the experience one bit, you've got another thing coming."

"Fine but if you get aspiration pneumonia, don't come whining to me."

"I'll be careful," her mom said immediately. "I promise. It's only one glass. And if you think I'm drinking from my plastic cup, or using a straw, you've got yet another thing coming." She moved her chair back and forth a few inches, like a kid fidgeting while waiting to be given a birthday gift.

"Fine," Jane conceded. "Can I just say—"

"No, you cannot," her mother interjected, grinning wickedly.

"It's-your-own-fault-if-you-break-the-glass-and-spill-the-champagne," Jane reeled off.

While she and her mother had been discussing the logistics, they'd been ignoring Morgan who'd unobtrusively heisted some food and moved to look at some framed photographs while she ate. Jane slipped to her side, a hand going automatically to Morgan's back. "Sorry, just the usual bickering."

"No problem." She turned her head, a smile already curling her mouth. "It's nice. Feels like home." After clearing her throat, she asked, "Shall we pour?"

Surprised by the emotion Morgan's observation evoked, Jane only managed a quiet, "Yes."

The tip of Morgan's tongue peeked out as she filled the three champagne bowls, carefully waiting until bubbles settled before topping up and checking the level in each one. As she passed Jane her glass, the tip of her forefinger glided over the back of Jane's hand. "It's your list, therefore it should be your toast."

Jane thought for a moment, discarded a couple of lame ideas and eventually raised her glass. "Here's to...friends." Wow. Because *that* wasn't a lame toast at all.

Her mom uttered her agreement as she tipped her champagne in Morgan and Jane's direction before bending her head slightly to sip.

"To friends," Morgan murmured, lifting her glass. Her expression was hard to read but seemed almost dissatisfied, as if she didn't like that word. Morgan sampled her champagne and made a quiet sound of approval. "Claude Moët knew how to make a fabulous vintage."

"It's incredible," Jane declared after her first mouthful.

Her mother mumbled her agreement and tried to lift her glass again but faltered, only managing to raise the glass an inch from her tray. Jane moved to help, but Morgan, sitting closer, was faster. She reached over and thumbed Jane's chin. "I can do it. You enjoy your champagne."

Jane wanted to gently push Morgan out of the way, step in and assist her mom, but Morgan's calm steady gaze, the one that seemed to say "Don't worry, I've got this, I'll take care of her" dropped Jane back into her seat. Morgan interacted with her mother as she did everyone else while at the same time being sensitive to her disability.

It'd become a joke between Jane and her mom—how will women I'm dating react to the mother in the wheelchair? Their unanimous favorites, if it could be called such a thing, were a woman who'd ignored Jane's mom completely, and another who'd spoken as if Jane's mother were deaf or didn't speak English until eventually her mom had piped up with, "I broke my spinal cord, not my eardrums…"

Now Jane couldn't stop watching as Morgan, her own glass untouched after that first sip, helped Jane's mother drink the precious Dom Pérignon. The weakness and lack of dexterity in her mom's hands was worse when she was tired, and Jane knew holding a glass stem would be difficult for her. When her mom slowly folded her hand around the stem, and curled her fingers closed with her other hand, Morgan said something to her, so quietly Jane didn't hear.

But her mom laughed and nodded. Morgan gently closed her fingers over the top of Jane's mom's—not forcing or pushing, simply helping unobtrusively yet clearly in a way that didn't make her mother feel helpless. Jane glanced away, not wanting to seem like a helicopter daughter, and when she turned her attention back to the others, Morgan had helped her mother bring the glass to her mouth.

Immediately obvious was how tender and confident Morgan was. Jane became aware of a slow building sense of rightness, of trust and a feeling that Morgan belonged in their house. She had to force the thought down before she started tearing up. Focus on the champagne, not the Hallmark scene in front of you.

She drank another small, slow mouthful, holding it in her mouth, savoring the fruit and surprising hints of vanilla. She almost shuddered at the taste, the crisp cleanness of it. Okay, so people were right when they said expensive champagne was better. She wanted to take her time to enjoy every note and flavor.

The thought was at once exciting and saddening. She was one of a small group of people who could say they'd drunk this exact vintage, yet the fact she would never drink it again felt like a metaphor for her life. Everything she wanted always felt just out of reach, or transient. Including the woman sitting three feet from her.

As if she knew exactly what thought had just passed through Jane's mind, Morgan turned slowly toward her. Her eyes were gentle and appraising, lips raised in a soft, almost sad smile.

Her mom lowered the almost-empty glass to rest on the tray of her electric chair. She sniffed and declared imperiously, "Well. It's nice. But tastes pretty much the same as the fifty-dollar bottles of champagne."

The glass on its way to Jane's mouth paused. "That's it. Next time you have an appointment with your specialist, I'm going to ask him to check your taste buds."

Morgan's grin was sly. "Does that mean you don't want the rest of your share of the bottle, Pamela? Because I'd be happy to take it off your hands if you don't like it." She turned to wink at Jane, drawling, "Assuming this one doesn't tackle me for it."

Jane's mom tsked. "Not a chance." She made another clumsy movement of hand toward mouth and would have dropped the glass if it weren't for Morgan who again moved with surprising intuition.

"Take your time," Morgan said quietly, helping her to raise the glass. As if Morgan wasn't wonderful in every other way, *of course* she interacted with her mother more naturally and easily than any other woman Jane had ever brought home. And, of course she seemed completely at ease, as comfortable as if it were her own home and Jane's mom a friend she'd known for years.

Maybe the emotion was just leftover sex hormones talking, like some sort of biological response to get humans to partner up. You've just had the most incredible sex of your life and the gorgeous woman who took you to her bed is treating your mother like a long-lost friend so of course it's natural that you're imagining wedding bells. Or, maybe it was just that Morgan really was an incredible woman. Either way, it didn't matter because nothing else could ever be between them aside from the casual, list-ticking sex they might enjoy a few more times.

By ten thirty p.m., the champagne was finished, Morgan had eaten two platters of snacks and Jane's mom was starting to flag. She stifled a yawn, and Morgan leapt up from her chair where the two had been discussing literature. Jane had joined in whenever she thought she could add something. But mostly she just enjoyed watching the two conversing and letting her mind wander to thinking about Morgan spending more time in their house.

Morgan was unusually flustered as she apologized, "I'm so sorry to have kept you up this late, I've had such a wonderful evening and I completely forgot about time. I'd best be going." She gently touched Jane's mother's hand. "It was wonderful to meet you, Pamela."

"And you. Please come and visit again."

"I'd like that, very much." It sounded genuine, not just polite.

As Morgan stepped away, Jane's mom blurted, "Are you any good at bowling?"

Morgan froze like a rabbit in a spotlight. "Pardon me?"

"Bowling. Ten Pin."

"Ah. I couldn't say as I've never tried it." She laughed. "I'd wager probably not."

"Mom," Jane warned, having the uneasy realization of where she was going with the line of questioning.

But she was ignored. "You see, Janie's in a bit of a pickle. One of her teammates is sick and they haven't been able to find a replacement for their bowling league this week."

"Mom! Seriously, you're going too far." She turned to Morgan. "Ignore her. She forgets that some people, unlike her, have social filters."

"I'm well filtered," was the indignant rebuttal. "You should hear all the things I *don't* say."

An expression of mild panic flashed across Morgan's face. "Um, well I'm not sure I'll be any good but if you need a warm body I'm sure I can, uh ten pin bowl?"

The eye-daggers Jane was shooting at her mom seemed to be flying past ineffectually as she barreled onward. "Oh, nonsense. I'm certain you'll be excellent. And a warm body is all Jane needs."

Jane almost melted at the mortifying innuendo from her mother of all people. Jane swatted at her, then leaned down to push the joystick to roll her chair backward. "Okay that's enough, no more champagne for you, ever." She turned to Morgan. "I'm so sorry about her, she thinks she's clever."

Morgan laughed. "She is."

"I am," her mom confirmed cheerfully, shooting Jane a cheeky look as she spun her chair around. "Safe travels home, Morgan, and please come back anytime."

Safely outside and away from her mother's meddling, Jane tried to repair some of the damage. "You really don't have to come to bowling, she was just trying to wind me up. Honestly, it's fine, we can just forfeit the week."

"Forfeit?" Morgan looked as if it pained her to say the word. "Oh, Jane. Never forfeit. I *will* be there, perhaps not in a helpful way, but I am certainly not going to let you down."

No, thought Jane. Morgan wouldn't let her down and would probably go out of her way to make sure she didn't, even if it inconvenienced or hurt her. She leaned against the wheelchair ramp railing. "You're just a little bit competitive, aren't you? This Employee of the Year thing, my bowling league."

Morgan grinned. "Oh no, not a little bit. I'm a lot competitive. Performance is everything for a perfectionist like me, in *every* aspect of my life…" She let the words hang as if she wanted Jane to take them.

Jane bit her lip, unable to stop the flood of memory of their time in bed earlier that evening. "Yes, I gathered that."

She took a small step forward. "Were you satisfied with my performance?"

"Beyond satisfied. Will I see you again this week?" When Morgan opened her smiling mouth to give what Jane knew would be a teasing answer along the lines of *yes every day at work*, she clarified, "After work. In a more intimate, naked kind of setting."

Morgan's mouth snapped closed and when she opened it to speak again her voice was tight. "Yes. That would please me a great deal."

"Me too," Jane breathed. "You can come around whenever you like in the evenings when Mom's asleep. What I mean is you can just…appear in my room. I'll be there."

Both of Morgan's eyebrows shot up. "Oh, no. I can't just come into your house. If I come over, I'll just text when I'm here."

"You can't come inside without being invited?" Jane glanced around, assuring herself nobody was nearby, yet the question was still an embarrassed whisper. "Like a vampire?"

"What? No. Goodness no. Again, total myth, that vampire thing. I can't come inside without being invited because that's really rude."

"Oh. Would you consider this a standing invitation?"

Smiling, Morgan shook her head. "I'm old-fashioned in some respects, Jane."

Jane grinned. "Just a little bit."

"Just a little bit," Morgan repeated. Her eyebrows drew together and her response was strained. "You and I are beyond a May-December relationship."

"Not really if you think about it in physical terms." Jane gestured. "That body is frozen at what, twenty-eighty years old?"

Morgan nodded, the edges of her mouth twitching.

"Right, so I'm actually older than you by three years. A regular cougar."

Laughing, Morgan raised both hands. "Fine, you've got me there." Her gaze wandered downward before coming back to Jane's face. "I think I like you being a cougar."

"I think I do too."

They stood comfortably for a few moments, leaning close without touching. Morgan broke the stillness first. "Thank you for inviting me in, I had a really nice time." Her voice softened, became almost wistful. "Your mum is amazing. And so much fun."

"She is." Jane glanced back at the house. "She's incredible. I don't know how she did all she did, charging through life as a single mom with me in tow while she studied and worked. I learned to just fit in with what she was doing, and I think she learned to do the same with my things." She paused, debating whether or not she should elaborate.

Morgan's gentle, genuinely curious expression made the decision for her, and Jane inhaled slowly. "Mom encouraged me to be curious. To ask questions. And I did, constantly. Why are the clouds floating? Do you think that man likes cats? Why does Sunday come before Monday? And when she had her accident I had all these questions I couldn't find words for. And it's only recently that I feel like we've found our way back to where we were before." Jane shook her head, laughing quietly. "Unfortunately, where we are right now doesn't leave much room for anyone else."

She bit her lip hard to stop herself from saying anything to embarrass herself further. To stop herself from blurting that she'd loved how Morgan had just…fit in to the space that was already there.

Morgan drew her fingertips down Jane's cheek. "She's incredibly lucky to have you as her daughter."

"Mmm, and I'm lucky to have her." Jane reached up to entwine their fingers, the smooth cool band of Morgan's ring a contrast to warm skin. She studied the backs of Morgan's fingers. "You know, I've always assumed this was some cheap piece of junk, but now I'm starting to think it's just very old and expensive."

"It is." Morgan turned their hands further so she could stare at the ring. "Cici gave it to me the year I decided to run away with her. She swears it belonged to Agnes of Beaujeu, who was Countess of Champagne in the early thirteenth century." Morgan grinned. "Worth a fortune, so if I ever find myself cast out of the Minion fold, homeless and penniless, I can always sell this ring and a few other trinkets Cici has bestowed upon me throughout the years."

"She wouldn't do that would she? Cast you out?"

Morgan laughed. "No, she wouldn't." She winked. "I'm the only one who knows how everything at Theda works. Plus, after such a long time I think she rather enjoys my company."

Jane replied before she could think about its context. "After our short time together, I enjoy your company too." Grimacing at her needy admission she hastily amended, "I mean, well I've really liked all the time we've spent doing not-work stuff."

Morgan's eyebrows slowly came down from where they'd shot up like a cat sprinting up a tree. "Me too. Very much. *All* of our time together." She rubbed her neck, as if she knew it was slowly turning pink and was trying to smudge the blush away. "So um, I guess I'll see you at work tomorrow?"

"You will. But I won't be able to do this until we're alone again, so let me just…satisfy a need to carry me through."

"And what need might that be?" Morgan asked, though the coyness of the question left no doubt she knew exactly what Jane was talking about.

"This one." Jane pulled her down, waiting a torturous few seconds before she slid her tongue along Morgan's lower lip, and kissed her.

CHAPTER NINETEEN

Naked except for a thong, and holding her tablet, Morgan carefully climbed onto the massage table and positioned herself with her face in the cut-out hole. Alanna, her masseuse, had long ago given up pointing out that working during a massage was counterproductive and offered, as she always did, a sigh that was maternally disappointed and disapproving all at once. Given the masseuse was in Morgan's house, Morgan felt she had some right to do as she pleased during the massage.

Alanna's fingers began to work their magic, kneading and digging into the knots of Morgan's back and shoulders until Morgan was cringing. Something that felt suspiciously like an elbow dug in. "Oof, you are so tense, Morgan. I swear, every time I see you it's like I've never worked on you. What do you do during the week to get you so tight? It's like you've been wrangling cattle all week instead of sitting in an office."

Alanna only knew a sanitized version of Morgan's job—as in I'm a manager, not I travel everywhere around the world and not-world frequently using nothing more than my own metabolism and energy, and oversee a group of sort-of-immortal people. Actually, overseeing Cici's underlings was a lot like wrangling cattle, or untrained calves would be more accurate. Morgan shrugged which earned her a hard finger dig from Alanna which meant *stay still and let me try to undo this mess you've gotten your body into yet again.*

Using a forefinger, Morgan input the passcode to send the afterlife package she'd just checked through to the servers. The movement earned her an elbow dig right below her scapula, which was Alanna's *punishment* for moving. She swiped again. Another elbow dig, this one hard enough to make her flinch.

After twenty wonderfully excruciating partly self-inflicted because-she-refused-to-stop-working minutes, Morgan had sent through enough packages to temporarily quiet her workaholic side, and her masseuse's barely concealed exasperation had reached the point where she could no longer ignore it. They played this game of chicken every session, and Morgan *always* broke first. She discarded the tablet and relaxed her arms by her sides. Alanna murmured her approval and said under her breath, which she probably thought Morgan couldn't hear, "About damned time."

Morgan let herself sink into the table, closed her eyes and tried to force herself to relax. Because forcing relaxation was exactly the right way to go about it. Blank mind, blank mind, blank mind, blank…Jane. Morgan let out a long exhalation, of which Alanna clearly approved, if the now-gentle thumbs in her lower back were any indication. The thought of Jane held a warm, soft feeling, almost as though she were wrapped in a comforting blanket. It'd been almost twenty-four hours since their lovemaking, and the lingering emotion had carried Morgan through a day that had been filled with screw-ups from Cici's underlings, uncooperative humans and not nearly enough work completed.

"Whatever, or whoever you're thinking about," Alanna murmured, "Keep thinking it. Your body just went from steel to solder."

Keep thinking about Jane. That was not a hardship. She spent the next half hour doing exactly that, mind slowly drifting until she almost fell asleep for the first time ever during a massage. Once she felt like a ball of clay that had been pummeled into a person-shape again, Alanna packed up her table and left Morgan with a pleading, "*Please* try to relax until I see you next week."

After agreeing she would try, Morgan took a shower to wash away the massage oil, and then pulled up some work on her tablet. She could relax tomorrow. At ten thirty p.m. when she'd sent through ten percent of the contracts she had to finalize, her door buzzer sounded. Morgan didn't need to look through the peephole, immediately sensing who was on the other side. The moment she opened the door, it was as if her world had been in disorder and now everything made perfect sense. "Jane," Morgan breathed.

"Hey. Sorry to appear unannounced." Jane reached up to tuck an absent piece of Morgan's still-damp hair behind her ear, her fingertips lightly tracing Morgan's jaw. "Mom's asleep. Can I come in?"

* * *

Morgan slid from the bed with the stealth of a spy, pausing as Jane shifted, rolled over and went still again. Morgan had to stop herself from leaning down and kissing her, from gently running her lips over the smooth, soft skin on Jane's neck and shoulders. Only the empty gnawing sensation in her stomach solidified her willpower. That and the fact their lovemaking had temporarily satisfied her more carnal hunger.

Rummaging in the fridge, Morgan absently ate a slice of cheese while she tried to find something more substantial. She ate two strawberries then tilted her head back and squirted canned whipped cream directly into her mouth. The *fffssstttt* sound echoed through the still, quiet house and Morgan cringed as she swallowed the mouthful. She paused, holding her breath as she waited for Jane to appear. When there was no movement from the bedroom, she squirted another portion of cream into her mouth, holding the dispenser down until her mouth was so full she was almost choking. She swallowed half, bit into a strawberry, squirted more cream, ate the other half of the strawberry. She heard footsteps a moment before Jane spoke, and hastened to swallow her mouthful.

"Until I met you I'd never been one for food porn," Jane observed from her right side. "But watching you eating at any time and especially now, standing there naked in front of your open fridge might be one of the sexiest things I've ever seen."

Morgan turned and before she could respond, Jane placed a hand on each of her shoulders, stretching up to lick the edge of her mouth. She lingered, first to suck Morgan's lower lip and then began kissing her with slow, soft caresses of lips and tongue until heat flared in Morgan's belly, and her legs were in danger of giving out. Jane's eyes were smoldering. "You missed some cream," she informed her, voice low and sensuous. "But I got it all."

Morgan held out a strawberry, arching an eyebrow in question. Jane nodded and leaned in, lips parted, ready to take the fruit from her fingers. Morgan swallowed, aware of both the hammering of her heart, and the excitement twisting through her belly. "Wait," she managed to say. She added a healthy dollop of cream and offered the morsel again.

Jane licked the tiniest bit of cream from the strawberry, then took it from Morgan's fingers, lips brushing skin. Jane ate the entire thing with a smile on those gorgeous lips. "Mmm, yum."

"Did you want another?" Morgan asked, unsurprised at the huskiness of her question. Watching Jane eat a strawberry was a divine experience that'd sent heat straight to her center.

"No. I want you to come back to bed with me." Jane smiled, reaching for Morgan's hand. "And bring the cream…"

The cream had been consumed and Jane's orgasm obtained when Jane hooked her leg around the back of Morgan's thigh and rolled them over until she was on top. She peered down, hair falling in a curtain. "Your turn," she whispered, the seductive note in her voice sending Morgan's stomach into a spin. Jane wasted no time, her hands and mouth working in a coordinated dance, and Morgan knew it wouldn't take long to reach her climax.

She lightly sucked Jane's neck, her earlobe. "That's so good. Keep doing that and I'll come for you." She lifted her hips into Jane's touch and just as she was about to begin her blissful spiral, became aware of someone else in the house. Morgan went utterly still. "Oh, for crying out loud."

Jane matched her for utter stillness. "What? Did I…do something wrong?"

Morgan framed her face with both hands and pulled her down for a lingering kiss. "Not at all. You're doing everything perfectly." She slipped out from underneath her lover, rolled off the bed and fumbled for her silk robe. "But I have a visitor. Unannounced and unwanted. I'll be right back."

Cici sat on one of the tall stools against the breakfast bar, one crossed leg bouncing impatiently. "Sorry to wake you," she trilled.

"You didn't wake me, and I know you're well aware of that." Despite her annoyance at the intrusion, and the interruption of her orgasm as her libido so unhappily reminded her, she kissed La Morte's cheek in greeting. "How can I help?" Cici must need something, and something big, if she'd taken a trip from Aether to see her in the middle of the night.

"It's Olivier. I'm sorry, darling, but I need you to go to Prague and fix his mess."

Morgan cinched her robe tighter. "What mess?"

"Among other things, he's bricked his tablet."

"Then he can bring it to me. And why didn't he call me instead of bothering you?" What a cretin, contacting La Morte for such a trifle.

"Ordinarily I'd agree and you know I hate making you do things unnecessarily, but I think you need to look at his operation and discover why he keeps making these mistakes." Cici's grimace was apologetic. "And he didn't call you because, I quote, you're mean."

"Ugh, really? Mean?" She'd show him *mean*. "My job isn't to be a bloody cheerleader, Cici. It's to ensure things are running efficiently for you."

"I know, darling, I know. So I need you to go and make things efficient again."

"I'm in the middle of something here. I have a guest."

"Ooooh! The delectable Ms. Smith?" Cici raised her voice to sport stadium level. "Don't you think it's about time you introduced me to your *amour*?"

"Shhh! And she is not my love." Even as she said it, Morgan knew how unconvincing she sounded. Being in love with Jane didn't make her Her Love. Did it?

Cici's expression confirmed that she was not fooled. "I don't think it's unreasonable for me to wish to meet this woman who has so clearly captured both your attention and your affection."

"No, it's definitely not unreasonable. But it's not happening, Cici."

Cici's eyebrow control was masterful. Her left arched so slowly it looked as though someone was dragging it up with a string. "Oh, really," she drawled. "And what makes you think you can stop me?"

Morgan rubbed between her own eyebrows. "Obviously I can't. But I'm asking you nicely to just…leave it alone for now. Please."

"You're going to have to give me a good reason if I'm going to deny myself such a delicious opportunity."

Morgan glanced over her shoulder, suddenly fearful that Jane might be listening. "Because she's special."

"Special." Cici said the word as a normal person might say *genital warts*.

"Yes. And I don't want to scare her off by introducing you two just yet."

Cici placed a manicured hand on her breast. "I'm wounded," she said, though she was smiling.

"Why do you need to meet her? You already know everything about her."

"True. But there is a large difference between knowing about a person and knowing a person. Therefore, I would like to actually meet her."

Morgan huffed. "I'm not sure why you even care. You've never shown any interest in anyone I've slept with before."

Cici was by her side before Morgan could blink, but the lightning-fast move was so familiar after so many centuries that she didn't flinch. La Morte placed a hand on Morgan's shoulder and leaned in to kiss her cheek. Voice low, she spoke against Morgan's ear. "Because. We both know that this is more than just sleeping, Morgana."

She knew the only way she could rationalize with Cici was if she remained calm and controlled. A slow breath helped. "Please don't meddle, not yet, not when everything is still so confusing and topsy turvy."

"Meddle?" La Morte threw her head back, her laugher rich and melodious. "Darling, I already have meddled. It's my *meddling* that set you on this path to being with Jane."

Morgan paused, trying to find the connection. She failed. "How so?"

"It was me who forced you to go when you really didn't need to. Not for the reasons I stated. I claim full responsibility for your current state of happiness." With her forefinger, she made a little tick movement in the air. "One point to me."

Morgan felt the blood drain from her face at the realization Cici had tricked her and basically set her up. "That was deliberate?"

"Of course." La Morte laughed disbelievingly. "Did you really think I of all people couldn't handle The Accountant if she queried your expenses? Ha! She wouldn't dare come after you. You're my special pet, darling. And I like to keep my pets happy." Then with a chuckle lingering in the air, she was gone.

Morgan blew out an exasperated breath. There was no time to mull over what Cici had said because she had to go and see useless Olivier Renaud. She gathered her hair up with both hands, trying to tame it as she walked back to the bedroom. Jane was sitting up in the bed, her body partially covered by the sheet. "Everything okay?"

"Big picture, yes, everything is fine. But I have to go to Europe, probably until at least dawn. And, I'm so sorry, but I have to go right now."

Jane's expression was a mix of disappointment, incredulity and awe. "Oh sure. No problem."

"It's a *huge* problem," Morgan corrected as she slipped out of her robe and rummaged through her walk-in closet. Olivier respected power, and though Morgan knew he was well aware of hers, it never hurt to look the part. "You and I were in the middle of something *very* important." She laid out her favorite dark gray pinstripe skirt suit on the bed.

"Mmm yes, we were." Jane's gaze lingered on the garment. "I love that one. You always look so hot and in command."

"Really?" She drew the word out until it hung in the air between them. "I didn't realize you'd been paying attention. In command is exactly the look I need right now, so, Ms. Fashion Stalker—which blouse should I wear for maximum *take no shit* effect?"

Jane didn't hesitate. "That crisp white one with the pearl buttons and your pearl cufflinks. Classic. And the plain black heels, the ones with the pointy toe."

"You really have been watching…"

Smiling, Jane shrugged. "Only every day since I started at Theda."

The admission made Morgan's toes curl. "Well that doesn't help."

"Doesn't help what?"

"My libido, knowing you've been secretly watching me as much as I've been watching you." Standing in the doorway of her walk-in so she could see Jane, Morgan pulled on underwear. "Just so you know, I am still so aroused I might actually die."

Jane grinned. "I highly doubt that."

"You shouldn't, it's a legitimate affliction. I'm this close to saying screw it and climbing back into bed with you because I want nothing more right now than to finish what you'd started, and then for both of us to start all over again. And then again."

Under the sheet, Jane pulled her knees up to her chest, and wrapped both arms around her shins. "Me too. But, you have an important job to do so we'll have to wait until after work."

"I won't last that long," Morgan whined as she slipped her blouse on. "I think I'm going to have to duck into the bathrooms during the day to take care of myself."

"No, you won't." Jane rose up onto her knees and beckoned Morgan closer. When Morgan moved to the edge of the bed, Jane began to fasten the buttons of her blouse. "Because if you do that, then you're going to spoil your appetite for when I finally get hold of you again."

"Unfair." She risked a quick peek down at Jane's gloriously naked body, then backed up and finished dressing. Jane watched silently, the expression one of intense concentration as if she were burning the image of Morgan into her consciousness.

After a speed application of makeup Morgan slipped into her heels, told Jane she could stay as long as she wanted and just lock the front door on her way out, gave her a thorough goodbye kiss which did nothing to extinguish her ardor and left for Prague. Maybe some distance would help.

Ha. Ha. Ha. Sure.

As it turned out, Olivier's incompetence was nothing more than apathy due to a bruised ego. He felt overworked, under-appreciated and all around neglected by Cici because surely *he* deserved special, personal attention. For what reason, Morgan wasn't sure. She thought she did a very good job of not only holding on to her temper, but also not reminding him of how much work was required of her without complaint or faltering, and also reminding him that as head of Europe he was a highly valued member of Cici's team of Minions and *of course* he would be allowed a break as soon as Cici could find a temporary replacement. And no, Morgan didn't know when that might be, as their boss's priority was currently finding someone to run The Americas which Morgan was currently doing. On top of her usual duties, she'd added sweetly.

She'd fixed his tablet and after a little more placation, a reminder about the operating systems and a quick demonstration, she deemed him mollified enough to not bother her for at least a few weeks and went home. It was almost six a.m. in San Francisco when she finally landed back in her empty house to ready herself for the day ahead, aware of how cool and empty the space felt without Jane.

Morgan wanted nothing more than to run a scented bath and wallow in it until her skin was so wrinkled one might mistake her for a prune, but duty called. Duty always called. Time for a quick shower, breakfast and then to the office. But first, a snack. She yanked open the fridge and immediately saw a plastic container with a handwritten sticky note on it.

Two grilled cheese ready to go. I had a feeling you might be hungry (haha) when you got home.

See you later.

-J xo

Morgan peeled back the lid to reveal absolute, thoughtful perfection. Two readymade sandwiches with buttered sides of the bread pressed together, and three slices of cheese—cheddar, Swiss and American—set on top. Heavenly. All she needed to do was separate the bread, drop the buttered side down and put the second buttered side on top. She turned the sandwich press on.

A persistent thought niggled. Traveling with Jane and all that entailed was one thing. Sex was another, utterly incredible, thing all together. Both things were comfortable enough. But Jane preparing food for her went far beyond the bucket-list guidelines. The most thoughtful gesture, sure. But also something far beyond that. Something, that for Morgan, was as intimate as lovemaking.

She knew she loved Jane, and that was fine, she could keep a lid on those emotions for as long as she needed to. But Jane was getting too invested, too involved. Best to pull back and get some distance while she could, and spare Jane the inevitability of having to break apart. But the thought brought absolutely no comfort or sense of resolution, only dread.

Morgan sighed. Jane, you are a saint. A saint whose heart I'm going to break. And I might just break mine all over again in the process.

CHAPTER TWENTY

Jane hadn't intended to buy anything for Morgan, but waiting in line perusing the wall menu, she'd been struck with a sudden urge to bring Morgan back a food-drink. It'd been the same the night before when she'd rolled out of bed after Morgan had gone to Prague, and had suddenly thought about Morgan coming back to her apartment, hungry and desperate for something to eat and having to scarf down butter or something.

Juggling her tray, Jane set the bigger cup on Morgan's desk. "Here, I got you something."

Morgan eyed the clear plastic vessel suspiciously. "What is this? Are you trying to poison me?"

Granted, the contents *did* look like liquefied mud. "If I was, I wouldn't do something so obvious and amateurish." Pleased by Morgan's grin, Jane went on, "It's from Smooth Operator. They call it The Beefcake."

"I see." Morgan raised the cup to peer at the contents. "Because it's made of beef?"

Jane laughed. "No, choc-peanut butter flavored. Full of carbs and fat and protein and a bunch of good healthy stuff, all blended in a tasty package for people who want something post-workout to help them get ripped." She cleared her throat, suddenly aware of Morgan's confusion. "I thought it would be something you could use?"

"You had me at choc-peanut butter." She had the straw between her lips before Jane could reply. "Oh hell. That's so good." With her eyes half-lidded as if she were experiencing a divine moment she drank a third of the beverage before reluctantly setting the cup on her desk. "Jane?"

"Yeah?"

Morgan's expression turned from food-orgasm to contemplative, as if she were deciding whether to speak her mind or not. "You know between the grilled cheese and this, I could get spoilt."

There was something in the tone that nudged at Jane. It was teasing, yes but with a seriousness layered beneath it. She lowered her voice. "Did I overstep? I mean, I just thought last night that you might appreciate something when you got back, that's all. And now too, I knew you'd probably be hungry, so I just grabbed something."

"I did appreciate it. I *do* appreciate it. Very much. It's just—" She clamped her lips together and smiling, shook her head. "Never mind."

Jane forced a smile of her own, and a light laugh. "It's just food, Morgan. It doesn't have to mean anything."

Morgan turned the plastic cup around and around, and when she finally looked up, her expression was pained. "But it does, Jane. Don't you see that?"

After a day of polite interactions between the two of them, Jane had decided that she really had gone too far. Gone was the ease and flirtatiousness. In their place was niceness. There was nothing wrong with niceness, but when you'd been writhing and slippery with sweat with someone, and they'd had their hands and mouth on almost every part of your body—and you theirs—*nice* felt cold. And cold was not nice.

Jane had just begun getting dinner ready, chopping cilantro when her cell rang.

"Jane, it's Morgan." She sounded almost breathless as though she was hurrying or trying to get the words out as quickly as possible. "I just finished a call with the air ambulance company and wanted to let you know to expect a visit from them tomorrow morning around ten."

Jane nestled the phone between her ear and shoulder as she moved to check her rice and bean mixture. "Oh, wonderful, that time is perfect. Thanks so much." Wow, so formal.

"No problem. It's just a consult to talk to you and your mum about what's required, and they will probably do a medical check and then it's full steam ahead." Morgan rushed on, full steam herself. "I've also arranged a bed for your mum in Connecticut but you'll need to let me know the address for delivery and if you need any other medical equipment. And if you want to talk to your mum's caretakers about going out-of-state with you we can cover that cost too, or hire caretakers in Connecticut. Whatever you want, it's your show. Just tell me the amount so I can arrange it and nearby accommodation for them."

Arrange it. "You're...not coming?" She was surprised at how hopeful, and tragically, how *disappointed* she sounded.

Morgan paused. "No, I hadn't planned on it." She cleared her throat then rushed ahead. "This is your family thing, Jane, not really something I should attend." Her laugh seemed forced and hollow. "Plus I have a mountain of packages to process that I should really get done before that award slips completely from my reach."

Oh, the award. The thing that had made Morgan agree to help Jane in the first place. An uneasy feeling snaked through her belly. It really was just an agreement, right? A mutual back scratching and nothing more. Could that be an explanation for Morgan's coolness during the day? Her knife on the chopping board paused as the realization hit. That *had* to be it. She had stepped over the unspoken boundary of the bucket list with the sandwiches and the smoothie and Morgan was freaking out at her neediness.

And! Morgan had been trying to tell her all day but was too polite to come right out and say it. Still, no matter how forcefully she told herself she didn't care, that she'd had what she'd wanted, the thought of Morgan not wanting her after telling her she did, stung like salt and lemon juice rubbed into an open wound. And Morgan not just coming out and being honest about it was equal parts frustrating and confusing.

So Morgan didn't want to come to Connecticut. No big deal, and her reasons were perfectly valid. And Morgan didn't want anything more than what they'd already had and done. Time to woman up and move on. She wilted at the thought. "Sure, okay then. I know you're busy." Jane scraped her sliced chicken breasts back into the skillet on top of the rice mixture.

"What are you cooking?" Morgan asked, apropos of nothing. Well, nothing if you weren't someone who thought about eating 24/7.

"Cilantro-lime chicken skillet. Mom's favorite."

A soft exhalation. "That sounds incredible."

"There's plenty if you wanted to drop by for dinner?" She'd spoken without thinking and the moment the words were out she wanted to grab them back. Slow clap, well done. Did you not just realize that you're going way too far with this whole I'm secretly in love with my boss thing, and that said boss is getting freaked out by your intensity?

Morgan sounded strained when she answered, "I...can't. But thank you for the invitation. I'm sure the meal will be wonderful, just like your grilled cheese." She paused. "Have a good night, Jane. And um, say hello to your mum from me?"

And then she was gone.

Once the dinner dishes were cleared and Jane had set up the board and tiles for a game of phonetic Scrabble, her mom pounced. "How's your hot Minion girlfriend?"

Distractedly, Jane shuffled her tiles. "Hot. Minion-y. Not my girlfriend."

"Clearly you and I are living different realities, Janie," her mom said as she opened the game with KRYSPEEE.

"I'll give you two E's but three E's is a bit much, Mom," Jane grumbled.

"Draw for it," was her mother's concession.

They each plucked a piece from the bag and when Jane's F beat her mom's S, her mom pulled one of the unnecessary E's from her word. Once Jane had recorded the score, her brain finally caught up. "Wait. You think she's hot?"

"I have eyes, Jane. She's gorgeous. I mean anyone can see that."

When Leah had expressed the same sentiment after Jane's southern hemisphere trip she'd been unable to do anything more than vaguely agree. But now she could actually express the wonder of Morgan's...well, *casing* as she herself called it. Jane's voice softened. "Yeah, she is. It sounds so clichéd but she's even more beautiful inside. The outside is literally just a shell, one that she can change on a whim, something to hold everything that makes her *her*. Just think, no matter what she looks like, she takes that beautiful, tender, caring, humorous, empathetic, generous soul with her. Isn't that an incredible thought?"

Her mother's eyes softened. "It is."

Jane fidgeted with the hem of her tee, trying to ignore the burn of threatening tears. "Mom...I've done something really dumb."

The tile arranging was abandoned and her mom moved herself closer. "What's that, sweetheart?" The way she asked it, and the expression on her mom's face told Jane that she knew exactly what the confession would be.

"I've fallen in love with her." She held her tongue on saying more because the reality hurt more than she wanted to admit aloud—that Morgan wouldn't or couldn't return her feelings.

"Yes, I'd figured as much," she said gently.

The rest of Jane's explanation fell out in a rush. "I mean, we know I've always had a kind of lame crush on her but it was all physical. I never realized before we spent time together just what a *good* person she is. Which is also weird, given her vocation. She's kind, compassionate, funny and so much more that I can't even begin to describe." Unimaginably incredible in bed, she added in her head.

"And does Morgan feel the same way about you?"

Jane's shrug was a stall, because she knew in her heart that Morgan didn't feel love for her. It was ridiculous to think that someone like Morgan would want someone like her, even if Morgan was emotionally available which—given everything she'd learned, and all of Morgan's hints—Jane was certain she wasn't.

Besides, how could she measure up to three hundred years of Morgan grieving for the love of her life? How could she penetrate those walls? She couldn't. "I don't know for sure, but I don't think so. She lost someone she loved, someone she *loves*, and I know love is frightening for her. But at the same time, when we're together I feel something from her." Her heart sank. She'd always known there would never be anything more.

"I think it's more than something, Janie."

"Okay well maybe just *like*? Or just some sort of lust even." Jane frowned, turning the thought over. "It's kind of weird because she's basically going to live forever and I'm not. And I know she knows when I'm going to die, and I just have this insecure doubt I can't shake that she knows I'm going to die soon and she's just…pity fucking me."

"Jane! Language. Anyone would think I raised you in a barn."

"Sorry," she said automatically.

Her mom smoothed her expression from *I can't believe this swearing child is mine* to *calm loving mother*. "I don't think she pities you at all. I've watched her watching you. I like the way she looks at you."

"I like it too. She makes me feel seen." Wanted. Desired. Her thoughts wandered off without permission. If Morgan's enthusiasm and reactions were anything to go by, she enjoyed their intimacy quite a lot. But enjoying sex wasn't a given gateway to a relationship, especially not when one party had huge reservations. Jane pushed back from the table. "Do you believe in soulmates, or whatever you want to call it?"

"You mean the idea that there's only one person in the entire world for you?"

"Mhmm, something like that."

Her mom paused, her thinking face firmly in place. "No, I don't believe so. Humans have such an incredible capacity for love that I don't think it can be assigned to just one person."

The comment gave Jane a small surge of hope. Maybe there *was* room for her in Morgan's heart after all. If she could only figure out how to show Morgan that. All she could say around the tightness in her throat was, "Mmm."

Her mom's look was knowing. "Does Morgan believe she had one soulmate?"

Jane nodded, and after swallowing a few times managed, "Yes. And she's lived with the pain of her dying for centuries, Mom."

"Then she is truly fortunate to have known such love. And is an incredible woman to have held on and stayed true to those feelings. But if she's had the capacity for that love, why can't she love like that again?" She reached out and clumsily wiped Jane's cheeks with the backs of her curled fingers. "I think the more time you spend with her, the easier it'll be for her to see beyond her hurt to the possibility ahead. It'll take time, but I really do believe she feels deeply for you even if she doesn't know how to put those feelings in place."

"But we have hardly any time left. We've completed nearly everything on the list." All that was left to do together were the coasters in Japan and Taiwan. Then it was back to *normality*. In appearance anyway. After everything they'd shared, even outside of their intimacy, Jane knew she would never feel how she had before they'd started the list.

"She agreed to join you for bowling. That's not a bucket list item, is it?"

Jane leveled a stare at her mother. "She agreed to that because you pressured her and she's too well-mannered to tell you to get lost."

"I doubt that someone like Morgan would do something she didn't want to." The smile started slowly, blossoming into full smugness. "She wants to spend time with you."

"See reasons above with the dying and pity."

Both hands came up a few inches in a *God help me* gesture. "You are utterly impossible sometimes, did you know that?"

"I get it from you." Jane worried her lower lip with her teeth. "Do you ever think about dying, Mom? Are you afraid?"

The answer came without pause. "I used to be. When you were younger and I didn't know who would take care of you. Then you grew up and I knew you would be able to take care of yourself. Then I just started worrying about you being alone. Now, with Morgan being around I'm starting to worry less about that." She reached out to clasp Jane's hand, and though the grip was weak, there was another kind of strength in the touch. "I'm not planning on checking out anytime soon. But it's childish to pretend I'm not going to die. We all do. I've lived a wonderful life, and I would give anything to have another lifetime with you, Janie, but when it's my time then it's my time. I'll die knowing I've raised a strong, compassionate and resilient daughter. When I go, I'll go knowing I've given you everything I possibly could and that you will go on to live as fulfilled a life as I have."

CHAPTER TWENTY-ONE

Right. What in all-the-hell dimensions were you supposed to wear to throw a heavy ball at some wooden lumps? Morgan considered texting Jane to ask, but a prickle of self-consciousness about being so clueless stilled her texting fingers. Only one option left—the thing which had revealed what one should wear for amusement park adventures.

Google.

The search yielded results like "Cute date outfits to wear ten-pin bowling". Shit. Was bowling actually a date? Had she agreed to something, stupidly not realizing the subtext? She opened another browser and swiftly typed *Is bowling a date?*

Oh, crap. Apparently bowling was a prime date activity. Sex was one thing, but dating was...well, it was an incredible, but unrealistic thought. Dating was far beyond what she was capable of giving anyone, including Jane. Over the top of that thought flickered a wistful idea that if she *could* date anyone, she would want it to be Jane.

She'd worked herself into a fairly good panic over dating, bowling and nearly everything in between when she finally remembered that it'd been Pamela who'd brought up the bowling thing, not Jane. Plus, it was a team activity which implied it was fun, instead of an intimate one-on-one experience. She was reading way more into it than she should have. She mollified herself by remembering that it'd been so long since she'd done anything like this, normal human activities, that it was understandable to be totally clueless. But the more time she spent with Jane and "being normal" the more natural it felt, and the more she wanted to be normal.

Finally she found a site that basically said wear whatever you want and be prepared for dorky bowling shoes. She could handle that. She took a couple of minutes to look at pictures of the bowling arena, and then watch a few videos on technique which served only to confuse rather than school.

Morgan slipped into her favorite jeans, boots and a vintage Siouxsie and the Banshees band tee she'd found while on a tea run to London in the eighties. She stuffed her credit card and ID—ha-ha, no really, I'm *definitely* over twenty-one—into the inner pocket of her leather jacket and left her apartment.

Jane's exuberant wave from a table overlooking the ten bowling lanes drew her attention the moment she walked in. She returned the wave to Jane and the stunning African American woman nursing a short glass of clear liquid and ice, who she assumed to be part of the team. The final teammate was apparently the blonde rummaging in her handbag. As she straightened, her face drained of color, expression changing like someone had flipped a switch. Her voice was ice and the short phrase she uttered an accusation. "I know you."

"No, I don't think so," Morgan said calmly and pleasantly, hoping denial would deflect Emma Matherson, aged thirty-one and nine-twelfths, who'd been assigned to Section F—a blandly pleasant afterlife realm where most of the millennial generation would spend their eternity after they'd died.

"Yes I do. You're…you're…" She could barely get the words out through spluttering rage.

Jane slid from her seat and barriered herself between the two, her expression one of perfect hospitality as if she had no idea what was happening, although she had to have an inkling. She gripped Morgan's forearm. "Morgan, this is Emma and Georgina." Jane gestured to each woman in turn, apparently having decided that despite Emma's reaction she should pretend it was a normal introduction. "Guys, this is Morgan who's here to make sure we didn't have to forfeit this week."

Georgina offered a cheery wave and casual, "Hey, great to meet you."

Emma, however, remained anything but cheery or casual. Her accusatory finger was thrust at Morgan's face. "I know what you are, and what you're doing. Stay away from Jane. And stay the fuck away from me."

Jane's voice turned low and soothing, "Hey, Emma. Relax. Morgan's a friend of mine, she's just here to fill in for Rochelle."

"She's a fucking monster. She's not even a person, is she?"

Emma's vitriol wasn't completely surprising, even though it wasn't the usual response Morgan got if she was recognized outside of her work. Even after all this time, understanding humans as she did, she still didn't know why some couldn't see past the fact she was just doing her job. A necessary job. A job that if not done correctly meant there would be untold chaos and disorder and billions of people suffering a rather unpleasant eternity in a shitty afterlife place. Morgan left her features neutral while Georgina just looked confused.

"She's not a monster," Jane said firmly. "She's my…friend, and she's here to help us out. So I suggest you get over it, or go home if you can't and then it'll be *you* who's made us forfeit tonight. Your call." The steel in Jane's voice was unmistakable and surprising. And kind of sexy.

Emma turned away without saying anything and dropped to a chair facing away from them. Morgan tried to cut through the tension with a bland question. "How long until we start the bowling?"

Jane turned her focus away from Emma's petulance and toward Morgan. "About thirty minutes."

She forced a bright smile. "Perfect. I'm going to the bar, what can I get everyone?"

Jane and Georgina gave her their drink orders. Emma mumbled without turning around that she was fine and didn't want anything. More likely she didn't want anything from Morgan. Leaning on the bar, Morgan drummed her fingers to try to work out some of the unsettled energy that had wormed under her skin, as a perky twenty-something took her order for drinks and fried snacks then flitted away. The bright smile she'd flashed at Morgan as she assured her the food would be brought to their table soon would normally have sent a warm glow through her.

But she felt…nothing. The encounter with Emma had left her drained and empty. Antsy and feeling out of sorts, Morgan tapped her credit card on the bar with one hand, and straightened piles of drink coasters with the other. She felt Jane's presence before she heard her step in beside her and turned around expectantly. Jane's hand touched her back. The effect was immediate. A slow flood of warmth, a burst of sunshine, a flower blooming.

She'd *never* had anything like that happen before. She'd known from almost their first interaction that she felt good around Jane and her seemingly eternal good mood and optimism, but she'd never felt this instantaneous burst of an almost static connection. Then again, she'd never been near Jane directly after someone had pulled her down.

The sensation Morgan had been trying to categorize suddenly crystalized into clarity. Connection. How or why she didn't know, but this thing she felt for Jane went far beyond simple lust or like or even…love. Morgan swallowed, trying to wrangle the mix of emotion which felt almost like the roller coasters she'd been on with Jane.

Jane's hand remained on her back, a soft comfort. "Hey. Thought you could use a hand." She looked up at Morgan, smiling sheepishly as she added, "Aaand Emma decided she wanted a beer after all."

"Ah, with the proviso that I didn't order it, pay for it, touch it or even look at it, right?"

The sheepish look turned to one of dismay. "Yeah…something like that. Look, I'm really sorry about her. I know it sounds typical and you probably can't believe it, but she's not usually like that."

"No I believe it. She was fine the last time we met." She paused. "Her cousin died last month in…not-nice circumstances. I suppose the pain of that death, coupled with seeing me with a friend of hers, and knowing what I am and what I do was a little too much for her to handle."

"Maybe, but that still doesn't excuse it. I'm sorry," Jane said again.

"Thanks but really, there's no need to apologize for her. Everyone is entitled to an opinion." Morgan's smile felt tight. "Even if that opinion is misguided."

Emma's demeanor was as cold as Morgan's beer while the group worked on their first round of drinks and snacks. Georgina on the other hand, was the model of inclusion, treating Morgan as if she were a long-standing member of their bowling team, laughing and even flirting with her. And Morgan swore Jane flashed her friend a few *cut it out* glances.

A voice that sounded like a bored pre-pubescent boy announced it was ten minutes until changeover. Jane leapt to her feet. "Time to swap footwear!" She glanced down at Morgan's boots, a faint flush dusting her cheeks. "Pity."

Once she'd changed her shoes and they'd stuck her fingers into six bowling balls to find the right one—while Morgan heroically held on to her innuendo—Jane guided her to the start of their lane. Morgan tried to sound casual instead of panicked when she asked, "Okay, so how do I do this? I Googled but it was more confusing than helpful. Who knew there were so many different ways to fling a ball?"

Jane moved to her side, gently positioning her arm. "A gentle swinging movement...but with some power." She grinned. "You don't want to hurl the ball down the lane, but you need to give it a bit of oomph."

"Like this?" Morgan made an awkward, straight-armed motion, trying to emulate what she'd seen online and what she'd observed everyone else doing.

Jane moved until she was pressed lightly to Morgan's back. "Not quite." Her palm glided over the back of Morgan's right arm until she was holding her wrist in a loose grip. Her left hand rested on Morgan's left shoulder, a reassuring touch. She could feel Jane's breath against the side of her neck and the sensation made her shudder inside.

"So, like this?" Morgan asked again as she swung her arm, trying to focus on how to bowl rather than the way Jane's breasts felt against her back.

"Close." Jane helped swing her arm forward and back, shaking it lightly. "Loosen up," she said, a hint of teasing in the command.

"I'm trying," Morgan complained. Easy for Jane to say *loosen up*, when she didn't have Jane Smith's warm body pressed to her back. She cleared her throat. "Everyone else's balls are spinning. Should I do that? Just a wrist movement right?"

"Sure, give it a shot." Jane took a step back and grabbed the ball they'd chosen for Morgan—a pretty pink and purple shiny marbled orb. "Ready to knock down some pins?"

"As I'll ever be." She stuck her fingers into the bowling ball holes, valiantly kept her juvenile thoughts to herself, and offered Jane a wide grin. "Just keep it in my lane, right?"

"That's it. Take a few big steps, then let 'er rip." Jane backed up to the u-shaped couches at the end of their lane and sat down. She leaned forward, elbows resting on her knees and gave Morgan an encouraging nod.

Morgan offered what she hoped was a confident smile but felt more like a grimace. Okay. She could do this. Just a simple physics exercise. She took a long slow breath, approached the lane, and flung the ball. Then she held her breath for the few seconds it took to spin right down the center of the lane. Most surprising was the thrill of anticipation as she watched the ball approach the pins. Then excitement turned into a sort of panicked excitement when she realized she *was* going to hit some pins after all.

The cheer from behind her came at the exact moment the ball careened into the stack, knocking over all but two of the pins on either side. She spun around, victorious arms in the air. Though she was smiling, Jane's clap was exaggeratedly slow. "Ohhh! A seven-ten split!" The smile grew wider, almost mischievous. "Probably one of the hardest layouts to pick up a spare."

"Well, I never like doing things the easy way." Morgan glanced back at the pins. "At least I didn't embarrass myself completely by missing them all."

"Give it time," came the snide reply from Emma.

Jane turned around lightning fast, making a gesture Morgan didn't catch but that made Emma look very contrite and mutter an apology. Jane put one hand on the small of Morgan's back, the other pointing down the lane. "You can try to spin it and you might scuttle one pin into the other. Or just try to get the certain pick up of one pin. Your call."

Morgan managed a tight, "Mhmm." The casual contact was turning her into a hormonal teen, unable to think let alone articulate. Get a grip on yourself, you're six hundred and eighty years past puberty.

Jane helped her get the correct grip on the ball again, then playfully patted her butt. "Go get 'em, tiger."

By the time they'd finished all their games, Morgan had perfected the seven-ten split. She'd also perfected the art of not hitting any pins at all, or only hitting one of the remaining pins needed to make the perfect score. When she'd knocked down all of the pins in one shot, she'd been treated to high fives from everyone—including a recalcitrant Emma—and a tight warm hug from Jane. Unfortunately, she hadn't been able to repeat her strike to earn another hug. By the end of the night, Emma had calmed down enough to at least have a conversation with Morgan, albeit stilted and uncomfortable. But she never relaxed, despite Morgan practically bending herself in half to put her at ease.

Strolling through the parking lot, Jane broke the silence first. "Do you want a ride home?"

"No thank you. I'll be home in two shakes of a lamb's tail." Home to her empty house and that feeling of something missing that she knew would come the moment they were apart.

"Isn't there a thing about not teleporting while drunk or something? Don't drink and teleport?"

Morgan laughed, genuinely amused at Jane's silly joke. "Not that I'm aware of. My main transport method isn't well known enough to become a national safety campaign. Plus, I'm certainly nowhere near drunk. I also have homing pigeon instincts, remember? I'll be home before you've even left the parking lot."

Jane's forehead creased, but she conceded, "Okay, all right then. If you're sure."

"I'm sure, but thank you for the offer." It was more than just being able to get home faster than if she were in Jane's car. Being in close quarters with Jane now, while her body was fighting need and want and rationality, would be a disaster. She stepped back. Jane leaned forward. Morgan shuffled backward again and felt the pain of moving away as if it were physical.

Jane touched her arm, tugged gently at her leather jacket. "Have I told you that I really like Casual Morgan?"

Taken aback by the out-of-the-blue comment, Morgan faltered for a moment before an unconscious smile formed. "You haven't." After another moment she added, "I think I do too. She's so rarely taken out in public."

Jane pointed the key fob at her Mazda. "Oh? I feel like I've seen quite a bit of her these past few weeks."

"You have." The smile faded as reality intruded yet again. They stopped near the driver's door, and everything she'd been thinking about all night fell out of her mouth. "Jane, I'm sure you've already gathered this but I don't…live a normal life. I don't socialize, I don't go out for drinks or dinners or bowl or go to theme parks. And the reasons I don't do those things are partly because they've never seemed important enough to me to carve out part of my already full schedule for, and partly because nobody has ever mattered enough to me to do those things. But since we started this, I have stepped so far out of my comfort zone that I almost need a map and compass to find my way back."

"Are you unhappy with where you are?" Jane asked tentatively. "In relation to you and me and your comfort zone I mean."

The question tripped her and she took a few moments to consider it. "No, I'm not," she said quietly. "It's definitely a new experience, but not an uncomfortable one." Morgan exhaled a long breath and decided to take a chance and share something she ordinarily wouldn't. "What is uncomfortable are things like what happened with Emma tonight. It doesn't occur often because Cici's staff are by nature, likeable people. It's part of what makes us so effective. Jane, I very much dislike people being uneasy in my presence. It makes me feel horrible. And to put it very simply, I don't enjoy feeling horrible." Morgan smiled wryly. "Stupid empathy."

Jane brightened as if she'd found the perfect solution. "Okay, so we stay away from people that make you feel horrible."

Morgan laughed. "If only it was that easy." She stepped closer. "Jane, you probably don't know this or haven't realized, but part of me being so empathetic is taking on the emotions of those around me, bad and good. And you're the good."

"What do you mean?" she quietly asked.

Fair question, given her vague and confusing explanation. "It's just…you change any horrible feeling *immediately* just by being near. It's like the moment you come near me or touch me, every bad or uncomfortable sensation I'm experiencing just melts away." She bit down hard on her lower lip, almost wincing at the pain. So stupid, why not just tell her you're in love with her?

If Jane realized what Morgan wasn't saying, she didn't let on. "Oh."

"And I can't keep using you as a crutch like this because it's not fair. Not fair to you or me."

"It doesn't feel unfair to me," she protested.

Jane's hopeful expression was everything Morgan needed to know. She was already invested in something beyond what they had, something Jane couldn't understand would never be the way she imagined. "It will," Morgan assured her. "It's an unspoken promise to you that I can never keep."

"I disagree." Jane's eyes held hers in a silent challenge. But she said nothing more and when Morgan remained quiet, the expression changed. Now there was an air of confirmation on Jane's face as if everything had slotted into place, as if she'd finally seen who Morgan really was and what she could never give her. It wasn't smug or knowing. It was resigned.

It was completely heartrending and made Morgan feel as if someone had hooked her insides and was tearing them out. But it was for the best. Best for Jane to realize now rather than later. Morgan made herself smile, but it felt so tight that the skin around her mouth seemed to be splitting. "Drive carefully. I'll see you at work in the morning."

Jane did nothing more than raise her hand in a weak wave before reversing out of the spot and driving away. Morgan slipped into the shadows, holding herself still. She felt cold and empty and it didn't take a genius to realize it was because Jane had gone.

Morgan rubbed her temples. You're an idiot and this has gone way too far. Putting some emotional distance between them was the right thing to do. She couldn't keep relying on Jane for comfort and to refill her empathetic bucket, because one day Jane would be gone and by then Morgan would have forgotten how to stand on her own.

But how exactly was she supposed to get some emotional distance when she saw Jane nearly every day at work, and with the last things they had to do for Jane's bucket list? And not to mention the sex. The sex... A slow wave of heat rolled over her body. Surely they could maintain some emotional distance while being casual bedmates, assuming Jane wanted to be casual bedmates. Morgan laughed aloud at the ridiculous notion that she could separate herself emotionally while being so intimate with Jane. No, she'd have to cut all emotional ties.

"Just do it," she mumbled to herself as if an audible pep talk might have a better effect than just thinking the words. "You're in way too deep. Jane is a mortal woman, remember? Do you remember what happened last time you fell for a mortal woman? You'd think that after so many centuries, you would have learned by now." Shuddering at the thought, Morgan closed her eyes and went home.

CHAPTER TWENTY-TWO

Now that the Smith shenanigans celebrating her mom's fiftieth birthday were over, the quiet stillness of Jane's aunt and uncle's house was unnervingly peaceful. Everyone had gone to bed an hour ago, and Jane had tried to do the same but was unusually restless and unable to sleep. She tried random Internet browsing, looking at memes, getting angry at people on social media, and reading articles about the latest advances in data storage technology. After a few hours, fed up with the Internet, she fetched her aunt's ever-present inch-thick Sudoku puzzle book to redo pages her aunt had messed up.

She felt like she'd chugged ten energy drinks and eaten an entire bag of candy, her body unsettled and almost…anxious. Anxious? Why should she be anxious among her family? Oh gee, I don't know, could it have something to do with a woman on the opposite side of the country? Jane didn't need a therapy session to pin down why she felt so unbalanced. She missed the woman who was clearly not interested in anything more than the casual whatever it was they were doing. And maybe not even interested in that anymore.

Since bowling late last week, whenever Jane suggested they get together after work, Morgan had immediately declined and with a smile explained she was sorry, but she had so much work to do.

After their incredible intimacy, this cool change stung more than she thought possible.

But Morgan had all but said it, hadn't she? There was no room in her life for Jane. Not in the way that Jane really wanted it. And that was fine. Really it was. Or, so Jane tried to make herself believe. She wasn't arrogant enough to think that she could be more than, better than a woman who'd held Morgan's heart for centuries. And she didn't want to be. She just wanted to be herself and to have Morgan want *that*.

Right, enough wallowing. Or wishing for things that would never happen. Leah was right, as she'd nudged her yet again the day before she'd left for Connecticut—she needed to move on. Best way to move on? Get busy. They'd cleaned up after the party so she couldn't procrasti-housework, especially not while everyone slept. She'd been sent automatic server reports from Theda a few hours ago, and everything was A-Okay so she couldn't procrasti-work. Television held no appeal. Neither did her portable handheld gaming console. The only thing she could think of was some fresh air and star gazing. Maybe Morgan was somewhere up there, zooming around the cosmos.

Ugh, stop it.

She grabbed the bags of party debris and had just raised the trash can lid when she became aware of someone lurking in the shadows of her aunt's climbing roses. Jane stepped back, clutching the bags tighter, as though she could somehow use them as a shield. "I, I… know self-defense! Black belt!" She was quite pleased when her voice came out steady instead of shaky. Of course, a steady voice telling a lie was not really an effective tool against a would-be assaulter.

The figure moved out of the shadows, both hands up at shoulder height as a familiar, British voice said dryly, "Really? Well, you learn something new every day. But please, Jane, I beg you, don't throw your dinner leftovers on me. I assure you, I'm completely harmless."

All Jane's adrenaline was replaced by pleasure. Accepting that Morgan didn't want her romantically would be so much easier if she didn't feel that little jolt every time she came near, like a quick tingle of static electricity. Jane dumped the trash and closed the few feet between them. She had to forcibly keep her hands by her sides instead of reaching for Morgan.

She'd clearly come from work, and was dressed in her usual impeccable office wear, which made Jane feel self-conscious in her old sweats, hoodie and the slippers she should really toss out. "Hey. What's up? Is everything okay? Is there a problem with something at work? I got a server report not long ago and everything looked fine but I know Jorge was grumbling about bank four before I left."

Morgan huffed out a laugh. "Yes and no. There's no problem except…" She paused for a few long moments and Jane could see her confusion and embarrassment. "I wanted to see you," Morgan said eventually, those simple words accompanied by a shrug. "I'm sorry, it's so pathetic and so incredibly stupid of me. And now that I'm here, I realize how intrusive and creepy this is, especially after the other night and what I said, and I'm so sorry to interrupt your family time." She produced a beautifully wrapped parcel which she held out to Jane. "This is for your mum. For her birthday. I know it was today so I'm technically late, and I was just going to leave it on the porch for you to give her but, well…you caught me."

If hearts could melt, Jane's would be like an ice cream dropped on the pavement in July. "You're not interrupting anything except everyone being asleep and me trying to find something to alleviate my boredom." She stepped into Morgan's personal space and took the gift, running her fingers over the smooth paper. "And thank you so much, this is incredibly sweet of you."

Morgan's response was husky. "It was my pleasure." After a beat she added a hasty, "It's a book. Well, three books technically."

"I gathered that, based on the bookish shape of it."

"Oh, of course." Morgan's eyebrows came together. "I really am sorry to intrude, Jane." She raised both hands, gesturing aimlessly as though it might help her find the words, and her eye contact was unusually absent. "As I said, I just wanted to see you. Or at least, be near you for a few minutes."

"Heyyy." Jane reached up, gently cupping Morgan's chin. "Look at me. You don't have to apologize for wanting to see me."

"No, I know that, it's just…I feel…" Morgan shrugged again as though hoping the gesture would speak in the absence of words.

"Lonely? Needy?" She took a chance, based on Morgan's expression. "Embarrassed about feeling that way?"

"All of the above. I wasn't going to intrude, really. I just had an urge to be near you, that's all," Morgan repeated. "I thought I could just stay here for a minute. You know, in a not-creepy outside-your-window kind of way." She laughed but it was completely without humor. "And I know that after what I told you about *not* doing this, not using you like my own personal feel-good service, me being here is, well…it's not right."

"I don't think it's *wrong*," Jane reasoned. "Can I tell you how I feel right now?" At Morgan's quick nod, Jane told her, "I feel special, needed, happy. Truth be told, I've kind of missed you. Are you hungry? There's enough leftovers from Mom's birthday celebrations to feed an army." Taking Morgan's hand, Jane began to pull her toward the back door.

Morgan remained where she was. "No, it's fine, thanks. I'm not really hungry, and I should probably head back." Despite her assurance, Morgan's stomach chose that moment to make a liar out of her and let out a grumble that Jane heard clearly. Morgan glanced down, frowning, and when she looked up she'd exchanged the frown for a sheepish smile.

"Are you sure? If you're worried about being tossed into the middle of a Smith family gathering, everyone's in bed."

"I think I'd like a Smith family gathering. Very much." She made a quiet musing sound, peering down at her hands which were finger-laced together and working nervously. "I have a problem, Jane, and it's not one I've ever encountered before and I'm really not certain how to approach it."

Jane leaned against the rose trellis. "Oh? Is this problem something I can help you with?"

"I don't think so, no." She paused, and in a rush said, "I'm so sorry. I feel like every time I'm near you I'm being tugged in two different directions. I want, but I'm just…I don't know how to do this thing. With you."

"What thing exactly?"

"I think you know," she said quietly. "Whatever is between us is now more than just friendship, or us being casual bedmates because of your bucket list." She offered no further explanation.

She didn't need to. Jane knew exactly what she was hinting at, and the thought of Morgan *wanting* as much as she did sent a thrill through Jane. "I do."

"Mmm," Morgan mused. "So, do you see my dilemma? A few days ago I literally told myself no more, that continuing whatever this is was only going to hurt both of us and that I would make an effort to return to the way things were before. And here I am, because I couldn't help myself. Because I'm like an addict. And it's you I'm addicted to."

The way things were before… Jane could never return to that. But she didn't want to spook Morgan by blurting that, so decided to play along with her thinking aloud. "Is there a solution to your dilemma?"

Apparently Morgan had decided to play along too. "There is. But I don't like it because it means no more…this. But this situation as it stands also feels somewhat untenable given my past."

Ah, a clue. She'd suspected as much, but having Morgan basically confirm that her relationship with Hannah, whatever had transpired, was affecting how she moved forward—or didn't—with Jane felt like a weight lifting from her back. "What about your past exactly?" Though she had an idea, she wanted Morgan to say it, to confirm it, to own it. Then she might be able to unpack whatever it was that she kept so close, and perhaps move away from it.

Morgan shifted nervously, and it took everything Jane had not to just hug her and tell her not to worry about it, that they didn't have to talk about it. But she didn't, because they *did* have to talk about it if there was any chance of something between them.

It was a while before Morgan answered, and when she did her voice was rough with emotion. "I feel like I'm carrying around everything that happened back then. All of my grief, and the emotional and physical pain. I feel like I *have* to hold on to it even as I'm trying to let go of it for you, for…potentially us. You keep breaking pieces of that pain off me, Jane. But it's been part of me for so long that every time I drop a piece I panic, and I feel like I simply must pick it up again. That if I let it go, then I'm going to fall apart somehow. My arms are getting very full." She smiled fleetingly. "Sorry, there's a lot of metaphors tonight."

"There's nothing wrong with metaphors. Especially if they help you express what you're feeling." Jane did touch her then, slipping her free hand into Morgan's. "Maybe I can help you. Maybe I could carry some of it for you, even if it's just for a little while."

"Maybe," Morgan agreed, her voice barely above a whisper. "Or maybe I'll just collapse under it the way I did in the past. Because what if you can't carry it either?" She reached up to hook her fingers in the trellis. "I'm just not sure I have the guts to say yes when I know what saying yes means for me."

"Then I suppose we'll have to figure out how to share the load so we're both comfortable."

Morgan's face relaxed as if she was trying to figure out how to fit that idea alongside her long-held ones. She nodded slowly but didn't say anything. But the hand Jane held squeezed her fingers lightly.

Jane squeezed back. "Do we have to make a decision right now?"

Morgan seemed confused by the question. "Well, not right now, no. But I think it's something that requires some forethought." She smiled a tight smile. "I'm sorry. This is quite possibly one of the strangest, most cryptic conversations I've had in a while. And I once had to administer an afterlife package to a gentleman who believed he didn't even live in this dimension."

She smiled at the thought. "Whenever you're ready to get less cryptic, I'm here."

"Noted. Good to know." Morgan's shoulders slackened a fraction. "I should probably get back, I really do have work to do. Thanks for, well, just being you."

"Anytime. I'm pretty good at being me." Jane leaned over and set the gift on the porch step. "Can I at least have a kiss goodbye?"

Morgan made a small helpless sound, dipped her head and kissed Jane with such tenderness that Jane instantly melted against her. She clutched her waist, pressing herself to Morgan, feeling her body soften, as if Morgan had let out a breath she'd been holding for hours. The kiss was unhurried yet filled with such passion that Jane was unable to stop her arousal building. They were in the shadows, nobody would notice if she… Jane parted Morgan's suit jacket and untucked her blouse from her skirt.

Her fingers found warm, soft skin and she stroked the small of Morgan's back. Morgan shuddered and relaxed for a few seconds before she went rigid. Gasping, Morgan pulled away. "I'm sorry." She paused, hastily kissed Jane's cheek, murmured a goodbye, took a few quick steps backward and disappeared.

Despite the warmth left by Morgan's sudden departure, Jane shivered, pulling the edges of her hoodie tight around her torso. She waited, stuck in place for almost ten minutes in case Morgan came back.

But she didn't.

CHAPTER TWENTY-THREE

Morgan had spent every minute since Connecticut chastising herself. What a pathetic, needy, borderline-stalkerish thing to do. And given that she'd sworn she was going to try to move their relationship back to the professional instead of personal, she felt like giving herself a massive forehead slap for doing *exactly* what she'd said she wouldn't. Age definitely didn't guarantee wisdom, and apparently affection or whatever it was didn't care about logic or basic things like convictions.

Since Jane had left for the east coast, Morgan constantly tried to reason that Jane was fine, as was her mum, that it was perfectly normal to miss her given the amount of time they'd been spending together for Operation: Jane's Bucket List. Eventually the reasoning had turned to anxiety so great she couldn't ignore it.

She'd decided to just make a quick trip—not to actually interact with Jane, no that was going too far—but just to be near her and to reassure herself that Jane really was okay. And leave Pamela's birthday gift of a first edition, three-volume set of Jane Austen's *Mansfield Park* somewhere in view. The night she'd delivered the champagne, she and Pamela had spoken of their mutual love of Austen, and Morgan decided that the books she'd purchased in 1814 would be a perfect gift and well-loved by Pamela.

When Jane had spotted her, Morgan's mortification almost made her blink herself away again, like a supernatural version of hide and seek. Until Jane had come closer, bringing that immediate sense of rightness, and Morgan's resolve crumbled quicker than a sandcastle hit by the incoming tide.

She really was stuck in some ridiculous reward loop: be near Jane, feel good, feel bad for the inevitable hurt that was coming for them both, want to be near Jane so she could feel good again. Inarticulately, Morgan had tried to explain the bond they had and told Jane she liked her—lamest and most understated explanation ever—and needed her nearby but couldn't keep relying on her for comfort. But then Morgan kept going back to her for comfort. Well done. Way to act like the Queen of Mixed Signals. But...at least she'd partially explained her feelings to Jane. Tried to explain what she was doing and feeling instead of just ghosting her.

As she pulled into her parking space, Morgan sensed Cici up in her apartment and was greeted by her boss reclining on her couch. Cici's otherworldly body was draped in an incredible patterned-silk Hermes dress. Morgan set her bags down and slung her coat over the back of a chair. "Well this is a pleasant and somewhat unexpected surprise." She kissed Cici hello. "To what do I owe the honor of your visit earth side?"

"I missed you." Cici's pout was well-practiced.

"Bullshit. I saw you less than twelve hours ago. I see you found my wine stash."

"It's not hard to miss, it's literally a wine rack in your living room." Cici raised the glass of Cabernet. "This is excellent."

"I know. I took it from your cellar a few months ago. Knew you wouldn't miss one bottle."

"Mm, well that explains it then." She raised the glass to her mouth. "Have a drink, Morgana. You look like you've had a hell of a day. Pardon my pun." Cici had a second wineglass ready and she nudged it closer.

"I've certainly had better." Between the usual Monday vibes at the office, trying to be cool toward Jane at work, a crying client, a combative client and her vacation from Olivier being cut short by his sending through a corrupted data package, she was about ready to scream. "So why are you here? Not that I'm not pleased to see you of course."

One of Cici's bare shoulders came up fractionally. "I thought you might like a chat."

A small sip of the excellent red eased some of the dryness of Morgan's mouth. "About what exactly?" She knew exactly what Cici wanted to discuss, and she could think of nothing she wanted less than trying to unravel the tangled and conflicting strands of her feelings for Jane. But if Cici decided a topic required a discussion, then a discussion would be had whether Morgan liked it or not.

"The state of the financial market. Which country will top the medal tally at the Summer Olympics this year. If the world really is heading for World War Three, which goodness I hope not because I'm going to be obscenely busy if that happens." Her eyeroll was exaggerated. "Or, we could discuss you and Jane Smith."

"What about us?" She tugged absently on her left earlobe, ran her fingers up the back of her ear to pull the top of her ear down then released it, hoping the familiar motion might calm her inner turbulence. "Or actually, more to the point, there is no us."

"Actually," Cici said. "There is, whether you choose to accept it or not. And you are miserable, fighting with what you want. You're punishing yourself for loving someone else who isn't Hannah."

"I don't. I...can't love Jane, for her sake and for mine."

Cici sighed, more a sound of sorrow than exasperation. "We have been over this until it's a raw bleeding wound and it is time to put a bandage on it so that it can heal." She raised a *don't interrupt me* forefinger. "You're afraid of feeling for someone again, you're afraid of loss. I know this. But, Morgana! Those things are what make you *human*. Granted, a human with an exceedingly long lifespan, but human nonetheless. And humans are the most remarkable species, so adaptable. And that's what you need to be."

"I barely made it last time, Cici," she whispered around the tightness in her chest. "You know that. I don't think I could do it again."

Cici laughed, a note of incredulity and some pride when she rebutted, "Oh yes you can. *You* are Morgana Ashworth. My right-hand woman and the person who singlehandedly revolutionized my operation. The woman who once broke up a bar brawl between raiding pirates. The woman who I have seen repeatedly throw herself in danger to protect others, even when you were human and mortal. I've seen you with more injuries than I care to, seen you endure more physical pain than any other human. Anyone else would give up, beg to be released from their immortality. But you keep fighting. Why is that?" she murmured.

"I really love my job." And I can't make myself let go of my memories, Morgan thought. She carefully schooled her expression. "And I love you. No brainer."

"I'm incredibly fond of you too. You are irreplaceable, Morgana, and not just professionally but personally. I dread the day you decide you've had enough of standing by my side."

"That day will never come, Mistress," Morgan said immediately.

Cici made a low rumble of pleasure. "Well, that pleases me." She ran her forefinger around the rim of the wineglass until the glass emitted a constant low crystal hum. "I think you keep going because deep down you've known that someday someone like Jane Smith would come along. Waiting for someone like her is worth the centuries of pain, isn't it?" Cici stilled her finger to stop the glass music.

But was it? Especially knowing what would come after. Was that to be her life? A cycle of love and loss waiting for the next woman who might heal her heart for the span of a mortal lifetime, before her heart was smashed all over again. She'd never survive. "How do you do it, Cici? Don't you get attached to people or things that you must leave behind?"

"Yes, of course. I feel emotion, though it is not the way humans do. Mine is with more intensity. Pain, lust, loss, pleasure, enjoyment, despair. All of it felt deeply. But, every one of my emotions is perfectly balanced by another. It may take time, but I always arrive at the counterpoint. As will you, if you have not already."

"I'm not so sure," Morgan mumbled. She sipped her wine and found Cici's eyes. "Could you go through my heartbreak with me again?" She shuddered at the memories. Too many nights to count.

"I will go through anything with you, my love. I would do anything, give anything for your happiness. You know that." La Morte drank an indulgently slow mouthful of Cabernet. "Why don't you use one of your saves?" Her ring-encrusted fingers twinkled through the air, as though her suggestion was magic. "All you need to do is submit your request and I promise I'll be very generous."

"I can't," Morgan whispered. She *had* thought about it for just the barest fraction of time, of asking Cici for one of her ultimate favors—to extend Jane's life. But as soon as she'd thought it, she'd almost choked on the idea. Jane would suffer not a whit, but Morgan would suffer for eternity when Jane had eventually and inevitably gone.

"And *why* can't you, exactly?"

"Because…" Morgan fumbled for something to say. "Because that would be selfish, and selfishness is a luxury I've been trying to give up ever since Hannah died."

"Please," La Morte scoffed. "Every time you save another cancer kid, or a grandmother who wants to see their grandchild come back from military deployment, or scientists making life-altering research breakthroughs, it's selfish."

"No it's not. That's entirely different. I do that for them."

"Sweetie," Cici drawled, the very picture of patience. "Remember who you're talking to and cut the crap. You do it because it gives you that warm tingle inside. It makes you feel good. It fuels that empathy engine of yours. Isn't that the very definition of selfishness? *Good* selfishness of course. So what makes this situation with Jane any different? You'll not only make her happy, but yourself as well."

Morgan delicately nibbled her lower lip. Make Jane happy... But would it really? Extending her life without being able to promise her anything wasn't a kindness.

La Morte reached for her wineglass. "Try again and give me the truth this time."

The truth felt almost as painful as the past. "You know the truth. At least if I stay away from her now it might be easier for me to move on. If I keep her for another fifty or sixty years, well you already know how that will end up."

Cici shook her head, the disbelief as clear as day. "Are you really so blind, Morgana, that you can't see what's staring back at you when you look in the mirror?"

"No. I see it. But I don't *want* to see it," she finally said. "I can't love her."

"We've been through this, my darling. You already do. You couldn't move on from her now even if you wanted to." Cici gently cupped Morgan's chin, raising her face. "Do you know, since she began working at Theda, nearly every time you've come to see me and report, you've mentioned her name? Jane did this, Jane and her team fixed that, Jane thinks we should... And every time you mention her, you get soft. Your expression, your voice, your eyes. You smile when you say her name. I've never seen that before. You've spent the past eight years learning to love her, even though you haven't realized it."

Morgan blew out a raspberry. "Softness, wonderful. Exactly what I'll need when Jane dies."

"There's nothing wrong with softness. It suits you, tempers your ambition and self-flagellation." She set down her glass. "Speaking of self-flagellation. Morgana, I know what happened in England."

Morgan cringed at the memory of her antagonistic stupidity. "Did Jane tell you?"

Cici baulked. "Of course not. I felt it. Felt your pain. And I was preparing to come to you when I realized I had no reason to. You had everything you needed right there with you."

"Jane," Morgan breathed.

"Yes. This has already gone beyond the point of no return. Use a save on her."

"You know why I can't do it."

"This isn't a *can't*. This is a *won't*. Have you told her about it? Explained yourself?"

Morgan tugged her ear again. "I mean I tried to but there's so much to unpack that I can't just unleash everything upon her. She'd run a mile. A hundred miles."

"Doubtful. And why ever would you not be open with her? Isn't that what people in relationships do?" The word *relationship* came out like Cici couldn't actually picture the concept.

Morgan offered an evasive, "I'm not sure."

"I am. It's because you assumed this would be nothing more than a brief fling, but it's turned into something big and important." Cici tsked. "She deserves to know, Morgana."

"Know what? That I love her so much that I don't want to spend more time with her? That concept is so illogical to a mortal that it's laughable. No matter what I say, how I try to explain it she will *never* understand because my reasoning is selfish—I can't deal with the aftermath and so Jane's feelings don't matter. Isn't that nice of me?" She ground those last words out. "Doesn't that just make me the perfect girlfriend candidate? A selfish emotionally stunted woman is just what every gal wants."

Cici waved a dismissive hand. "Fine then. Do whatever you want to. Stop seeing her and spend the rest of your time alone, never risking your heart. I'll admit that I'm glad you won't subject me to another two hundred and fifty years of your ridiculous misery." The words were gentle and teasing, but Morgan still felt the bite of Cici's truthful rebuke.

"All right then, I will." She almost crossed childish arms across her chest.

La Morte sighed. "I feel her through you, Morgana. Faintly, but I feel it. And if I can feel it then I know that you are carrying Jane's emotions around as if they were your own. What you are doing to her now—this yes-and-no business—is cruel and causing nothing but hurt for both of you. Either commit to it or leave her be so that she may find someone else. I mean it. I'll not have you doing this to her and yourself and by extension pulling me into your emotional maelstrom."

Morgan felt like she'd just eaten a whole lemon.

Cici laughed softly. "Ah. Look at that expression." La Morte's smile was lazy, a light seeming to flicker in her eyes. "Perhaps I'll just extend her lifespan anyway, regardless of what you think."

"You wouldn't dare," Morgan spluttered, utterly incredulous. "You can't do that. You have no right!"

Cici's eyes flashed emerald with ire, her accent growing thicker as her voice deepened to authority. "Morgana Illiana Rochefort Ashworth. I love you more than I have ever loved anyone or anything for thousands of thousands of years, across all the galaxies and realms both known and unknown. But right now, you forget yourself. You're overstepping, and your temerity regarding this woman tells me all I need to know. I have *every right*. Do not test me on this one. And do *not* forget who I am."

Morgan ducked her head, trying to suppress the shudder running down her spine and the sensation of a hand closing around her throat. Cici rarely wielded her power with Morgan, but when she did it was intense, overwhelming and calculated. She fought the urge to drop to her knees and beg mercy. "I'm sorry, Mistress. So very sorry. Forgive me, *please.*"

As quickly as it'd appeared, her boss's anger dissipated along with the aura of power. "Oh, enough with the submissive routine. I love it when everyone else does it, but when you do it, it makes me feel I've been an ogre. Just behave yourself."

"I will, Mistress. Sorry," she couldn't help adding.

La Morte used a forefinger to raise Morgan's chin. "Do you know how I know she means so much to you?" She raised an eyebrow, waiting for Morgan to respond, and when Morgan remained silent, she continued, "Your anger, your defiance. It is more telling than any of your words. You are one of the most serene people I know, Morgana. The only time you show anger is when you are afraid. And I know exactly what you are afraid of now."

Morgan slumped forward and buried her face in both hands. "I can't deal with it. I just can't. I think it would really kill me." She raised her head again, hoping to find an answer in Cici's expression.

"Then what about something more...permanent." A manicured nail tapped against Cici's chin. "I really do need someone to run The Americas, as you keep reminding me, and that would solve this issue of your loss."

"No!" She grasped at every excuse she could find, which weren't many. "She's not...capable. And, and...what about her very mortal mother who she would leave behind. You'd give Jane an eternity of grief."

Cici's sigh was long and exasperated. "Morgana. All of *Mes Minions* have lost family and had to live with grief for their long life. That's a poor reason. As for her being *capable*?" La Morte laughed. "Bethany Harris was a professional tennis player. You will need to do better if you think you'll change my mind. So why don't you cut the teenaged run-around and tell me exactly why you don't want me to give you one of the greatest things I can."

"What's that?" Morgan whispered.

"Eternal love."

She tried to fight the wave of tears and when she finally managed to articulate one of her fears, Morgan's voice broke. "Because what if she doesn't want me for an eternity?"

Cici's hands came to her cheeks, thumbs wiping at tears. "Oh my dearest love, it's not an eternally binding commitment. Simply an opportunity if you both want it." Her expression, though still soft, grew shrewd. "Which you both do. Besides, *I've* managed to put up with you for all these centuries. You're very loveable. In fact, you're such a catch, they should have you on the first lesbian dating television show."

Morgan coughed out a laugh. "Oh, wouldn't that go down fabulously? I can see it now. Some eligible woman asks me, 'So, what do you like, Morgan?'" She adopted a vacuous expression, twirling a piece of hair around her fingers. "Ohhhh, you know, this and that. Talking to people about death, teleporting around the world and into realms nobody has ever heard of, eating everything I can get my hands on, and being an emotional cripple."

La Morte snorted. "At least you're honest." Her expression turned pleading, an odd look on someone so powerful. "Speaking of honesty. You need to tell Jane about your past, tell her all of it, tell her every nitty gritty reason why you're so afraid. Then let *her* decide."

CHAPTER TWENTY-FOUR

When Morgan had texted first thing Saturday morning asking if Jane could come around to help her with something, she'd left home right away. A monstrous television was mounted to the wall in front of Morgan's couch. "You bought a TV!" Jane said, and immediately felt idiotic. Excellent observation, Captain Obvious.

"Yes, I did." Morgan ran a hand over the back of her neck and up to tug at her ear. "I had to do some work over the weekend and one of my clients was going on and on and on about a show called *Killing Eve*. And I thought it actually sounded rather interesting. Ergo, television purchased and I signed up for some streaming services that she recommended in order to get maximum cross-coverage. The salesman said this model was very good, and the image looked quite realistic in the display room, so I just said yes. I also bought a Blu-Ray DVD player. Apparently very few people use DVDs now, and I didn't know if I would or not so I decided to err on the side of maybe I will purchase DVDs and got a player."

Morgan's rambling explanation of her first television purchase was endearing, and Jane snuggled an arm around her waist for a brief side-on hug. "Look out, couch, you're going to get some serious usage." Wow. That could be taken so many ways. Ahem.

It seemed Morgan agreed, if the faint pink of her cheeks was any indication. She indicated the television with a sweeping arm. "I've already found about sixty programs I want to watch. How does anyone find time for it? Hence why I need your help. I don't know where to start." She cleared her throat. "I thought, maybe we could watch a program together?" Her expression was charmingly hopeful, her demeanor unusually shy.

"Sure. Do you need a hand setting anything up?"

Morgan arched a haughty brow at her. "Please. I was assembling computing devices before you were born."

Laughing, Jane held up both hands. "Got it, never get in the way of a woman and her electronics ego. Shall we break the seal on this new setup?"

"Sounds like a wonderful plan."

When Morgan moved to plonk down onto the couch, Jane stopped her. "You know, you need popcorn for TV binge sessions. It's a rule, sorry, even if it's barely past breakfast."

"Oh! Well that's a rule I can get behind."

Jane hung around the kitchen while Morgan microwaved popcorn and assembled a snack platter laden with cheese, crackers, deli meats, vegetables, chips and dips. There was a bashful wariness about her, as if she didn't quite know how to act or what to say. The only thing Jane could put it down to was uncertainty about this activity which was novel. Morgan carried a double armload of food and drinks to the living room, arranged everything on the coffee table then offered Jane the remote. "Here, you decide."

Jane held up both hands in refusal. "Oh no, no, no way. Your house, therefore you are queen of the television. And besides, this is a huge deal, Morgan. There is no way I am going to get in the way of the beginning of your love affair with Netflix."

"Okay then." She spun the remote over and over in her hand. "What kind of shows do *you* like?"

But Jane only shook her head.

Morgan flashed her the cutest helpless look. "I, um…found some documentaries before, about history, that I wanted to watch. See how accurate they are." She chanced a glance at Jane, who kept a deliberately neutral expression. "Um, and there's some dramas that I thought looked good too? Also comedy and movies, and uh…shit, I just don't know."

Jane decided to put her out of her misery. She slung an arm over the back of the couch and softly touched Morgan's shoulder. "What do you feel like watching? A series or a movie?"

Her relief was palpable. "I think a series would be good to start with?"

"Seriousness or laughing? Action? Drama?"

Morgan's smile was immediate. "Laughing. But action and drama are fine too."

"Okay. And romance or not?"

"I don't mind." She laughed. "Sorry, I'm not being very helpful, saying everything is okay by me."

Jane grinned. "No, you're not. But trust me on this one and I'll give you something you won't forget." Wow, more unintended innuendo. She cleared her throat. "Do you want reality or complete fiction?"

"Fiction first up. I want to see what's so great about this visual escapism."

"Got it." Jane placed her hand over Morgan's and helped her move through the Netflix menu. "Thank you for filling in my television questionnaire, Ms. Ashworth, if you'll just navigate to here…and then here, we can get you on your way."

Morgan laughed. "You sound like me, administering afterlife packages."

"Then maybe I should give it a shot sometime, if you're ever looking for a vacation from Minion-ing."

Morgan stiffened as if electrocuted. Her quick smile seemed forced. As did the brightness in her voice. "I don't think vacations would be the same without you."

The tone was slightly off and Jane couldn't figure out if her lame joke or alluding to more vacations had caused the mood shift. She took a chance it was the latter. "I don't think my vacations are going to be the same without you either."

Still smiling tightly, Morgan nestled one of the popcorn bowls between them, passed Jane a Sprite and changed the topic. "So, what are we watching?"

"*Jessica Jones*." Jane hoped the combination of action and dark humor would appeal. "Superheroes, villains, epic friendships and sisterly love, and a hot take-no-shit lesbian lawyer character. Win and win."

"Sounds like it."

By episode two, they'd moved so Morgan was sprawled on the couch with Jane leaning against her. By episode four, Morgan had declared herself a *Jessica Jones* fan and murmured that snuggling on the couch watching TV was indeed an excellent way to spend time.

Morgan ate most of the snack platter and popcorn and when she got antsy they ordered food and ate it while glued to the couch.

As the light outside faded, Jane asked reluctantly, "Do you have to leave?"

"Oh no, not until I've at least finished this season." Her forehead furrowed, lips moving silently before she said, "It'll be nearly ten p.m. by the time we're done, but Cici can wait." Morgan's eyes widened. "Are you okay to stay?"

"Yep, I'll be fine." She'd already texted her mom to let her know she might be late home to help her to bed and had received a *GOOD!* in response.

"Great. I can see why people like this so much. Jane, I think I'm hooked on television. My productivity is going to take a nosedive."

"Ah, so buying the TV was a mistake?"

Morgan's grin was wicked. "Absolutely not." She started the next episode.

After thirteen episodes back-to-back, broken only by bathroom breaks and food-delivery drivers, Jane felt like she'd aged a century from so much sitting. She rolled over so she wasn't using Morgan as a pillow and tried to massage the knots from her shoulders.

Morgan stretched, exposing a few inches of bare skin over her stomach. "Oh my God," she groaned as she raised arms over her head. "That was fabulous. And the ending? *I love you* as a code for *not* being mind-controlled?" Her eyes went wide. "And the way Jessica said it to Trish? I think my heart skipped a few beats."

"Yeah, it's one of my favorite TV moments of all time." She smiled, almost to herself. "So simple. Just...I love you." Jane froze. She'd never said those words aloud in front of Morgan, and though she was just talking about what the character said, *obviously*, saying those three words cracked something open inside of her.

I love you.

I love you.

I love...you.

Oh shit. Don't do it, Jane. Keep it to yourself. She clamped her lips together but her brain clearly had other ideas. Other not so smart ideas. "Morgan?"

"Mmm?" she responded, absently scrolling through the menu. "When can we start season two?"

"After work one night, or if you're desperate you can watch it by yourself." I love you...

"I'll wait until you're ready. I think it's better with you here."

"Mmm." Jane placed her hand over the remote. "Morgan. I want to sign."

Morgan went still. "Excuse me?"

"I'm ready to complete the afterlife package."

Recognition dawned in her eyes. "Really? But we're not done with your bucket list yet, we're leaving for Asia next week."

"I know, but I still want to."

"Why?" She set the remote down beside her and turned to face Jane. The hurt in her voice wasn't quite disguised when she asked, "Do you not want to finish the bucket list things with me? I mean I know it's only one more trip, but…"

Jane almost laughed at the absurdity of that question. If only Morgan knew. Jane frowned. That was just it, Morgan *didn't* know, and she maybe should. "No, that's not it at all. I want nothing more than to keep spending time with you. It's been the most wonderful time of my life, and not just the adventures and travel."

"Me too," Morgan agreed quietly.

"But it's too hard to keep pretending, to act like I don't…like we haven't shared intimate and exciting and fulfilling times together. Like this has all just been a deal we made, when in reality I think it grew into something so much more from our first adventure together." She swallowed. "Moments like this, quiet intimate times together are precious and I don't want to hide my feelings behind the charade of my bucket list anymore."

"Why not?" she asked, voice a tight whisper, as though she feared the answer.

Jane considered not answering, considered brushing the truth aside for a half-answer or even a lie. But she knew she couldn't do that. What did she have to lose by telling Morgan her deepest feelings? They'd already shared so much, and her heart was already halfway out the door, skipping merrily toward Morgan.

Jane bit her lower lip, terrified yet desperate to verbalize her admission. "Because I'm not built that way. I'm not the kind of person who can pretend one thing when I'm feeling something completely different. I've tried for the last who-knows-how-many-months and it's just too hard and too confusing. You've given me number four as a freebie too. So, it's only fair that you get your package completed and my signature."

"Four." The word was fearful, open and loving all in one, and Jane knew that Morgan knew exactly what she meant. She sucked in a breath. "That's—"

"Yes. Fall in love..."

The admission came out thin and wavering. Jane scrunched her eyes closed, drew in a long breath, then opened her eyes and tried again.

"I love you. I'm in love with you."

CHAPTER TWENTY-FIVE

No matter how many times Morgan turned the word over in her head, she couldn't quite make sense of it. Love. In love with. That phrase from Jane's lips was simultaneously the most terrifying and thrilling thing Morgan had ever heard.

She knew she should call Jane, explain why she'd disappeared, but she couldn't quite do it. Ugh, you are such a selfish shithead. Just because you're too chickenshit to face her doesn't mean that Jane shouldn't know at least that you're okay and haven't blinked out somewhere between here and who the hell knows where.

Compromise. She sent Jane a quick text. Yes, she was definitely a chickenshit. *It is the oldest line in the book but it's not you, I promise – I tell the truth always, remember?* Truth always, unless you counted omitting things. She tapped the top of the phone with her fingertips and after a brief internal debate decided that would do for a starting point. Send.

Three dots appeared almost immediately to let her know Jane was replying. Then the dots disappeared. Morgan stared at the screen, willing them to come back. Willing Jane to say something, anything. After a few minutes, Jane's message landed. *I believe you. But I thought we'd agreed in Connecticut to talk about this thing.*

They had. But how could she talk about it when she had no idea how to say what she needed to. Morgan flung her phone and heard it thud against the wall then fall to the floor.

The soft crackling hum of Cici arriving jolted Morgan from her near catatonia on the couch. La Morte leaned down, her face six inches from Morgan's. "Neat vodka, darling? Are we really doing this?"

Morgan waved the bottle cheerily. "If it's good enough for the Russians then it's good enough for me! And I'm using a glass, so it's classy. Glassy."

Cici's lips set in a thin line as she hmmed. "Morgana, this is not like you, and frankly I'm concerned about you."

Morgan coughed out a laugh. "Really? Why would you be concerned?"

Cici chose her words carefully. "Firstly because you didn't come to Aether this evening, and I sensed something amiss. And secondly, because the last time you were like this…" She didn't need to finish her sentence—Morgan knew exactly what she was talking about.

She grinned sloppily. "Don't be. Everything's dandy. I'm relaxing, just like you said I should when this whole mess began."

"This was not what I meant, and you're well aware of that." Cici arranged her flowing dress before settling beside Morgan. "So why don't you tell me why you're drinking yourself into a clichéd stupor?"

Morgan shrugged and nearly fell off the couch. "She told me that she's in love with me."

Cici had an excellent poker face, but her feelings broke free for a fraction of a second before she schooled her delight and hopefulness back to calm thoughtfulness. "I see. And what did you say in return?"

Morgan's face heated as she dragged her mind back a few hours to Jane's sweetly hopeful expression, the openness and trust she'd placed in Morgan by telling her something so real, so personal. And what had Morgan done? The most idiotic, bland and thoughtless thing in the world. She'd panicked. Then she'd forced a bright smile, kissed Jane on the cheek much the same way one would kiss a long-lost aunty, and said, "Thank you."

Thank you. So cringeworthy. And as if that wasn't bad enough, she'd slid backward on the couch, and made an absurd excuse that she had to do some work. The dual hurt and understanding in Jane's eyes was like sticking a knife into her own gut. But there was no other way. Being in love with Jane was one thing, something *she* was responsible for, a load she had to carry. But having Jane love her was unfathomable. It was too much.

Jane had kissed Morgan and left. Her kiss was less like a family member's and more like... Morgan pushed the image of the kiss away and cleared her throat. "Um, nothing much really." She poured another half glass and downed a quarter of it, shuddering as the liquor burned its way to her stomach.

"*Please* tell me you gathered her into your arms, told her you were madly, deeply in love with her too and then carried her off to your bed."

"Not exactly..." Another burning mouthful.

Cici held out a hand, fingers waggling. "Give that bottle to me, please. This is not the solution to your issues and clearly your mind is addled enough."

Morgan almost snarled as she held the bottle to her chest. She stood...okay, stumbled to her feet and backed a few feet away from Death.

Both of La Morte's hands came up in exasperation. "Fine. But when you wake with a hangover so bad you want to die, don't come crying to me. And when you've given yourself liver damage bad enough that you must find a new host body, I don't want to hear you complain about *adjustment*." It was an idle threat, the liver in this body would be unaffected, even if she pickled herself in one-hundred proof alcohol.

"Who cares? Mistress. La. Morte." Morgan spat out those last three words, crisply biting each one off. She was well aware that she was not only being petulant and insubordinate, but that she was slurring and swaying. "I'll just ruin this body and get another and then another and another ten or seventy or a thousand after that. And maybe if I change bodies enough I might lose that stupid fucking part of myself that makes me keep falling in love with mortal women. And maybe in five hundred years I'll forget about Jane Smith and learn to stop falling in love with people I can't keep." She drained the glass and left her apartment without saying goodbye.

She hadn't thought at all, just *left* and trusted her brain and body to take her somewhere, anywhere away from Cici and the grim reminder of the things she wanted and couldn't have. Morgan knew her subconscious would never let her teleport any place that was dangerous, so it came as no surprise that she found herself standing in the darkness on Jane's front porch. "Absolutely bloody perfect," Morgan muttered. Jane was light in the darkness, right?

Now that she'd moved away from Cici, the frustration and anger and sadness that had caused her to flee in the first place exited as suddenly as it'd flared. Morgan closed her eyes, inhaling deeply. She could sense Cici had left the earth realm, and not having to confront her own petulant, childish behavior was small relief. What the hell was wrong with her? She'd never been so bratty, not even after Hannah. Morgan flung her body through time and space, back to her apartment.

The bottle of vodka was still clutched in a white-knuckled grip. Excellent. She grabbed a bag of potato chips, a box of cereal and the packet of cheese from her fridge and threw herself down on the couch for some serious wallowing. All she managed was the reminder of sitting on her couch watching television with Jane and that this was the exact spot where Jane had so hopefully proclaimed her love.

Ugh. She slid from the couch to sit on the floor.

When she came back to consciousness, Morgan was aware of two things simultaneously. One, vodka was evil and not the cure-all she'd hoped. And two, she really wanted to die. The empty bottle had rolled away from the couch and there were chips and cereal remnants all over the floor. Perfect.

She took stock of herself. As far as she could tell, nothing was damaged. Though if you counted a horrendous hangover as damage then she was shattered into a million pieces. The conversation she'd had with Jane in the hotel after their *Valravn* day, where she'd almost kissed her for the first time, came flooding back. *"And I get hangovers."*

Morgan groaned. She tried to chase a thought hovering just out of her reach, but it was gone. All she knew was that pretty much the first coherent thought she'd had upon regaining consciousness was about Jane. Jane. She was always present. Even when Morgan was trying so hard to keep her away.

It took her half an hour before she felt controlled enough to move, and even then it was only from the floor beside the couch to the cold tile floor beside the toilet. Thankfully, she tended to recover fairly quickly from illness, including self-inflicted misery and after another hour of enjoying the coolness of her bathroom tiles, Morgan staggered to her feet, cleaned up her living room, showered, and prepared a late breakfast.

She considered taking a trip to Aether to apologize to Cici but immediately decided against it. She needed to talk to Jane first, unpack some of...whatever this was before throwing herself upon Cici's mercy.

She was midway through her third bowl of cereal and second pot of tea when the doorbell rang. The spoon froze midway to her mouth. The one person she most wanted, yet also was afraid, to see. Morgan left the bowl of cereal on the counter and rushed to her door, not even bothering with the peephole.

Jane's nervousness was clear, but she relaxed slightly when Morgan took her hand, pulled her close and kissed her lightly. She couldn't help herself. All Morgan wanted was to touch her, feel her warm comfort and return it. "Come in."

"Sorry to just appear like this but I called and texted you last night to apologize for springing the l-word on you, and again this morning and there was no response and I got worried you'd been hurt." Jane smiled sheepishly, as if aware of how unlikely that was.

"Ah. No, I'm fine. But thank you. And sorry if I worried you." She peered around. "I don't know where my phone is, so I've not received any messages." Morgan gestured vaguely. "It's somewhere within these four walls, that I know. Likely in a very safe spot. So safe I cannot recall where exactly."

"Oh, right, I get it." Jane reached for her, then seemed to reconsider. Her hand dropped back to her side. "Are you okay?"

Morgan made a see-sawing movement with her hand. "Yes and no. I'm sorry about yesterday. I kind of, well, as I'm sure you noticed, I panicked."

Jane smiled. "I did get that vibe, yeah. Do you want to talk about it?"

Talk. Could she talk honestly and openly about the thing Jane needed to know? A rhetorical question. Of course she *could*. But did she want to? Part of her said no, but only for the pain she knew it would cause. The surprising thing was that the yes part was easy. For some reason, she wanted Jane to know about this repulsive part of herself, the disgraceful selfish time in her life. But even as she knew she wanted to tell Jane, she couldn't understand why exactly.

She tucked her hands into her armpits. "I…Jane, I just need you to listen to me without judgment. Can you do that for me? Can you keep an open mind for me while you listen? If you want to be angry or disgusted after I tell you what I need to, then I accept that. But I would be grateful if you could just listen first."

Jane nodded, looking suddenly uneasy and as though she already regretted her agreement. But her voice remained steady. "Yes, I can do that."

"Thank you." Morgan gestured to the couch, and once they'd both settled, opened the floodgate, her hands twisting together with unusual nervousness as she spoke. "After Hannah died, I was a mess for a very long time. I even asked Cici to release me from this…life or whatever I exist in. I asked her every day, begged her even, and she refused every single time. She is privy to strands of time that I can't even imagine, she *knows* things and she told me the pain would ease if I could just hold on, if I could wait, then peace would come."

Morgan blew out a long breath. "Yet despite her refusal I tried to die, so many times. During the day I worked, administering contracts and filing packages, and then every night I put myself into dangerous situations. Bar fights, street brawls, boxing matches which was novel at the time given my gender, jumping from heights, trying to drown myself, weapons, fire, gas…you name it and I tried it. And if it didn't work, I used a, uh, tried and tested method to end myself. And every single time, Cici came to me. Picked up my broken body and carried me to a new host."

"Sweetheart…" Jane's voice trembled. She slid closer but as if afraid she might spook Morgan, she touched her with such caution it barely registered. "I'm so sorry. I can't even imagine that emotional hurt."

Morgan reached up to where Jane's hand rested tentatively upon her shoulder and squeezed it. "Eventually it hit me and I went to see a man they called The Butcher—highly unoriginal, but apt for a murderer. For a fee, he decapitated me with pleasure. And I *still* didn't die. Cici came, as she always had, within minutes of my should-have-been-death. I could still see, hear, taste and feel even though I was looking at my body lying three feet away. It was surreal, horrible, something I never wish to experience again in a million lifetimes."

"What happened?" Jane whispered, wiping under both eyes.

"What always happened when I was unable to move my hands. Cici took my Animus and moved it to a new host." Morgan inhaled a shuddering breath. "She is *so* very powerful, beyond imagination. And she told me, as she had done the hundreds of times prior that she'd rescued me from myself, that it would pass. One day. This feeling would pass and I would heal." She raised both hands, palms up as if surrendering all over again. "And I gave in. After that…incident, I realized that she wasn't going to let me go."

Jane's question was tight. "What did you do? How did you accept it, or move on?"

"It took some time until I found what I needed." Morgan picked up her teacup, drank a cool mouthful, then set the cup back down on the coffee table. "Irene Dawkins. Sixth of May, 1846. I had to administer a package for her. She was in her mid-thirties, with a broad Yorkshire accent and a penchant for feeding stray cats. She had tuberculosis, and seven months left, though she and her husband didn't know it would be so short. I'd been busy and had left her contract late, right on our minimum time frame for pre-death. She looked...she looked as if her skin didn't fit her, as though it'd continued to grow, leaving her flesh and bone behind to shrink. It creased and flopped loosely around her joints and face.

"She offered me tea and freshly-baked scones with cream that she'd churned that morning from cows she'd milked herself even though her hands were so weak she could barely manage it. She'd lived such a wonderful, fulfilled life. Her husband, Peter, sat beside her holding her free hand as she worked through the document. They discussed every aspect of it, and how best to match up their answers so they could be together in the afterlife. He wrote down her answers so that he could put in the exact same ones in his package. So in love, so...staunch despite everything.

"And when she was done, she handed me back the papers and told me to come out into the garden with her and smell her roses, her jasmine, her lilacs. And she stared up at me with these sickly watery blue eyes and she told me in this weak hoarse voice that she knew she was dying but she wasn't afraid because..." Morgan faltered. "Because love is eternal, even if you have to be apart for a little while until you can meet again."

"That's beautiful," Jane murmured.

"It was. It is. This woman, having had confirmation of her fading mortality, healed me. She seemed to know I was broken and she knew exactly what to say to help me at the time I needed it the most. It was miraculous in its simplicity. I try to remember to stop and smell the flowers, to appreciate the things I've been given because I've been given a great many things, but lately I think I've forgotten that. I think I've forgotten it right at the moment I needed to remember it."

"What do you mean?"

She drew in a slow breath. "I've learned over the years that the universe always gives you what you need. It might not do it when you think you need it, but it always provides." Morgan finally looked up and met Jane's eyes, instantly comforted by the empathy she found. "It's given me you. But I don't know what to do with it because I still don't feel ready, I still don't feel...deserving of it. What kind of person does what I did to myself, Jane? I'm not what you think I am. I'm weak, and cowardly and not what you deserve."

"What about what *you* deserve? You deserve to be loved, Morgan," she said forcefully, though the words broke around her tears. "And you deserve to love without fear or remorse or guilt. And I would love nothing more than to give you that, but if it's someone else who can or will then that's okay. It doesn't matter who or how, as long as you get the peace and love you're worthy of." Jane closed the final inches between them, reached up and pulled Morgan's face down and unhesitatingly kissed her.

She felt like she'd already kissed Jane a million times and hundreds of thousands of different ways. But this kiss was entirely new. It was as if Jane wanted to absorb Morgan's pain into herself to keep it away from Morgan. Her lips, soft as they were, moved with fevered urgency and she pressed herself to Morgan in a way that felt like she wanted them to fuse.

When they drew back from the kiss, Jane remained close, her hands stroking up and down her back. Morgan bowed her head to rest her forehead against Jane's. *The love you deserve*. But what about the love Jane deserved? Her lower jaw worked back and forth, trying to shake the words loose until eventually she spoke, her voice a rough whisper. "Cici offered me something, Jane. Something for me. Something for you."

CHAPTER TWENTY-SIX

Jane reached up to stroke the tight line of Morgan's jaw. "What did she offer you exactly?"

Morgan's expression turned inward, as if she was sorting through her thoughts and trying to decide which ones to put into words. She slid backward a few inches on the couch. "She offered to save you." Morgan clearly picked up on Jane's perplexed expression and went on, "That means she can extend your lifespan beyond your predetermined death date. It's a thing we may request for people whom we would like to live longer than they have been allocated."

"A save? I…see." And Jane did, in a slightly unclear, unfocused way. "So how does it work when you *save* someone? They still die, right?"

"Yes, of course. It's an extension rather than an indefinite delay. Let's say a person's death is in a year's time." She shot Jane an eyebrow-raised look and added a quick, "Purely hypothetical. If I choose to use a save, then I submit a request to Cici. She takes data compiled over the years, mean life expectancy of genders for certain geographic areas and that sort of thing. Then she usually adds a few years as a bonus of sorts for her employees, and for me, a few more on top of that. Then the *saved* person will live a life without health complications until the new date of their death, which I can choose to know or not."

Well, that sounded absolutely incredible. "Okay then, if she offered it for me, sign me up," she said, unable to keep the enthusiastic cheer from her voice. "I am totally ready to be saved."

There was a long, uncomfortably silent pause until Morgan's tight response. "I refused, Jane."

The admission was like a punch to the solar plexus, stealing the air from her body. It took a few moments for Jane to suck in enough breath to say, "Oh."

"Jane," Morgan pleaded softly, both hands reaching for her then pausing to hover ineffectually in the air as if Morgan just didn't know what to do.

"Okay, I get it. You don't think I'm worth it, worth using this magical save on and that's fine, we've only been friendly and…intimate for a short time. And now I've scared you off by telling you that I'm in love with you." Embarrassment wormed through her body, mixing with the confusion until Jane really felt like she couldn't breathe.

The grinding of Morgan's molars was audible. "It's not that."

"Then what is it?" The words hurt her, but she had to say them. "At least have the guts to be honest. I'm an adult, Morgan. I can handle truth. I'd prefer it to not knowing. All I can assume is that you just don't think I'm worth it."

Morgan's jaw tightened, her words came out clipped. "And that right there is the issue with making assumptions. I do think you're *worth it*. Worth using a save on, worth spending another fifty or sixty or seventy years with. And it is an enormous, heartbreaking problem."

"I don't see the problem here. Unless you're disgusted by the thought of being with me when I'm eighty and wrinkled, and you still look—" She swept her fingers up and down the image of Morgan in front of her. "…like that."

For the first time since she'd know her, Morgan looked angry, and it was like a bucket of ice water had been thrown on her. "Please," she spat out. "Do you honestly think I'm that shallow?"

Jane sighed. "I'm sorry. No, I don't but I can't think of any reason other than you don't want me."

"I do want you, badly, as I keep saying, and that's exactly the issue here," Morgan ground out. "I don't want to feel this way but I can't help myself." Morgan grimaced, her face contorting into something pained. "I'm in love with you and it's going to kill me, Jane. *Literally* kill me. I can't do it again, I can't stand it and when you're gone I *will* tell her I'm done with this job, this immortal life because I can't live another three centuries feeling like part of my insides are missing, like my whole body is an open festering wound. When I'm away from you, it hurts, even if it's only the shortest amount of time. Can you imagine what that will be like for me when you're gone?"

"Not really, no because I've not lived the life you have. But that doesn't mean I don't deserve a say in this, or an explanation that's more than just you're going to find it hard when I'm dead. Everyone finds loss hard, Morgan. In every relationship, someone dies first." She knew she was oversimplifying things and even dismissing Morgan's obvious pain.

"You want an explanation? Fine," Morgan spat out. When Jane recoiled at the venom in her voice, Morgan instantly apologized, reaching out to touch her hand. She inhaled slowly and released the breath even slower. "I did it once, used one of my saves to extend Hannah's life. We'd already been together for eight years and she was what I felt to be my once-in-a-lifetime love. She knew what I was and she didn't care. I loved her with that intense kind of love that feels like it's oxygen, and I couldn't think of being apart from her for even a day. So I did it, I asked Cici to give us more time even though I had an idea of what it would do to me when Hannah died."

Jane's frustration deflated like a pricked balloon. "Oh."

"Yes. *Oh*. But I didn't tell Hannah what I'd done because I didn't want her to think about things like her mortality. We spent another sixty-three years and eighty-seven days together, and every day I fell a little more in love with her until I honestly thought my heart could not get any fuller. And then the inevitable came closer, and for the years leading up to it I became obsessed with the date, trying to chase it away, trying to stall it, anything. I spent years focusing on the fact she was leaving me instead of enjoying those precious moments, and she couldn't understand why I'd become so frantic, so...strange. I wasted those years and then she was gone, and every single one of those days loving her came back to crush me."

Jane opened her mouth to say something, but no words would come out.

Morgan's inhalation was ragged. "And that's the problem with love that's like oxygen—when it's gone, you suffocate. I was strangled by my loss, Jane, and it's only recently that I've begun to feel like I can breathe again. And if I let you become my new oxygen..." She let the implication hang.

The way she'd put it made perfect sense, and all the things Morgan had alluded to about Hannah, about her past suddenly dropped into place. Everything she might say felt hollow and meaningless, and the only thing that felt even remotely adequate was, "I'm sorry."

Morgan's voice was tremulous. "I can't do it again. I can't handle the weight of loving you for so long and then having you leave me. I can't. It's already going to be hard enough, feeling as I do about you, but at least I might be able to keep living if it's not so long. I already need you like I need air, and I've hardly even…been with you. And if I feel this way about you now, more than I ever have with anyone, *including* Hannah who I thought was my soulmate, how am I supposed to survive being left again? I won't. I'm not strong enough, Jane. I'm not."

Jane slumped back on the couch. What could you say to something like that? To hear that you're *too* worth it. Her brain had registered Morgan's usage of the word love as it applied to her, but having heard it, she felt hollow. "When is it for me?" she asked, almost afraid to hear the answer.

But Morgan just shook her head. "You know I can't tell you." She dashed both hands under her eyes.

"It has to been soon-ish though. You just said it—*if it's not so long*. So my death is soon."

"Don't. You'll drive yourself insane." Morgan stood, and went to the kitchen where she pulled a paper napkin from a kitchen drawer and wiped her eyes and blew her nose.

Emotions whirling, Jane tried desperately to ground herself in something, to find something that would tell her exactly how she should feel in this moment. Because all she really felt was empty. Finally she managed to grasp an emotion. "This is fucking bullshit!" Anger, okay, not quite what she'd thought but why not roll with it for now. She cringed internally as if her mom was about to come zooming up out of the blue and slap her hand for swearing.

Morgan, halfway back from the kitchen, actually recoiled as if she'd hit her. "I—"

But Jane cut her off. She stood, closing the distance between them. "You want to know what I think? I think you're being selfish and one-sided. You've made this choice with no thoughts as to my feelings about it. You're a gutless coward."

Morgan's response was immediate. "How dare you." But the words lacked bite. "You have no idea what you're talking about."

"Maybe I don't. But I do know that loving people, no matter for how long, is always hard when you lose them. Twenty lifetimes wouldn't be enough with you, Morgan, and to deny me more time with you is cruel. Even if it's only a few more months." Jane straightened, placing a hand on her chest as if that would calm her racing heart and ragged breathing. "So, I call bullshit."

"You have *no* idea what it was like for me, Jane. I'm not a regular person, I don't experience things the way you do and the thought of living that again is horrifying."

"I can understand that, really I can, but you're taking a possibility that you're going to react as you did before and turning it into a certain thing. I'm not Hannah, I would never try to be, and I would never presume to tell you how you feel about Hannah. But—" Jane searched desperately for the right words. "This thing is not the same as what you had with her, and don't you think whatever is happening between us deserves to be given some time? Do you think the thought of me dying and leaving you doesn't hurt me as well? I mean I know I'm not going to live forever like you, but still..." She sucked in a quick breath. "I'm in love with you, you're in love with me as you've plainly admitted. I'm not asking for any promises, just say that you'll try. Just *try* and we'll see where that takes us."

Morgan's expressionless face was a mask, and her words were flat and forced. "I think you should go home." She backed away.

Jane followed. "Please don't. Please don't push me away. Please don't run away from me."

Morgan took another few steps backward. "I'm not, don't you see that?" She swallowed hard. "I'm running away from myself, because I can't stand feeling this way. Falling in love with you is unforgivable when I have nothing to offer you."

Unforgivable? What the actual...? Jane laughed dryly. "You're apologizing for having feelings for me? And nothing to offer me? I can't even begin to unpack that. Don't you get it, Morgan? You've made me live. You've given me everything I ever wanted and things that I didn't even realize I wanted until you showed them to me. I don't want to go back to the way things were. Dull. Stagnant. I can't."

"You have to. There's no other way. I can't do this." Morgan's voice cracked as she offered another, "I'm so sorry, Jane."

* * *

By Sunday afternoon, having spent all day inside her head running through the day before and all possible courses of action, Jane decided she had two choices. She could accept things as they were, accept

Morgan's word that she would never, could never love another human woman again. That would be the respectful thing. But it didn't feel like the right thing.

Or…she could try to show Morgan exactly how things could be. Show her what she could give her, what possibility and what intense love she could fill Morgan with to carry her beyond Jane's mortal life. Charging ahead regardless of Morgan's protests and explanations because Jane thought she knew better would be the disrespectful thing to do, the selfish thing. But *was* it selfish or disrespectful if it could give Morgan something beyond what she thought she'd ever have? If she could pry open Morgan's armor and show her that she would soothe her wounds rather than making new ones, then surely that was better. Because weren't two people who were in love a perfect starting point for something incredible?

Jane laughed sardonically. Sure, in a normal world which Morgan didn't seem to inhabit.

This was an impossible situation with no good solution and really, no matter what she did, it couldn't get any worse. But there *was* a chance it might get better. Jane shot a quick text to her mom, out having dinner and a movie with friends, then grabbed her keys.

On the drive to Morgan's, Jane tried out and promptly discarded various platitudes.

"Hey, let's just see where this goes."

"Love really can conquer everything!"

"I don't need a save, I just need you."

The door opened within a second of Jane pressing the doorbell, but it was not Morgan who opened it. Jane was greeted by an ethereally beautiful woman with the most startling green eyes. Hair a few shades off black fell in waves to her shoulders, brushing the neckline of a dress that looked like it cost more than what Jane earned in three months.

The woman's posture was relaxed yet absolutely confident and the moment she saw Jane, her full ruby-red lips lifted into a smile. She exhaled, as if relieved. "Ah, at last," the woman said, her voice low, melodic and with a sensuous European accent. She reached for Jane's hand and pressed a soft kiss to the back of it. "It is a pleasure to finally meet you, Jane. I'm Death but you, my darling, may call me Cici."

CHAPTER TWENTY-SEVEN

Morgan rubbed the back of her neck, trying to massage away the tension before making the trip home from Tennessee. Alanna was going to have a field day when she came next week, and Morgan wondered if her masseuse would accept love as the reason for all the knots in her body. It was a laughable notion, but the truth.

A day of distance from Jane had brought some clarity but no comfort. She now knew a handful of things for certain. She knew she shouldn't have sent Jane away after she had come to ensure Morgan was all right. But having her nearby overthrew every ounce of her rationality and ability to think. She knew she'd hurt Jane and wanted to apologize and tell her that everything would be fine. But that was a lie.

She also knew unequivocally that she loved Jane, was in love with her. And Jane was in love with her. But none of these facts had brought clear answers. She should have been leaping for joy—the first hurdle of *I love you and you love me* had been cleared, but all it left were miles of obstacles.

Yet the more she tried to remain steadfast in her conviction, the more she wavered. *Was* this new love enough to overcome centuries of hurt and wariness? *Could* she set aside deep seated, reactionary fears and throw herself into a relationship again? Am I ready for that, she wondered? Do I even want it? Can I do it? Every cell in her body screamed yes and no simultaneously.

The moment she arrived in her kitchen, she heard voices in the living room. Cici—not entirely unexpected. Jane—not at all expected. Morgan remained still and quiet, just listening. Cici's laughter was high pitched and genuine as Jane recounted the unfortunate events of Morgan's first roller coaster ride.

"She vomited? In public?" Another loud peal of laughter. "Oh, poor Morgana. Or rather, poor Morgana's ego. You know, she once *insisted* on trying a new drink Anne Bonny's pirate crew had concocted. She vomited for *days*. That is, once she stopped hallucin—"

"Hello," Morgan interrupted the embarrassing story about her one and only encounter with pirate liquor. Those were horrendous days which she would rather forget.

"Morgana," Cici purred as if she'd only just realized Morgan was nearby. "We were just talking about you. I hope you don't mind but I was here waiting for you and let Jane in." Her expression was far too innocent, which meant Cici had sensed Jane would go to Morgan's and made the trip from Aether to sit and wait for her. Sneaky.

"I know. I heard you. And of course I don't mind." She crossed quickly to her couch where the two women sat, leaning down to kiss Cici's cheek. She debated for the briefest of moments before turning her attention to Jane, who wore an expression of wariness mixed with lingering enjoyment. Too physically and mentally exhausted to control herself or think of the consequences and yet another mixed signal, Morgan bent to kiss her softly and felt the rightness the moment their lips brushed. "Hello," she murmured.

Jane's wariness melted away. "Hey yourself."

Cici offered Morgan a knowing look then leaned back, an arm lying along the back of the couch, her posture screaming satisfaction and pleasure. Morgan surmised that despite her initial reluctance to meet Cici, Jane seemed relaxed. Morgan confirmed they were comfortable then excused herself back to the kitchen. As she poured a can of Guinness into a pint glass, she could hear Jane and Cici resume their amused conversation.

"Does anyone need anything to eat or drink?" she called. At the double no thank you, Morgan left them to their conversation and turned her attention back to the fridge where in between large gulps of beer she ate a container of cold Chinese food, then a four-slice sandwich of bread hastily slathered with peanut butter and honey.

The moment Morgan returned to the living room, Cici stretched, a vision of almost feline contentment. "Well, I'd best be off. I have some people to do, things to see." With a lascivious wink, she rose gracefully and held out her hand to Jane. When Jane stood and took her hand, Cici pulled her forward, right into her personal space. Interesting. "Jane," Cici purred. "It was marvelous to finally meet you. I do hope we can chat again soon."

Jane ducked her head shyly. "Me too."

Cici swept her up in an embrace, which Jane returned without hesitation. Doubly interesting. Cici lowered her head to whisper in Jane's ear, eliciting a nod, before Cici released her and turned her attention to Morgan. "Walk me to the door, Morgana."

Jane's quick nod in response to Morgan's eyebrow-raised silent question indicated she'd be fine for a few minutes. Morgan guided Cici to the entryway where they would have privacy. She held Cici's camelhair coat so she could slip into it. "Enjoy your visit?"

One of Cici's dark brows flicked upward. "I certainly did. It was very…enlightening."

"Mmm." There was no point in digging any further when she had a guest. This was a conversation for later. Soon later.

"Take care of her, and yourself, darling." She presented her cheek for a kiss, which Morgan gave and then with a dazzling smile, La Morte disappeared.

Two things to process. Firstly—Jane had come to her apartment to see her despite the fact Morgan had been acting like a person even *she* didn't like. And secondly—Cici La Morte did not touch or allow others to touch her readily. Even some of her Minions, whom she'd known for centuries and who were bonded to her weren't granted the privilege. Yet there she was with Jane on their first meeting, acting as if they were bosom buddies.

Morgan let out a breath and strolled back to Jane standing at the French doors, looking out over the view. "You're here," Morgan said dumbly.

Jane turned and offered a smile. "Yes, I'm here."

"Did you enjoy your brush with Death?"

She laughed, and the sound was like a warm embrace Morgan wanted to wrap herself up in. "Actually I did, very much. It was intriguing. And fun."

"I told you she was easy to talk to."

"Yes you did, but I still couldn't quite get over the image in my head. She is nothing like I'd thought."

234 E. J. Noyes

"I'd imagine not." She stepped closer, debated kissing Jane again and thought the better of it. First, talking. Then, maybe kissing. "I really didn't expect to see you here tonight." After a pause Morgan added quietly, "Or anytime soon, really."

"I'm persistent. And something occurred to me today, well many things really but this thing in particular."

"What's that?"

"I didn't complete my afterlife contract the other night."

"No you didn't. And you want to do it now?"

Jane's smile was sly. "No. I want one more thing from you. You said it yourself, you wanted to be sure that I was completely satisfied with number twelve. And I have to say," she mused. "I'm not really. Not yet."

The tight knot in Morgan's stomach unraveled a fraction. "Ah. I see."

"If you're agreeable that is."

Saying yes was *such* a bad idea but saying no didn't feel like an option. Silently, Morgan nodded.

"Okay," Jane breathed, her shoulders dropping. "Just one more and then I'll do what you want and stay away from you outside of work, and we can forget about this thing between us."

Why couldn't Jane see that *wasn't* what she wanted? Not at all. She was doing this for both of them. Morgan started backing toward her bathroom. "Do you mind if I shower first? I've been everywhere from Boise to Bogotá today."

"Go ahead. If you don't mind me watching you…"

"That doesn't sound nearly as fun as you joining me."

"Oh it might be," Jane murmured. "And it's my bucket list, remember?"

Jane stood by the shower as Morgan began to undress, and she made no secret of her interest. Morgan took her time, sliding her skirt down her legs and unbuttoning one slow button of her blouse at a time, though she wanted to tear her clothes off and pull Jane to the bathroom floor. She turned slightly and caught sight of herself in the mirror.

The reflection made her pause and she clenched her teeth in dismay as the panic rose. Not now, not here with Jane. But she couldn't look away, couldn't stop the slow spiral of anxiety. Morgan traced the shape of her own body with her eyes, trying desperately to ground herself again. Yet the more she stared, the greater her disquiet became until it felt like a beast clawing at her breast.

The sound of the shower running, and Jane's quiet, "Morgan? Are you ready?" snapped her from her intense panicked self-scrutiny.

"Yes, I am," she said, her earlier idea of performing a striptease forgotten. She slipped out of the last of her clothes and stepped into the shower. Jane leaned against the wall, eyes roaming slowly over Morgan's body. Every now and then, through the steamed-up glass, she could see Jane smile and make a swiping motion, and each time Morgan complied and cleared the glass with her palm.

Slowly the discomfort ebbed, helped in part by Jane's unabashed gaze sliding with lazy pleasure over her body, until the earlier anxiety faded and was replaced by an unbearable desperation for Jane's naked body. She shut off the water and before she could grab her towel, Jane was in front of her, holding it. "Let me," she murmured. "Stand on the mat, hands on the wall, face forward."

Arms braced against the wall, she let Jane towel the water from her skin. The towel slid over her in long, slow strokes—the only thing touching Morgan—and she wished with all her being that Jane would touch her, really touch her.

"Spread your legs," Jane said against her ear, voice low and rough.

Morgan did as she was told. Her fingers curled and straightened against the cold tile seeking, and failing to find, something to grasp. The towel moved down her back, over her ass until Jane had to kneel to dry her calves. Morgan closed her eyes. If she kept them open, watched Jane kneeling between her legs, she would lose all control. As it was, the denial and anticipation had her nerves sparking and the excitement curling through her depths was growing dangerous.

Jane on the other hand, seemed to have infinite control. Still without skin-to-skin contact she drew the towel up the inside of first one thigh then the other, each time stopping just short of where Morgan most wanted her to touch. After an eternity, she heard Jane stand and murmur, "There, all dry."

Morgan opened her eyes. "Is this where I make a silly joke about how I am actually rather *wet*?"

Jane adopted a mock-surprised look, though the expression was somewhat weakened by the desire burning in her eyes. "Are you?"

"I think you already know I am."

Then they were kissing, a frantic clash of lips and tongue as they moved toward her bedroom. But it was too slow, too torturous, and Morgan bent to pick Jane up and whisk her to the bed, until Jane's soothing hands and her whispered, "Wait…just wait," made her pause and take a breath. Two sets of hands found synchronicity to remove

Jane's clothes along the way and they landed on the bed, both naked, with Morgan on her back and Jane pressed full length on top of her.

Morgan tried to roll them over so she could be on top but Jane resisted, holding firm. She kissed Morgan with a delicate, barely-there brush of lips. "Oh no. I think it's my turn to be in charge." Jane slid a hand along Morgan's side, continuing up her arm until she grasped a wrist and held it pinned to the bed. Her eyes were molten with desire. "Can you let me be in charge? Can you let me make love to you?"

The nuance was clear. Morgan propped herself up on her free elbow. "Is that what you want? To control me?"

Jane's eyes widened. "No, never. I just want you to let go."

"I can let go," Morgan asserted, though she knew it sounded more petulant than confident.

"Mmm. *Maybe* you can." Jane leaned down, deliberately keeping herself from touching Morgan. "But I think you might need a little help." She kissed the base of Morgan's throat, licked along her collarbone.

Morgan arched her body up, offering herself. But Jane refused. Morgan tried to pull her down and again, was deftly outmaneuvered. "Not fair," she complained.

"It's plenty fair. Stay there." Jane rolled from the bed and crossed the bedroom to the hat stand in the corner where Morgan draped her scarves.

And suddenly Morgan understood. Jane was going to give her no choice but to relinquish control. The thought was thrilling, terrifying and incredibly arousing. She sat up, watching as Jane's feminine hands traced over Morgan's scarves of silk, satin and wool. After a minute's deliberation, she selected a single silk scarf of Tyrian purple and brought it back to the bed, drawing it between her hands. "Do you trust me?"

"Yes," Morgan breathed, meaning it with every cell in her body. When she'd realized Jane was going to use her scarves, she had expected Jane to bind both hands and feet to the bed. But the single scarf implied she would be free to move *something*. What would it be?

Jane's face softened, as if Morgan's trust meant something precious to her. "You only need to tell me, and I'll take it off and the game is over, okay?"

Morgan nodded, her throat suddenly closing around her words. She didn't want to say no, but she wasn't sure she knew how to say yes to this. To giving over all her control, leaving herself completely vulnerable. When was the last time she felt truly vulnerable? Perhaps never.

Jane folded the scarf over and over and then kneeled behind Morgan. She placed the folded scarf over Morgan's eyes and tied it behind her head. Ah. The effect was instantaneous. Not total dark blindness, but simply a dulling of her sight which negated any fear. It was as if Jane knew exactly how far to take their play.

Jane's hands brushed over her shoulders. Lips on her neck made her shudder. She could feel Jane's breasts against her back, light breath whispering over her skin. "You wore this scarf the day you told me who you were."

"I did?" She turned her head, seeking Jane and finding nothing. "Is covering my eyes with it a payback of some sort?"

Jane laughed softly. "Oh no, anything but. I chose this one because I love the way it looks on you."

"Well then I'll try to remember to wear it more often." A promise. Did she have any right to offer such a thing?

"Mm, good." More light kisses, this time over the back of her shoulders. "Lie down and get comfortable."

Morgan felt the bed shift, hands guiding her to lie flat on her back. She stretched her legs out as her hands searched blindly for Jane, again finding nothing.

"Hands on the bed." It was a gentle command, but a command nonetheless. "If you touch me before I say you can, the game is over and I'm going to go home."

"Understood." She paused a beat. "What about with my feet?" she asked facetiously.

"Morgan…" Jane's no-nonsense tone was stomach-curlingly sexy.

"Okay, okay. Sorry." Morgan curled her hands in the sheets.

A long slow breath near her ear. "Where to start?" Jane murmured. A finger glided up Morgan's forearm, the touch a whisper on her skin. "Here?" The finger moved higher, over her bicep and up to trace the line of her collarbone. "Or here?"

The light touch somehow stole Morgan's words and all she could do was nod. She couldn't get the words out that she just wanted to be touched anywhere as long as Jane was touching her. A second set of fingers joined in, making twin paths down Morgan's chest to brush over her breasts. A soft, teasing pinch of her nipples rippled excitement through her stomach. Jane's hands stroked gently, first her breasts, then down her stomach and over her thighs.

She felt Jane's breath against her face a moment before she kissed her. "I think you like it," Jane murmured against her mouth. "Being helpless like this. Having someone in charge for once. Letting me control your pleasure."

Control.

She so rarely relinquished it, in any aspect of her life. Yet here she was, giving it willingly to Jane. The game was an illusion of helplessness, with the safety of trust—Jane's control was firm, at the same time there was no abuse of power. Jane had stripped her down to her base self, left her completely vulnerable yet safe. Along with Morgan's knowing she could stop the game at any time, Jane's tenderness was trust. Her caresses were soft, not rough, her mouth warm and wet as it mapped Morgan's skin.

"Do you like this?" Hot lips around her nipple, a grazing of teeth, a touch of tongue.

Morgan clenched the sheet in tight fists and managed a choked, "Yes."

The mouth moved to her other nipple, repeating the same exquisite touch of lips, teeth, tongue. "And this?"

"Yes."

A light touch on her stomach, the flat of palm gliding down over her belly button until the hand nestled between her legs. Morgan lifted her hips, seeking firm pressure and finding only the softest touch. A single stroke over her clit, then the touch withdrew and Morgan was smothered by a sense of nothingness. She knew Jane was still in the room, still nearby, but the absence of her touch was devastating. She raised herself up onto her elbows. "Jane?" Morgan asked, voice hoarse with need and an edge of panic.

"I'm here," came the quiet reply. "I'm just…looking. You are so fucking beautiful."

Morgan could imagine her, the heat in her gaze, the flush on her skin. She wanted to see it, and the desire to tear the silk from her eyes and declare the game over so she could free her hands from their voluntary inaction was so strong she actually raised her hands off the bed a few inches to do just that.

No word from Jane, just the quiet sound of her breathing. And the sound was enough to make Morgan recall the way Jane's breath had caught when she'd slid her fingers through Morgan's heat. The sound Jane made, part moan, part groan and all delighted when she'd stroked Morgan's clit. And Morgan recalled the way *her* nerves seemed to catch fire, and how every sense strained to discover what would come next—the arousal, the delight, the spiraling pleasure of *not knowing* what would follow in the wake of Jane's calculated touch.

Not knowing.

Without warning, Morgan was struck by the horrible sensation of not knowing who she was. That anxiety rose, threatening to choke her and she turned her head in the direction she'd heard Jane's voice. "What…what do you see? What do I look like?"

Jane inhaled sharply, and when she finally spoke an eternity later it was in a low, husky voice. "You look—" An exhalation. "Sexy. Needy. So beautiful. I see a woman who's struggling to let go, struggling to let me be in control but isn't fighting me. I see a woman desperate to climax. Morgan, I see something incredible."

Morgan relaxed her grip on the sheets, lowered herself back down to the bed and surrendered. The weight on the bed shifted and breath whispered over Morgan's neck. "You're flushed. Your hair is messy, disheveled and that golden color it shines when the light hits it just right."

A kiss was pressed just under Morgan's ear and she jumped at the unexpected touch. More kisses followed, making a pilgrimage to Morgan's mouth and stopping just at the edge. A light tongue traced her lower lip. Morgan turned her head and found Jane's lips for a long, heated kiss. Her hands tangled tighter in the sheets as they kissed and the whole time Jane's fingers were busy. Jane's breathing was ragged and shallow. "Your skin is shiny and slippery with sweat…"

The fingers brushed over one nipple then the other, gently pinching and sending shivers of pleasure rippling through her. Then Jane moved until she was pressed against the side of Morgan's thigh, the heat of her arousal evident on Morgan's skin. "Your nipples are tight, hard. A perfect color, like rose pink or something." She laughed quietly. "Sorry, that's not a sexy description of nipples. I sound like I'm trying to write a Harlequin romance."

"It's very sexy," Morgan countered instantly. "Can you keep touching them?" The question came out surprisingly tentatively.

Hands closed over both of her breasts, cupping them as Jane's fingers teased softly at her nipples. Morgan clutched the sheets, using the leverage to push herself upward into Jane's touch. Her senses were razor sharp. Every sensation—touch, sound, scent and even taste were amplified. She could hear the rapid thud of her heartbeat in her ears, feel air moving across her skin.

The unknown, Jane's touches and her words all combined to arouse her in a way she'd never felt before. It was consuming and maddening all at once. A soft kiss on one, then the other breast. Jane exhaled, the sensation of air gliding over Morgan's breasts. "Your muscles are tight and get tighter every time I touch you. Your knuckles are white, hands gripping the sheets. You have gooseflesh all over your body." Jane paused, swallowed. "Morgan. You're exquisite. I don't really know what to say, how to describe it."

But Jane *had* described it, described *her* with such detail that she could see herself, know herself. And the knowing made the anxiety melt away to be replaced by certainty. "Thank you," she breathed. Not for the compliments, but for the gift of seeing herself without eyes. For seeing herself through another's eyes.

Jane's mouth closed around her nipple, sucking and biting as her hand roamed Morgan's torso to lightly stroke her skin. Fingers slid briefly through her pubic hair then continued down to stroke her. Just once, a single pass through her heat and then the touch withdrew again. Groaning with desperation, Morgan squirmed, seeking Jane and failing to find her.

Morgan felt Jane's tongue, her lips, her teeth as she explored skin and heat. "You're so wet, swollen." Jane's breath blew over Morgan's flesh. "You look like you want me to fuck you."

"I do. Please," she begged, straining upward until she felt the muscle and tendon in her hands scream for her to let go. But there was nothing. No touch. No words. Again, just the sound of Jane's breathing, ragged and unsteady now. And suddenly Morgan truly understood. Everything before this had been nothing more than a test. But would she pass?

She dropped back to the bed, released her hold on the covers and placed her palms flat on the bed. She offered herself to Jane, giving her body in silent supplication. Barely a heartbeat passed before heat engulfed her. The sensation of Jane's tongue making slow passes through her folds had Morgan on the verge of hyperventilating. Without her sight, she was hyper-focused on the touch, the sounds, the scents. Jane licked her clit as she lightly teased her entrance, then with agonizing slowness entered her with a single finger.

How could something Jane had done many times already feel so entirely new? She thrust gently, and the whole time she worked her with that torturous, teasing, tantalizing mouth.

"Jane. *Please.*"

The finger and tongue stilled. "Please what, baby?"

But Morgan didn't even know what she was asking. Please let me touch you? Please let me come? Please, just...*please*. She made an indistinguishable sound, part mewling cry, part desperate begging. Another brief moment of panic smothered her. Then gone again as Jane shifted to bring skin to skin as she moved up Morgan's body, pausing to kiss or touch wherever she pleased. A brush of fingertips along Morgan's cheekbone and the edge of the fabric. "Do you want me to take this off?"

Morgan swallowed the lump in her throat, body straining almost unconsciously upward. She wasn't sure what she wanted, just that she *wanted*. She'd never felt so completely, utterly undone before. Nor so desperate. "I want to see you, but I…"

And as if Jane understood what she was saying without words, she murmured, "You can see me anytime. I want you to *feel* me now." She straddled Morgan's thigh, sliding up until her own thigh nestled against Morgan's wetness.

"I do. I can feel you," Morgan choked out. "Oh God." She lifted herself, pressing her thigh more firmly between Jane's legs.

Jane's low moan went straight to her core. She rocked slowly against Morgan's leg, a soft panting exhalation on every back and forth. Fingers danced on her skin, slid through her wetness then inside her again. Jane thrust slowly, languorously stroking every millimeter of her. A slow, soft touch on her clit. Hot mouth on her neck, her ear, her lips. And Jane kept stroking, kept rocking, kept…knowing.

Morgan's arousal peaked suddenly, a white-hot ball spreading outward, and in the space between one thrust and the next she let go. As she climaxed, the heat moved from her belly, spreading down her legs right to her toes. Morgan's body arched like a bow, her grip on the sheets so tight she feared she might tear the material. Jane's low hum of approval sent another thrill through her core and it was all she could do to hold on as wave after wave of pleasure pulled her under.

When she could finally think and speak, she managed, "Can you take the blindfold off now? Please. Please." The words choked out with urgency and she almost raised her hands to do it herself until she realized that might break the rules and mean Jane wouldn't let her do what she most wanted to.

The fabric fell away. Jane's beauty was a punch in the gut, and Morgan had the sensation that she'd never truly seen her until this moment. Jane moved quickly to straddle her hips. "Touch me," she said, and despite her demand, there was an edge of desperation to the words. "Put your hands on me, Morgan."

She sat up, curling an arm around Jane's waist to pull her close. The kiss was furious, possessive and hungry. A moment of uncertainty, of not knowing what to do or where to begin. Then Jane, precious, knowing Jane, kissed her as she lifted herself slightly from Morgan's lap. She guided Morgan's hand between her thighs, against her slick folds and ground herself in a steady rhythm.

Jane kept an arm slung around her shoulders, fingers tangling tightly in Morgan's hair. Her breathing was loud and erratic, low gasping moans and sharp exhalations as Morgan's fingers danced over Jane's clit. Jane gripped a tight fist of hair and pulled Morgan's head back to feast on the skin of her neck as Morgan slid into her heat.

Skin slipped and slid. Jane moved until their bodies pressed close, shifting her legs until she settled fully in Morgan's lap with legs wrapped tightly around her waist. She held on around Morgan's shoulders, face buried in the skin of her neck as her fingers moved restlessly over Morgan's skin. Morgan's fingers were not restless, they were steady and unerring.

Jane tightened around her, rocking forward as her breathing hitched and she shuddered through her climax, a low moan vibrating against Morgan's neck. Jane's breathing slowed and steadied, her mouth still pressed to Morgan's skin as she came down from her release. She kissed her way along Morgan's shoulder and whispered, "I love you."

The words were so quiet that Jane probably thought she wouldn't hear them, but Morgan did and those three words were like a jolt. Morgan felt like they were fused. And she felt like *herself*, perhaps for the first time in centuries. A small sob burst out before she even realized it was happening.

Jane started, shifting back slightly. "What is it?" She eased herself from Morgan's fingers, but remained on her lap.

"I'm sorry." She tried to push the emotion aside, to take them back into the moment but instead of calming herself, all she managed was to make herself sob even louder. "I'm sorry," she repeated, bringing a hand up to cover her face. But the hand wasn't enough. She was still too exposed, and she buried her face in the curve where Jane's neck met her shoulder.

Jane stroked her back with soft rhythmic movements. "You don't need to apologize. Do you want to talk about it?" Jane moved back carefully and pulled Morgan's head from her shoulder. Jane gently wiped the tears then kissed each cheek, Morgan's forehead, and finally her lips with such slow tenderness that Morgan settled.

"I just—" Morgan inhaled a shaky breath. "Do you remember when you asked me what it's like to move into new physical bodies and I said it was no big deal?"

"Yes, I remember that."

"I mean, it isn't really but at the same time it's...like sometimes I don't feel like myself. Not often," she added quickly. "But every now and then I'll see my reflection or some part of my body, and I just don't know who I am. And it's like I've lost myself and there's no real way to find myself again except to wait until the feeling passes."

Jane stroked her face gently, fingertips lingering on her jaw. "Oh, Morgan. I can't even imagine how that must feel."

"Awful." She captured Jane's hand, kissed her palm, each fingertip before twining their fingers together. "But I always feel like you see *me*, not just this body I happen to inhabit at the moment and which could change at any time. And that feels so incredible, I can't even describe it." She bit back another sob. "You help me feel like myself."

"I do see you, Morgan. I see your kindness, your humanity, your generosity, your humor...and so much more." Jane smiled. "I mean don't get me wrong, I like this body very much but if you were to inhabit a new one I would love that one just as much because you're inside it."

Blinking to clear more threatening tears, Morgan got out a hoarse, "Thank you."

Jane studied her face intently. "For what?"

"Tonight. For somehow knowing what I needed." She shrugged, feeling so suddenly emotionally spent that she didn't know how to say what she most wanted to. Thank you for helping me let go of a part of myself. Thank you for seeing me.

Jane's gaze softened as if she'd read something in Morgan's expression, and she murmured, "See? You can let go." Jane kissed her softly and pulled her close so Morgan was once against nestled in the comforting softness of Jane's neck.

Morgan had no idea if Jane truly understood the depth of what she'd done. *Let go.* Maybe, just maybe, if Morgan could let go of one thing at a time, leave it to fall away without being picked up, then there would be nothing between them but love and trust. And hopefully that would be enough to keep her alive when Jane left her. If she could only be brave enough to say yes.

CHAPTER TWENTY-EIGHT

When she and Cici had said goodbye at Morgan's apartment, Cici had whispered in Jane's ear that if she ever needed her, Jane should just think about her and ask her to appear. Well, Jane really needed Death now. She closed her eyes tightly and clenched her fists as if that might make the signal send better to wherever Cici La Morte might be. She had no idea exactly what thought she was supposed to use so she tried imagining Cici, then thinking her name and then after thirty seconds of weirdness she whispered loudly, "Cici La Morte, I need you!"

Nothing.

Jane tried again and again, changing her intonation, her words and even holding her arms out like an antenna, but still nothing happened except embarrassment. Sighing, and feeling like a complete idiot, she dropped back onto the couch, snugged her headphones over her ears, grabbed the game controller and started killing demons. She'd almost finished the level boss when movement in her periphery made her drop the controller. And she was dead. In the game. Jane yanked off her headset and squeaked out her hello.

"Hello, Jane." Cici La Morte's smile was both brilliant and contrite. "I apologize for not getting here sooner, but I was caught up and it didn't seem as if you were in imminent danger." She delicately drew her thumb around the outside of her lower lip. "I do hope I'm not interrupting anything?"

"Um, no problem. Thanks for coming. And no, you're not interrupting at all. I was just, um…relaxing." Jane hastily cleared away some magazines, her dinner plate and the dropped PS4 controller.

"Mmm, very good. Relaxation, I approve of. So many people just don't take the time to enjoy the things they have. A pity, and something I believe shortens already too-short lifespans." Cici glanced at the television where Jane's character lay slain among the hellscape, the image making the edge of her mouth twitch. After a few long moments of studying the screen, Cici murmured, "A fascinating likeness. Researching Morgana's work?"

Jane stared at the hulking horned hellbeast looming over its hemorrhaging victim. "Really?"

Cici's Mona-Lisa smile made it impossible to know if she was being truthful or simply teasing Jane. She said nothing more, leaving Jane to pick up the conversation.

"I just enjoy killing pretend demons, that's all," she finally said, aware of how foolish it sounded. At Morgan's, Jane had relaxed immediately with Cici, but now she was in her house she felt awkward.

"Ah, very well then. Everyone needs hobbies. I actually rather enjoy knitting myself."

Death. Knitting. "How did you find me?" Jane asked, knowing it was a stupid question to ask someone who Morgan had said was so in tune with the world.

The smile turned mischievous as Cici held up both hands, fingers twinkling. "Touch. Once I've touched someone I'm linked to them and can find them anywhere instantly. Anyone I haven't touched takes slightly longer."

"Oh, right." She indicated toward the kitchen. "Can I offer you something to drink?"

"No I'm fine, but thank you." Cici peered around the living room. "This is a lovely house. It has a very good feeling to it." She brought her focus back to Jane, a soft smile playing about her lips. "Happiness lives in here."

Jane's discomfort fell away at the sentiment. "Yes, it does."

"I can feel why Morgana enjoys it here. Being surrounded by the love you and your mother share would be like receiving a turbo boost for her." Cici's eyes went toward the closed door of her mother's bedroom. "And how is Pamela?" The way she asked was like she was inquiring after an old friend.

"She's very well. Thank you for asking." After a beat she felt compelled to clarify, "She's in her room. She got a new book she can't put down, and apparently I make too much noise when I'm gaming for her to concentrate out here."

"I can imagine how reading and gaming in the same space would not work. And I'm pleased to hear she's well," Cici said, the words laced with sincerity. "Now, how can I help?"

Suddenly the reason felt silly and the words stuttered out of her. "I was just wondering, um, Morgan mentioned something about a save thing that you can do?"

Cici's face relaxed into understanding. "Ah. I see."

"Morgan said you'd offered it and she said no. I was just wondering if maybe you could do it anyway?"

Cici settled regally on Jane's couch, somehow looking both completely at home yet out of place. "I wish I could, sweet one. But Morgana must ask me for it."

Jane's stomach fell to her feet. "Oh." She dropped onto the couch with far less grace than Cici.

"Yes, and unfortunately, Morgana has twisted herself into such a state over the situation that she can't tell up from down and certainly cannot think rationally about such things. She cannot see what is right and good at the moment, and so she is refusing." Dark eyebrows drew together and almost to herself, Cici murmured, "But she will see. And maybe then she will ask me for you."

"But you *could* just do it, right? I mean I was under the impression that all she had to do was ask, she doesn't have to actually do anything to make it happen."

"Of course I could, but I will not. I have rules in place because otherwise there would be anarchy and I cannot have that." Her tone was matter-of-fact, yet kind.

Jane swallowed, feeling so suddenly desperate that she blurted, "I'll give you anything for more time with her, anything at all. Even my…" Her fingers fumbled the air as she searched for a word. "My *soul* if that's something real."

Cici La Morte's eyebrow arched regally. She raised her chin. "And what makes you think your soul isn't already mine, Jane Gabrielle Smith?"

Jane felt the blood draining from her face. She tried to respond but only managed a choking squeak.

Cici laughed, the sound soft and musical. She leaned forward and patted Jane's arm. "I'm kidding. Just a little Death humor to brighten my day." Her mischievousness faded to seriousness. "Jane, has she told you what happened after Hannah died?"

"Yes."

"I see. And did she tell you all of it?"

"I...I don't know. I assumed so?" Jane cleared her throat against the sudden lump of nausea. "She told me about The Butcher."

The expression on Death's face could only be described as horror. She exhaled the two words, "The Butcher." Cici slid closer, until her thigh was barely two inches from Jane's, and took both of Jane's hands in hers. The grip was warm and strong and immediately soothing. "Jane, I have existed for longer than you could imagine. I have witnessed things you could not fathom, been part of and shaped events throughout history which disgusted and horrified me. And not one thing in my almost infinite lifespan has ever made me feel as completely ruined as Morgana did in the months after Hannah died.

"After Hannah, Morgana begged me repeatedly to let her die. And every time she asked, I refused. And so, every single night for three hundred and twenty-six days she tried anyway. And on every one of those nights, I went to wherever she lay broken and trying desperately to leave her life and I picked her up, and I gave her a new body and I pleaded with her to stop doing what she was doing. But she didn't. It was as if she hoped that one day I'd lose concentration and she could just...slip her death past me."

She shook her head, a mirthless laugh slipping past her lips. The laugh caught, and Cici pulled her hands away from Jane's and clapped them over her mouth, but it didn't quite muffle the sharp sob. She exhaled, and it was as if this simple action took some of the pain and enabled her to speak. "Being tied up in the cause as I was made it even harder. I mean, I *am* Death and the woman she loved had died."

Jane's hands hovered in the air, feeling more useless than they ever had. Watching this poised, elegant woman, Cici La Morte, *Death*, unravel made Jane feel as if her heart were being slowly dragged from her chest. She swallowed, took a breath, tried desperately to calm herself. "Then why did she keep doing it if she knew you would never allow it? Wasn't she telling you that she wanted to be done with life and shouldn't you have just...let it happen?" The thought of Morgan feeling that way was so heartrending that Jane didn't know how she could stand it.

Cici gently wiped tears from Jane's cheeks. "No, sweet one. That was her grief speaking, overwhelming everything else until it was all she could see. Grief speaks loudly, but not always truthfully." Cici's eyes were a warm shade of green, soothing like soft moss in a forest. "I believe she wanted to hurt on the outside to match the inside. She needed a greater pain than what she felt from Hannah's death. Honestly, I've never seen pain like it. It was literally as if someone had cut a part of her away and she simply couldn't function without it.

"I'm sure she's told you that I'm endowed with a certain sense of foresight. Not always immediately clear, but always true. And I knew that if she would just *live* then she would heal and find something greater than what she'd known with Hannah. I tried so hard to make her see, but she couldn't. There was nothing I could do, nothing that would ease her pain. So I did the only thing I could—kept her alive knowing what would come. And here it is, she has arrived at the point I knew she would. Morgana has found a woman who I know can give her everything she needs, and she's still trying to run from it."

Jane exhaled. "Is there anything else *I* can do? I've tried to show her that I'm here, tried to make her see that the thing we share goes beyond me dying." She paused. "But still, knowing how it'll end for her I can't help wondering if my selfishly wanting this with her is cruel. Even if she says yes, will she spend the next however many years thinking about my death?"

Cici's laugh was dry. "Selfishness. I know that feeling. For so many years I wondered if I'd done the right thing by refusing her request. If I'd been selfish because of my connection to her. And now I see you and I know I did the right thing. I don't believe love like this is selfish." She smiled but it was not without a touch of sadness. "When she's with you I can feel the change in her, even from another dimension. And when she is not with you, I feel how that hurts her."

The quiet pensive truth from Cici had Jane's heart racing with joy but the feeling was tinged with pain. "I hate that loving me hurts her. Hurts to be away from me, and will hurt when I die."

Cici's expression turned introspective. "Perhaps it will, but also perhaps not in the way she thinks. Morgana has always been a curious mix of maturity and childishness when confronted with something difficult. I don't wish to be flippant or diminish her experience after Hannah because it truly was horrendous, but she can't see that it doesn't have to be the way it was before, that it might not end the way she thinks it will."

"Do you really think that?"

"I know it." Cici's gaze made Jane feel as if she could read her thoughts. "You care about her."

"Yes."

"And you love her."

"Yes. Maybe more than I should for such a short time of us being together as, you know, friends and lovers or however you want to define it, but..." Jane shrugged, feeling utterly adrift. "I can't help myself."

"No, I believe you can't. Morgana inspires love but this thing between you goes deeper. She's in love with you, Jane. More than *in love*. You must understand that she fears only one thing. Loss. And that's why I know this is real, and that all her protests are nothing more than feeble attempts to rationalize what she's feeling. She is terrified."

"I can see that."

Cici sighed. "Morgana *feels* so deeply. She has always had an intense empathy, and that is simply *her*, not anything to do with me or the life I have given her. Morgana is the purest soul I've ever met, a truly unselfish person. The thing is, she believes she's selfish because she wants to be happy, because she does things that make her happy. But because of who she is, her happiness is always tied up in another person's, so it's as if she feels she's only trying to make others feel good so that she may also feel good. It's a ridiculous circular logic."

Jane frowned. "She mentioned something like that, that her relying on me for happiness was only making things harder. Does it really?"

"I can't answer that, because I am not Morgana. But I do know love is one of the most powerful things humans can experience."

"I don't think love is enough in this case." Jane's chin trembled and she fought to regain composure. "She's so afraid of me dying that she'd rather walk away and have nothing than risk feeling something. It's basically pain at every turn, no matter what she chooses, and I don't know what more I can do because I don't quite understand her reasoning for not wanting to have me around for longer. Isn't having more time, any amount, better than not?"

"I believe so, yes." Cici smiled wryly. "But my perception of emotions and time are not the same as yours or Morgana's."

"No, I guess not. So I'm stuck with her having made a choice I don't like or agree with." Jane tried to force out a laugh, but her throat closed around it and when she spoke it came out choked and hoarse. "I've tried everything I can think of, but it seems love doesn't really conquer all."

"Oh, sometimes it does." Cici brushed down the front of her silk blouse. "Quite frankly, Jane, all of this simply strengthens my conviction," she said, somewhat cryptically.

When Jane raised her eyebrows in question, she received no answer. "I suppose I have to accept Morgan's decision and that there's nothing I can do except learn to live with it." And maybe get a new job. In another country.

Cici raised her chin, her gaze unwavering as she studied Jane. "You're right, perhaps there isn't anything *you* can do. But there is something I can do. Something far better than a *save*." She gripped Jane's hand, squeezing it. "I'd like to discuss something with you…"

* * *

It took Cici La Morte half an hour to lay out her proposition, which made perfect sense to Jane. She'd listed all the reasons why she thought Jane would be the perfect person to be her newest Minion and take over The Americas, and the more she spoke the more Jane realized how much Morgan must've told Cici about her.

Cici uncrossed then recrossed her legs. "I need a *people* person, Jane. Someone who knows how to communicate, who's good with time management, and has the ability to take on new skills. You fit the bill, and more besides. The skills you'll need to learn will come easily to someone like you, and the fact you're comfortable with technology is also a huge bonus." She laughed. "You're not going to give Morgana an ulcer because of technical ineptitude like some of *Mes Minions*."

Morgan. The one thing that rose above all else. "Will my decision affect Morgan's future happiness?"

"I can't answer that. My role and by extension, the role of Minions has never been to influence a decision, simply to provide as much information as we can so that you may make the decision that feels right for you." Her expression blanked for a moment as if she'd had a thought, then turned back to its previous attentive calmness.

"But what if I accept and live for centuries but she doesn't want me for all time? It's one thing to think about just letting me live a few more years but this is…I, like…what if something happens between now and…later and we end up fighting or something?"

Cici laughed brightly, shaking her head. "You and she are so perfectly suited that you even have the same ideas."

"What do you mean?"

Cici shook her head again, though this time it was an indication she'd chosen not to answer Jane's question. "I don't believe either of those things you mentioned to be an issue. And besides, I still need someone in charge of The Americas. Regardless of how things stand between you and Morgana, you are eminently suited to the task." She waved a nonchalant hand, yet her tone was anything but. "The other things are merely bonuses."

"What about my position at Theda? I don't want to sound ungrateful, but I would like to continue working there."

"Are you concerned about money, Jane? As one of mine, you and by extension yours will be exceedingly well taken care of financially, physically, emotionally."

Jane's ears heated. "No, it's not that. I just really love my job."

"Ah. Well I see no reason you can't remain as you are. You will find that if you accept my offer then your need for sleep will diminish. I have every confidence you can do everything you need and want to." She leaned in, clasped Jane's hands. "If that's your only caveat for not accepting then I'll personally guarantee your job at Theda. If you find you need to decrease your workload or perhaps delegate more to your team, then between you, Morgana and myself, I am certain we can reach an arrangement that you're happy with."

Jane took a few moments to run through the proposal and what it would mean for her. How her mom would react. And, most importantly—the opportunity it would present to her and Morgan. A lifetime of positives outweighed any negatives, but...she still needed to discuss it with her mom. Hoping she wasn't trampling over Cici's generosity, she quietly said, "I don't want to sound ungrateful, but I think I need to talk to Mom first before I agree."

Cici eyed her shrewdly. "Ah, but you want to agree."

"Yes. I just need a little time. Please?"

"Take the time you need. I'm finished with all of my...engagements for now, so I will come the moment you call for me." Cici bestowed a lingering kiss on Jane's cheek, took a few steps backward, then disappeared.

After a quick knock, Jane slipped into her mom's room. "Do you have a minute?"

"For you I have two." She lowered the e-reader to her chair tray. "You look like you've seen a ghost."

"No, just Death." Jane sat on the end of the bed.

Her mom paused, processed, then smiled as if she'd just heard her favorite celebrity was in town. "Here? Why didn't you introduce us? Is she still here?"

"She's gone. And if you want to meet Death so badly then you summon her."

"Perhaps I will." She moved the chair closer, bumping Jane's leg. "What's up? Considering you're still here, I assume she didn't come to kill you."

"Death doesn't actually kill anybody, that's a myth." Jane blew out a breath, still not fully able to wrap her head around Cici's offer. "She asked if I wanted to be one of her Minions."

"And? What did you say?" Jane's mom's voice had risen two octaves.

"Tentatively yes, pending talking with you."

"Well I suppose my first Mom question to you is, will it make you happy?"

Jane didn't even think before answering, "Yes."

"Then why are you even asking me?"

She fiddled with the corner of the throw blanket. "Because you're my mom. We've always made all our big decisions together. And I need to know you'll be okay with it."

"Obviously I'm okay with it. But, Janie, it's not my decision. It's yours. I'll support you and be happy for you no matter what you choose, but you have to make the decision that you can live with. Perhaps for a very very long time," she added with a laugh. "What does Morgan think?"

"She doesn't know. But it seems so simple, solves all the problems between us so I can't see why she wouldn't be thrilled."

"Then why are you hesitating?"

She shrugged. "I guess I don't know how I'll deal with missing you for the rest of time. Morgan says it's hard living for so long because you keep living while those you love are gone."

"I suppose that's true. But I also know if, heaven forbid, I lost you, that I would want to live for as long as I could so I could remember and relive all those moments of love we shared. You may move on as time passes, but you don't forget. And even if the pain is immense, you'll learn to cope and you'll have Morgan with you every moment."

The emotion she'd been fighting since her disagreement with Morgan bubbled over, and all she could manage was a tearful nod.

"Remember what we do with opportunity?"

Jane wiped her eyes on her shirt. "We grab it."

"Yes, with both hands. So go get it." She made a clumsy gesture. "Lean close."

When Jane did as she'd been told, she received a forehead kiss. Her mom made a shooing motion. "Now go do whatever you need to do."

"Okay." Jane bent lower and hugged her mom tightly. "Thanks, Mom. For everything."

She patted the small of Jane's back. "How exciting. My immortal daughter. I'm going to be the envy of the movie club."

This time when Jane thought of Cici, the woman appeared within seconds. "You've spoken with your mother and made peace with your decision?"

Jane exhaled. "Yes I have, and I accept. Minion me up."

Cici's delighted smile was so broad it displayed nearly all her teeth. "I am absolutely thrilled to hear that. Shall we begin, or do you wish to take a moment to prepare yourself?"

There was nothing to prepare for except a world of possibility before her, which was wonderful rather than frightening. "Mhmm, let's do it." She paused. "It's not going to hurt, is it?"

"Not in the slightest. In fact, you might even enjoy it." She leaned in to whisper in Jane's ear. "Now, Jane, don't be alarmed, but I'm going to kiss you."

Jane leaned back. "Ohhh, um, mmm, I don't mean to be rude and you're incredibly attractive but I'm strictly the monogamous type and Morgan and me right now are, well, you know…"

Cici threw her head back and laughed. "I know that. But this is how you will become one of mine, Jane." She leaned in, eyes twinkling, and when she spoke again she lowered and deepened her voice as if pretending to be sinister. "The kiss of Death. It's the quickest and easiest way to transfer a portion of my Animus to you." She offered a teasingly seductive smile. "Though if you'd prefer, we can do it more…intimately."

"Oh, no no no. A kiss is fine then, if that's what it takes. I mean I'm sure that, um, other thing would be great, but see aforementioned statement of strictly monogamous."

Cici's laughter was loud and mirthful. She wiped delicately under her eyes, still chuckling. "Oh I can see why she loves you so. You are so good for her." Gently she cupped Jane's face in both hands, leaned down, and kissed her.

The actual kiss itself was unremarkable. But the heat that flowed through Jane moments after it was beyond remarkable. She still felt like herself, but a mix of sensations flooded her. She felt simultaneously weightless and grounded. Gentle yet powerful. And she felt connected to the surroundings, to Cici, to…Morgan.

Cici pulled back, exhaling a surprised breath. "Ah, you can feel her too?"

Jane's hand came to her mouth, muffling her answer. "Yes."

"Hmmm. How very interesting. I can sense her through you."

She pulled her hand away. "Is that normal?" Jane squeaked.

"Not really, no. In fact, it's the first time that it's ever occurred. Your link with me, our bond is as it should be. But for you to have a link with Morgana is extraordinary." She shrugged. "Though perhaps, given the circumstances, not all that extraordinary after all."

"Really?" Maybe this thing between her and Morgan was more than she'd ever dreamed, more intense, more connected. Maybe it meant that things really would work out as she hoped.

"Yes." Cici rubbed her hands together. "And this simply confirms that not only have I done the right thing for both of you, but that I'm a genius."

Jane had no idea how to express her gratitude, and eventually offered an emotional stuttering, "Thank you. I'm very grateful and I swear I'll do my best."

"I know you will, darling." She cupped Jane's chin gently. "And I'm going to need you to do your best to soothe Morgana."

"Why?"

Cici laughed. "Because she is going to be very mad at me."

"For the kiss, or because of…this?"

But Cici simply smiled that inscrutable smile again. "Go to her, Jane. And I will see you very soon."

"How do you know that?"

"Because Morgana will want to yell at me, and she won't be able to leave you behind." She leaned down and pressed a soft kiss to Jane's cheek. "Do be sure to eat something before she drags you to Aether." Cici tilted her head, her gaze again going to Jane's mom's closed bedroom door. She smiled. "Ah. I have a meeting to attend now, so I must dash, but tell Pamela I'll come back next week so we can meet properly. I'll bring my knitting."

Then she was gone. But also…not gone. Jane could feel the tether, though indistinct and fuzzy. She felt another thing, definitely not indistinct or fuzzy, but as strong and real as anything she'd ever experienced. And she knew only one thing—she had to see Morgan. But…maybe she'd drive there instead of testing out her new abilities.

Oh God. Her new abilities.

CHAPTER TWENTY-NINE

The moment she opened the door, Morgan paused. Every muscle suddenly felt like it was vibrating and she knew immediately that Jane was different. And she knew the reason why. "Sonofabitch," she griped under her breath. "When did she do it?"

"Just before I drove here." Jane paused, mouth edging into a frown. "Are you angry?" She shimmied out of her jacket and hung it in the entryway.

"I am. But not at you, not at all. I'm angry at her for doing something she knew I was opposed to." Morgan rubbed between her eyes, trying to force the tension away. She'd forgotten the most important thing in her fit of temper. She lowered her voice and stepped close to Jane, grasping both of her hands. She turned them over, kissed each palm. "Are you okay?"

Jane peered down the length of herself. "Yes, I think I am. Better than okay."

"Good." Morgan exhaled, still trying to tamp down the lingering anger. She was almost successful. "She had no right to do this."

Jane stretched up on tiptoes, and after a brief kiss, said, "Morgan, I love you but I don't belong to you. Cici asked, I consented. I made this choice for myself because I saw no reason not to take an opportunity that would give me everything I've been looking for." She paused, looking suddenly very uncertain and her voice grew tremulous as she asked, "And what you've been looking for too?"

The fact Jane was uncertain about such a thing melted Morgan's annoyance at Cici, and the idea that Jane had done something so monumental for *them* sent the remnants of her fears scurrying into a dark corner—not gone, but no longer in her way. "Your logic makes it very hard to hold on to my grumpiness." Smiling, she ran her hands down Jane's sides. "As does your love. And *of course* this is what I've been looking for. Thank you for this. Thank you for being strong enough to carry my old burdens." She kissed Jane again then dipped her head to let lips linger against Jane's neck. "Mmm."

"What?"

"You still smell the same." Morgan kissed under Jane's jaw, inhaling the familiar scent of her. She kissed her way to the edge of her mouth and paused. Jane turned her head until their lips brushed, and Morgan let her lead the kiss. Jane pressed against her in that way that was so familiar, her arms coming around Morgan's neck as she parted her lips. Their tongues met, stroked lightly against each other. The connection was as strong as it had always been, but now there seemed to be a confidence in Jane—not from her transformation, Morgan realized, but from the knowledge that they would have time to explore that connection.

"Do I taste the same?" Jane whispered teasingly once they'd broken from the kiss but not each other's embrace.

Morgan grinned. "I'm pretty sure you do. But I might need to check a few more times to be certain." This kiss was softer, sweeter, a reminder of what had always been there and was now strengthened. When Morgan had satisfied herself that Jane was indeed unchanged—except for the immortal-ish Minion thing—she pulled back. "Are you sure you're all right? Did she pressure you into this?"

"I am all right, yes and no she didn't. Morgan, I *want* this. It's the perfect solution to what we both want, while circumventing one of the things that was an issue between us."

"No, I know that." She made herself smile. "It's an excellent solution. I'm thrilled."

A dubious eyebrow rose. "Thrilled? Then why do you look like someone just spoiled the ending of *Jessica Jones* for you?"

There were so many reasons, so much past doubt to unravel that it took her a minute to figure out her thoughts. Jane remained silent, watching her with a calmly expectant expression until Morgan finally managed to articulate, "I didn't want her to do it because I was terrified that you wouldn't want what this implied."

"Which is?"

"A thousand lifetimes with me." She felt tears threaten, and tried to chase them away with another smile, though it felt weak. "It's one thing to say you want a normal lifetime with me, but this is far beyond that."

Jane's expression melted into softness. "Oh, Morgan. I can't think of anything I want more than that. Don't you feel it when I'm with you? It's like a great big billboard screaming *I love you*. Even when I'm away from you I've always felt some part of you nearby."

"I do feel it, I've always felt it." She paused, dipping her head to catch Jane's eye. "I wanted it so much, this life with you, and it was selfish of me to put something like this on you. The last time I was this selfish, it ended in heartbreak, and I was trying to stop you from getting hurt as much as me."

"Umm, I think I've just proven you're not the only one who can be selfish." She smiled. "But if it's selfishness in service of another's happiness then I think it's not so bad."

Morgan mused her agreement, leading Jane to the couch and settling her on it. "Have you told your mum?"

"Yeah, we talked about it beforehand."

"What did she say?"

"Nutshell version—do what makes me happy."

"And does this? Do I?" She was surprised at how tight her throat felt as she asked the question.

Jane's response was immediate. "Yes, incredibly so. That's why I did this, Morgan. It was for us. The immortality and superhuman stuff are just bonuses." Her mouth worked as though she was trying to figure something out and failing. "Wait, aren't I supposed to feel stronger and faster and…better and all that?"

Morgan laughed. "You're not suddenly a superhero, Jane. Give it a few weeks, and even then remember, it's only a twelve if normal humans are a ten. And I'm only a twelve because I am old."

Jane's grin was naughty. "Twelve is my new favorite number."

She matched Jane's grin. "Mine too, but only as of recently." The grin faded. "Are you *sure* you feel okay?" It'd been so long since her transformation that the details of the time immediately after were vague. She didn't recall feeling bad, so much as discombobulated.

"I'm sure. I feel…likeable, which is weird."

"Jane, you've always been likeable, incredibly so." She kissed her gently. "What has she told you about what's required and the things that you're now capable of?"

"Nothing really but when she was offering the Minion deal, she said you would explain the mechanics and teach me the whats and hows of how to do my job and use my new abilities."

"Really? She's not sending Serena to you?"

"Who's that?" Jane's forehead furrowed as she rubbed her stomach absently.

"Newbie coach. When we first decided that we needed to expand the Minion pool in 1682, Cici had me run a workshop to bring the new ones up to scratch. It was a disaster. I had people everywhere across all realms, stuck, not knowing how to get back. And I swore I was done with trying to teach. So Serena took over because she has the patience of a saint and is also a brilliant teacher."

"Oh. Well if you don't want to do it, I could ask Cici to get the *real* teacher to help me." There was a teasing sparkle in her eye.

Morgan scoffed. "Please, I think I can handle one freshly created Minion."

"Little bit cocky, aren't you?"

Morgan tried for stern but got laughter. "Quiet, newling." She stole a kiss. "And I'm a lot cocky."

Jane nestled against her side, tucking her feet up. "Okay, so give me a quick primer. The teleporting thing. What if I get lost, or stuck somewhere in the bit between here and everything that's out there?"

"It doesn't matter." Morgan slid an arm around Jane's waist and pulled her closer. "I'll always find you."

"What about me? Will I get that finding skill?"

"Maybe in a few decades." She stroked the bare skin of Jane's arm, irrationally wanting the reassurance that she was still *Jane.* "Do you want to practice?"

"How?"

Morgan slipped from under Jane and stood. "Like this." The moment she'd finished talking, she ported away. "Easy as walking."

Jane's tone was dry. "I can hear you in the kitchen, Morgan. Not exactly far away."

"No it's not," she agreed. "Do you want something to eat?"

"Actually, yes please. That would be fantastic."

"Then come here and get it yourself. But the floor is boiling lava so you'll have to get in here some other way…" Morgan called back.

"Don't think about it. Just imagine being in my kitchen. Think about my voice and being here with me."

Almost two minutes passed before Jane appeared, standing barely a foot in front of her. Morgan couldn't help her squeal of delight. "You did it! And first attempt too! You're a natural."

Jane was a most interesting shade of green. "Holy fucking shit." Her face contorted then she clapped a hand over her mouth.

Morgan moved to her side, light fingers stroking up and down her neck. "Relax. Don't think about it. Just breathe."

Jane's grunt sounded less like trying to breathe and more like trying not to vomit.

Morgan kept stroking. "Jane Smith, conqueror of the world's scariest roller coasters, gets sick at a little teleporting?" Morgan peered through her apartment. "…over a distance of approximately fifteen feet. Cute."

"Not funny," Jane gurgled.

Morgan resumed her gentle stroking of the damp skin at the back of Jane's neck. "Just breathe, sweetheart. Breathe and relax. Focus on where you are right now, not where you've been."

After a few minutes, Jane's skin returned to its usual color and the tremor in her hands subsided. "Is it always like that?"

"In the beginning, yes. But it'll pass as you adjust, as you grow more comfortable with interstitial travel." Morgan sighed. "Speaking of travel, there's someone I need to see."

"Time to have a word with the boss?"

"Yes. Many words. If I come back flayed, well…it's been wonderful."

Laughing, Jane swatted at her. "Behave yourself. I happen to like your skin where it is." She kissed Morgan's neck. "And I happen to like how much it responds when I touch it."

"Me too." Morgan paused as a thought popped into her head. From the couch to the kitchen was one thing. Morgan's house to Aether was another, huge thing all together. But she didn't really want to leave Jane, not now when she'd just undergone a huge change, physically and emotionally. "Want to practice that interstitial travel?"

Jane spluttered, "How exactly? I mean, Cici said you would bring me with you when you came to yell at her, but I thought she was joking. I mean, I don't even know how to get there or where it is or anything like that."

"Basically the same as what you just did. Close your eyes, think about Cici and where she is. You want to be there, and you will be. It's as simple as that. And I'll hold on to you the whole time like a little booster."

"I'm not sure I can," Jane said, panicked.

"You can. I promise." After a beat, she grinned. "Well, after you've had something to eat. I can help you get there, but me dragging you through time and space to Aether won't be a pleasant way to remember your first journey." Laughing, Morgan added, "And I might make something ready to eat when we get back."

"Okay…"

"Trust me, Jane," she murmured. "I've got you."

Jane's shoulders relaxed. "I know you do."

Once they'd eaten, Morgan pulled on her shoes and grabbed the *Valravn* cap from its permanent place on the hook near the door. "You ready?"

"As I'll ever be."

"Remember what I said, just think about being with Cici. Focus on her energy and wanting to be with her."

Jane's expression was dubious. "Mhmm?"

Morgan took her hand, interlacing their fingers. "Ladies, please fasten your seatbelts, stow your tray tables and prepare for liftoff."

"Takeoff," Jane corrected.

"How do you know we're not going to outer space?"

"We are?"

Morgan couldn't help teasing, "Maybe." She bent down and whispered in Jane's ear, "Jane? It's time to go. Three…two…one. Liftoff."

The sensation of Jane's body touching Morgan's, their hands gripping as they traveled to Aether filled her with such a sense of rightness that she let go of the last of her misgivings about Jane's transformation. When they arrived, Morgan turned to face Jane, who this time didn't look queasy so much as shellshocked. Morgan ran her hands up and down Jane's biceps, trying to rub some warmth into her. "Are you all right?"

Jane shivered despite Morgan's attempts to warm her. "You weren't wrong about the cold," she said around chattering teeth.

"Come on, let's get moving and get you something to eat." Wrapping an arm around Jane's waist, she pulled her tight against her side and led her toward the concierge desk. "Jonathon, this is Jane. Jane, this is Jonathon who can get you anything you require at any time. He's an absolute magician."

Jonathon dipped his head, clearly pleased. "Hello, Ms. Smith. It's lovely to see you here."

Jane leaned into Morgan. "Uh, thanks. It's nice to be here?"

He smiled knowingly. "I'll have some food sent to her study right away."

Morgan squeezed his shoulder. "Thank you."

Jane echoed the thank you to his departing back, before turning to Morgan, eyes wide. "Oh my God. I'm so hungry. Is this what you feel like every time? How do you stand it?" She placed both hands on her stomach. "It's like there's a bear in my stomach. Growling after it's eaten everything in there. I literally just ate and now this?"

Morgan couldn't chase away her frown. "I'm sorry, I thought you'd eaten enough."

"Morgan, I feel like an entire buffet wouldn't be enough right now."

"Then next time, we'll eat two buffets. Each." She raised their joined hands and kissed the back of Jane's. "Come on, time for me to face Death."

Morgan knocked on Cici's closed door, and pushed it open at the summons to enter. Cici rose from the couch and flung aside the papers she was reading. La Morte didn't bother trying to disguise her glee, clapping delightedly. "Ah, if it isn't my oldest and newest Minions come to see me. What a pleasure." She held up her hands, feigning fear as her lips twitched in amused delight. "Morgana, are you going to challenge me? Shall I fetch those two prototype pistols Herr Peck created before he presented Emperor Charles the Fifth with his personalized pistol? We can have a duel at twenty paces! Though I admit, unlike you I've never actually used a wheellock pistol, so you will probably have a distinct advantage over me. Do you remember that brawl in Munich in the mid-fifteen hundreds? Hilarious."

Morgan strode toward Cici, who stood completely relaxed as if she feared nothing, especially not Morgan's potential annoyance. When she reached her, Morgan placed a hand on each of Cici's shoulders and placed a lingering kiss on each cheek. "That *brawl* was your idea, not mine. And you're fortunate Herr Peck showed me how the damned things worked or we could have had a serious incident to clean up."

"All in good fun, Morgana."

"You find everything *in good fun*." Morgan lowered her voice. "I'm upset with you."

Cici's smile held no contrition, simply self-containment. "I wouldn't know what to do if you weren't, darling love." She peered around Morgan and held out a hand to Jane. "Come here, sweet one. You look a little stunned. Is Jonathon taking care of refreshments?"

Jane took Cici's hand. "Yes, I think so."

"Good. Let me look closer now that you've had time to settle." She turned Jane side to side, musing her approval. "Being one of mine suits you, Jane."

"Thanks?"

"How are you feeling?"

"Good, I mean aside from hungry."

Jonathon thankfully arrived with two platters of food, and Morgan heard Jane's relieved sigh as he set them down. Cici made a sweeping gesture. "Dig in, Jane."

Jane barely said a thank you before she'd nabbed a plate of pasta. Morgan chose a grilled cheese and ate one half in two huge bites as Cici watched on like a lioness who'd just delivered a baby zebra for her cubs. Once Morgan had finished, Cici took a few steps toward the door and gestured for her to come along. "Come take a quick walk with me, Morgana." She glanced over Morgan's shoulder. "Jane, will you be all right here for a short while? Eat, and regain your strength for the journey home. You can call for Jonathon if you require anything more."

Jane nodded, her mouth too full to reply. Morgan smiled, recalling exactly how she'd felt after her first trip to Aether. Cici smiled too but hers was soft, indulgent, like a mother looking upon a favored child. Morgan blew Jane a kiss and followed La Morte. Cici moved gracefully down the hall toward her private quarters, silent for the thirty-meter walk.

The moment she'd closed the door, Morgan pounced. "Why did you do it?"

"For the same reason I do everything—because I wanted to. We both know I need someone to run The Americas, and she passed every one of my tests. She's *perfect*, Morgana. And honestly I can't stand the thought of endless centuries of you being miserable. But also because you've earned it. More than earned it." Cici lowered her voice to a whisper as if she thought the walls had ears and someone might catch her admitting a weakness. "And I like her. She's sweet and kind and amusing. And most importantly, you seem to *really* like her, if the expression you've been wearing for the last few months is anything to go by."

"Yes, but she's a data nerd, not a human resources person."

"But nothing, Morgana. Some people just have innate skills, and Jane Smith is one of those. You've said yourself she has fabulous organizational skills, good interpersonal skills, is excellent at team management *and* she knows all the technology back to front. It's done, she is one of mine, and I suggest you get used to it and focus your energies on helping her adjust." Cici clapped excitedly, barely restraining her squeal. "Oh I'm very excited to see what she can do!"

Morgan had to admit, "I am too."

"And I'll have a Minion *couple*. It's going to be fabulous, the two of you working side by side! I cannot *wait* to tell the Committee. Hera is going to be so jealous."

"I wonder how people would react if they knew the Afterlife Committee deciding their post-life eternity is basically a bunch of immortals behaving like a group of teenagers gossiping."

"Basically, yes," La Morte confirmed cheerfully.

An unpleasant thought intruded. "Did you enjoy kissing my girlfriend?"

"Your girlfriend." Cici drew the word *girlfriend* out, making it sound both schoolyard-teasing and intensely pleased.

Morgan grunted, then aware it made her sound like a Neanderthal, tried a more articulate, "Yes, she is."

"Good, I agree. And yes, I did rather enjoy our very brief and chaste and totally not sexual kiss. She tastes like sunshine." Cici settled on the edge of her bed, crossing her legs. She patted the cover beside her.

"Yes she does." Morgan exhaled a long sigh, sitting where Cici had indicated. "Is everything okay? Is everything...as it should be?" She couldn't bear to ask the questions outright, to hear perhaps that Jane's transformation hadn't gone well.

"Everything is perfect. Her bond to me is strong." Cici raised her chin, eyed Morgan shrewdly. "She is also bonded to you in a way I've never experienced. I could sense you *through* her."

"Really? That's never happened before, has it?"

"No, it has not," Cici confirmed. "Any guesses as to why?" The way she asked it told Morgan that Cici knew the exact reason.

"I—" Morgan was about to brush the question aside with something flippant. But what she had with Jane was too important for her to be anything but truthful. "I've always felt close to her, connected to her in a way I haven't with anyone aside from you." She waited, expecting the sharp pain in her chest. But it never came. Simply a soft sensation that felt like acceptance. "Not even Hannah, not like this."

"No. Ergo, you belong together." Cici stretched luxuriously. "I really have outdone myself this time." She pinched Morgan's cheeks. "Look at you, so very content."

"Mmph," Morgan managed around the facial intrusion.

"Contentment looks wonderful on you, Morgana."

Contentment *felt* wonderful. Morgan reached up to where La Morte was still jiggling her cheeks and grasped her wrists, stilling the movement. She turned her head and kissed La Morte's palm. "Is it just me, or has this all worked out rather easily and quickly? Such a simple solution to one of my fears and boom, it's done and we can move forward."

Cici's shoulder lifted in a lazy shrug. "Perhaps it was a quick and easy solution in the end. But don't you think it's time you had something like this come easily, especially after the journey you've had to get here? You deserve it, Morgana. You deserve every happiness in the universe and I for one am simply grateful that I could help with one portion of it."

Morgan blinked away rapidly forming tears. Hadn't Jane said something similar? That Morgan *deserved* happiness. Whatever she had done to deserve Jane, she would be eternally grateful. "Cici?" That single word was hoarse with emotion.

"Yes, my dearest love?"

"Thank you."

La Morte flashed her a dazzling smile that didn't quite conceal her emotion. "You are so very welcome." She leaned back on her hands. "You know, something occurred to me when I was discussing this change with Jane. She wanted to know what she should do and I had to explain we are not here to influence decisions, merely provide options. And it occurred to me that was perhaps why you declined my offer in the first place. You didn't want to influence how Jane might feel."

"Partially, yes." Morgan agreed, unsurprised that Cici had unraveled more of her torment. "On top of everything else, if I forced her into a decision because of my actions, I believed I'd spend the rest of our time together wondering if she'd really wanted it, or merely felt an obligation."

"Love really did blind you to the obvious, Morgana." Cici pulled Morgan close and kissed her quickly. When she pulled back, she flicked the brim of Morgan's *Valravn* cap. "This really looks ridiculous."

"I rode roller coasters for her." Morgan grinned. "Love makes us do weird things."

La Morte's gaze softened. "Indeed it does. Now, when was the last time you were in my garden?"

Morgan frowned, trying and failing to recall. She had no need to go outside Cici's mansion when she visited, and it had probably been at least fifty years since she'd strolled through the immaculately maintained gardens and lawns. "Quite a while," she finally answered.

"Everything is blooming and it's truly magnificent. Why don't you take Jane for a walk and show her the garden." She smiled a Cheshire-Cat smile as she passed Morgan a small folding blade. "And do be sure to stop and smell the flowers."

CHAPTER THIRTY

Jane had eaten more than she'd ever eaten in a single sitting and only *just* felt full. She had tidied the remnants of her meal…s when she sensed Morgan's proximity. Morgan smiled knowingly. "Feel better?"

"Much."

"Good." Morgan held out a hand. "Come walk with me. I want to show you Cici's garden." She laughed at Jane's doubtful expression. "Trust me, it's magnificent."

Acres of sprawling lawns and beds of every flower imaginable encircled what Jane realized was a large gothic mansion. Morgan paused to smell a brilliant white rose in a bed of ten or more rosebushes bursting with blooms. Smiling, she pulled out a small pocket knife and cut the rose stem. She seemed content in a way Jane hadn't witnessed before, as if being among the flowers brought her a sense of peace. "You know," Morgan mused. "I don't think I've felt this…light in centuries." She exhaled a contented breath. "You were absolutely right."

"About what?"

"Letting you carry some of my pain makes it easier." Smiling, she indicated a yellow rosebud. "Smell this one."

Jane bent to sniff the flower, surprised by the strength of the beautiful scent, as if it was a flower on steroids. Perhaps Cici would let her take some home for her mom. She straightened again and was face to face with Morgan. "Will you tell me what year it was going to be?" When Morgan arched an eyebrow in question, Jane explained, "My death year."

Morgan stopped beside a rosebush that held the most incredible deep-red roses Jane had ever seen. "You really want to know?" She softly fingered the petals before slicing the stem.

The question made Jane pause. "I don't know. I feel like I should even though I know it doesn't really matter. Don't worry about it."

"It was...far enough away that you would have had a wonderful and fulfilling life, but close enough that it was too soon for me." Morgan sighed, turning the rose around and around in her fingertips. "Honestly, even the eternity we're going to have now doesn't feel like long enough."

"Then we'll just have to make the most of every minute."

She smiled. "Yes, we will." Morgan exhaled slowly. "Jane?"

"Mmm?"

"Thank you for helping me to breathe again."

"Thank you for letting me."

Morgan dipped her head for a kiss, her free arm sliding around Jane's waist to pull her closer. This kiss felt like a new beginning, exciting yet familiar all at once. Chuckling, Morgan disengaged. "Come on, if we keep this up we're never going to leave this garden." She took Jane's hand and guided her to another bed of brilliant roses.

Slowly they wandered the grounds. By the time they'd completed a full circuit, Morgan had collected another rose and held all three by the stems she'd been carefully paring thorns from as they walked. Jane had hooked her hand in the crook of Morgan's elbow, and gently nudged her to get her attention. "About that whole eternity thing..."

"What about it?"

"You agreed to spend eternity with me, but I probably should have told you that when I eat Mexican, it's a warzone the next day. I *hate* doing laundry. I'm a total television hog, and you're going to have to put up with me playing PlayStation every free moment I get. When Jennifer Lawrence dies—I want her body. Just for a little while. Ohhh, maybe Beyoncé! And where are we going to live?"

Morgan spoke with exaggerated slowness, as if trying to process Jane's verbal stream. "Okay, well, thanks for the heads up on all of that. I assumed we would stay in your house or find somewhere big enough and suitable for us and your mum. And Jennifer Lawrence, well…you're going to have to fight Imogen in the UK for that. As for Beyoncé, I think Bethany Harris put a claim on her a while ago."

"You're the boss, Morgan. Surely you can tell them too bad, so sad, those celebrities are mine." Jane raised herself up on tiptoes. "Because that's what you have to do when your wife wants something."

Morgan pulled her into a hug, nuzzled her neck. "Wife?"

Jane leaned back in the strong, comforting circle of her arms. "Well yes, eventually. You can't tote me around as your hot bedmate forever. You need to make an honest woman of me, Morgan Ashworth."

Laughing, Morgan agreed, "Mm, I like the sound of that." Her expression turned serious, earnest as she presented Jane with the three roses. Morgan's thumb brushed over the petals of each rose as she explained, "White is for our new beginning. Orange for my desire. Red is for my love."

Heart. Melting. Jane had to put a lid on tears and it took a few long moments before she felt controlled enough to ask, "When did you get so romantic?" Jane inhaled deeply, savoring the mixed scent of the three rose blooms.

"What? This? This is nothing. I couldn't give you *all* my suave moves, Jane. You'd have fallen head over heels with me the first time I swept you off your feet." She bent to kiss the soft skin under Jane's ear.

"I fell head over heels for you the first day we spent together."

"I think I did too," Morgan admitted quietly. "There's something so bonding about roller coaster nausea, isn't there?" She interlaced their fingers and they walked toward the rear of Cici's mansion.

"When will I officially take over from you as an actual working Minion for The Americas?"

"I'll start teaching you the ins and outs over the next few months and when you're ready, we'll phase me out and you in." She smiled down at Jane. "I'll be with you every step, every time you travel around earth or to here, or administer a package, until you're comfortable on your own. I'm not going to leave you alone. And maybe you'll be able to beat Bethany Harris because she's going to be insufferable once she gets that award this year and will need to be brought down a notch or two."

"Really? You mean she's going to beat you after all of…this? But you've been working so hard."

Morgan shrugged. "Not that hard. These past few weeks made me realize there were more important things to worry about than *another* useless trophy."

"I'll avenge your loss, I promise." Jane slipped her fingers from Morgan's so she could slide an arm around her waist. Pressed close, they climbed a set of stone stairs. "What about me moving into a different body?"

A blonde eyebrow went skyward. "You want to do that now? What about everyone you know? You can't just turn up in a new casing without telling your mum what's happening. And those two you mentioned aren't for some time yet."

"Well not now *now* but I'd like to know the hows of it."

Morgan huffed out an mmph. "I'm not sure I like the thought of you changing this body for another. I'm rather fond of this one."

"Well I'm going to have to deal with you swapping yours, aren't I? Fair's fair." She laughed as the scenario popped into her head. "Can you picture it? Us going around together to find new bodies that we *both* like."

"True," Morgan said eventually. She sighed. "I suppose I'll have time to get used to it."

Jane pulled them to a stop at the top of the stairs. "It's okay." She twisted the *Valravn* cap around so she wouldn't have a brim poking her in the face, and kissed Morgan until she felt her knees wobble. She wondered if she'd ever tire of that feeling, smiling when she realized they really did have forever to test the theory. Jane kissed her again. "We have all the time in the world, right?"

Bella Books, Inc.

Women. Books. Even Better Together.

P.O. Box 10543
Tallahassee, FL 32302

Phone: 800-729-4992
www.bellabooks.com